girl unwrapped

girl unwrapped

GABRIELLA GOLIGER

ARSENAL PULP PRESS .
Vancouver

GIRL UNWRAPPED

Copyright © 2010 by Gabriella Goliger

ARSENAL PULP PRESS
#102-211 East Georgia St.
Vancouver, BC
Canada V6A 1Z6
arsenalpulp.com

The publisher gratefully acknowledges the support of the Canada Council for the Arts and the British Columbia Arts Council for its publishing program, and the Government of Canada through the Book Publishing Industry Development Program and the Government of British Columbia through the Book Publishing Tax Credit Program for its publishing activities.

This is a work of fiction. Any resemblance of characters to persons either living or deceased is purely coincidental.

Editing by Susan Safyan
Cover design by Mauve Pagé

Printed and bound in Canada on 100% PCW recycled paper

Library and Archives Canada Cataloguing in Publication:

Goliger, Gabriella, 1949-
          Girl unwrapped / Gabriella Goliger.

Also available in electronic format.
ISBN 978-1-55152-375-0

          I. Title.

PS8563.O82848G57 2010   C813'.6   C2010-903224-1

Recycled
Supporting responsible use
of forest resources
FSC   www.fsc.org Cert no. SGS-COC-003153
       © 1996 Forest Stewardship Council

For Barb, love of my life.

ACKNOWLEDGMENTS

I am deeply grateful to all those who helped me through this journey. Thank you to the writers and friends who read the manuscript at various stages: Frances Itani, Debra Martens, Alison Gresik, Anne Whitehurst, Dawne Smith, Cheryl Jaffee, Gary Kellam, Deborah Gorham, and James Deahl. Thanks to Mary Borsky and Nancy Baele for the support and good talks; to the other members of the Ottawa Women's Writers' Group for all their feedback; and to the wonderful members of my family who always asked "how's the book coming" in the most encouraging way. I received generous financial support from the City of Ottawa, the Ontario Arts Council, and the Canada Council for the Arts. Thanks also to the Banff Writing Studio, especially Stan Dragland and Edna Alford, and to Humber College. My editor, Susan Safyan, was a joy to work with, as was the entire team at Arsenal Pulp Press. My deepest debt is to my partner, Barbara Freeman, whose faith in me never wavered and who stood beside me through the ups, downs, sideways, and inside-outs of this crazy ride.

part I

The Mountain

chapter I

"Choose life!" Lisa says.

Her motto, her toast, her battle cry, as she raises the glass of wine, clutches the stem so tightly the glass trembles and red drops spill down the side. "*Nu?* Chews life," she crows again in her German-accented English, giving Toni the "look," fierce and filled with a terrible pride but also with sparks of accusation that make Toni squirm and kick her feet against the crossbar of the dining room table. The Sabbath candlesticks wobble and the flames twitch. Toni grabs her egg-cup-sized beaker to shrill in response, "Choose life!"

"Ai!" Julius protests, steadying the candles with one hand while his other flies to his temple. As if his daughter's voice were an arrow penetrating the soft, vulnerable depths that lie beneath a thin layer of skull and bare skin. "Calm down, both of you."

Friday night, the grand moment of the week has arrived, when the three of them sit down to the big table, set with the embroidered cloth and the gold-rimmed dishes, and they linger over the meal, enveloped in candle glow. On Friday nights especially, the invisible Others are present: the uncles who live across the ocean in Italy, Grandma Antonia and Grandpa Markus who were snatched away, Minka the cat, Julius's childhood companion when he lived in Vienna long, long ago. They are here, along with a slew of lost relatives—the ones who couldn't escape—because Lisa has a way with ghosts. She pulls them in through the cracks in the walls. She talks to them, calls them by name, or simply mentions "our loved ones" in a voice thick with sadness and an unsettling rage. Julius grunts and shifts, uncomfortable with such displays of emotion, but his discomfort makes Toni feel the Others all the more, as if their shadowy selves crowd him, and that's what makes him cringe. Her papa doesn't care for company much.

On Friday night, there's food enough for a tribe, more food than the three of them can possibly eat at one sitting. Noodle soup, a whole chicken roasted to golden-brown perfection, dumplings, red cabbage with caraway seeds, fruit compote and Bohemian *Mehlspeise* for dessert. There are blessings, whispered like magic spells, over candles, wine, and *challah*, while Julius taps an impatient forefinger against the table. All ceremony irritates him, but Lisa insists. There are the happy kinds of arguments between Toni's parents, their voices flying across the table like ping-pong balls. There are chances for Toni to boast about her tree-climbing prowess and to pretend she is drunk, falling under the table in a fit of giggles. Sometimes, after dinner, if her father can be persuaded, there's a paper hat made out of a napkin and, if her mother is in the mood, a fortune read from a deck of cards. The only thing that can spoil Friday night is when, as on this night, Lisa has come home with a cardboard box from the store where she works—Shmelzer's Ladies' Fashions—and a gleam in her eye, as if she's already won the argument that will erupt after dinner. *After dinner, you'll face the music.* The box will be offered like a gift. The contents will be wrapped in rustling layers of tissue paper. Inside will be the Loathsome Thing. Toni shuts her mind against what's to come and concentrates instead on her thimbleful of sweet, fiery wine.

Mumbling a quick *l'chayim*, Julius sips from his own glass, then quietly translates, as his mouth curls in a skeptical smirk and his eyebrow lifts. "To life" is the correct meaning of the Hebrew toast. You could also say "*Prost*," which is Latin for *pro sit*, or "*Zum Wohl*," or "Cheers." *Your mother has her fixed ideas, but we'll go along to keep the peace*, the raised eyebrow says.

Toni probes the burning liquid with the tip of her tongue and wonders. She's already alive. What is there to choose? To be sharp. To be a Somebody. To be as lovely and darling as the Nutkevitch twins next door. To be the miracle child her mother insists God delivered at Toni's birth. The infant Toni inched into the world, blue in the face, the umbilical chord wrapped around her neck, a terrible silence locked inside her. But the doctor worked with clamps and suction pumps while Lisa struggled to call out through her swoon of fatigue. Finally, baby Toni filled her lungs and wailed. Then, though half dead with childbirth, Lisa had bellowed, "Bring her, or I'll get up and fetch her myself." So they brought the red-faced bundle with the tiny trembling fists. On the spot, Lisa chose the name Antonia, after Grandma, who hovered above in the air, waiting anxiously for her namesake to arrive. Whenever Toni's mother tells the story, she gazes tenderly past her fidgety present-day child at a vision of the perfect little bunny that once was.

The chicken, gravy-soaked dumplings, and braised cabbage fill the room with savoury aromas. Eat, eat, eat. But eat with understanding. Lisa demonstrates with a skinned morsel of chicken breast, her lips pressed together, her eyes shut. The mind must be filled with beautiful thoughts while the mouth is filled with the mushed-up stuff. For years, your Mama and Papa went without, and now they slave to put this feast on the table. We have meat every day, we have to, otherwise we might as well be back in the internment camp, that long-ago time before you were born. *You don't know how good you have it.*

Julius eats slowly, methodically, with deft movements of his knife and fork, chewing every bite thoroughly, wiping the plate clean with *challah.* Then he bites off the ends of the chicken bones and sucks out the marrow, the most nutritious part. He accomplishes all this without a sound and without a fleck of grease falling onto his neatly trimmed salt-and-pepper goatee. He washes down his food with glasses of red wine. Now and then he dabs his lips with the corner of his napkin. Dinner is serious business. It's a sin to waste. Abundance may be here now, but you never know.

Their plates rest on the white Sabbath tablecloth that Lisa embroidered with images of birds, flower baskets, and ribbons, all finely cross-stitched in blue and gold thread and just like the one Grandma Antonia once made and was lost. Along with everything else from the olden days. The china they use now was bought at the bargain basement at Ogilvy's. One bowl in the package was chipped, one saucer was missing, but it's still a fine set. Plain white with gold rims, nothing kitschy, giving the table dignity. Sadly, there are no mocha cups. Lisa keeps her eyes peeled, scans the department store ads in the *Montreal Star*, but though there are White Sales, Spring Sales, and Wedding Bell Sales, mocha cups are not to be found in this primitive land. This country with one foot still in the Ice Age.

In the kitchen, the stainless steel percolator perched on the low blue flames of the gas stove sings its merry song: *pok, pok, pok.*

"Canadians know nothing about real coffee," Lisa pronounces with a vehement shake of her head. "They just shoot a bean through the water. Back home in Karlsbad—"

"Pah," Julius interrupts. "Don't tell me about that provincial town you came from. In Vienna, we knew coffee."

His eyes, a pale, frozen grey behind his glasses at the beginning of the meal, have slowly melted into a warmer colour. Loosening his tie, he reveals the knob of Adam's apple in his throat, leans back in his chair with his long legs stretched under the table, and winks at Toni. The fun begins.

"What are you talking about? Karlsbad, provincial! Royalty came to Karlsbad. Princes and princesses, all the cultured greats of Europe." Lisa's eyes flash and her chin quivers with holy indignation. "On Sundays we strolled the colonnaded promenade. We stopped at Café

Imperial. We always got the best table because the owner's daughter was in love with our Franzel."

"Your fat *shlemiel* of a brother?" Julius says.

"Don't listen to him, Toni. Don't let him fill your ears with poison. Both my brothers are handsome men. They take after my Papa, may his soul rest in peace. Even in the internment camp, girls were after my brothers."

"All in your head! Anyway, that was when the war had trimmed a few pounds off their guts. Which have come back with interest in the meantime."

Julius grins so that Toni can see the gold tooth winking at the back of his mouth.

"Tell about the coffeehouses in Vienna, Papa," Toni shouts. "Tell about the whipped cream."

"*Quatsch!*" Lisa says. "When did he go to coffeehouses? He never had two cents to rub together. He was a clerk in a hole-in-the-wall bookshop."

"I was a senior employee in a distinguished publishing and bookselling firm in the 9th district." Julius clears his throat and looks annoyed. Then the laughter comes back into his eyes. "The coffee in Vienna had mounds of *Schlagsahne*," he says with reverence. "Whipped cream that shook like a belly dancer when the white-aproned waiter approached with his tray. But in your mother's town, all they gave was a thin squirt of foam."

So the banter continues while the cuckoo clock ticks, the radiators clank, a stiff March wind rattles the loose windowpanes. The conversation, in German with bits of English, Yiddish, and Italian mixed in, flits back and forth between Karlsbad, Vienna, Trieste, Bolzano, Ferramonti, Cortino, Fossoli, the Umbrian hills—towns in Italy to which her parents drifted after the war, or places where they lived separately, before they met. Some weren't towns at all, but camps or prisons or places with caves for hiding during the war, when they had to go underground. Toni gets mixed up with before, during, and after the war, with all the names, the episodes, the rules that kept changing, the mysterious words. There was running, escaping, shooting, like in an episode of *Gunsmoke*, but with something else going on at the same time, something dark and shameful and unfathomable, like the headless man behind her bedroom wall. *You can't know how it was, and it's good you can't know.* Best to listen quietly to the bits and pieces that slip out and to wonder. The War. That was long, long ago, before she was born, and yet it is still happening, isn't it? Questions are dangerous. But sometimes they jump out anyway.

"What does internment mean?"

There, she's done it. A sudden silence fills the room, along with what she thinks of as the Brown Smell. Those words she understands, but not quite—"interned," "imprisoned," "underground," "house arrest," "displaced"—change the quality of the air. Instantly the atmosphere becomes like that cold, damp, and queasy-making place beneath the outside cement stairs where cats pee and the Brown Smell lurks. You aren't supposed to notice. Noticing makes the changes in the room more terrible, yet strangely thrilling too, so she can't help but ask again, her voice high, insistent: "Tell me, tell me!"

Lisa rears up in her chair, her chin trembles, her mouth opens. She is ready to spit out words like gunshot, the whole wretched story, but Julius flaps his hand and makes rough gurgling sounds—*harrumph, harrumph*—as if something is caught in his throat. His face grows pale. He is choking, drowning.

"Never mind," Lisa hisses, rising from the table. "Help me clear the dinner plates. Hurry up."

When the dirty dishes have been stacked beside the sink and the glass bowls set out for the sugar dumplings, Lisa says: "I have something for you, *Bubbele.* Come with me."

Her tone coaxes. Her expression has changed from thunderous to sly.

"What about dessert?" Toni cries, sensing the new danger.

"Come with me first. Then dessert."

Toni's heart sinks as she follows her mother through the door of her parents' bedroom, where, in the centre of the big bed, the cardboard box from Shmelzer's awaits. Lisa opens the box with a flourish and fishes out a girl's dress that she holds up in the air between pinched fingertips.

"*Nu?* What do you say? Lovely, isn't?"

The dress is blue-and-white-checked cotton with a wide flared skirt and petticoat underneath, bands of rickrack along the hem and sleeves, a Peter Pan collar, a cinched waist, and a cloth belt that ties in a bow at the back. Toni knows her mother went to a lot of trouble to make the dress with her own hands during moments stolen from her long day's work at Shmelzer's where she sews alterations in a curtained-off alcove. Toni's closet is full of similar creations. Last month, Lisa brought home a tartan jumper with a pleated skirt. Before that came the despicable dirndl dress with the polka-dot skirt, laced bodice, and white blouse with puffy sleeves. Toni's mother can't understand why her daughter would prefer to wear trousers and T-shirts, filthy with grass and mud. Why scuffed up sneakers and hair like a rat's nest? Such attire is *schlampig*.

"People judge you on your appearance," she always says. "The world respects you if you look your best. You can never have enough respect."

Lisa herself is always well turned out in good quality suits and dresses—bought at a discount at Shmelzer's—brooches and necklaces (costume jewellery, but no one would know), powder, rouge, and a bold slash of lipstick for a smile to conquer the world. Julius is an elegant dresser too, in neat, dark suits, the pants crisply pressed, white shirts, sober tie, highly polished shoes, and a matching felt fedora with a tiny flared feather tucked into the band. He never appears on the balcony on hot summer evenings in an undershirt as do the other men of the neighbourhood. His shirts, long- or short-sleeved, are always done up to all but the very top button, even when the stifling heat of August blankets the city. So how did Julius and Lisa Goldblatt, refined and cultivated people in the old European style, get such a gypsy of a daughter? This is the question her mother sometimes throws at Toni and offers her own answer. It's this shabby neighbourhood the family's stuck in for the moment. It's that gang of boys Toni runs around with. The janitor's son and the other fellow with the flat feet and the odd boy with the shifty eyes—juvenile delinquents in the making, the lot of them, and none of them Jewish either. *Stay away from those little hooligans.*

Her mother holds the new dress aloft in one hand, clamps Toni's shoulder with the other. "Don't make such an ugly face. Go ahead. Try it on."

"Do I have to?"

"I would have jumped for joy to receive such a lovely gift when I was your age. I would have fallen to my knees and kissed my mother's hand. Put it on!"

After many sighs, Toni stands before her mother with bowed head. The stiff new material itches, the waist pinches, the collar chokes, the skirt and petticoat billow and rustle, and everything is wrong. Toni feels like a badly built kite, certain to plunge nose-first into the dirt after the first attempt at lift-off.

"Hmm. You grew behind my back. I'll have to let out the hem and sleeves." Lisa peers at Toni, puzzled, as if she were expecting a somewhat different child to be standing before her. "Still, it's very nice. Look in the mirror."

She pushes Toni toward her vanity table with its army of makeup bottles and perfumes and its large, oval mirror that tilts up and down so you can see yourself from different angles. There she is, trussed in checked cotton, wrists dangling, scabbed and knobby knees exposed. Every dress she's ever worn makes Toni feel both confined and naked, aware of the great, empty spaces between her legs and the folds of material waiting to tangle her up when she walks. She thinks of Mabel, the chimpanzee who appears on the *Ed Sullivan Show* clad in frilly dresses and matching bonnets, strings tied in a bow under her chin. Mabel looks very black and hairy against the pale, flimsy material of her outfits. Her trainer, who is dressed in a tuxedo, invites Mabel to dance, and they shuffle around to waltz music, he taking graceful steps, she shambling awkwardly, the dress flapping around her bowed legs. At the end of the performance, Mabel curtseys, blows hideous smacking kisses at the roaring audience, and lurches about as if yanked by an invisible chain. All the while she stares directly at Toni through the TV screen, her dark eyes knowing and sad.

Toni fumbles for the buttons behind her back.

"Can I take it off now?"

But Lisa isn't ready to release her from the frilly prison.

"Leave it on. You keep that dress on if you want your dessert."

"But that's not fair!"

The outrage! The unbearable trickery! Her mother's cool, unyielding eyes. The same adamant expression is reflected in the face of Grandma Antonia as she stares out from her pewter-framed picture atop the bureau. Those two are always ganging up on her. Dashing down the corridor, Toni throws herself at her father's feet.

"Please, please, please, please, Papa," she wails. Hot tears splash down her cheeks. He gazes down miserably, biting his lips. His hand clutches his temple, *Ai, ai,* it hurts right there above his eyebrow where her unhappiness has lodged itself, burrowing deep and growing bigger than any suffering she can possibly imagine.

"Stop that. Look how you aggravate your poor Papa."

Lisa shouts. Toni screeches. A shudder runs up Julius's long limbs. He can't bear a scene. *Go away, go away.* His hands flap as if shooing off a swarm of flies, but it is he who leaves, hurrying down the hall to shut himself in his study, a tiny nook between the bathroom and the fire escape, which is crammed with books, two towering shelves of them, that form a solid barrier against the noises from the rest of the house.

Sent to bed early, Toni clutches her teddy bear in one arm, her golliwog in the other, and sucks her thumb—she knows she's too old for this, almost eight, but sometimes you need extra comfort. It's not her fault that Papa got a migraine. It's not fair that Mama is so mean. Soon she won't be allowed to be a tomboy anymore. She will have to wear dresses every day instead of the clothes that she considers like a second skin, the shirts, dungarees, and scuffed-up sneakers that smell of basement corners, bubble gum, street gutters, coal dust from the furnace room, and the big, wild woods.

From their place of banishment behind the dresser, the unloved tribe of dolls snickers. Some are girlie dolls with long-lashed eyelids that fly open when you tip them, exposing their foolish blue eyes. Some are bald-headed babies with outstretched arms and puckered lips that form a perpetual "Oh" of want for the bottle that never comes. They are birthday-present disappointments, one and all, the results of Mama and Papa's and the faraway uncles' good intentions. She had to smile and say "thank you" for each doll, while her heart sank at the stupid, oh-so-pretty faces. Only Teddy and Golly are real chums.

The neglected dolls jeer and mock: *You can hide us, but you can't get rid of us.* Same with the dresses that crowd the closet. What to do? Her one-eyed Teddy, old and wise, doesn't mince words. *Run away. Build a shelter of pine boughs in the woods. Live like Radisson, the explorer.*

Leave right now. I dare you. But it is cold beyond the edges of her covers. The bare linoleum would send shivers up her legs. The woods on the Mountain are still soggy with snow. Above her head, a long finger of yellow light slants across the ceiling, making the darkness in the room lonelier than ever. But worse is the sound behind the wall. The headless man has begun to moan. His strangled cries reach out through the plaster, and all she can do is burrow down beneath the covers, pressing Golly and Teddy to each ear, while chanting "Mama-PapaMamaPapa" to drown him out.

chapter 2

Melt water gurgles in the roof gutters. The dregs of winter drip away. Toni opens her eyes on a bright April sky and wisps of clouds like horses' tails. She leaps out of bed to press her nose against the window. From her vantage point at the back of their third-floor apartment, she has a good view of sooty buildings like their own, of wash lines, fire escapes, congresses of pigeons, muddy lanes to gallop through and puddles to stomp in and chainlink fences to climb.

As far as Lisa is concerned, the apartment on Maplewood Avenue is a stopgap measure, a step up—but only just—from the downtown slum in which they used to live. Their first home, when her parents got off the ship in Montreal harbour, was a room in a cold-water flat with rickety staircases and thick lips of ice along the bottoms of the windows in winter. Toni was too small to remember, but Lisa tells stories. The streets overflowed with immigrants, "greeners" like themselves from every blasted corner of Europe. *Fellow Jews, yes, but dingy synagogues, men in black coats, the babble of Yiddish. We didn't go through what we did to end up in Borscht Alley. You want to be with your own, but you want a bit of lawn in between.* Their current neighbourhood facing the back of Mount Royal is neither one thing nor another, Lisa says. Not a slum, but not an up-and-coming suburb either. The apartment buildings look worn out and listless, like people just trudging along to the end of their days.

As far as Toni's concerned, there can be no other home, no other street, no other neighbourhood in the whole world. All imperfections are perfect. All belong to her: the cracks that zigzag up the walls, the gaps in the kitchen linoleum, even the creaking floors that scare her at night. These things are as much her possessions as her trove of cat's-eye marbles and her Dinky Toy cars. In the dimly lit basement of the building, pipes snake along dark ceilings, a coal-fired furnace roars, and a big pile of coal fills the air with a peppery smell. But best is the Mountain. Their street hugs the wild side of Mount Royal: miles and miles of trees, bogs, ponds—Radisson and Davy Crockett land. If you follow a path through the tangle of woods, you emerge on a wide, stony plateau beneath a semi-circle of cliffs that rise high as skyscrapers. Toni and her gang often scramble up the sheer rock face for the lick-in-the-belly danger sensation and the view from the top, the north end of the city spread out before them all the way to the faint glimmer of the river in the distance. It seems to Toni that her parents' wanderings from place to place had a single purpose: to bring her to this place beside the Mountain.

She squints through the window to see whether her gang is down in the lane yet. Soon they will assemble—Peter, Nicky, Frank, and their captain, Arnold, good old Arnold. With whoops, whistles, and Tarzan yells, they'll dodge the street traffic and charge into the wild frontier. Saturday morning. Spring at last. Time to be Daniel Boone.

Still in pyjamas, she begins to wolf down her breakfast of cooked oatmeal from the bag with the Quaker man on it, his fat red cheeks setting a good example. Her father, dressed for work, studies the *Gazette*, neatly folded into quarters and held close to his face, while the radio mutters in the background. In the evenings, Julius reads the *Montreal Star*. Though most of it is bad, there can never be enough news for some reason. Lisa patters around the kitchen in her rose-coloured wrapper and high-heeled mules, her head bristling with rollers beneath a hairnet.

Toni contemplates her bottomless bowl of porridge as Saturday excitement boils in her chest. *The guys, the woods, the Mountain.* While her mother's back is turned, Toni slips spoonfuls of breakfast into the plant on the kitchen table and covers the gluey mess with damp black earth. Were her parents to see, they would both have a fit, in their own individual ways: Lisa roaring with outrage, Julius convulsing in private grief. A sacrilege, to waste food. However it tastes, however much excess exists, food must be treasured. Regiments of carefully labelled leftovers cram the Goldblatt fridge. Hardened bits of bread crust and rinds of cheese wrapped in wax paper lie hidden in the pockets of her father's well-pressed suit jackets. *One never knows.* Her mother now swoops forward to inspect Toni's bowl.

"Finished eating? Good. You're going to play with the Nutkevitch girls."

"What?"

"It's all arranged. They're waiting."

Howls of protest are to no avail. Her mother's flinty eyes and iron grip mean business.

"You will play with the Nutkevitch girls. You will wear your nice new dress."

Double outrage.

"I hate the twins!"

"Nonsense. What's to hate?"

As far as Lisa is concerned, the Nutkevitch twins, who live in the apartment building next door, are cute, chatty, charming, good at everything girls are supposed to be good at. They take ballet lessons, they play piano. They go to a special Jewish school where there are no *goyische* hooligans. The Nutkevitch family are *Ostjuden*, eastern European Jews, but it doesn't matter, you can't have everything. Such nice girls.

Lisa pushes, tugs, brushes, fastens—brisk, efficient, merciless. Captive in the billowy-skirted dress, her hair tightly pinned with two butterfly-shaped barrettes above her ears, Toni shuffles toward the twins' house next door, while her mother glares like a tiger from the front walk.

Their names are Ashie and Shevie, but Toni calls them Assie and Shittie. With their snooty, better-than-you attitude, they try to make Toni feel she's the one who's all wrong. Her buddies hate them too, because not only are the twins girly-girls, they are weirdly foreign, using Jewish expressions and speaking in sing-song voices. On the Jewish high holidays they go on foot to attend a synagogue many blocks away. Dressed up and marching briskly, their noses in the air, the twins push their baby brother, Yankele, in his carriage and act as if they think everyone else is being lazy. The guys understand Toni isn't Jewish in any way that matters, just as she's not quite a girl. She's a tomboy. Her family never goes to synagogue. They keep holidays quietly, behind closed doors. The boys pump her back, saying "Good old Toni, good old sport."

Now, Toni stands on the doorstep of the Nutkevitch apartment, summoning up the nerve to ring the bell. She can never tell the twins apart, which adds to her disadvantage. They wear identical clothes and high, bouncy pigtails, their hair parted perfectly to create a straight, narrow road of pale skin up the backs of their heads. Behind the door she can hear their baby brother bawling. *Assie and Shittie*, Toni chants in her mind as she stabs the doorbell with her finger.

Mrs Nutkevitch answers. She is big-chested, flushed and sweaty, wearing a flour-speckled apron and smiling distractedly. She jiggles Yankele on her shoulder with one hand and holds a cloth diaper in the other. The watery-eyed baby gapes, hides his face in his mother's neck, and sticks out a bare red bum. Greeting Toni with little cries of welcome, the twins hook their arms into hers and escort her down the hall to their room. White and gold furniture, frilly curtains, two sets of identical hairbrushes, combs, and hand mirrors on the dresser. On each of the identical beds, a row of dolls arranged according to size, confronts Toni with glassy stares.

"How nice of you to visit," says one twin in a phony grownup voice.

"Have a candy," says the other, offering Toni a LifeSaver from a multi-coloured roll.

"*Oy*, I love your dress. It's gorgeous!"

They bob their heads in agreement and finger the rickrack on Toni's sleeves. Clearly they are under orders to be nice.

"Let's play house. We'll be mummy and daddy and Toni can be baby."

"I don't play house," Toni growls.

"Oh," says the twin who made the suggestion. She sucks her cheeks around her LifeSaver while raising her eyebrows and exchanging a look of astonishment with her sister. What kind of girl refuses to play house? "So what do you want to do?"

Toni shrugs. To say, "I want to go home" would be to sound like the baby she doesn't want to pretend to be.

"We could have a game," says the other twin in an encouraging tone. "We could play rummy."

Toni nods, grateful. Card games are neutral, neither boys' nor girls' territory. Cards can be played without shame even while wearing a flare-skirted dress with a white petticoat underneath. The three of them sit cross-legged on one of the beds and play round upon round of five-card rummy, then hearts, fish, war. Toni wins as often as either of the twins, so they're not cheating or ganging up on her. Toni notices that though the twins have no toys she would consider playing with, they do have some of the same Walt Disney books she has on her own shelves. In the kitchen Mrs Nutkevitch is baking something for a midmorning snack, something the twins call *rugelach*.

"You've never had *rugelach*?!"

The twins stare incredulously, as if Toni were an ignorant country mouse. They explain about the yummy rolled pastries filled with raisins, nuts, and chocolate powder.

"You haven't lived until you've had *rugelach*," says Ashie—or is it Shevie?—with a cute toss of her head that makes her seem almost a teenager instead of eight years old and in grade three just like Toni. From the heavenly aroma seeping beneath the door, Toni thinks they may be telling the truth, and that it's worth hanging around until the snack is served.

When they've tired of cards, the twins again propose a game of make-believe, and once more Toni shakes her head. She would like to explain about being a tomboy, but that's easier to do while wearing dungarees and surrounded by the gang. So she pulls the hem of her dress over her bare knees and decides to stop talking altogether. While Toni remains sullen and cross-legged on the bed, the twins spin their stories, chattering merrily, and hop around the room, pigtails dancing. Here comes Papa, home from a long day's work at his butcher shop. Mama greets him at the door with joyful cries. Now they will dress up for a party. But before they can go out, they must attend to baby. "*Schluf, schluf, kindele,*" the twins croon in high, squeaky, lullaby voices. Toni squeezes shut her eyes and claps her hands over her ears until she feels a hand lift her dress. Her eyes snap open.

Two identical, gleeful faces grin down at her. One twin holds a diaper, a real cloth diaper like the ones Yankele wears, the other has talcum powder and petroleum jelly. Toni flings herself backward and hits the wall, which pushes the bed sideways and makes the entire row of dolls tumble to the floor. Still on her back, she bucks, kicks, roars. The girls shriek. The bedroom door flies open.

"*Kindele!* What's going on?"

Mrs Nutkevitch stands in the entrance, a flour-dusted oven mitt pressed against her cheek, an expression of alarm on her face as if she cannot believe such havoc can be happening within her four walls. From the kitchen comes Yankele's rising wail. Before the twins can spew out a malicious tale, Toni bolts. Down the hall she runs, out the door of the Nutkevitch apartment, down the stairs, heart racing. On the front walk she pauses for breath, then turns toward home at a more leisurely pace, exulting in her freedom, until she hears them chant in unison behind her: "Toni the freak! Toni the freak!"

There they stand on the steps with their hands on their hips and their grinning faces thrust forward. Without stopping to think what she's doing, Toni bends over, pulls down her underpants, and moons them with her bare behind. There's a moment of stunned silence, then the eruption of a new chant, voiced with frantic hilarity: "Garbage bum! Garbage bum!"

Their vengeful delight makes Toni wonder if mooning the twins was such a brain wave after all or the sort of dumb move that haunts you the rest of your life. Suddenly she feels squishy inside, foolish and naked and wrong. Suddenly she's Mabel the chimp, all bowed legs and shambling feet and hairy humiliation in front of an audience collapsing in hysterics. Pretending a dignity she doesn't feel, she walks stiffly away while her hair, loosened from the barrettes, flops in her face and the wide ship of her dress wobbles in the air.

But later she gets even. Dressed again in her proper tomboy clothes, Toni swoops upon the twins as they play skipping games on the three squares of walkway in front of their house. She plasters two identical wads of Dubble Bubble onto the backs of their two unsuspecting heads. From their hiding places in the hydrangea bushes, the whole gang bursts into cheers as Assie and Shittie wail for their mama. Before the posse can arrive, four boys and Toni race across the streetcar tracks to the waiting embrace of the spring-green woods.

chapter 3

Grandma Antonia is a flame in a glass, a dancing tongue of fire above thick white wax. When Toni bumps against the kitchen counter, the flame body twists, writhes, as if angry at being disturbed.

"Hold still," Lisa hisses, pinching Toni's arm. "Stand and listen while I say the Kaddish. And when I'm done, you say 'Amen.'"

This evening is the start of Yom Kippur, the Day of Atonement and a day of remembrance for all those without a final resting place. In the Goldblatt family household, it is a day to spit on Hitler and to mourn Grandma's death.

The memorial candle sits in a small glass jar with the blue Star of David and Hebrew letters printed across one side. The flame will burn all through supper, through their television shows—*Gunsmoke, Country Hoedown*, the CBC evening news—and throughout the night, filling the kitchen with a spooky glow. All day tomorrow, the flame will sway behind its sooty glass walls, finally becoming nothing but a tiny blue eye in a puddle of wax, clear as tears. And still it will endure, on and on, refusing to disappear until well after dark. Once a year the candle is lit, allowing Grandma, whose spirit lurks in mysterious corners of the house, to come out into the open. She fills the kitchen with her eerie light, her brazen presence, tingling the skin at the back of Toni's neck.

On Yom Kippur, Lisa fasts, "for my own reasons," she says, but cooks meals for Toni and her father, just as on any other day, and joins them at the table to make sure every morsel goes down as it's supposed to. They all stay home for the day, don't troop off to synagogue like the Nutkevitch family does. Papa works, just not where people can see. On Yom Kippur, he works at home, in the silence of his study. To do otherwise would be disrespectful, he says, though Toni isn't sure why. Disrespectfulness extends to shopping in stores and playing in the streets. It is a strange day of being holed up together. Of waiting. Of hiding.

"*Yit'gadal v'yit'kadash sh'mei raba...*"

Mumbo jumbo falls from her mother's lips. The Kaddish prayer. Lisa closes her eyes. Her voice rises, defiant against the twilight gloom of the kitchen and the everyday noises, the patter of October rain in the gravel lane outside, the gurgling fridge inside, and now the clang, whirr, "cuckoo" from the brown clock, shaped like a fairy-tale cottage, on the wall above the kitchen table. Toni wants to jump onto a chair and push Cuckoo behind his door before Mama loses her temper and rips him out of his hidey-hole once and for all. Toni strains forward, but her mother's hand yanks her back.

"... *Yit'barakh v'yish'tabach v'yit'pa'ar v'yit'romam v'yit'nasei.*"

Grandma's flame rears straight up, sending a long wisp of smoke toward the ceiling.

What happened to Grandma?

A bad question. Whenever Toni dares to ask, her mother spits out the answers: "She was taken," or, "She perished," or, "She was swept away." Then Lisa's body quivers as it does when she's about to give Toni a smack for being saucy, but instead her hands ball into fists and her lips form silent words meant for Grandma alone. They speak to each other all the time, a conversation that goes on just beyond the range of Toni's ears.

Where did they take her?

That too must not be asked. Toni knows Grandma was killed, but it was not an ordinary sort of killing as on cowboy shows when the outlaw in the saloon gets a bullet in the chest. Her dying must have been more like when the bad guys tie up and gag the schoolteacher, so that all she can do is roll her eyes and make strangled sounds. "Gag" is what happens when you've got to throw up but can't, and you feel like you're drowning from the inside out.

The Kaddish drones on. The flame winks, flows, changes shape, transforms itself every instant. Toni remembers a scene from a Walt Disney film where a single flame with an innocent, smiling face swayed on the end of a match. The flame split, became two laughing faces, then they divided and divided again and soon hundreds of wild, cackling flames, their eyes slanted upward with evil, danced all over the forest.

After she died, Grandma's soul floated straight to heaven. Whenever Lisa says this, her jaw clenches and she glares down, as if Toni were giving her an argument. Grandma whispers warnings, advice, hovers at the ends of Lisa's fingers when she lays out rows of cards on the kitchen table and turns them over one by one to tell fortunes. Julius has nothing to say about heaven and he pooh-poohs the fortune-telling cards. He doesn't believe in ghosts, visions, conversations with the dead. What moans through the cracks in the walls and between the floorboards is mere wind, he'll say. All that exists are the solid things you can hold or touch—the floor, walls, the antique books he collects—or what science can explain—that fire, for example, is a mix of fuel, heat, and air, nothing more. One candle flame is pretty much like any other.

"… *aleinu v'al kol Yisra'el, v'imru amen.*"

Lisa's fingers prod Toni's shoulder, prompting a loud "Amen." Toni turns her head and blinks away the tears that blurred her eyes after so much hard staring, but Lisa continues to gaze intently for some moments, lips moving, muttering in German, while the flame answers her in a series of winks and nods.

A terrible wonder holds Toni to the spot as she waits for something to happen: an outburst of anger, a torrent of strange words, upraised hands that command the heavens to do their bidding. In the Disney movie the wizard stood on the mountaintop while lightning flashed, bats whirled, trees bent double in the wind. Lisa sucks in her breath. Is it possible that instead of grand anger will come tears? But her mother never cries. *If I cried, I wouldn't stop.*

"Bring Grandma's photo," she now says, lowering herself onto a kitchen chair.

Toni dashes to her parents' bedroom to fetch the pewter-framed photo of Grandma Antonia that stands on the bureau. She wasn't a grandmother then, Toni remembers, just a thick-waisted lady in a dark, sack-like dress that came to her ankles, pearls around her neck, her hair done up in a tight bun. Lisa distends her lips like a fish and blows mist on the glass and wipes it clean with a cloth. She admires the photo as if for the first time.

"*Mutti* was our rock. She took care of everyone, never complaining. She was wise, clever with her hands, industrious. You bear her name."

Now the stories flow. On Yom Kippur, Grandma kept several of her famous homemade bread sticks in her handbag. At the end of the long fast day, coming down from the woman's gallery to the outside steps of the synagogue where Grandpa Markus stood waiting, she slipped him a few for sustenance. Otherwise Grandpa might have fainted from hunger before she could get him home. Grandma herself had no trouble fasting as her constitution was strong as a goat's, just as Lisa's is now. Grandma could add up columns of sums in her head. She helped Grandpa Markus in the store that sold fancy linens, tablecloths, runners, lace doilies, finely finished bed sheets, and embroidered blouses. If a crooked dealer came with shoddy goods, Grandma could tell before he unpacked his wares. She could sniff out a shoplifter too. Grandpa Markus would say, "Never mind. If the poor girl pinches a scrap of cloth it's because she needs to."

"He was so kind, your Grandpa," Lisa says, as if kindness were not entirely an admirable thing.

All this—before-the-war—is one story. Then comes how Antonia said, "Go, go, go. They won't bother with us old folks, but there's no future here for the young." So Lisa and her two brothers, Wilhelm and Franz, travelled by train to the coast of Italy, where they boarded a boat for Palestine. But it turned out to be a swindle. The boat chugged out to the open seas, then turned back that very same night so that when they looked out the porthole in the morning they saw, not the wide, blue Mediterranean, but the barnacled hull of the same Russian tanker they'd docked beside the day before. The captain had disappeared. Their money was gone. After that it was out-of-the-frying-pan-into-the-fire. Banishment, arrest, release, internment, escape, hiding, hiding.

"All in all, the Italians were human. It could have been worse. How? Don't ask! We found good people to help us. *Mutti's* voice told me who to trust. We hid with poor farmers, high in the mountains. I learned to take care of the cows. Can you see your mama pitching hay?"

Toni can. She imagines her mother brandishing a pitchfork at German soldiers who run down the mountainside, their hands shielding their bums.

At the end of the war, Lisa and her brothers landed in a DP camp, which was not a prison exactly, just a place to wait, to rot, until some country, somewhere, was willing to take you in. Lisa worked as a nurse's aid in the clinic where she tended to all kinds of miserable souls.

"Unbelievable stories. You can't imagine, and it's good that you can't."

They were mostly *Ostjuden*, speaking a babble of tongues, but one was a long-legged fellow from Vienna—practically a countryman! It was Papa. He languished on a cot and he was white and limp as cooked asparagus, his eyes like spent bullet shells. Dysentery. Plus something else that caused the doctor to shake his head. A collapse of the spirit. While others groaned endlessly and clamoured for attention, Julius disappeared into the silence of his bones. Not the most appealing sight, you would think, but he had beautiful hands, and after all that time with sausage-fingered peasants, Lisa was susceptible to a pair of elegant hands. And she liked the length of him. Tall as an American if you could stand him up. While she held a cup of water to his indifferent lips, Antonia whispered that this was the one. So he became Lisa's project. She had will enough for them both.

"I cooked a hearty broth and fed him spoon by spoon. I knew if I could get my soup into him, one thing would lead to another, and I was right. After a while—" a sly smile plays around Lisa's lips—"after a while he became hungry on his own."

She stares down at the photo on the table.

"I knew there was no point in going back to Vienna. I read the cards. I knew all we needed to know, but he wouldn't listen. He had to go back. To look. We lost our place in line at the embassies."

"To look for what, Mama?"

Her mother starts, as if surprised to hear Toni's voice. She digs her fingernail into the crevices of the photo frame to remove bits of caked-on polish.

"Always we were very close, *Mutti* and me. We were like one mind in two bodies."

Toni slips off her chair and stands beside her mother to see what she's talking about. The woman in the photograph is not as beautiful as Toni's mother, but she does seem to have the same will of iron. Her back ramrod straight, she stares fiercely out of the photo and right into Toni's heart. *I know you hate the name Antonia. What kind of granddaughter shuns her Grandma's name?*

In her mind Toni argues that "Toni" sounds nicer and could even be a boy's name, while "Antonia" sounds creaky and old. Grandma's photo-face remains unconvinced.

One mind in two bodies. The thought makes Toni feel left out. She flings herself against her mother, who still holds the picture in her hands.

"Oof, careful, you'll break it," Lisa grunts, shoving Toni away. But the next moment she has scooped Toni into her arms and clutches her hard, squeezing the breath out of her, causing a hot, bright warmth beneath Toni's ribs and a smothered sensation too, so that it is she who must push away at last.

"Lay the cards, Mama. Please," Toni begs, seized with longing for magic and revelations. "Maybe you have to warn someone they're going to die."

"Nonsense. I wouldn't do such a thing. I only tell good fortunes." Lisa narrows her eyes at Toni. "So you want to know what lies ahead, do you? All right then, fetch the cards."

Toni hands over the deck. Her mother lays long rows face down on the table. "Hmm. Interesting." She sucks in her lip as she peers first at the card she's turned over, then at Toni over the tops of her reading glasses.

"What? What?"

But Lisa shakes her head. Let's not be hasty and interpret too soon. One card means nothing on its own. More must be turned over to know whether there is a pattern here, a story, or only random bits of cardboard on the table. Aha, the Queen of Diamonds. Now all is revealed. A progression, see? A three of clubs grows up to become a lovely feminine face card. There can be only one meaning—a wedding foretold. Toni will one day become a beautiful bride in a frothy white gown. The guests will cry "*l'chayim,*" they will dance the *hora*. Her mother's eyes shine with happily-ever-after.

A frothy white gown, Toni mutters under her breath as she lays the table for supper. She shouldn't have asked for the cards to speak. Now she's stuck with this picture in her head of the gown coming at her with outstretched sleeves, the spooky veil floating over a cold, dark emptiness. Over on the counter, the flame in the jar convulses in silent laughter.

Julius sits at his desk, bent over his ledger books. His shoulders are hunched, his long back curved like the arch of the goose-necked lamp that casts a glow on his bald head. Papa's skull is like a delicate shell, with bumps and indentations and a thin, tight layer of skin—the same aged, yellowish colour as the pages in some of the old books he collects. *Tappa, tappa*, go the fingers of his left hand, dancing over the keys of the adding machine, *tappa, tappa, kachunk,* while his right hand makes neat, precise entries in the ledger squares, never straying over the lines. Now and then he tugs the short grey hairs of his goatee and sighs. Her father is a bookkeeper, which has nothing to do with real books; it means keeping track of other people's money and not seeing much of your own. During the day, he hurries on foot or by streetcar from one client to another, carrying two bulging leather briefcases that knock against his sides.

"You can come in if you stay quiet," he says without lifting his head. "Sit in the corner and read."

The room embraces her, a narrow, cosy cave, crammed with Papa's things, but with everything in its place, shipshape. Books stand at attention on bookshelves that rise from floor to ceiling on two sides. The wide wooden desk by the window has a view of stained brick walls, backdoor landings, metal rails, and circular stairs that wind down to a tiny courtyard between their apartment building and its twin next door. Through the raised window sash comes a faint smell of garbage and cement moistened by October drizzle. Toni takes a seat on a stool in the corner. The books on the shelves that tower above her are Papa's treasures. They are mostly in German with dense print, old-fashioned Gothic letters, and impossible words. Books are precious, Julius says, and their value can't be reckoned in dollars. Once, Hitler's men burned books in huge bonfires because they were written by Jewish writers or because they said things Hitler didn't like. His men hunted down books just as later they hunted down people. But they couldn't burn everything everywhere. If Lisa had her druthers, the books in the study would be much fewer so she'd have space for an ironing board. "He hardly reads them anyway," she says. "He collects. And they collect dust."

Which isn't true, of course. Julius does read, sitting still as a statue in his chair, a position of deep devotion, while the flicker of his eyelids and the slight movement of his lips tell you he's very much awake and, *um Gottes willen*, don't interrupt. He keeps everything on the shelves clean and perfectly arranged according to rules Toni will never understand. If she pulls out a volume and shoves it back in the wrong place, he rushes to fix her mistake. Ignoring her own stash of Walt Disneys in the corner, she attempts to remove one of Papa's books now, a fat cloth-bound tome with gold lettering on the spine, like something a wizard might own.

"What are you doing?" Julius spins around in his chair.

"Show me, Papa," Toni pleads. Not that the books themselves mean anything to her. She just likes how he shows them, how he becomes a different Papa when he does. A soft gleam has already dawned in his eyes. He hesitates, twiddling his pencil, but he can't stop himself.

"Ah, by instinct you have found a jewel. Jakob Wassermann."

He gingerly places the book on the desk in front of him and draws her close. "A great novelist. One of the best of his era. When this book came out in 1928 we filled our whole display case at Stubling's with copies. This is a first edition."

His eyes have gone from washed-out grey to silver-dollar bright.

He enfolds Toni in the crook of his arm, keeping her still, while his right hand gently turns pages with the tips of his fingers. Her father handles his books as if they were butterflies that could be crushed by a clumsy gesture. He can spend hours poring over inscriptions with a magnifying glass or gazing at a decorative border. What a book says, he explains, is sometimes only a small part of what makes it beautiful or important. He loves typefaces, bindings, paper, ink. He loves how a fine book is put together, how it rests in his hands, the musty smells of old paper and glue, a black-and-white photo of the author's face beneath onion skin paper, an engraving of a maiden posed beside a well. He loves the surprises that sometimes tumble out of the pages: a piece of a moth's wing, a single white hair, a yellowed newspaper clipping, a grocery list from the olden days—signs the book had another life, in another time.

"Papa, how many books were in your store in Vienna? A million?"

She could listen forever to his tales about Vienna, a place of towers and spires, boulevards and cobblestone streets, the emperor's palace and the giant Ferris wheel in Prater Park. A whiff of long-ago, never-again beauty comes through in her father's recollections. Once Julius sat on his own father's shoulders to see the emperor's plume-bedecked carriage pulled by six prancing white stallions. Once he worked in a bookshop with golden letters on the plate-glass windows and oak display shelves and famous customers, like a certain Dr Freud. Those were the days, when lilting Strauss waltzes poured from outdoor band shells, when smells of roasted coffee, crusty rolls, and fine cigars mingled with the scent of hyacinths from the palace grounds, when people dressed for the theatre or for strolls on the promenades. *Ach*, those were the days.

"A million books!" her father now chuckles. "A million is a very big number. And besides, it wasn't my shop. It belonged to my employer. But I was his right-hand man. In those days, in Europe, one had to study to be a bookseller. Not like here where you encounter some half-wit clerk who could just as well be selling matchboxes as books. I took courses after high school. My father was dead set against it. He wanted me to follow him into the banking profession. *Ach, ya.* He was right. A very uncertain business it turned out to be, selling books."

Julius heaves a great gust of a sigh, sad, but also strangely comforting, like a breeze that stirs the bedroom curtains at the end of the day, telling you nothing else interesting is going to happen, you might as well shut your eyes and go to sleep.

"Tell about Minka the cat."

Toni settles herself against his chest, her head under his chin. She likes the smell of him, the clean cotton of his shirt and the faint, minty trace of aftershave. He rocks back and forth in the swivel chair as he speaks.

"As a boy I wasn't a good student like you, *Mausie.* Although I liked to read, I found it hard to apply myself, especially in mathematics, which was a great disappointment to my father. The irony is that after all these years, here I am, making my living with numbers after all. All right, all right. Minka. When I hid in my room in shame from a bad report card, she rubbed herself against me, purring like an engine. She knew I needed comfort."

"I wish we had a cat. Why can't we, Papa? Why?"

His mouth closes tightly, his encircling arm drops. Toni isn't sure whether he's annoyed by her question or troubled by the absence of a cat in their lives.

"The cat was actually supposed to be for my sister. To keep her company. She was often ill."

"What was wrong with her?"

He doesn't answer. He stares out the window at the dark brick wall. Then, after a long uncomfortable silence he says, "The cat was afraid of her."

"Why?" Toni shrills. Suddenly, she, too, is afraid, because of the hollow sound of his voice and the sudden stiffness in his limbs. He turns from the window and fixes her with the strangest expression, as if he sees not Toni, but some terrible ghost, and this look takes her voice away, so that while she wants to call out to him, she can't. The cry lies frozen in her throat. Now he turns away again, his eyes blank and empty, his body like unfeeling wood, all of him unreachable. *PapaPapaPapa.* The words knock against each other but can't find their way to her lips. She slides from his knee.

"There's a good girl," the hollow voice says.

"Show me another book?" she manages to whisper.

But nothing moves in his face except for the blink of eyelids over cold grey jelly. She slips away out of the room, closing the door noiselessly behind her to shut out the unbearable sight of her absent Papa. The spell could last a minute or a long, long time. Somehow it's her fault. She made him disappear. Her wrong question, or maybe it was just her careless jostling against his shoulder, broke some invisible string. One moment he was her Papa, the next moment a puppet severed from the things that hold him up and make him work.

In her parents' bedroom, in the closet behind her mother's dresses and her father's suits, lies a metal chest about the size of a breadbox. Toni knows how to creep unseen into the closet, half closing the door behind her, unlock the chest with the key from the hook in the corner and settle herself noiselessly on the dusty floor. Inside the box, among bundles of uninteresting papers, is an envelope with a few cracked photos. Toni slips them out one by one and holds them up to the shaft of light. The lost relatives.

They wear old-fashioned outfits like in a Major Hoople cartoon: the men have waistcoats, fedoras, round spectacles; the women wear long, dark, tight-fitting suits and hats like bowls pulled down over their ears; and the children have round, shocked eyes and serious mouths.

Among the children in the photos she recognizes her father, though there's no beard, of course, no furrows across the brow. What connects that face with her papa now are the pale, moody eyes and the long reedy body. In one photo, he wears a sailor suit and holds the hand of a blonde little girl in a white dress, white stockings, white shoes, and an absurd white bow like a huge butterfly perched on her head. Is this the girl who scared the cat? She looks no stranger than any of the others. We should put them into an album, her mother sometimes says of these photos, but her father looks away. One time he did consent to tell Toni who was who. *Sister, mother, father, uncle this, auntie that, cousin so-and-so.* He jabbed his forefinger at the people, spoke in a flat, weary voice, as if they were strangers to him, too. Now she can't remember any of what he said. A washed-out, grainy blur of faces gazes back at her.

chapter 4

June has come. The breezes that blow through open windows smell of earth, dust, lilacs, cut grass, the meaty turds left curbside by the horse that pulls the Borden's Milk truck through the streets. At Goyette's corner store, they've started selling ice cream cones again—vanilla, strawberry, chocolate, Neapolitan—a nickel apiece. At Saint Joseph's Oratory, pilgrims recite a prayer on each step while ascending a long outdoor stairway on their knees. The Mountain is in bloom, and that great blue sea of time—summer holidays—beckons.

Nine-year-old Toni gets ready for her school day with the resignation of a soldier preparing for the trenches. Slipping on the uniform— white blouse, pleated navy blue tunic, and spit-polished Oxfords—she becomes that other self: quiet and studious, good sport, blackboard monitor, nobody's special friend, but nobody's enemy either. In the bathroom, she scrubs her hands to raw pinkness. Her mother, rushing by in her housecoat, pauses by the open bathroom door to comment.

"Amazing. Such a *schlump* on our street, such a neatnik at school."

Lisa smiles a knowing smile that says: *You're not such a lost cause as you pretend to be. You really are my little girl at heart.* There's no way to explain to her mother about the two separate realms that require Toni to be two different people. And even if she could explain, it wouldn't change a thing. She checks her nails for stubborn bits of grime. Their teacher—the frosty, aloof, and terrible Miss Muir—once stopped at Toni's desk while patrolling the aisles.

"My, my, what filthy nails!" Miss Muir exclaimed.

Her tone made Toni feel the hold-your-nose horror of the unclean, and everyone snickered. There were boys with grubbier paws in the class. Miss Muir was so offended because this particular set of nails belonged to a girl, which made the dirt beneath them inexplicable and especially dark. Toni made an inner vow to never again give cause for such scorn.

Surveying herself now in the bathroom mirror, Toni decides a tunic is not as bad as a dress. A dress is nothing but a flimsy curtain, insubstantial as the little pig's straw house, whereas a tunic is made of solid, dark, pleated, no-nonsense material that falls to her knees. And the crisper the pleats, the tidier the belt, the shinier her shoes, the better the outfit can be imagined into the uniform of the Lone Ranger. It's a stretch. It requires eyes-squeezed-shut concentration until the dream takes hold. *Hi ho Silver, away!*

Before leaving the house, Toni pauses in the doorway of her parents' bedroom to watch her mother at work on herself with creams, powders, lipstick, pencils, pincers, tweezers, and inky black stuff from a tube with a tiny spiral brush. Putting on a face, it's called. As if Lisa's morning-pale cheeks and unpainted lips were not the real thing, the face, but instead, a filmy, ghostly mask that could vanish in the bright light of day. Seated at the dressing table in her peach-coloured slip, Lisa brings a pinching apparatus up to her left eye and squeezes down on the scissors-like handle. She holds the pincer in place while her eyelids quiver.

"Doesn't that hurt?"

Lisa's free eye slides sideways to observe her daughter watching.

"We must suffer to be beautiful."

She smiles. Her mouth, not yet coated with lipstick, looks soft, naked, and vulnerable, like a flower petal about to fall off its stem. With deft strokes of the little spiral brush, Lisa lengthens and blackens her eyelashes, then flutters them at Toni, who turns away.

"Yech!"

"One day soon you will be begging me to let you put on makeup. Oh yes, you will. A mother knows."

Toni says nothing. When Lisa moves to the closet to choose her outfit for the day, Toni snatches one of the golden tubes of lipstick from the dressing table and slips it into her book bag. The gleaming finger of red, so much finer and brighter than a crayon, will come in handy. Later.

In the alley behind their apartment building, Toni meets tubby Peter and squinty-eyed Nick, two boys from her gang who go with her to Jubilee School. Her other buddies, Arnold and Frank, attend a Catholic school beside a tall-spired church run by black-robed nuns. Ashie and Shevie—the Nuts, as the gang has come to call the Nutkevitch twins— head off early with their father on a bus every morning to a remote, mysterious part of town to attend a school for Jewish kids only.

During the entire long, carefree walk toward Jubilee, through the tree-lined streets and vacant-lot short cuts, Toni, Peter, and Nick amble and tumble together. They bump shoulders, take turns kicking stones, and share licorice strings like the best of pals. But the moment they reach the outer edges of the school yard, the brotherly trio comes apart. Peter and Nick dash off without a word to join a ball hockey game in the area that by common understanding belongs to boys alone. This territory takes up a broad semi-circular swath, stretching to the fences, fields, and streets—the outer borders of school premises—while the girls' sphere consists of that inner space near the doors and walls. There's no question of Toni following the guys. Nothing personal. Just how it is. At school, the divisions are plain and firm.

Instead, Toni heads for the Double-Dutch skipping game in progress near the steps beneath the doorway engraved with the words

"Girls' Entrance." Though she never skips—those silly, mincing hops are beneath her dignity—Toni doesn't mind turning rope. She whirls them in fast-moving arcs, standing with legs slightly apart like a cowboy who rustles steers. As feet scuffle and voices chant, Toni dreams herself back into the world of the Lone Ranger until Karen Weissbloom appears. When she sees Karen, Toni's heart goes "plop," like a puppy falling into a bath of cold water, and then beats hard. Her palms tingle as if something's about to slip from her hands. She has to concentrate to make sure the two whirling ropes don't collide. What is it about Karen Weissbloom? She's the girliest of girls, yet in a totally different category from the squealing, giggling Nutkevitch twins. Karen is the angel on the Christmas tree, the Sugarplum Fairy, Tinker Bell, and Snow White, all rolled up in one. She has silky tresses of honey-blonde hair, dimpled cheeks, tender eyes, and a mouth like a cherry lollipop. Karen isn't just pretty, she's sweet, with a warm, trusting smile for everyone, as if she couldn't imagine a mean thought in anyone's heart. Toni never speaks to Karen. Just watches her, aware of Karen's halo glow.

Miss Muir is teaching geography. Who knows the names of the Great Lakes? Would someone please do her the favour of raising a hand? With arched brows, she eyes the bowed heads, the squirming bodies trapped behind desks. She makes an "O" of disappointment with her lips. But it's not real disappointment. There's haughty triumph in the way her graceful head swivels on its long neck when she scans the class for someone reckless enough to think they know the answer.

Miss Muir hails from Scotland, the pink place at the very top of the pink expanses known as Britain and Her Dominions on the map of the world. She is tall, slender, and beautiful in an evil-queen sort of way, with pencilled eyebrows, ice-blue eyes, porcelain skin, and chestnut hair done up in a tight French roll. In the lapel of her tweed suit jacket a silver brooch shaped like a thistle sends out dark gleams. She's a stickler for spelling.

"Gels and boys," she often says. "Nothing so marks you as an ignorrramus as the incorrect spelling of homonyms."

She utters the "g" of "gels" deep in her throat, like a growl.

Now, as Miss Muir prowls the class, she wonders aloud why no one knows the answer to her simple question. Has no one done his homework? Toni has. She could rattle off, "Ontario, Erie, Huron, Superior, Michigan," because those big, fine names have sunk into her mind along with the names of the explorers and *coureurs du bois*. But she doesn't raise her hand because the words disintegrate on her tongue under Miss Muir's cool, amused, unnerving gaze. And anyway, Toni would rather vanish into dreams. *A fiery horse with the speed of light, a cloud of dust and a hi ho Silver, away! The Lone Ranger!* It's easy to disappear. She's been playing that trick ever since she can remember, slipping out of her body, leaving a ghost of herself in the chair. She appears to be completely present, hands folded on her desk, back straight, while her mind splits: one part keeping track of Miss Muir, the rest taking a holiday wherever it pleases. The seat she's chosen helps: front row, off to the side near the window. She's just a blur in the periphery of the teacher's vision.

Flinty eyes sweep the room in search of a victim. Miss Muir's voice rings out above the shuffling and uneasy whispers.

"Karen Weissbloom," the teacher commands. "Stand up, gel. Tell me the names of the Great Lakes."

The chair legs scratch across the floor as Karen rises. Toni's dream flies away, and she focuses on the girl whose pretty face pales, then blushes red, a flood of hot colour rising up from the tender V of chest framed by her regulation white blouse.

Silence. Heavy, monumental silence.

"Well?" Miss Muir's eyes bore into their victim. "Surely you know at least one of the names."

Karen's lips move, but no sound comes out. Her inability to speak prolongs the torture. She's too delicate a lamb, too much the gentle princess, sweet and unsuspecting and used to adoration, to deal with the likes of Miss Muir. Cupping a hand to her cheek, Toni frantically mouths the answers, but Karen doesn't see. The golden head hangs, hiding the angel face behind a curtain of hair. Toni wants to put her hand up—*Choose me, choose me instead*—and save her darling from further disgrace. But what if that's the wrong thing to do? What if everyone thinks she's just showing off? Worst of all, what if Miss Muir, with her uncanny knack for peering deep into the dark corners of the heart, roots out some blemish of the soul, some bit of filth that escaped Toni's notice until now, and blows it into daylight on a wind of cruel, disdainful remarks, and it is Toni twisting, cringing, blushing, and suffering in front of the class instead of Karen? What if?

Tap, tap, tap, goes Miss Muir's wooden pointer, a relentless beat against the linoleum floor. Karen's classmates squirm in sympathy, but not a word emerges from anyone's mouth. Finally, the teacher lifts a weary hand to her brow.

"Oh, sit down. Really, this class is tiresome today."

A sigh whispers through the room, the expelled breath of thirty-one pupils who have been sitting on the edge of their chairs. When the recess bell finally rings, even Miss Muir's dagger eyes can't keep them all from exploding from their seats and stampeding out the door toward the brilliant June sunshine. In the yard, a cluster of friends circle Karen, touch her hands and hair, murmur words of consolation in her ear. Toni watches from a few feet away, hands in her jacket pockets, one of which holds the treat she has been saving, a Lowney's Cherry Blossom. She likes to savour it slowly, to eat with understanding as Lisa puts it, by nibbling a hole in the chocolate shell, sucking out the cream, and squeezing the maraschino cherry between her teeth. But the thought now comes that she could offer the Cherry Blossom to Karen. "Here!" she'd say, and the soft blue eyes would melt with gratitude. As she starts to walk over, the friends press closer so that Karen disappears behind a wall of bodies. The huddle becomes a single creature with many giggling heads. Giggling at Toni? Telling secrets? A chant rises up from the huddle:

"All in together, girls,

It's fine weather, girls,

When is your birthday?

Please jump in!

January, February, March … "

Indeed they are girls, the whole stupid bunch of them, Karen included, singing one of those cutesy skipping songs that sets Toni's teeth on edge. They don't know that's how she feels. They don't know a thing about her, and that's just fine. She doesn't care. School is in-between time anyway.

Off with the tunic, on with the real clothes, the rumpled trousers and T-shirt that lie on the floor of her closet. They are soft with use, smell of grass, dirt, gum, and have absorbed the neighbourhood into their fibres. Heart singing, muscles on fire, Toni races across the street and into the thick, green woods. Whooping and wild like a TV Indian she runs, crashing through the underbrush, stumbling and muddying the heels of her hands on the path. *Coming, guys. Coming, coming.* Golden light pours down out of the late afternoon sky, making the leaves overhead glow like jewels. Gasping for breath, she arrives at the meeting place, the pond circled by mud-caked rocks, swarming with tadpoles and water-bugs.

"Yay, here's Toni," yells Peter, clapping her on the shoulder and making her stumble, though he doesn't mean to. Peter's like Tubby in the Little Lulu comics, a bowling ball of a kid, heavy and clumsy, charging blindly in their games and taking others down with him. Nick, the Greek, is skinny, quick, and cunning with his feet, one of which he now winds around Toni's ankle while his hands shove. It takes all her will to keep from flying sideways into the pond. They shuffle and grunt for several moments until Toni takes advantage of her greater height to regain ground and gives Nick her wild dog look—teeth bared, face steaming. He breaks into a just-kidding grin. He knows she's capable of a sudden burst of fury that can undo his manoeuvres and deliver painful kicks to the shins. Standing back, he lets rip with the first half of the Woody Woodpecker cry: "Hee, hee, hee," then stops so she can finish it. "Haw, haw," she shouts. They both convulse in giggles. From his perch on a flat-topped rock, Frankie, "the Squirt," watches this out of his pinched, serious face and his forever-smeary glasses. Though Frank's a pipsqueak, there's never been any question about him belonging to the gang. The gang was formed long ago, before any of them can remember, and once you're in, you're in for good. Arnold, their captain, leans against a tree and whittles arrows out of saplings. Whip, whip, goes the blade of his penknife, stripping off grey bark to expose the moist, white wood. Toni approaches to get a better look at the arrows and the beautiful, slicing blade.

"Hey, Arnold. What are we playing? Indians and Settlers?"

Arnold shrugs. "Maybe," he says.

He likes to keep his men in line. He likes to keep everyone guessing. Arnold is half a year older and half a head taller than the rest of them. He has a narrow, foxy face, dark curly hair tumbled over his brow, and a know-it-all smile. But he does know things: wrestling moves, how to pinch candy from under Goyette the grocer's nose, how to sneak fags from his dad's overalls, and what the "F" word really means. Arnold's father was wounded in the war, so now one leg is shorter than the other, but that doesn't stop old man Mackay from booting his son to kingdom come when he's mad. Sometimes Arnold wears purple bruises all over his body. And that makes him even more of a captain.

Whipping out a slightly flattened pack of Players Navy Cut from his back pocket, Arnold doles out cigarettes to each member of the gang. He lights his own by flicking a match against his thumbnail, sucks in smoke, and exhales it through his nostrils. No one else can match this feat, but the other guys push out their lips and attempt to blow smoke rings. Toni takes short, shallow puffs that burn her throat and curdle her stomach, though she'd never let on.

"Know what happens to girls when they grow up?" Arnold says in a thoughtful tone while gazing up at the patch of sky between the trees. "They pee blood."

There's stunned silence for a moment, then Nick and Peter explode into hooting laughter while Frankie stares goggle-eyed at Toni through his smeared glasses.

"Bullshit," Toni says.

"Nope. Got it from a very reliable source."

"Load of hooey," Toni says.

"Peeing blood. Yech!"

Nick makes retching sounds.

"Tell you something else," Arnold says coolly as smoke curls from the sides of his mouth. "Girls get hair between their legs. I know it for a fact 'cause I've seen it myself."

"Who? Who'd you see?" Frankie shrills, leaning so far forward on his perch it looks like he's about to topple over.

Arnold ignores him. His eyes flick up and down Toni in a funny way as if he's trying to tell whether she too has sprouted hair in unspeakable places. There's only one answer to this. She flings her burning cigarette into the pond, springs to her feet and kicks Arnold in the thigh. Maybe she got him in a spot already sore from his father's beatings because he gasps and clutches himself and has to concentrate on the pain. But in another moment Toni's on the ground, straddled, arms pinioned above her head. The other boys crowd around chanting, "Bellybutton, bellybutton."

The bellybutton treatment is Arnold's special brand of torture, reserved for times when extra discipline is in order. He grows one of his thumbnails especially long for this purpose. Still pinning her arms with one hand, Arnold lifts up Toni's T-shirt with the other and digs into her navel with his long, sharp nail. She squirms and bucks, but Arnold holds her firmly in the vice of his knees and the grip of his fingers. The thumbnail burrows deeper, igniting an astonishing flash of pain. The surprise and misery come not just from the hurt—which is bad enough—but from *where* it hurts. The sting travels right down to her privates as if the damp little hole in her belly were connected to her peeing place by a taut, invisible string. The sensation creates a fierce need for release. If Arnold decides to keep the pressure up long enough, he could make her piddle her pants. That's the brilliance of the bellybutton torture—that it can end in a smelly, humiliating mess. And what if this time there was more than just pee? What if she gushed a bright red, stinking stream out of her privates, making them shamefully visible? It's bad enough she has to crouch in the bushes while the guys can stand tall and aim their little water pistols straight ahead.

The thumbnail drills down. Arnold smirks as he waits for her whimpered plea for mercy. Abruptly, Toni stops struggling. She lets herself go limp and stares right into her tormentor's eyes. Without moving a muscle, she floats herself away, high into the treetops, and the pain changes from a red-hot fire to a small yellow ball behind her head. It's a trick that came to her some time ago in the dentist's chair when the whine of the drill was so unbearable she just had to escape. Suddenly, amazingly, she could, she did. Now she continues to stare at Arnold with deadly calm, letting him know she can wait him out. The gleeful certainty in his face becomes confusion, his eyes drop, his grip loosens. Finally he rolls off her, with an embarrassed shrug. When she's on her feet again, he claps her back to show there are no hard feelings. She's one of his men, after all.

"Anyway, even if girls do pee blood when they grow up, that won't happen to me," Toni crows. "I'm not like other girls."

"That's true, you aren't," Arnold admits, but there's an unsettled question in his voice.

The game of Indians and Settlers begins, a game of stealth and strategy, of hiding, searching, and killing with pointed-finger guns. The boys whoop as they give chase through the underbrush. The woods resound with yells and mouth explosions, the snap of twigs, the splash of rocks in the shallow pond. Everyone except Toni is caught and killed and freed and killed again. None of the boys can hide as well as she does. They give themselves away, almost immediately, with an impatient grunt, the need to taunt their pursuers. They never *want* to stay hidden for very long, whereas Toni does. Stretching out on the ground behind a log, she covers herself with branches and disappears. She becomes a thing, hard, impenetrable, unmoving, just like the dead tree that shelters her. She knows that once, long ago, her father flattened himself into a paper-doll figure and lay, barely breathing, under a tumbled heap of books in the attic of his shop while the Nazis crashed around in the room below. Papa, too, knew how to leave his body.

In the distance, she hears her name.

"Toni! Toni! We're going home without you."

The calls become fainter and fainter. She falls into a great, deep, tranquil silence that wraps itself around her like an eiderdown quilt. Dampness from the ground seeps through her trousers, bugs crawl about, but she is happy and busy within herself. All that exists is this little patch of earth beneath her elbow. Look at last-year's leaves that have been disintegrating into the forest floor. They are stiff, stark skeletons, intricately branched. Look how one leaf vein connects to another and how they spread out to mirror the shape of the full-blown tree.

"Toni! Toni!"

An anguished voice punctures her dream world. Peeking through the brush, she spies a hat, a long lean figure, and a grimacing, ashen face.

"Hi, Papa," she says sheepishly.

He sucks in his breath with a strangled sound. His eyes hold horror. They are fixed upon her face, but it's not his Toni he sees. There's no daughter here, no precious little girl. Instead, he sees a sight so dreadful it eats him up from inside.

"Wha ... what?" he gasps. He points a long shaking finger. "What have you done to yourself?"

She touches her face and her hand turns red. She sees what he sees: blood, gore, mutilation.

"It's okay, Papa. It's just the lipstick. We put it on our faces for war paint."

She wipes her face with her arm to demonstrate the truth of her words. They walk out of the woods together in shamed, crushing silence. How could she kill her papa yet again?

chapter 5

The landlord wants to raise the rent by five dollars, and the Nutkevitches next door are on the move—two facts that send Lisa into a rage.
*How dare that skinflint ask more for an apartment with gaps, cracks,
rust stains, pipes that groan like old men complaining, and windows
with broken pulleys that could crash down and chop off your head?*

*How dare the Nutkevitches find their dream house in the suburbs
first?* Lisa learned about their neighbours' happy prospects after running into Mrs Nutkevitch at the produce section of Steinberg's. Mr
Nutkevitch—a *shoichet*, a butcher, and before that a common rag ped-
dler—has bought a split-level bungalow in an up-and-coming west-
end suburb to which Jews are flocking in droves. The other bit of news
that Lisa has divined was that another little Nutkevitch is on the way.
The twins' mother looks exactly the same as ever, as far as Toni can tell,
but Lisa *knows*, she can smell the baby coming. To top it all off, a sleek,
brown Chevy sedan from Harold Cummings' used car lot stands in
front of the building next door waiting to carry the burgeoning family
off to their four-bedroom palace with the basement den.

"Good riddance," Toni chortles into her cup of cocoa. But Lisa bristles with the energy of discontent. She gulps her morning coffee at the
kitchen counter while shredding a large head of cabbage. The cuckoo
clock warbles and Lisa barks, "*Verdammt!*" and Toni stifles a giggle because her mother's curses are hilarious when not aimed directly at her.

"Now's the time to buy," Lisa declares, knife poised in mid-air.
"Now."

Julius continues to read the paper, folded twice to make a neat parcel he can hold steady in front of his face while his other hand lifts the coffee cup to his lips.

"We could get a nice bungalow in Côte Saint-Luc for about twenty-thousand dollars."

"Twenty-thousand dollars?" Julius tears his eyes away from the newsprint and stares at her, incredulous. "That's what you call affordable? Twenty-thousand dollars?" He speaks the number slowly as if trying to get a grasp on that huge tower of money.

"We get a mortgage. We put a little down, the rest monthly. It wouldn't be so much more than we're paying now."

"Yes, of course, a mortgage." He taps his forefinger to his temple to show what he thinks of such a notion. *Verrucktheit.* Madness. "You want to ruin me with debts."

"Everyone here has debts. That's how people live in this country. That's how people get ahead."

"*Naturlich!* Buy now, pay later. Pay with my blood."

If they'd just ask Toni her opinion she'd tell them they can stop fighting right now, because she has no intention of moving. She glances around the kitchen, cosy and crowded with familiar objects—the Arborite-topped table, the vinyl-covered chrome chairs, the sputtering gas stove, the fat-tubbed wringer-washer, and the dear old cuckoo clock on the wall. Where could be better than here? But Mama and Papa are too caught up in each other to pay attention to Toni. So she turns back to the book she's reading, *Black Beauty,* about the adventures of a lovely young horse who must deal with the injustice of bad masters in a harsh world.

The argument does not go away. Day after day, at breakfast, at supper, through the bedroom walls at night, her parents raise their voices against one another. Lisa cajoles, loses her temper, hurls sarcastic barbs. Julius meets her with crossed-armed silence or mocking remarks of his own. "Indeed, Xanthippe!" he mutters. One morning he reminds her of Uncle Alfred, ruined by debts, besieged by creditors, consumed by shame, and driven to fire a bullet through the back of his mouth with his World War I revolver. Debt is a cancer, Julius's father used to say. And even he, a well-established bank employee, lost barrelfuls of money.

"That was the Inflation, the Depression. That was Europe in the dark days. Now there is prosperity, opportunity, the New World, in case you haven't noticed, Mr Head-in-the-Sand. Where would we be if I didn't push you forward? Still in some stinking back alley in Rome waiting for the right moment to leave. It was *I*," Lisa strikes her fist against her chest, "*I* who got us the entry papers. *I* who made the arrangements."

She glares across the breakfast table. A series of incredulous chuckles falls from his lips, a sound like bubbles bursting. He rolls his eyes. Her version of events is too preposterous.

"She forgets how she nearly lost us our chance to come to Canada because of all her scenes at the consulate. We were nearly blackballed."

He addresses these words to Toni, speaks quietly, reasonably, hand on his cheek, head shaking, as if the two of them were consulting over a mental case. Toni doesn't allow herself to crack a smile. She locks eyes with her father's and nods. Then she stares down at her plate and focuses on her bread and butter so she doesn't have to see her mother's wounded expression. *My own daughter betrays me.*

The hostility between her parents gets worse. Every day, accusations fly back and forth. The conflicting stories about how they got to Canada get mixed up in the argument about moving. Her mother corners Toni in her bedroom after school as she's changing out of her tunic.

"Listen to me, *Bubbele*, it was like this. A nasty little man at the consulate—an anti-Semite, you could see it in his eyes—tried to get in our way. 'Wrong papers,' he said. 'Stateless.' Of course we were stateless! Who wasn't stateless? I stormed out of his office and slammed the door behind me. I threw myself at the feet of the consul himself. 'Madam, you must not upset yourself,' he said. A proper gentleman."

The moral of the story? Never deal with underlings. Too much caution can kill you. And: Your father needs a fire lit under him.

But no, it was like this. Julius takes the opportunity while Lisa's in the bathroom to explain what really happened.

"There were quotas, even after the war. The Canadians wanted immigrants with certain trades, like furriers, hat-makers, garment workers. The fact that your mother could sew wasn't good enough because the men, the breadwinners, had to find jobs. A crowd grew unruly in the embassy corridor—not just Jews, regular Italians and DPs from all over. They didn't understand the procedures, they didn't know English. Some got hysterical. I put myself forward as an interpreter for the overwhelmed official and was able to calm the mob, and so I made a good impression. The official put me on the list."

And the moral? Keep your head. Don't act rashly. And: Your mother gets carried away.

Confusion buzzes in Toni's head. Even the cuckoo seems overwhelmed. He peeps feebly, retreats slowly behind his door to the sound of groaning springs. What does it matter how they got to Canada? What matters is that the family is here now and not moving ever again, plain and simple. What matters is the adventures of a plucky little horse in old London town. While Black Beauty pulls an overloaded cart up a hill, Lisa ambushes Julius in the corridor.

"An investment in a house is money in the bank."

"Ha! Money *for* the bank. The *bank* will own the house."

He retreats into his study. She follows and pushes open the door he closed so firmly behind him. She is like a terrier with a bone. But he is made of unyielding material, like wood turned to stone through eons of sediment.

One evening, planting herself in front of the television screen and blocking out the announcer on the news, Lisa yells, "And, by the way, another thing, in case you haven't noticed. My clock is ticking. I'm running out of time."

"Time for what?" Toni asks, wrenching herself away from her book. Two horses have been talking about what it's like to have a bit in your mouth, and Toni can feel the cold, cruel iron against her own tongue. Yet she is forced to lift her eyes from the page by the mystery in her mother's words, the sound of a desperate plea.

Lisa glares at Julius, a look of smouldering resentment, while he regards her with a strange mixture of pity, apology, and pained embarrassment.

"Time for what?" Toni asks again. Neither of them answer.

A story in the *Montreal Star* changes everything. Her parents lean over the front page spread out on the kitchen table. Julius sits, Lisa stands by his side looking over his shoulder, her jaw clamped shut. There's a deadly stillness in the room. No sound except the rustle of the paper and the dull ticking of the old, brown clock.

Still in her pyjamas, Toni watches their curved backs. She creeps forward and peeks at the paper. There is a picture of a balding man in a dark suit, with thick, dark-rimmed glasses like her father's, standing with his head turned sideways and slightly raised as if someone is talking to him and he's listening very carefully to each word. Behind him, a man with a peaked cap like a policeman's sits on a chair looking bored. Above the photo, the headline reads: "Court's Authority Challenged as Eichmann Trial Begins." A smaller headline states: "Nation Aware Israeli State Also on Trial."

"They should hang him from the nearest lamppost," Lisa growls with animal fury. "They should hang him upside down and use his head for a football."

"Hush. That would be wrong," Julius says. He rakes his fingers across the furrows in his brow. "Eichmann must have a fair trial. Due process. The Israelis have to prove we are a civilized people. There's enough controversy already about the abduction. The government says it wasn't the Mossad that did it. Volunteers, they say. But everyone knows."

"Right they were to hunt him down. He'd still be dancing in Argentina if they hadn't."

"The defence says the judges are biased and the court has no authority and Israel has no jurisdiction. Listen to this: 'Since Israel did not exist at the time of the alleged offences, it has no jurisdiction to hear the case.' They will have to make an iron-tight case, otherwise he'll become a martyr."

"That monster, a martyr? What are you saying, you of all people? *Mutti, Mutti,* listen to this madman, he defends Satan."

"Hush, hush, don't excite yourself. I'm just saying how the world might see it."

"Who cares what the *farshtunkene* world thinks?"

"We can never ignore what the *farshtunkene* world thinks."

He speaks quietly. He touches her arm, then takes her hand, balled into a fist at her side, and encloses it within his long fingers. He does all this without removing his eyes from the paper.

"Who's Eichmann?" Toni asks.

Her father's head shoots up. He whisks the newspaper off the table and refolds it into a small package. "Go, go, go. Get dressed. You'll be late for school."

When Toni returns, her mother has dismantled the burners on the stove and scrubs the tarnished rims with Dutch cleanser, as she always does when particularly upset. Her father eats scrambled eggs and toast, chewing with his usual care, but his eyes are unfocussed, and a bit of egg is caught in the bristles of his goatee. Lisa brings more toast to the table. She too seems lost in brooding silence. Neither of them takes notice of the rogue bit of egg in his beard.

There are no more fights. There are murmurs and long silences behind the wall that separates Toni's bedroom from that of her parents. One Saturday morning, Toni finds her mother in her flannelette housecoat humming happily as she tends to her plants.

"Grow. I command you to grow. It is spring, and you must grow," she warbles to the African violets lined up along the windowsill. Her flushed face appears softer and more rested than it has for a long time. More astonishing for Toni is to see her father emerge from the master bedroom still in his rumpled pyjamas. Usually he's up and dressed before anyone else. The open V-neck shows the crinkled black hairs on the white skin of his chest. He seems a bit sheepish to have slept so long, but also, like her mother, unaccountably cheerful. When he's been to the bathroom and put on his Saturday clothes—pressed pants, white shirt, grey wool cardigan—and is seated at the dinette, Lisa plants a kiss on his bald head. She brings the newspaper, but instead of handing it to him, as usual, she spreads it out in front of herself, open to the classifieds. Her finger runs down the columns of ads.

"'Three-bedroom upper, bath, kitchen, sun porch. Parking available,'" she reads aloud. "A sun porch would be nice for my plants."

"What's going on?"

Toni looks from her mother to her father, sipping his coffee contentedly. Avoiding Toni's eyes for a moment, her father clears his throat and tugs his goatee, while an embarrassed grin plays at the corners of his mouth.

"We have come to a compromise," he says. "We'll look for a duplex in Snowdon. The prices in Snowdon are still quite reasonable. Especially for a duplex."

"What!"

"No harm in looking." Her father lifts his palms in the air, the gesture half hopeful, half surrender.

Toni turns from her father to her mother.

"Snowdon is a good neighbourhood," Lisa declares. "Not so good as Côte Saint-Luc or Saint Laurent, but still … Nice stores, synagogues, schools, a Jewish Y."

"What about my friends?"

"High time you made new ones. Enough with those hooligans."

"What about the Mountain?"

"The Mountain? The Mountain is not going anywhere. You're never far from the Mountain in this city."

"Papa," she chokes. He waves his hands in front of his face. *Don't start, don't spoil things.* He seems not the least bit perturbed that they are about to fall off the edge of the world by leaving the only home she has ever known.

On a blustery Sunday morning in mid-March, the three of them go duplex hunting in Snowdon, strolling long blocks lined with squat one- and two-storey buildings and mature trees. Julius and Lisa stop to admire large balconies, picture windows overlooking neat front yards with waist-high clipped hedges and fir trees standing like sentinels on either side of walkways. Although the lawns still lie brown and battered after the long winter, her parents seem not to notice. They absorb all with keen, possessive eyes.

"A bit of the Bauhaus there," says Julius, pointing to a curved overhang above an entrance.

"No clutter on the balconies. Not like in the old neighbourhood," says Lisa.

The old neighbourhood. Already the ground has shifted under Toni's feet. To her, this Snowdon is all cold, dreary sameness and strangeness; neat, boxy-looking houses, secretive blinds, sober, too-quiet streets without alleys, courtyards, vacant lots, or woods. Even the trees—big, bare-limbed maples plastered against an overcast sky—are tidy and tame. She lags behind while her parents surge ahead, eager to behold what wonders await them in the next house.

They come to a rectangular building divided into two mirror-image duplexes, with wide stone steps and blue-painted front doors, each door set with three rectangular panels of glass. Lisa checks her newspaper clipping. Yes, this is the one. They enter a tiny lobby, climb the stairs to the upper apartment. The owners haven't moved yet. The housewife—a breathless, exuberant woman wearing black stretch pants, a white turtleneck, and hair that looks like it came out of a spray can—welcomes them with a toothy smile. She ignores Lisa's attempt at a formal introduction and Julius's graceful removal of his hat.

"Hey, come on in, make yourselves at home," she sings, as if they are all old pals.

They stumble out of their boots and tramp in sock feet over a plastic runner and onto the powder blue wall-to-wall carpet of the living room. There's a plush, white, plastic-covered couch and matching armchairs, a shiny-wood hi-fi set, and the biggest TV Toni has ever seen. The room is bright and airless and Lisa harrumphs as if to say, *These Canadians, they never open their windows.* Toni is suddenly aware of how stiff and foreign her parents seem, how grating their accents compared to the woman's easy drawl. She is aware of her father's long unshod feet stepping carefully over the carpets and polished floors. At home he always wears closed-back slippers.

Lisa pokes her head into closets, sniffs, checking for unacceptable smells. In the bathroom, she wrinkles her nose at a whiff of sweetish air freshener but otherwise seems satisfied. She comments approvingly on the spaciousness of the rooms, the cute breakfast nook in the kitchen, the gleaming electric range: *You don't have to strike a match to light a gas burner.* The woman smiles back at Lisa in a pitying way to hear of something so backward as gas. When they reach the bedroom belonging to the household's teenaged daughter, Toni hangs back because, though the girl is out at the moment, she could suddenly return and stare with frosty astonishment at this strange kid peering in at her things: the white plastic portable record player and stack of 45s, the pictures of the idols—Elvis Presley, Richard Chamberlain, Bobby Vinton—on the walls. Toni can't get out of there fast enough. Back on the street a couple of boys around her age have started a game of pitch and catch. One of them glances over briefly, and the blankness in his eyes tells Toni what he sees—a nonentity. He doesn't know Toni is a tomboy and wouldn't care if he did. A tomboy doesn't fit in Snowdon.

Next stop is the Jewish Y. It takes up a whole block on Westbury Avenue, bustles with activity and resonates with voices in the big, marble-tiled lobby. A large glass case displays an assortment of trophies, and all the important men who donated money to the Y gaze down from a gallery of portraits on the wall. There are also faded black-and-white photos of athletes. One shot shows a group of women wearing long skirts down to their ankles, cardigans, funny hats with ear flaps, and lipsticked smiles. The caption reads, "Ladies Hockey Team, 1925."

"Baloney. How can they be hockey players?" Toni says loudly to her father, but he's busy studying a display titled "Our Community Is 80 Years Young." Lisa meanwhile has disappeared into an office to ask about programs. She returns clutching a bouquet of coloured, mimeographed sheets. So much going on: an Israeli coffee house, a Purim party, folk dancing lessons for boys and girls.

"I'm *not* taking folk dancing."

Her mother and father look at each other over her head in a meaningful way. She bolts out of the building. She doesn't know those two people who call after her. They don't belong to her, nor she to them. She belongs nowhere and with no one anymore.

When the phone rings at supper time, Lisa leaps from her chair to answer it. She prances back into the kitchen, eyes aglow.

"They've agreed to our terms. We've got it."

Without bothering to tell Toni what's been agreed to, she pirouettes around the room, then hauls a startled Julius to his feet and makes him polka with her up and down the hall. The transformation of her parents into prancing ponies is almost as unsettling as the announcement that finally bursts from Lisa's breathless lips:

"We move the first of May."

Toni attacks the lukewarm potato dumpling on her plate. Have they forgotten the importance of eating food when it's hot? Is everything to be upside down from now on? Someone has to maintain proper order.

Toni tries. Over the next weeks, while her parents are busy, busy, working overtime to earn some extra dollars, Toni comes home promptly after school to bring the empty apartment back to life. She waters the plants, straightens cushions, puts casseroles in the oven, gives the stopped cuckoo clock a tap so that the pendulum resumes its back-and-forth journey and the kitchen is filled with the familiar tick-tock. Despite all her efforts, home becomes transformed into a place of chaos. Cardboard boxes from Steinberg's crowd the hall and are gradually filled with newspaper-wrapped knick-knacks, dishes, towels, clothes. Cupboards stand open, exposing naked hooks and yellowed shelving paper. Blank rectangles of emptiness stare from walls denuded of pictures. A vast machinery of change is in motion. All protests are useless, ridiculous, like Wile E. Coyote churning his legs in mid-air above the vast canyon that he pretends not to see, because as soon as he does, he will drop like a stone.

"Now is the time for a clean sweep," her mother says, handing Toni a large paper bag. "Throw broken toys or the ones you don't want in here."

Though the remnants of Golly and Teddy have gathered dust in a corner of the closet for ages, Toni hates to toss them out. Even the mutilated tribe of dolls tugs at her heart. She wants to keep everything, the tattered board games, cracked water pistols, ripped rubber balls, even gumball-machine charms that litter the bottom of a drawer. Her mother taps her foot with impatience.

"They're only things. Don't get attached to things. I left home at sixteen with hardly more than the clothes on my back. Everything comes and goes."

One day, Toni finds the cuckoo clock in a box of odds and ends relegated to the garbage. It gives her a strange feeling to see the clock, which once hung grandly on the kitchen wall, lying on its back amid stinky rags and clutter, its pendulum chains spilling out of the bottom. The clock hasn't worked right for some time; still, the outside is the same as ever, a dark brown wooden house with a steeply sloped roof and a trap door under the eaves. Behind the door, the tiny bird that once seemed so real to her is just a flimsy bit of papier-mâché. She rips the frail body off its perch and crushes it between her fingers. Suddenly enraged, she gallops through the half-empty rooms, hitting the walls with her fists, while part of herself looks on from afar and says scornfully, "You're really much too old for such nonsense now."

She'd imagined that on the day of the move all the guys of her gang would gather round on the front walk, long-faced, giving one another comradely slaps on the back to cheer themselves up. Arnold would give a captain-style speech about how the gang would always stick together no matter what, and Toni would say she'd be back to visit soon. But the first of May turns out to be a Monday, a school day. No one is around except a whimpering baby in a stroller and its bored-looking mother.

Toni has to help carry down boxes, which they pile beside the curb until the moving van arrives. Then there's nothing to do but stand and watch as the two brawny hired men take over, emptying the apartment with surprising speed. When her parents' mattress appears—naked, sagging slightly in the middle, looking not entirely clean—Toni has to turn her head and is suddenly glad none of her chums are here to witness the sight. Finally, the van doors slam shut and the truck roars off carrying practically everything her family owns within a space not much bigger than their balcony. After the van leaves, Julius, Lisa, and Toni stand at the bus stop with suitcases of newspaper-wrapped fragile or precious items Lisa didn't trust to the movers. The other passengers on the bus stare as they heave their bags inside, stumble forward, try not to bump any elbows, and wrestle the suitcases into the narrow aisles between the seats. One man smirks a little, as if he knows all about people like them and is not impressed.

Part II

Camp Tikvah

chapter 6

Overnight, Toni's become a beanstalk, long, gangly, big-footed, everything stretched out and wrong. Clacking across the kitchen floor in high-heeled mules, Lisa turns on the light, then starts back at seeing her newly hatched giant of a daughter, an overgrown dinosaur, cracked out of its grotesquely large egg, lurking in the shadows by the fridge.

At thirteen-and-a-half, Toni is five-foot-eight and still shooting upward, towering over her mother and approaching her father's height, but there's no advantage to being tall. Instead, she feels exposed, naked, every inch open to her mother's scrutiny, to say nothing of the scrutiny of kids at school and strangers on the street. Everyone can look her up and down, there's so much to see, and it's hard to say which is worst, her mother's anxious appraisal, the withering glances of classmates, or the coolly curious gaze of strangers. Her body betrays her in other ways too: feet that trip over themselves, hands like bunches of bananas, hair where no hair should be, curling under her arms, fuzzing her legs, sprouting from her private parts. And then there are the breasts she's supposed to be proud of but that feel like something soft and vulnerable has leaked out from inside her.

For weeks she's been dismayed to see that the flat pennies on her chest have risen to become two swollen bumps, which could officially be called boobs. *Boo-boo, booby prize, booby trap.* She tries to hide them under her navy cardigan buttoned to her chin, but her mother crows, "My little girl is developing," as if it were an achievement, and drags her off to see Nadia, the saleslady at the lingerie department of

Zellers. While the two women discuss the virtues of double-stitched reinforced cups, elastic backing, and adjustable straps, Toni huddles in the corner of the dressing room avoiding, as best she can, the sight of the long, pale stalk with the stricken face in the mirror. She is measured, prodded, jerked this way and that and finally trussed in her first bra, size 32A. Itchy and tight around her ribcage, the bra sports two dunce caps in front that end in squishable cones of empty air.

"Room to grow!" her mother chirps.

Dressed once more, slouching along the street behind her mother, Toni feels the presence of those dunce caps beneath her cardigan, pointing, thrusting, announcing themselves to the whole world. And the world stares back in bone-tickled astonishment.

At school she's among the outcasts, though not openly tormented. She doesn't merit such attention. Despite her long, galumphing body, the boys barely notice Toni, and for this small mercy she's grateful. The girls have a more pointed way of dismissing her. They size her up, exchange glances, arch their brows, and look away as if offended by the sight of her, then turn back to their intimate huddle. She pretends not to care, shuffling down the hall with her nose in a book, but can't help sneaking peeks at her classmates. What are they saying? What are they thinking? Sometimes the need to know is so fierce, she'll drift toward the edge of their circle and then have to endure the sudden turn of a head, a sarcastic, "Ex-kyoose me?"

Gym is agony, not just because she can't accomplish a single movement with grace, but because of the humiliation of showers. She emerges from her towel at the last minute, dashes under the stream, trying not to look at who is looking, trying not to let her eyes register the sight of her classmates' nakedness. But there they all are, soft-skinned, bare-bummed, bare-boobed, shining under streams of water, setting off an uncomfortable commotion in her chest.

Her mother brims with advice and hopeful projects. She comments, criticizes, coaxes, cajoles, clips out magazine articles about makeovers. Here's a photo of dowdy Sue with the horsey face, lank hair, downcast eyes—the "before" shot. And now, look! The "after" Sue, with hair clipped and puffed, kiss-curls caressing her cheeks, drawing attention away from that long, unfeminine jaw line. The new Sue smiles into the camera, eager and bright as a squeaky-clean plate. She has been groomed.

"Stand up straight, for God's sake. You look like a question mark. Tall can be lovely. Models are tall. Maybe my daughter will become a model. Hmm? Don't hide your face. Be proud."

Her mother delivers this lecture after her own recent makeover, which includes a powder-blue jersey-knit dress—the latest spring fashion from Shmelzer's—a hairdo of high, stiff, lacquered waves, and nails gleaming with Coral Dust polish. Since moving to their Snowdon duplex three years ago, her mother's hair has gone several degrees lighter, from muddy brown sprinkled with grey to Mahogany Lustre to Chestnut Glow to Arresting Auburn. But newly awakened to ugliness—her own and the rest of the world's—Toni sees what Lisa wants to hide; the spidery lines around her eyes, the tiny, fleshy protrusion by the side of her nose, the way her feet bulge out around the straps of her high-heeled shoes, and the raw look of her fingers despite the gleaming nail polish. Toni sees, and she's not sure what she hates more, her mother's ugly parts or the way she stalwartly, triumphantly denies their existence through the feminine arts of makeup, dress, and charm.

Reaching up, her mother tries to brush away the thicket of bangs on Toni's forehead.

"Get away from me!" Toni shrieks. She crashes out of the kitchen, slams her bedroom door. A few minutes later, her mother knocks—a firm, unapologetic rap—and enters the room without waiting for an answer.

"That was not my daughter talking," Lisa pronounces, bristling with offence. From a Zellers bag, she produces a new, downy soft, egg-yolk-coloured mohair sweater, the kind that is all the rage. Toni can just imagine how big and yellow she'd appear in one of those. Like a giant "caution" sign.

"*Nu?* What do you say?"

Toni squishes her face deeper into the pillow. Even more infuriating than the appeal for gratitude is her mother's troubled gaze, the anxiety flickering beneath the surface. Peeking out from the folds of her pillow, Toni sees her mother fish something else from the paper bag, a bottle of Arrid Junior Deodorant, which she places in the middle of the bureau. The Arrid bottle stares down accusingly. Lately, Toni has been lathering her underarms with the Mennen Deodorant from her father's side of the medicine cabinet, always careful to put it back in the exact same spot, but apparently her mother has noticed.

"Leave me alone," Toni rages.

Her mother's hand flies to her breast where the arrow of ingratitude has lodged.

"I lost my mother when I was not much older than you. I'm glad I have no such cruel remarks on my conscience."

Her voice quivers with grand tragedy. She wheels around and marches out of the room.

Later, at lunch, devouring blintzes and sour cream (her appetite is huge these days, she can't control it), Toni avoids her mother's gaze. *You see how good I am to you*, those dark eyes telegraph. *How good my blintzes are?* Toni would like to go on a hunger strike, but her mother lays traps of irresistible food.

These days, when Lisa isn't hounding Toni about one thing or the other, she's busy with work at the store, where she's been promoted from alterations to sales, with Hadassah committees and bazaars, and with her bridge club ladies, who come on Thursday afternoons and leave before Julius arrives home for supper—it's understood he doesn't want to run a gamut of ladies. On the surface, Lisa is relentlessly cheerful—the family is finally getting ahead—but Toni suspects fraud. Something is wrong, something is missing, disappointment and bitterness fester beneath Lisa's polished surface. *You're not really happy, you're just pretending.* Toni wants to hurl the accusation, but this could bring revelations and Toni doesn't want to know what's bothering her mother. She really doesn't want to know. She assumes it's got something to do with her mother's nature, her impossible expectations. Always pushing—pushing and then furious to encounter a locked door.

Her parents don't fight, they side-step one another. Her father absents himself as much as possible, leaving the women to sort out the messy women's business. He now has an office above a shoe store on Queen Mary Road. After dinner, he disappears into his study with a guilty but determined air, especially on evenings when discontent seeps out of Lisa's pores and she bangs around with pots in the kitchen. His study is in what was supposed to have been the nursery for a baby. No one has told Toni there was supposed to be another child, but she knows, just as she knows the reason for its absence. Her parents are too old. Younger people have babies, not people as battered-looking as Lisa and Julius. And that's fine with Toni. She certainly never wanted a baby in the house.

Her father bothers her too these days: the dry click when he swallows, the pouches under his eyes, the parchment colour of his bald head, the aging, used-up look of him. She resents his general pessimism, the sarcastic remarks that reveal his anxiety about money. "Do you own shares in the electric company?" he asks with a grimace when she forgets to switch off a light. Yet, according to her mother, he's doing well, having recently completed exams that allow him to call himself an accountant, not just a bookkeeper. New clients and bigger fees are just around the corner, but you'd never know it by the way he carries on. Plus, his feeble attempts at humouring her drive Toni crazy. When Toni mentions that she's bored, he says, "Good." Why good? Because it means he's achieved something after all to have settled in a country where his child can be bored. He turns back to his dense columns of newsprint, the reassuring reports of catastrophes elsewhere. She wants to pummel those clean-shaven cheeks above the neat goatee, but what's the use? She lurches from the table to escape to her room, stumbling on the rucked-up carpet along the way.

And then there are the moments when he departs from his body. She looks up from her breakfast toast to find a mannequin in a suit across the table. Frozen limbs. Eyes of stone. Immediately she busies herself with stabbing her finger into toast crumbs along the rim of her plate until a dry cough and a creak of the breakfast-nook bench tell her it's safe to lift her head. Her mother sips coffee as if nothing happened. None of them speak about these little absences. Do they really occur, or does she dream him into an impenetrable black-and-white photo, one that reveals less and less the more you stare? She is no longer frightened, as she used to be, just a bit sickened, as when the bus gives an unexpected lurch, making her momentarily nauseous.

Her mother is delivering another of her lectures about eggs, blood, babies, what's nice, what's not nice. She sits at the breakfast nook opposite Toni, who hunches over her cocoa and tries to lose herself in the sweet, milky liquid. Lisa's voice is that of a faraway carping crow. A crow with neat rollers, a hairnet, and pencil-thin eyebrows that leap up and down. Her face is flushed with self-importance. Her forefinger stabs the air.

"Are you listening?"

"Yes," Toni sighs and looks back at the chocolaty bottom of the cup. Seems she'll be captive a while longer.

"Look at me when I speak to you."

Toni looks. She sees creases under the foundation makeup, red lines in the whites of the eyes, shiny brown circles surrounding dark holes. That's what the pupils are, holes, empty space. Mr Blake, the biology teacher, told them the word "pupil" comes from the Latin, meaning "little doll," because, if you look carefully, you should be able to see a tiny reflected image of yourself in someone's eye. Of course, as soon as he said that, everyone in class tried to peer into one another's faces amid yelps of laughter. It was only when Toni examined herself in the bathroom mirror at home that she saw what Mr Blake was talking about. A miniature, shadow self looked back at her. She doesn't see anything like that as she stares into her mother's eyes now, just black spots floating together. This staring is a new trick, a nice one, because her mother is forced to draw back a little.

"Do you understand?"

Toni nods.

"Do you have any questions?"

Toni shakes her head.

It is Lisa's turn to sigh.

Five weeks later, a baffled Toni finds the toilet paper in her hand stained red. Another unpleasant surprise from her body. Growth spurts, pimples, unwanted hair, and now this, a hidden wound. She wipes herself as thoroughly as she can and hopes whatever has been torn will heal by itself. She feels no pain, so it can't be too serious.

On her next trip to the bathroom she discovers that not just her underpants but also the crotch of her slacks are soaked through with dark-coloured blood. Something inside has ruptured. Yet, marvellously, she still feels nothing. Maybe this is what death is about: going numb, dribbling away, disappearing. Lately, she's fantasized often about dying, but in spectacular ways. A girl called Judy at school, who is even more of a bookworm and pariah than herself, has told Toni about spontaneous human combustion. People have exploded into flame for no reason while sitting quietly in an armchair, burning down into nothing but a pile of ash and maybe a lone, singed foot still wearing its shoe. Proven scientific cases, Judy says. Toni likes to imagine erupting thus in front of her classmates when their eyes flick over her in disdain. She envisions them scattering through the hall, clutching their heads in horror.

The drops of blood blossom in the toilet water like strange aquatic plants with long stems and spreading pink faces. She must tell her mother. But how? She can't think of the words. Her pondering is interrupted by thumps on the bathroom door.

"Have you fallen in? Come out already."

How can she tell her mother, "I'm bleeding to death. I'm bleeding to death *down there*"? This fact is too hideous and crazy, worse than any of Judy's wild stories. And despite the gush of blood, Toni feels shamefully healthy. She'd have to pull down her pants to convince her mother something's wrong. Impossible! She hurries to scrub away every sign of her new affliction, rolls her underpants in a washcloth and hides the bundle in the back of the cabinet under the sink. Then she slips her slacks back over her bare thighs. The crotch is stiff, but the stain isn't visible. Maybe she can sneak into her bedroom unnoticed.

"Finally!" her mother says, pushing right into the bathroom as soon Toni unlocks the door. Her mother swivels her head in all directions, sniffs the air.

"Ha! I knew it. You have your period." When Toni stares back blankly, she says: "Come, come. A mother knows. Didn't I tell you it would happen soon? *Mazel tov.*" She pats Toni's cheek. "When I got my first period my mother gave me a smart *klatsch* across the face. That was the custom in those days. It didn't hurt. I felt proud."

Lisa marches Toni into the master bedroom, shuts the door, opens

74

the closet, and brings out a large brown paper bag. She and Toni sit together on the double bed near the pewter-framed portrait of Grandma Antonia, who is staring fiercely down from the bureau.

Inside the paper bag is a blue cardboard box with a picture of a white rose.

"Deep Downy Soft Impressions" is written in fancy letters across the top. And at the bottom, "Kotex Feminine Napkins." Her mother pulls out a thick, white cotton wad with tapering tabs at each end—not quite a bandage, not quite a diaper, something in-between—and an elastic belt with metal fasteners.

Back on the toilet, Toni examines the pamphlet that comes with the box.

"*Are you in the know?*" it asks mockingly. She is not.

She reads, "You can always be your own gay self when calendar qualms are off your mind. With our exclusive Kotex safety centre for extra protection, there's no ceiling to your confidence. And because Kotex comes in three sizes, there's a Kotex napkin just perfect for you."

There are diagrams for attaching the napkin to the belt. After much fiddling, Toni succeeds and waddles out to the hall where her mother relentlessly waits.

"*Nu?* Isn't that better?"

How can it be better to be made so aware of this place of mysterious, oozing wounds? "No one can see a thing," her mother says cheerfully. "My little girl is becoming a woman. Now, remember what I told you. You don't use the word 'period' in public. You say 'I'm unwell' or 'I'm indisposed.'"

Toni can bear it no longer.

"But Mama, isn't there a cure?"

Lisa's mouth drops open and she looks as if she's not sure whether to laugh or to scream. "*Mutti! Mutti!*" She addresses Grandma's stern, unsmiling face. "How is it possible?"

And so Toni is marched back to the bedroom to hear again the lecture about eggs, blood, and babies from beginning to end. An undeniable fact becomes clear. The wound isn't temporary but will open month after month, be a part of Toni's life for as far as she can see into the future. She's not dying or suffering or special. In fact, she's a bit late in experiencing what must be routine by now for most of the other girls in her class. Which she would know if she ever dared talk to any of them other than wacky Judy, encyclopedia of bizarre but useless information. Dimly she recalls her old buddy Arnold's crazy tale about girls peeing blood when they grew up. He knew a kernel of truth, more than she did, anyway.

After reviewing the basic biology lesson, Lisa zeroes in on hygiene and discretion. This is women's business with which men—her father, in particular—are to be spared any contact because men have lofty minds and delicate stomachs. Hide the Kotex box in a brown paper bag. Bring your fresh napkin to the bathroom hidden under an article of clothing. Wrap the soiled napkin in newspaper and throw it into the garbage pail on the landing outside when her father is out of the way.

There are more lessons, vague but disturbing, which her mother delivers uneasily, alternating between stern looks and troubled sighs. Boys take what they can, they are unable to help themselves, so the girl is responsible and has to watch herself. Bad girls get into trouble; does Toni understand? But Toni is still thinking about foul blood and soiled napkins. Napkin is the word for what you use to wipe your mouth. How awful!

A few days later, Lisa hands Toni a slim paperback.

"Here! Read! You prefer to read than to listen to your mother. Maybe something will sink in."

The book is called the *Facts of Life and Love for Teen-agers: What Every Teen-ager Should Know.* After closing her bedroom door, Toni hunches up on her bed and reads for the rest of the afternoon. She reads about breasts and brassieres, hips and girdles, skin troubles, grownup hair, menstruation. Everything is perfectly normal, nothing to worry about, even growth spurts before a girl's first period when she "may become as tall as her mother." (But what about the girl who's as tall as her father?) Normal too is the "filling out period." The mounds on Toni's chest haven't risen much lately. They're neither one thing nor another. Her long, angular body isn't right, but curves would seem stranger still.

She reads, "The length of time spent in the process of growing up varies widely among girls, yet eventually almost all emerge as grown women ready to fall in love, marry, and have families of their own."

"Almost all." Therein lies cause for hope and dread.

"Above all, be glad that you are a girl, and don't start feeling sorry for yourself. You'd be a lot sorrier if you never did menstruate, but remained an 'It' (whatever that would be!) without any of the normal manifestations of being a growing-up and grownup woman."

She skims quickly through the chapter on "Where Babies Come From," the tedious details about the egg in the womb, pregnancy, and birth, hearing her mother's lecture again, seeing her mother moving her hands around her own belly with such a self-satisfied smile. The paragraph about birth defects is mildly thrilling—some babies have six toes—but too brief, and she learns that what mostly occurs is "the miracle of normality." Finishing the chapter, she realizes she missed something and goes back to the discussion of eggs, cells, sperm, tubes.

"*Sperms are deposited in the vagina during coitus … the penis is inserted into the vagina …* " So it's not quite as Arnold once said. In his version, a man and woman rubbed their naked bellies together while grunting like pigs. This "coitus" stuff seems quieter, more business-like: a key inserted into a lock, money deposited in a bank. She tries to imagine the sperm with his little suitcase of genes, the egg with hers, spilling their belongings together to make a person. A split-second later or earlier, a different sperm would be first in line, and a different person would be formed. Would she have been herself, or would she not have been born? Would it have been some entirely other baby? At what point does the "me" happen? She feels strange, at the verge of some great discovery, but then dizzy, weary. She flops backward onto her pillow, reads on through less mysterious, more depressing chapters.

Behold the great ladder of love: the infant's self-love, then love of parents, friends, crushes, mature love for a partner of the opposite sex, and finally, near the top of the ladder—just one rung below Love of Mankind—love of babies. Toni drops the book. She has never been drawn to babies; she finds them too helpless, frightening, demanding, blubbery. When her mother sees a neighbour's new baby in a pram, she exclaims in rapture, "*Dass süsses Würmchen!*" The sweet little worm. The phrase sounds nice in German, but in truth, there is something grub-like and wormy about babies.

Babies are born to become grownups who fall in love and get married and have babies in turn. On and on, as in the long, dreary list of "begats" of the Bible. Grandchildren for her mother, great-grandchildren for Grandma Antonia: She imagines the two of them holding hands and beaming the same ecstatic smile over a crib full of squirming, pink descendants. Suppose she were to die tomorrow and there were fewer "begats" in the world? What would it matter? Besides, she is not, as the book assumes, obsessed with boys. She's seen girls in her class giggle and swoon over Manny Mendelsohn, who's in grade eleven, student president, and considered a dreamboat because of that indefinable smirking something called "cute." She wouldn't mind being able to enter a room with Manny's confident swagger and be gazed at by adoring female eyes. But she doesn't care about the cycle of life. She's nowhere on the ladder of love.

Which means she must be an "it." Whatever that may be.

Huddled on her bed, one ear buried in the pillow, the other plastered to the transistor radio, Toni rocks back and forth to the Top Forty. *Twist and shout*, the Beatles urge. She imagines herself as Ringo, on an elevated chair at the back of the band, facing a set of drums and cymbals that she thwacks and pounds.

"And coming up very soon, for all you dedicated rock and rollers, the pick of the charts. Stay tuned. Don't touch that dial."

Toni wouldn't dream of it. She's addicted to the thump and whine, the swinging rhythms, the DJ's frantic shouts. But now the bedroom door opens and here comes her mother wearing a sour-puss face. Startled, Toni drops her transistor onto the floor. Her mother bends down, clicks off the twanging guitar, and tugs the roller blind so that it flies upward, letting in a relentless flood of winter sunshine.

"I did knock. You didn't hear. Mooning and wallowing. Are you sick? No? So what are you doing in bed on a beautiful Saturday afternoon?"

Toni surprises herself by sitting bolt upright and blurting out, "I wish I was dead."

Silence follows this declaration, then a hand swoops through the air, a slap rings out across the room. Toni's head is knocked sideways. It takes her a moment to connect the hand and the tingling in her cheeks with her mother, who stands quivering with outrage.

"You do not say such a thing! You do not think it! You have everything—a beautiful room, a lovely home, family, school, opportunities. We have struggled to give you all that you could possibly want, and this is your answer? Let me tell you a story." Lisa's chin juts out and her voice crouches low in her throat. "I think you know your father had a younger sister, Ida. She was not quite right. Never mind what was wrong—this we don't need to talk about—the point is, because she was unwell, the parents could not easily leave Vienna and they were among the first to be taken away. She was just thirteen, your age, when they tore her from her home. A pretty child, frail, sweet, gentle. Your Papa told me of her in the days after the war when we were still looking, hoping. How that child must have suffered is impossible to imagine, and your father, though he never says a word, suffers every day thinking of her, especially now, seeing you with your long face, mooning about, instead of being a picture of youthful joy to distract him."

These accusations and more rain down on Toni's head. A flood of stories is unleashed, fragments of stories that have no beginning or end or clarity and are all the more horrible for this confusion.

Her mother and other refugees cower in a cave. Armies approach. Germans? Americans? It isn't clear from her mother's blast of words. The refugees are on the wrong side of a battle line, in any case, and catastrophe lurks beyond this hole in the hills. They have nothing but mouldy bread and a little water. The stink of diarrhoea. The overpowering heat. How will death arrive? So many ways. And her father? It's no picnic for him, either. To be in that prison in Bolzano, for example. He hears screams. He escapes from the prison, but never, never from those screams.

"But do we ask death to take us? No! Not even in our darkest moments! To die is to give Hitler victory."

Panting from her exertions, satisfied that she's finally made an impression, Lisa stomps away. Toni sits on the edge of the bed in a daze, unable to run after her mother and tell her the blow was unjustified. Her mother has all the ammunition. Be grateful, her mother says. What Toni is grateful for, what she likes best about her so-called beautiful room, is the door that shuts her parents out (if only it had a lock), the roller blind, the bed covers into which she can tunnel. She never really cared for the pale pink of the walls, the ivory-coloured furniture, the flounced curtains, none of which were of her own choosing.

Sometimes she imagines herself a space alien, kidnapped by earthlings and wrenched from her small, one-person planet (they are reading *Le Petit Prince* in French class) to be imprisoned in an atmosphere where she can't properly breathe.

Now, shrugging on her duffel coat, she gallops downstairs and outside to roam the snowbound streets, her left cheek carrying the memory of her mother's slap. She tries to envision the lost Ida, with whom there was something terribly wrong and whose ghost her father sees when he looks at his daughter now. Perhaps Ida, like Toni, was an oversized grasshopper of a girl, clumsy, conspicuous. Perhaps they all tried to hide when the Nazis came, but Ida's impossible feet stuck out from under the bed, causing the family's downfall.

Toni won't, can't, ask for clarity about Ida. She has learned over the years that certain corners must not be poked into, for the result will be hard, blank silence or a punishing burst of emotion. Every so often, as today, a detail pops up like a Punch-and-Judy puppet, dances briefly in the stage lights of conversation and vanishes back into the shadows of the forbidden. Toni thinks she might have heard before that Ida was a problem in some way, but she can't be sure. She forgets bits of her parents' stories. They have the power of being always shockingly fresh and depressingly familiar.

Instead of dwelling on Ida, her mind turns to the Anne Frank story she's been reading. She imagines her and Anne together in that attic, Anne's lovely brown eyes gazing at Toni with helpless appeal as the Nazis approach. Toni flings a hand grenade into the Gestapo men's faces, killing them instantly, and at the same time blows a hole in the wall through which she carries the swooning Anne to a rowboat in the canal. The scenarios change half a dozen times as Toni stomps along the icy sidewalks, while the crowds of shoppers and buildings barely register in her vision. But suddenly the bubble of fantasy bursts and she finds herself far up Decarie Boulevard, miles from home, feeling like the empty paper bag that's being blown along the gutter. She longs desperately to leap into another body, another existence, but there's nothing but this stick-figure of a self. She stops in the lobby of an apartment building to warm up her cold ears for a few moments. The lobby is dark and shabby, with battered mailboxes and tracks of slush on the buckling tiled floor. A gloomy silence presses down.

"I wish I was dead," she yells and flees out the door, the echoes of her own voice chasing her through the gathering dusk.

chapter 7

Dear Diary,

I'm 15 now and still a mess and it makes me want to jump off a cliff or stick a dagger in my heart. I wish I had a gun. My favourite books are: To Kill a Mockingbird, Quo Vadis, The Three Musketeers, and Kon-Tiki. I wish I could travel the South Seas in a raft like that guy Heyerdahl. 'Bye for now. Love and other indoor sports, T.

The diary goes beneath the corner of the carpet that's under the bed to keep it safe from Lisa's prying eyes. Even so, Toni imagines the diary in her mother's hands, the naked words exposed to her mother's pained and scornful scrutiny. Lisa has a nose for secrets and a knack for schemes to make Toni miserable. She arrives home with a brochure that's become slightly crumpled in its journey from the hand of Mrs Rajinsky at the Jewish Y to Mrs Shmelzer, to Lisa's purse.

Lisa smoothes out the folds, flattening the pamphlet against the dining room table so that Toni can admire the glossy black-and-white photo of a posed shot of about a hundred kids and teenagers arranged in a wide semi-circle, youngest in the front, oldest in the back, angled slightly so they all fit in. They wear a uniform of sorts; dark pants, crisp white shirt, neckerchief with a crest. Some kids also wear an Israeli-style, thimble-shaped hat low on their foreheads. One and all, the faces look depressingly cheerful. Despite the grainy quality of the photo and the creases in the paper, the group's smiling eagerness and togetherness shines through. Beneath the picture the caption trumpets, "Camp Tikvah: Nourishing Jewish souls in the heart of the Laurentians."

And the blurb exults, "An opportunity for Jewish boys and girls from various backgrounds to meet and live together in healthy, happy surroundings. They will form a bond with Israel, gain a love of our people and heritage, build lifelong friendships." Inside the brochure, more promises, including "swimming, canoeing, arts and crafts, ping-pong, drama, socials, Israeli dancing, to name just a few of our exciting activities. Kosher meals planned by a home economics teacher ... the pristine waters of Lac Sainte-Cecile."

Toni's chest tightens and a dreary gloom presses against the back of her eyes. She knows everything she needs to know about these Camp Tikvah kids. She can feel their easy camaraderie through the page, how they've grown up together, gone to the same schools, belonged to the same clubs, danced the Twist at the same bar mitzvahs. They have aunts and uncles or Hebrew school teachers or friends of friends in common. They form a smooth wall of cemented bonds while she, Toni, remains loose debris. Bad enough to be an oddball at school, where at least she's found her niche, become used to her spot on the margins. She couldn't bear to start all over again in another hostile environment. No point in voicing such thoughts to her mother, though. To do so would unleash another lecture about what real hardship and starting over means: war, horror, DP camp, wandering through countries, coming here with nothing, and learning a new language. Her parents think fitting in means having money in the bank, a roof over your head, and a textbook grasp of English.

"I'm not going," Toni says, crossing her arms over her chest.

"What do you mean?"

The bright, expectant look in her mother's eyes dims to incredulity. "Have you even read the brochure? What they offer? Swimming, canoeing ... "

"I don't want to go to camp."

"Well, you can't moon around here all summer again."

"I won't moon around."

"Look at you. Pale as goat cheese. Miserable and lonely. You think I don't know how lonely you are? You think I don't hear you sniffling in your room? It breaks a mother's heart."

Toni is shocked into silence at the thought of her mother, ears cocked by the bedroom door, for how else would she know? How else would Lisa be aware of Toni weeping quietly into her pillow at night? Toni tries to summon her anger, but her mother, leaning across the table with her face full of outrage and a mother's heartbreak sucks the life out of Toni's unvoiced reproaches.

"You have no friends," Lisa continues, merciless and accusing. "At camp you'd make friends."

"I have Judy," Toni counters, without much conviction.

Toni has chummed around with Judy Rothstein off and on since grade eight. Judy is cross-eyed, brainy, talks a mile a minute, and has odd obsessions such as Catherine the Great, Lewis Carroll's nonsense rhymes (many of which she's memorized), ghoulish songs, her restaurant napkin collection, scratching doodles on her skin with a needle, and lighting fires in ashtrays. They do have fun together sometimes when they lock themselves in a dark basement room at Judy's place, eat raw weiners straight from the cellophane package, and howl out the words to the Lizzie Borden rhyme: *Lizzie Borden took an axe / And gave her mother forty whacks.* They sterilize a needle in a candle flame and play X-O on their arms, and Judy, oblivious to pain, often pricks deeply enough into her own flesh to draw blood. Out in the world, Judy likes to pretend she's a madwoman, muttering the "Jabberwocky" poem on the bus or in the school hallways, relishing the startled looks she garners. For years, Toni has wavered in her feelings toward Judy between admiration and protectiveness, on the one hand, and horrified embarrassment on the other. Her friend doesn't seem to realize when she's gone too far, and Toni can't help but wonder whether Judy just pretends or really is crazy after all. Toni resolved to give Judy the shake by her fifteenth birthday, but that birthday came and went three weeks ago and nothing has changed. Toni is as dependent as ever on wacko-Judy for company.

"The Rothstein girl!" Lisa scoffs. "She's not normal."

"So what?" Toni growls, though normality is what she longs for and what eludes her because of Judy's friendship, along with her own freakish body and general weirdness.

"You can do better. Anyway, she's going to Girl Guide camp this summer. Haven't you heard?"

Toni has heard. Judy told her the news quite cheerfully. She said she looked forward to campfires and learning to tie knots and would probably be able to apply her new knowledge to crafting a hangman's noose. Toni briefly toyed with the idea of asking to go to the Girl Guide camp too, but the thought of a whole community of Judys made her think twice. A summer without her old standby pal, without anyone at all, seems equally unbearable.

When her father comes home and reads the brochure, he sighs over the price of the camp—$400 for the two months—but his lips curl in a wan smile at the magic words, "lake," "country," "Laurentians," "fresh air." Julius remembers the rambles he took in his youth through the Vienna woods, the cool breezes, scent of pine, troops of children in knickerbockers singing wandering songs as they marched along the path. The word "wander" has a different meaning in German than in English, although it's spelled almost the same, he tells Toni. The English word has connotations of being lost, whereas the German suggests freedom and exploration.

"Edelweiss, edelweiss," Toni trills mockingly, but Julius hasn't even heard of the saccharine Julie Andrews musical set in the Austrian Alps, and the irony goes right over his head.

"They make a big deal about Israel at this camp," she says. "Listen to this: 'Some of our best and brightest have gone on to make *Aliyah*.' Is that what you want? That I'm brainwashed to leave home and live in Israel?"

He gives Toni a sidelong glance.

"You don't have to swallow every word they say. Enjoy the mountains and the lake. Learn to swim. That's what I'm paying for."

"Of course you must visit Israel some day," Lisa says as she sails into the living room and plops down into her corner of the couch. "It's a wonderful place."

Instead of her usual housedress, she's wearing a blue T-shirt and white peddle-pushers, as if she herself were getting ready for the Tikvah experience. A kerchief twisted into a turban caps her head because she's put some new stuff into her hair and it needs to seep in. A sheen of cold cream glistens on her cheeks and a smug, everything's-settled smile sits upon her lips.

"Can you imagine a country where everyone around you is Jewish? The policemen, the bus drivers, the radio announcers, the government officials, the ..."

Lisa's hands grope in the air as she searches her mind for more categories of Jews.

"The Santa Clauses!" Toni offers and guffaws.

"You see? She has no Jewish pride," Lisa says accusingly to Julius, who has picked up the *Montreal Star* and begun to scan the headlines through the bottoms of his bifocals. Toni knows he's not as enthusiastic a Zionist as Lisa is. He grudgingly makes annual donations to various Jewish organizations and wonders how much really goes to planting trees in the ancestral land and how much into the *schnorers'* pockets. "Israel is a necessary evil," he sometimes says, quoting Einstein. What he means is that, though the establishment of the state was a practical necessity after the war, a country chock-full of fellow Jews holds no great appeal for him. He also worries about Israel's vulnerability. He's not keen on so many Jews being gathered together on one miserable spit of land amidst a sea of hostile Arabs. Beginner's luck is how he regards Israel's successes in battle so far.

"What's so great about being Jewish?" Toni demands. "I mean why is it a bigger deal than being left-handed or having a name that starts with 'T'?"

Her own words strike her as a brilliant, self-evident heresy, like the child's revelation that the emperor had no clothes.

Lisa glares, speechless for once.

"Jewish, shmoo-ish!" Toni adds. The phrase pleases her and she repeats it more loudly. "Jewish, shmoo-ish!"

"Shame on you! Shame! To spit on your own people!"

"I'm not spitting. I'm just saying—"

"After all the sufferings of so many millions!"

Lisa rears up on the couch. Her finger jabs at Toni, seated cross-legged on the carpet. "In my wanderings, in those years when we were hunted like animals, I met a few Jews who—"

Oh, here it comes. The damning tone, the deluge of stories.

"—never could say a good word about their own kind."

"What's so great about it? That's all I'm trying to—"

"Believe me, these are the most pitiful of people. Not the ones burnt in the ovens. No! Not them."

"What does Jewish mean anyway? It doesn't mean anything. It's, it's …"

"…blessed compared to those others, the self-haters, the ones without a soul."

"It's just a stupid word."

Toni is walking around in circles now, plucking at her hair, hardly aware of what she's saying, just wanting to drown out her mother's voice. Out of the corner of her eye she sees her father's face twisted in a grimace. His hands push at the air in front of him. He gets up and rushes off down the hall, and in his haste leaves one slipper behind so that he walks to his study with a lop-sided shuffle. Before Lisa can begin blaming Toni for upsetting her father, she decamps too. She makes sure to slam her bedroom door extra hard.

Some time later comes a gentle knock. She's surprised to hear her father call her name. He enters and sits on the edge of the bed and strokes her forehead with his long, tapered fingers.

"Your mother puts things in extreme terms sometimes, but all in all she is right. One must have pride."

"I'm not ashamed. You both don't understand." Toni kicks the foot of the bedstead. "I just don't see why I have to call myself Jewish. I'm not religious and neither are either of you."

"It's much more than religion and you know that. We have a history, a culture, so many great—"

"Okay, okay. So I can read Jewish books. And English books, and French. And Chinese, if I want. There's culture everywhere. What does that have to do with *being* something. What if I just want to be an ordinary Canadian?"

Julius sighs and tugs at his goatee. And then comes that soft, dry, helpless click produced at the back of his throat when he swallows, a sound that's like a tickle in the small of her back where she can't reach and that makes her want to jump out of her skin and makes the desire to kick him almost irresistible. She can't, of course, because he's delicate, her papa, he wouldn't fight back, he'd run away, and it's been such a long time since he's sat at the edge of her bed like this. And she doesn't want her papa to leave.

"I once thought exactly as you do," he says at last. "I considered myself a citizen of the world. Vienna was a cosmopolitan city. I read English papers, listened to Italian opera, drank French wine, went to a nightclub where good Austrian citizens applauded Yiddish wit."

He draws himself up as he speaks, his voice swells with the rhythm of his story, speaking to her equal-to-equal, instantly erasing that volcano of irritation within her that was about to erupt. Suddenly she's full of wonder at that younger man she glimpses: clever, carefree, and at ease in a place of mystery called a nightclub.

"I voted for the socialists who promised that all mankind would be as one if only the filthy capitalists could be toppled from power. And then, one day, there were no more filthy capitalists. Only filthy Jews. No. No. I know what you want to say. You are thinking: 'This is so negative. Why must we allow others to define us?'"

He holds a raised palm in the air, as if to stop her in mid-protest, though no such objection has occurred to her.

"And you are right, in principle. But the world does not operate in principle. In the end, you cannot choose whether to be Jewish or not. You can only choose *how* you will be Jewish. Those ordinary Canadians you mention, they have their Christmas trees and their churches and their Thanksgiving dinners. Everyone belongs to a tribe of some sort. Like it or not, and I don't, that is human nature. When the Nazis ordered the Jews of Germany to wear the yellow Star of David, one of our leaders said, 'Wear the yellow star with pride.' A bit quixotic, no? To make a mark of shame into a badge of honour? Not very effective. But noble, nonetheless."

Julius smiles broadly so that the gold tooth at the back of his mouth winks at Toni.

"When the day comes that race and nationality are meaningless everywhere in the world, then you can choose to be nothing in particular. In the meantime, you can't throw away your Jewishness like an old coat. First of all, as I have explained, the *goyim* won't let you. But more important, you must be proud of who you are for your own sake. You must not renounce your people. To do so is to live without honour. It is to lose your soul, as your mother says."

He cradles his chin and looks down at her gravely, the evening light reflecting off his glasses and the taut skin of his bald head. She tries to fathom this old-fashioned word, "honour." She rather likes the grand sound of it and how her father suddenly appears to her a bit like Yul Brynner in *The King and I*. At the same time, the unfairness of what he has said sinks in. *You cannot choose.* Isn't that always what grownups say?

And so, her fate is sealed. Toni allows herself to be dragged by her mother to buy new shorts, T-shirts, a bathing suit, and a plain white bathing cap (she will *not* wear the one covered with yellow rubber daisies) for summer camp.

According to the brochure, the word "*tikvah*" means "hope" in Hebrew. The camp's name echoes the title of the Israeli national anthem, "Hatikvah." Toni feels anything but hopeful as the date for her departure approaches. Her gut churns with grim foreboding.

chapter 8

Their new names are Angela and Sharon. They've developed into teenage goddesses, the kind that gaze out of magazines, perky and bright, yet with a glitter of insolence that seems to say, "Go ahead and stare. We're used to it."

They set the pace among the girls of Cabin Eleven, determining when it's time to get up and go, whether it will be a pedal-pushers or a Bermuda shorts sort of day, whether a boy's joke is hilarious or deserves just a weary smirk. They are the sun around which the others spin, even their counsellor, Lorna, who is just a couple of years older than the rest and has squinty eyes and a residue of yellow where she's dyed the fuzz on her upper lip. When Lorna gives an order, all eyes turn to Angela and Sharon to see how they'll respond.

Toni knew from the moment she laid eyes on them on the first day of camp that's how it would be. Everyone stood outside the bunkhouse, waiting for the trunks to arrive, and introduced themselves. There was Deena, a cute, pixie-faced girl with a breathless manner; Faye from Cape Breton—a place none of the others had heard of—speaking in a strange accent and wearing braces and a good-natured smile; heavyset Marion, blotchy red under the afternoon sun, but with pretty forget-me-not blue eyes. They offered eager or bashful grins as they spoke their names and looked appealingly around the circle. When it was Toni's turn, she kept her eyes neutral, her back stiff. Her name came out gruffly, a crow's hoarse croak. Angela and Sharon registered no surprise. Their glances flicked over her, cool and bland. Speaking to the others out loud, they said, laughing, "You can tell us apart by our rings," and presented their soft, golden hands to be admired. While Toni remained aloof on the sidelines, the others twittered and crowded around, in awe of the thick signet rings each of the twins displayed on the middle finger of her left hand. Going-steady rings—one with an onyx stone, the other with the McGill crest—proof of college boyfriends back home.

"Don't worry if you mix us up," they said graciously. "We're used to it."

Toni remembered how they used to live next door on her street and how, egged on by her buddy Arnold, she used to throw dirt at them when they passed by. She remembered their hoity-toity airs. *Assie and Shittie.* The kindergarten insult floated into Toni's mind to mock her, not them. They no longer dressed identically or wore the same hairdos (Angela had a bouncy, shoulder-length flip, Sharon's was slightly shorter and turned under). Still, they were a picture of mirror-image loveliness. They both had well-cultivated tans, as if they'd worked on themselves with sun reflectors before coming to camp. Pearly pink nail polish winked from their toes. Maybe it would have been better to admit she recognized her old enemies, but the opportunity passed, and then it was too late. She was trapped by her own falseness. The twins exchanged a look. They telegraphed some kind of understanding between them. *We know you,* their pitying smiles said, *we know you know us, but if you want to pretend otherwise for some twisted reason, that's your business.*

Now Toni hears the twins chatter a few feet away as the entire camp assembles in a giant "U" around the flagpole, the oldest groups along the sides, the youngest in the middle, for the morning routine: roll call, pep talks, exercises, anthems. Kids shuffle into place on the grassy slope above the lake and turn to face uphill where Myron, the camp director, stands at attention, beaming down on them. He's a swarthy, thickset man, barrel-chested, with gleaming white teeth beneath a toothbrush moustache. He generally looks like a jolly uncle, except when the sarcastic edge creeps into his smile. He raises his hand for *sheket*, silence, and the counsellors all shush their charges. Angela and Sharon lower their voices but continue with their business of sorting out the guys—who's cute, who's a drip, who's merely so-so. What does it matter, since they already have boyfriends to whom they write letters sealed with big, pink lipstick smears on the back flap? It matters. Their voices hiss with urgency. They deliver judgements with confident authority. They ignore Lorna's feeble attempts to hush them up.

Myron launches into a speech about Camp Tikvah's goals—sound minds in sound bodies, Jewish identity, love of the struggling, heroic, new-born state of Israel—as his voice grows husky, his barrel chest swells, and his face gleams with the perspiration of earnest effort. How dearly he wants his campers, his 120 "Tikvah-maniacs," to understand the importance of Israel, far away in miles but close to our hearts. Imagine, he implores, that they are in two places simultaneously. They are here at this beautiful spot on Lac Sainte-Cecile in the Laurentian mountains, surrounded on all sides by spruce and poplar forests, but they are also in the ancestral Promised Land. Look beyond the Canadian bush to another landscape of orange groves, sand dunes, ancient hills. Admire the pioneers with sun-bitten faces, work-hardened hands, the modern-day Davids and Sampsons who carry rifles on their shoulders and books of poetry in their hands. Remember the great ones of history—Moses, King Solomon, the Maccabees, Theodor Herzl, Ben Gurion. Think of the countless other heroes, the kibbutzniks, the citizen soldiers, male and female, and even the children, the bold, miraculous new generation.

"Him? He's got tits. Didn't you notice at swimming? And Hank? Oh, Hanky Panky? He's O.S.I."

A burst of giggles sweeps through the row of Cabin Eleven girls.

Toni does what she's been trying not to do; she leans over to look at the twins, as if looking will tell her what O.S.I. means. The twins clutch their stomachs and slap their thighs and catch her watching, and their grins turn doubly wicked. *We know you don't know, and we're not telling.*

A stiff breeze flaps the flags, Canadian and Israeli, on top of the pole, and the loose ends of the ropes ching-ching against the metal. Grey clouds scud across the sky. Beneath the grassy slope on which the assembly stands lies the lake, ruffled and purple and cold looking. All around the lake, the forest crowds up against the shore, the trees seeming to huddle together as if they too have goosebumps from the chill morning air. Toni shivers. She can't swim. She will never learn to swim. She ventured into the lake up to her knees, hugging herself, while Hank, the waterfront captain, tried to coax her to at least dunk her face in. When she did, water leapt up her nose and down her throat.

"Your head is like a coconut. It floats," he assured her. His hand strayed over the hard packed muscles of his chest as if he loved the feel of himself, couldn't resist it. Dreamboat Hank. The whistle that dangled from his neck was shaped like a miniature pistol. Little kids half her size walloped the water around her, while in the deep end of the roped-off swimming area, all her bunkmates swam laps, arms churning, pink heels flashing. Rooted to the spot, her toes clinging to the muddy lake bottom, she cringed whenever she got splashed, and trembled with self-loathing.

It's time for the pledge. One-hundred-and-twenty campers and counsellors put their right hands on their hearts, raise the other in the air and chant, first in Hebrew, then in English: "If I forget thee, O Jerusalem, let my right hand forget her cunning. If I do not remember thee, let my tongue cleave to the roof of my mouth."

One half of the "U" lags behind the other in the slow, mournful chant, so there's an echo at the end of every line and then another hollow murmur, ghostly and mocking, that seems to come from the lake. Toni pretends to chant along, but she doesn't know the Hebrew and, even during the English part, her voice remains frozen in her throat.

Myron likes to end the morning assembly with a show of camp spirit in the form of a cheer. Nothing is as important as spirit, which means frantic happiness, and unabashed, shrieking, frenzied enthusiasm bursting forth from every mouth. Their cheer comes from the Bible, from the phrase Moses used to urge Joshua into battle: *chazak v'amatz*, be brave and strong. Myron calls out the first word and they all answer with the second.

"Can't hear you," Myron bellows, cupping his hand around his ear.

One-hundred-and-twenty Tikvah-maniacs yell out the response.

"Louder!"

Kids bend their knees, put their hands to their heads, scream with every ounce of their lungs. The girls of Toni's group join in, Angela and Sharon shout with savage glee, everyone howls like escapees from the Verdun Asylum, but it's Toni who's the weird one. She stands woodenly, with lips pressed together. She lacks what it takes to cheer her head off.

When the assembly dissolves, the girls of Cabin Eleven, all except Toni, form a chorus line, arms draped over shoulders, and march down the hill toward the dining hall singing: "I go to Camp Tikvah, O pity me, There ain't a damn man in the vicinity."

Some of the boys of Cabin Twelve lean over the rails of the dining hall veranda and hoot about the cleavage they pretend they can see. Toni lingers behind, having sloughed off Lorna's attempts to force her in with the group. You're supposed to sparkle, bump hips together. You're supposed to be like Alka Seltzer fizzing in a glass. That's how it's done when you're normal.

Dear Diary,
It's the second week of camp: forty-two days, 1,008 hours, 60,480
minutes of Hellfire to go.

During after-lunch rest period, while the other girls sprawl on their beds with magazines, letters, and toe-nail polish, and a drowsy heat fills the cabin, Toni goes over her lists:

The things I hate:
1) No privacy. I have to hide under the blankets to get dressed and undressed. There's just a thin piece of plywood between the toilet and the rest of the cabin and nothing at all around the sink area so everyone sees everything. If I have a pimple or that morning gunk in the corner of my eyes, they all can see me looking at my icky stuff in the mirror.

2) The annoying routine. We're up at 6:30, with Myron singing a peppy song over the loudspeaker. Assembly, breakfast, Period 1, Period 2, Period 3, etc., until lights out.

3) The endless togetherness. I'm not allowed to wander off by myself. When I try to escape group activities, Lorna hunts me down and herds me back, making "tsk-tsk" sounds.

4) The requirement to be smiley. If I don't have a grin plastered on my face like everyone else, some counsellor gives me a phony friendly hug and yammers something cheerful in my ear.

5) The twins. I hate their beauty-queen guts.

6) Trying to swim. Hank says everyone can float, but I can't. I sink down to the muddy green bottom of the lake and the water squeezes my head, the noise is awful and it lasts forever.

7) _Folkdancing._ They've got this frantically happy accordion music blasting from the record player. We're in a circle holding hands and whirling faster, faster. Everyone stamps in unison, everyone except me, because my stupid body jerks the other dancers off balance. They snort with laughter and the twins roll up their eyes. I pray for the music to end, but when it does all I hear are the giggles and all I see are my big, long ugly feet.

The things I like:
1) _My bed._ It's the upper bunk, in the corner, close to the rafters, so almost like a hiding place. Above my head, a daddy-long-legs dangles by an invisible thread. It's a creepy old thing, that spider, but nice somehow with hinged, hair-thin legs spreading out from a body like a blob of spit. It sways in the breeze, defying gravity. The thread comes from its abdomen. I read that somewhere.

2) _The food._ My parents think Canadian food is inferior but I think it's great. I love the pancakes with corn syrup, hotdogs, peanut butter and jelly sandwiches on white bread, and Jello instant pudding.

3) _Baseball._ It's the one sport I'm good at. The first time I swung the bat like crazy and missed and the boys on the other team made fun of me by covering their heads as if they were about to get beaned. But the next chance up I connected and did their jaws ever drop.

4) _Faye._ She's goofy and sweet and so easy-going. When the other kids screw up their faces at Faye's Cape Breton expressions ("knickers" instead of underpants, "mitts" instead of hands), she just grins and puts on her broadest accent: "Youz turkeys ain't heard nuttin' yet." She sleeps in the bunk below me and always calls up, "Sleep tight, Toni," every single night. She taught me

"O.S.I." means "over six inches." (Yuck!) Faye would like to be a bridge between me and the twins. She wants everyone to be one big happy family. Silly, kind-hearted Faye.

5) Beauty. In nature. I've read about beauty in books and thought I knew what it meant, but I didn't until now. It floors me how beauty sneaks up, jumps out. One morning there were swirls of mist on the lake, and the far shore was blotted out except for the dark green pointed tips of the fir trees. A loon called. It felt like there was this huge, looming thing in the silence of the forest. Another time, I saw pale green sparks winking on and off in the thick darkness beyond the cabin. Fireflies. How do they do that? How do they transform their insect bodies into light?

Things I'm not sure about:
1) The singing program.
2) The singing instructor, Janet Bloom.

This Friday evening begins, like all others, with welcome-the-Sabbath ceremonies. Three junior girls wearing white dresses and crowns of daisies giggle on the dining hall threshold: the Sabbath Queen and her attendants. All other Tikvah-maniacs sit in their groups at trestle tables and crane their necks. "Aw," the crowd murmurs in unison. The hall breaks into a hymn as the trembling procession advances up the aisle. "Come, my beloved, with a chorus of praise, Welcome Shabbat, the queen of our days."

For Friday evenings, the long tables wear white paper cloths and plastic tumblers of wildflowers whose heads flop forward on wilting stems. Decorations adorn the walls; hand-drawn menorahs, dreidels, golden coins, and the ever-present, somewhat misshapen Star of David. The theme is Hanukkah in July. All the major Jewish festivals will find their way onto the agenda during the course of the summer. Toni had no idea there were so many.

Myron rises from his place at the head table in the front of the room to say a few words about the significance of Hanukkah, the ancient revolt against oppressors and a demonstration of Jewish *ruach*. "What does the Hebrew word *ruach* mean?" Myron asks them, but doesn't wait for an answer. "Spirit and breath. Which brings us to the meaning of Sabbath, too. God's *ruach* created heaven and earth. God's *ruach* blew into Adam's lungs. And do Tikvah-maniacs have any of that *ruach*? Do they?" Myron cups his hand to his ear.

"Yes!" the hall thunders. "Yes, yes, yes!" Feet stamp, fists pound the tables and make cutlery clatter. The hall erupts into chants of, "We want Janet, we want Janet."

Myron's chief ally in the *ruach* department sits at the end of the head table with her chin in her hands, looking dreamy, as if none of this commotion has anything to do with her. She heaves herself up at last and shuffles slowly down the centre aisle. Her face is rosy, freckled, and unremarkable. Her figure is slight, with pink, sunburnt legs sticking out of khaki Bermuda shorts. The hall simmers down. An expectant hush descends.

Janet makes them wait a few moments longer, then opens her mouth and belts out a line of song. "David, David, King of Israel," she sings in Hebrew. Her voice reaches from one end of the room to the other, hits the rafters, rich and clear, high and sweet. A voice so much bigger than the rest of her. She repeats the line, excruciatingly slowly this time, groaning out the words like a record on the wrong speed. The little kids hoot with laughter. Finally, she delivers the song for real, at its proper peppy tempo, her hands waving for them all to join in. Voices blend and swell into a tide. Faster, faster, Janet urges them as she hops up and down the aisle, her hands clapping, her frizzy red hair springing free from the bobby pins that held it in place. One song melts into another. "The hills skipped like rams," they sing in Hebrew.

"Hava nagila ... "

"Tzena, tzena, tzena ..."

"Michael, row your boat ashore, Halleloooooya."

Hating her own froggy voice, Toni resists the pressure to sing, but she sways a little; she can't help herself, the wash of voices sweeps her along. Now arms drape over shoulders, she's included in the circle, with Marion on her left, Faye on her right, as the whole group rocks together and warbles for all they're worth. A pleasant vibration rises in Toni's chest. Her tiny drop of sound flows with the rest. How good when the whole hall unites, when the girls hold onto one another, glowing with goodwill, smiling like angels, all trace of snootiness gone. The room is one great heart, one gust of wind, *ruach, roooo-ach.* Myron waves his hands as if he's orchestrating the songfest, but it's not him of course, it's Janet, that brilliant spark in the middle of the room.

Then it's over. Back to the chatter, titters, whispers, gossip, head tossing, exchanges of superior looks.

After the prayers that conclude the evening meal, the entire assembly storms outside onto the lawn and the big wrap-around veranda to await the evening program, a play about the battle between the Greeks and the Maccabees. Toni slips away to the far end of the beach, where overturned canoes and rowboats lie. Secluded from view, she settles on a cool aluminium hull. The water is still as molten glass and dark, except for a path of gold spangles cast by the setting sun. Across the lake, the lower slopes of the forested hills drown in shadow, while the tops glow like candles. On the far shore, the white houses of the village of Sainte-Cecile cluster together. All this beauty is right in front of her, yet a million miles away, beyond her grasp. Loneliness bites deeper than ever.

"Pretty damn gorgeous, eh?" someone beside her drawls.

Toni whips around to see Janet Bloom standing above her. Janet's bare feet must have whispered along the grass, but Toni heard nothing. The song instructor studies Toni for a long moment, then plops down onto the boat. Fumbling in the pocket of her shorts, she fishes out a matchbook and a somewhat flattened cigarette, which she moulds back into shape with her thumb and forefinger. Casually, she lights up. A cigarette on Shabbat! Instinctively, Toni cranks her head around. She's become so used to spying eyes everywhere. Janet winks.

"Nice spot you got," she sighs over a deep drag.

They sit in silence for a while, Toni holding herself very still, as if an exotic butterfly had come to rest beside her and she mustn't scare it away. Janet lets coils of smoke unfurl from her half-open mouth. Out of the corner of her eye, Toni steals glances. Janet is better looking than she realized. Her loose hair sticks out on both sides of her head, a wild, coppery mass blazing in the evening light. Her ruddy face swims with freckles, pulsing like dark lights beneath the fine skin. There's even one funny freckle in the bow of her lip, like a spot of chocolate.

Catching Toni's gaze, Janet winks again. A surge of heat flares up Toni's chest, neck, and ears, but if Janet notices, she doesn't let on.

"I could just sink into that, couldn't you?" Janet waves her hand at the panorama before them. "Makes me want to do something wild." She takes another drag. "How 'bout you? A sunset do something special to you?"

"It makes me feel blue," Toni stammers.

Janet nods her head slowly, as if Toni had just said something very deep. There are freckles on Janet's knees and between the knuckles of the hand holding the cigarette. Her bare feet have high arches—deep, audacious curves—and bright red toes, as if the blood pulses close to the surface. The word "sassy" comes to Toni's mind. Those feet are sassy. It's not a word she can remember ever thinking of before. Her heart flutters strangely.

"You put your finger on it," Janet says and Toni stares in surprise. "Heartbreakingly beautiful. A view like that makes you want to weep." Janet sweeps her cigarette hand in a wide arc. They watch while the sun shrinks into a twinkling green eye atop the hills, then vanishes, leaving behind layers of crimson clouds and dark silhouetted humps.

"Shit. I'm supposed to be introducing the play," Janet says, flinging the smoking butt end into the lake. "Toodle-oo."

She rests her hand on Toni's shoulder for a moment, perhaps just to get her balance as she stands, but the hand seems to be saying something more, that it belongs there. Then she's gone, walking swiftly up the grassy slope. Toni watches Janet join the streams of campers heading back into the dining hall. What just happened? What? Something amazing. She blinks hard. Green and gold sunspots still dance before her eyes. Janet never addressed her by name. Does Janet even know her name? Doesn't matter. A connection has sprung up, a connection beyond ordinary words. She is lost yet knows exactly where she is. She pulls in the moment like a newborn with its first gush of warm milk. She feels she has swallowed the sun. Then, for no reason she can fathom, Toni leaps from her perch on the up-ended rowboat and marches directly into the lake with all her clothes on, her Bermuda shorts, T-shirt, bra and underpants, sneakers and socks, ploughing forward against the resisting pressure until she stands up to her neck. Only her head sticks up above the glassy surface. Her clothes feel both heavy and light, clinging here, billowing there, while the water swirls, flows, nudges, tugs, and is transformed from the first shock of cold contact into a pleasant bath-like temperature. If a counsellor came by now ... there must be a rule against walking into the lake with your clothes on. She'll have to sneak back to the bunk to change. It pleases her immensely to break this unknown rule. Janet would understand.

chapter 9

Dear Mama and Papa,
Camp is better now. My swimming is coming along swimmingly
(ha, ha) since I graduated from the dog paddle. I've learned to
canoe. Also, I'm production assistant for the musical, Fiddler
on the Roof, *which is being directed by Janet Bloom, the Sing-*
ing Instructor. I've told you about Janet. She's very talented and
creative and will be famous some day, like Joan Baez, except her
style is more bluesy and beautiful, I think, more real.

Toni lifts her pen from the writing block that rests on her knees and
gazes at the rough-hewn beam above her head. Afternoon heat has
gathered beneath the rafters. The whole cabin roasts, especially the upper bunk, so that sweat trickles down Toni's neck and moistens her
palms. Down below, her bunkmates scribble away, filling pastel sheets
of paper. Letters home. Letters to cousins and friends and boyfriends.
Angela's toenails glisten with a fresh coat of candy-pink polish, each
tanned toe separated with a wad of cotton wool and wafting a sweetish
chemical smell directly into Toni's offended nostrils. Janet's toes are
ruby red. Janet's eyes are smoky green, the entrancing green of fir-clad
hills. Toni furiously scratches out the sentence that wrote itself upon
the page. The blatant words seem dangerous, and besides, what would
her parents know, stuck as they are in the grooves of old 78 records,
Strauss waltzes, and Marlene Dietrich songs? But once again, the pen
in her hand moves of its own accord, forming the letters "J-a-n ... "

Marion's transistor radio buzzes, crackles, then picks up the faint chorus of "Mrs Brown, You've Got a Lovely Daughter" by Herman's Hermits. A cheer goes up in the cabin and the girls join in. "Luvely daaawter" they sing in fake British accents. A month ago, Toni liked this group too, but now the sequins-and-lollipop sound grates on her nerves. Janet has introduced her to *real* music: Folkways records of *authentic* artists who sing Negro spirituals or old English ballads, accompanied by acoustic guitars and the autoharp. Some evenings, a few devotees gather in Janet's room in the staff house amid candle glow and cigarette smoke to listen to her record collection and talk the kind of serious talk that must grace the air of Greenwich Village coffee houses.

Last night, the conversation touched on civil rights marches, ban the bomb, the Mariposa Folk Festival, dropping out of college to live on a kibbutz, and rival interpretations of the liner notes of *The Times They Are a-Changin'*. The in-crowd consisted of a few counsellors, a French-Canadian guy, Alain, who works as kitchen staff, a senior boy, Samuel, who always wears a *kippah*, a skullcap, and is one of the most religious kids at camp, plus Toni. A bottle of wine in a brown paper bag passed from hand-to-hand, but Samuel bristled and shot Toni a warning look, and she too declined, feeling noble. She wouldn't do anything to get Janet into trouble. From her place on the floor in the corner, Toni absorbed every silvery, tremolo note of Joan Baez singing "Babe, I'm Gonna Leave You." Arms wrapped around her legs, chin on her knees, she peered from under her bangs and watched Janet who sat cross-legged on the bed with her head thrown back in ecstasy. "You play now," Alain, the French guy, had said, handing Janet her guitar. Janet's fingers dancing over the strings produced a stream of golden notes, and even the little squeaks her left hand made as it slid up and down the frets sounded exquisite. Then Lorna rapped with uncouth knuckles against the screen door. Her white cats-eye glasses caught the glare of the porch light.

"Come on, come on! Curfew!" she hollered, clapping her hands sharply as if Toni were a dog to be brought to heel.

"Good grief," says Lorna now, bringing Toni back from her reverie. She fans herself with a magazine. "Can you believe this heat, girls? My *kishkes* are boiling away."

Toni turns back to her letter. "I hope Papa's ulcer will be better soon," she writes. "Looking forward to seeing you at Parents' Day."

Should she drop a hint about the generous tip that is the song instructor's due? Maybe not. Better to work on her father in person. If he decides to be cheap she will die of shame.

But now there's time before next period to run an errand. Janet had asked her to stop by the kitchen and collect a couple of big pots to use as pails for Tevye the Milkman in the play. Toni clambers down the bunk-bed ladder and shoehorns on her sneakers with her forefinger. On the way down the aisle, she accidentally hooks her foot against the leg of Angela's cot, sending a bag of jumbo rollers tumbling to the floor and bouncing in every direction, including into the dusty gloom under the bed. "Oops, sorry." Toni holds back the smirk that creeps into the corners of her mouth.

"Well, isn't someone in a hurry?" Angela drawls, without looking up from the Harold Robbins paperback she's reading. Then she raises her head to fix Toni with a gaze of cool appraisal.

"Such an eager beaver. You do have it bad," she says in a pitying tone.

Toni stares back coldly, as if she has no idea what Angela is talking about. *Of course you know. And I know you know.* Toni's eyes are the first to drop. "Got a problem?" she stammers, but before Angela can answer, Toni lurches out of the cabin and lets the screen door slam. *An insect compared to Janet!* But Angela's words and the look of penetrating intelligence eat into her anyway. She must race down the hill to be rid of them.

She stands outside the empty Culture Hall clutching two enormous, battered soup pots along with their lids. Sweat pools in the hollow of her throat, trickles down between her breasts. The pots had bumped against her thighs as she ran, and twice a lid fell off and rolled along the dirt path. A note on the door reads, "No rehearsal today. See you tomorrow, Fiddlers. Love, Janet." Everyone except Toni seems to have known about the cancellation because not a single cast member has shown up, not Tevye and his daughters nor any of the little kids in rubber boots and shawls or vests who play the villagers. Why didn't Janet tell her, why? A sense of betrayal stabs Toni's heart. She had imagined how she would place the pots very carefully at the back of the room so as not to disturb Janet in the middle of directing a scene, then would lean quietly against a wall and wait to be noticed and thanked, maybe with a hug. She'd imagined the hug, Janet's arm encircling her waist and pulling her close. But Gita, the dance instructor, has taken over the Hall with records and posters of Israeli dance troupes and peppy music. Numb with disappointment, Toni bangs the pots down and sprints away so as not to have to meet Gita's startled glance. She stops in mid-stride, sneaks back to snatch the piece of paper off the door. She wants that note, written in Janet's bold, loopy hand, especially the part that says "Love, Janet."

She wants to tell Faye as they paddle together in a canoe on the still, glassy lake in the shimmering heat. On her knees in the stern, Toni arrows the canoe forward with brisk, firm strokes while Faye dips her paddle more tentatively. They make good canoeing mates: Toni supplies direction and muscle and Faye manages to hold the rhythm, following Toni's lead, humming as they skim along. Now and then Faye slaps nervously at a deerfly and apologizes for making the canoe wobble. Or she'll ask if it's okay to rest—as if it's up to Toni to grant permission—then lay her paddle across the thwarts and trail her fingers in the water. She doesn't feel obliged to chatter, is content to sink into the dreaminess of the afternoon. Her faded blue thimble hat, too big for her head, lies low over her ears, shading her elfin face. A large dragonfly quivers on the hat's crown, which would make Faye jump if she knew. Her parents sent her half-way across the country, far from the sea-washed shores of her island home, so she could meet Jewish kids from Montreal, expand her horizons. Faye has confided to Toni that she wept into her pillow night after night the whole first week at camp.

Because of all this, words rush to the tip of Toni's tongue. *Have you ever felt … I know it's weird, but … do you think I'm crazy?*

She steers the canoe toward a secluded bay with a raft of water lilies whose pads scrape softly along the hull and whose long stems coil around their paddles. Hundreds of glossy green lily pads spread out around them, some with fat, yellow, multi-layered flowers, some holding well-camouflaged frogs that utter tiny shrieks as they leap away. The docks of camp, all the other boats, all signs of civilization have vanished. This place exists for itself alone. Toni rests her paddle on the gunnels and Faye turns to face her.

"Are we stuck?" Faye asks anxiously.

"'Course not."

"We better go then."

"Don't be such a scaredy cat. It's nice here."

Toni speaks gruffly, but in thinking over what she wants to say her throat has gone sandpaper dry.

"But the period's almost over. We'll be late."

A touch of panic strains Faye's voice, and there is a doubting look in her eyes, as if she's not so sure about Toni after all, whether she's the right kind of person to hang around with. Nothing to be done, Toni realizes, but to dig her paddle into the mass of lily pads, work the wobbling canoe around, and retrace the journey. There is no one to tell.

Every step holds danger, every twist of the hard-packed dirt path that runs down the hill from the bunkhouses to the quadrangle of buildings around the flagpole. Any moment her breath could freeze, her heart could leak out through her pores for all to see. Fists thrust deep into the pockets of her shorts, Toni shuffles along trying to look like someone without a care in the world. She keeps her eyes straight ahead, but she's aware of every flicker at the periphery of her vision. Every shape could be Janet. Any moment Janet could appear and ignite the air, blast the ground beneath Toni's feet. Yet every moment of Janet's absence is an abyss. Oh beautiful, terrible anticipation. Hope soars to the stratosphere, crashes to the depths, rises again—and oh, my god, what if someone sees how she trembles? And she is only halfway down the path.

Supper is creamed salmon on toast. Toni looks down at her melamine plate, at the pinkish milky sauce dotted with grey-green peas. The fierce hunger she felt a moment ago has vanished, replaced by a rising tide of nausea. Her face burns. Sweat trickles down behind her ears. Yet a fine breeze blows through the picture windows of the dining hall, dishes clatter, and merry voices hum. She should ask to be excused.

Instead she barks across the table, "What did you mean just now? About being a case? What do you think you're talking about?"

Angela's fork stops in mid-flight toward her mouth. Her eyes gleam as if she's been dealt a winning hand. Everyone falls silent.

"I didn't mean anything. Don't get yourself all hot and bothered."

She and her twin sister exchange glances of suppressed hilarity.

"A case of what?" Toni growls as she stabs the underside of the trestle table with her knife. She's aghast at her own question. How could she leave herself so open? The knife thrust is meant as much for her own guts as for Angela's.

Sure enough, Angela gazes back calmly and asks, "You really want to know?"

Toni grabs the table edge to steady herself. She swallows hard.

"You better not mean anything," she mutters. She picks up her fork and pokes around in the mush on her plate.

In the thick darkness beneath the rafters, Toni hearkens to the snores and snuffles of her bunkmates. Eyes wide open, pulse racing, she slips her hands under the blankets and pushes down on the waistband of her pyjamas. Carefully she eases her legs out, trying not to wiggle the bed. *Ho, ho, ho*, a monkey chorus at the back of her mind hoots. *Look at you.* She's got a brief spell of time before the counsellor on night duty swings through the bunkhouse, flashlight beam bouncing along beds and walls to check that all is well with the sleeping angels. Perhaps only a few minutes, but it should be long enough. She thrusts her pillow between her thighs and props herself on her elbows and begins to gently rock. Who cares about the jeering voices? Who cares about anything now? She sees herself as Ari, the Jewish resistance leader from the movie *Exodus*. He stands on the cool sand of a moonlit beach as a red-haired girl runs her hands up and down his bare sides. Up and down. Their lips meet. Luxurious flames lick inward. Miracles happen. *Ah yes, any moment now, any moment.*

"Toni? What's wrong?"

Faye's hoarse whisper pierces the black stillness. Toni freezes, holds her breath. But Faye persists, calling up from the bottom bunk. "Is everything okay?"

"I'm fine," Toni gasps.

"But you were shaking. You were shaking the bed."

"I'm okay. Go to sleep!"

Toni slumps forward, crushing her damp face against the mattress.

"Are you sure?"

"Yes!"

Well-meaning, good-hearted Faye. At this moment, Toni wants to take her by the throat and throttle her.

Angela begins a story. There was this creepy girl at school. Liz.

"Oh stop!" Sharon squeals from the neighbouring cot.

"Liz the Lezzie," Angela grins.

"Don't say any more. Just that name gives me the willies."

Sharon pretends to clap her hands over her ears, but her dark eyes dance with mischief and delight as she looks around the room to see whether the others have taken the bait. Indeed they have. They lean forward on their elbows. "Tell, tell, tell," they chorus like baying dogs. Someone switches off the tinny transistor radio, and the cabin goes quiet. Toni in her upper bunk shields her face with her open paperback, though she peers over the tops of the pages.

Angela sits up straighter, adjusts the pillow behind her back, and launches into her tale. This Liz had a beefy face, hefty shoulders, walked like a gorilla, and reeked like piss. Worse was how she stared at the popular girls, especially at Angela and Sharon, with big cow eyes. Angela bugs out her own eyes and lolls her tongue at Sharon to imitate the hideous, gawking Liz. Sharon waves her hands in front of her face, pushing away the appalling vision. Whenever Liz approached, Angela continues, their friends would form a protective circle around them. Unable to take a hint, Liz would try to wriggle her way into the group. Everyone would let her know she was a pervert. She would slink off like a big lump of misery. But then, just as the twins thought she'd got the message, she'd ogle them again from across the classroom.

But that wasn't the worst, Sharon tells them with a shiver. No, Angela agrees. The worst was how she played with herself. In public.

"In public?" Marion exclaims in disbelief.

"In the toilet stalls. That's public enough, don't you think?" Angela grimaces.

"Some girls peeked in on her. Not us, of course," Sharon says quickly.

"Besides, you could smell it," Angela says.

"Yes! The leftovers." Sharon shrieks at the memory.

"Yech!" the others chime in.

"She got weirder and weirder."

"Her parents finally took her out of school, thank God."

"What happened to her then?" Faye asks in a serious tone.

"I dunno," Angela shrugs. "Probably the mental asylum. She's probably still groping her petunia."

Everyone howls with horrified laughter, even Faye. The twins never glance upward in Toni's direction as they speak. They don't have to. She can feel Liz, the ape-girl, the mental case, raging and hideous, inside herself. Her heart flutters like a trapped moth. She wishes she could summon righteous anger—*You, you are the ugly ones, you alone*—but the best she can do is feign indifference, gripping her paperback between sweaty fingers. For the past couple of days, during lulls between activities, she's been devouring *Exodus*, swept along in the thrilling saga, fighting alongside its heroes through every chapter, burning with their loves. But now Liz the Lezzie takes over. The printed words swim on the page.

In the days that follow come more Liz stories. There are dirty jokes, whispered secrets, sudden bursts of laughter that erupt at the mere raising of an eyebrow, the mouthing of code words, the flick of a lizardly tongue.

chapter 10

Fish like black needles flit near Toni's feet. Lacy shadows ripple along the sandy bottom of the little bay, and beyond, the silvery lake shimmers beneath a hot blue sky. Toni rubs her mosquito-bitten legs against sun-warmed granite. Nice spot she's found. Private. The yelp of kids at Camp Tikvah sounds like the mew of far-off gulls. She takes another swig from the bottle.

It is pleasing to put her lips to the glass mouth, to tip her head back. It is rude, wild, naked, and angry. Wine pours in a silky gush into her belly. The first gulps had made her sputter. They burned her throat and made sweat pour from her forehead into her eyes. Then a pleasant numbness spread through her limbs, her tongue grew large, likewise her hands. Invincible. She drinks with understanding. She has a plan: to get very, very drunk.

To find this secluded bay, she'd hurried along a muddy track behind the boathouse through a half-dried-up marsh and then fought her way through tangled bush. She pushed at the branches with her free hand while clutching the wine bottle hidden beneath her shirt with the other. Just when she thought she could go no further, she glimpsed the beckoning rock, a bare, pink-veined boulder overlooking the bay.

The bottle she'd snatched so quickly and carried away beneath her shirt turned out to have a screw top. Lucky! She didn't expect to feel so good. Just wanted to feel not so bad. She's surprised now at the laughter at the tip of her big, floppy tongue, and how the village across the lake seems to float in the air. She glugs down some more of the wine. A brown duck lands, feet first, in her little bay and begins to paddle toward a clump of arrow weeds.

"Cheers," Toni calls out. The startled creature takes off again with a nervous flutter of wings. Toni clutches her sides. Too funny.

Perhaps she will go into the water. That would be nice, to float on her back and gaze at the clouds, to lie there until the sky turns indigo and the winking stars appear.

"To life," she howls.

"Ai, ai," the lake softly echoes.

Back at the Culture Hall, they're rehearsing *Fiddler on the Roof.* Golde asks Tevye if he loves her, his daughters beg the matchmaker for husbands, the entire village, in shawls, rubber boots, and cotton-batten beards bawl out the chorus: "To life, to life, *l'chayim.*" Janet coaxes music out of their throats. But where is the papier mâché goat? Where is the production assistant who was supposed to bring the goat from the arts and crafts room? Missing. Oh no, our Toni is missing. Send out a search party. The entire cast, Janet out in front, runs toward the woods. Maybe an angel will lead Janet to this spot. *Oh, I was so worried.*

Maybe.

Or maybe no one has noticed. Maybe no one misses the goat, either. It wasn't finished anyway, was still a stiff wad of drying newspaper in the arts and crafts room. So Toni took a detour. She approached the staff house, tapped at a certain door, entered Janet's room. Janet's guitar lay on the bed, its neck resting on the pillow, as if it were taking a nap. The sight of the lovely blond-wood instrument brought a new ache into Toni's heart. She lay down and curled around it, drawing her knees up beneath its curved bottom. The strings uttered a soft murmur as she settled in. She pressed her cheek against the tuning keys and lay for a long time as the cool wood absorbed the warmth of her thighs and fused with her sweaty skin. Now and then she plucked a string.

The vibrations soothed her aching chest. When at last she shifted her body, she heard a clunk and a rolling sound beneath the cot. She put her eye to the gap between the bed and the wall and saw a wine bottle rolling back and forth among the dust bunnies.

"Ha!" she yells now, throwing her head back and looking straight up at the sun.

"Ah, ah," the lake responds.

She flings the empty bottle onto the pebbled shore where it shatters with a satisfying crash. Heaving a great sigh, she staggers on Franken-stein legs into the bush, both arms flailing. She plunges from woods into marsh.

Tall reeds surround her, blocking her way. Knife-sharp edges slice into her skin. Blood mingles with sweat on her arms and legs. Ooze sucks at her feet. Something furious buzzes in her ear, takes a juicy bite out of the side of her neck. Where in this stinking swamp is the high ground with the solid track? Vanished. Shit, shit, shit. She is drowning in reeds. Within the fog of confused thought, a hard, alert kernel of fear awakes. She's in trouble. *Help!*

And then she's on hands and knees, panting and laughing, howl-ing with laughter, because the marsh has given way to a grassy bank, beyond which she sees the familiar green boards and white window frames of the boathouse.

"Pick myself up. Start all over again," she chortles, shouldering a paddle plucked from a hook on the boathouse wall. She stomps along the dock where the canoes are moored. She has a date with a canoe. She will cross the lake, find the stream that snakes into the wilderness, follow the current like the voyageurs of old. "Radisson, oh Radisson," she sings as she struggles with the knot on the mooring line. But who's this calling her name? Why, it's Faye! Little elfin Faye has come up behind her on the dock and wrings her hands in the most comical manner.

"Hi there, Faye. Wanna come for a ride?"

She barely gets the words out. That floppy, furry tongue!

"Oh, Toni! You're all wet and muddy and bleeding. What happened? I was looking all over. Lorna sent me to find you."

"Where's Janet?" Toni sighs, sinking onto her backside.

"Janet? I guess she's in the dining hall with everyone else."

The dock sways crazily when Toni springs to her feet. Canoes clunk together as she lunges past Faye. Up the slope she marches, on ground that heaves like a sea. Onto the dining hall veranda, her soggy sneakers slapping the boards. She flings open the door. From the hush in the room she can tell they are about to recite a Sabbath eve blessing. There is the white-garbed Sabbath Queen, having just lit the flickering candles. And there's Janet. Lovely, flaming-haired, freckle-cheeked Janet. *Blessed are you, Lord of the universe ...*

A roar rises in Toni's throat. Heads turn, faces freeze. Nothing matters now but to tell the true story. There may never be another chance. She needs to explain that, despite all the weak-willed, shameful, under-the-blanket episodes (which she has renounced finally, for good and all, she swears it), her love is pure, decent, undying, worthy. Far worthier than anything any dumb guy like Hank or Alain has to offer. She's not the Lizzie type, nothing like that. Furthermore, the twins are cockroaches. A torrent of words pours from her mouth.

Janet looks like the woman in the horror movie who has just seen Godzilla loom into view and whose fascination is about to turn into terror. *No, no, Janet! Please understand!* Toni lunges. Arms restrain her. Someone pinions her to his side, shuffles her out the door. Someone's saying "Whoa! Whoa!" as if talking to a runaway horse. She's half-dragged, half-carried along the veranda, down the steps, her head bouncing like a rubber ball. "Stop," she manages to gasp. They come to a halt, and her bearers allow her to sink to her knees.

The world goes black.

Myron's office is stifling, cramped and crowded with shelves, a filing cabinet, and an oversized desk, behind which Myron sits in his swivel chair, regarding Toni gravely. Perched on the edge of a metal chair, she looks down at her scratched, welted legs. She wishes Myron wouldn't stare so intently, as if he wants to bore a hole in her skull and examine the contents. The oscillating fan on the window ledge stirs the papers on the desk and the tufts of hair on the sides of Myron's otherwise bald head, but the breeze doesn't reach Toni. Sweat trickles down behind her ears.

A dish of shelled peanuts sits amid the papers by Myron's elbow. He runs his tongue along his teeth and lifts the dish toward her, inviting her to partake. Her throat constricts at the odour of masticated nuts on his breath. She began her day with her head bowed over the infirmary toilet.

"Sorry. Forgot." Myron utters a sympathetic groan. "I know just what that's like. The self-inflicted wound."

She looks up quickly and sees how his brow knits and his mouth scrunches up, as if he can feel the pain at her temples. Then he smiles broadly. There's peanut goo in his teeth.

"I tied on a few when I was a freshman at McGill. In the morning, I'd wish I hadn't been born."

He chuckles softly at the memory of those raucous nights and wretched awakenings. It's hard to imagine Myron as anything but what he is now, plump and balding and slow-moving, like a walrus.

"Of course, I was much older than you. I was legal, at least." He cocks his head, still smiling but narrowing his eyes, as if taking aim. "Where in heaven's name did you get that stuff, whatever it was you drank, to get so drunk?"

Toni's shoulders stiffen, she ducks her chin and mutters.

"What?" He cups his hand around his ear. "Can't hear you."

She repeats, more audibly this time, "I don't remember."

Her eyes fix on her jiggling knees. She hears his doubting grunt and his fingers scrabbling in the dish, the crunch of peanuts. She remembers more than she cares to. It is true that whole swaths of yesterday have vanished, but certain moments leap out of the dark. A chaos of scenes. The marsh, the whipping reeds, a flapping duck, Janet's frozen horrified stare. Toni can smell rotted vegetation, wine, and vomit beneath the odour of peanuts.

"Did someone give you liquor?"

"I don't remember."

"What did you actually drink? Beer? Spirits? Wine?"

"I don't remember."

"Who else was with you?

"No one!" she says, glancing up in surprise. "I was by myself."

"And that you *do* remember?"

She ducks her head. She twists her hands together in her lap.

"Look at me, please, Toni. That's better. You're protecting someone. I wish you wouldn't. I'm not seeking to lay blame, I'm just trying to understand what happened."

As he studies her, Myron pinches his fleshy lower lip between his thumb and forefinger, tugs it outwards and lets it snap back like a piece of rubber. The silence in the room stretches out for what seems an eternity.

"Would you feel more comfortable talking to Shirley?" Myron asks in a gentler tone.

Toni shakes her head hard. Not Shirley, the infirmary nurse (and Myron's wife). Toni doesn't want to meet those frank appraising eyes, that annoyed expression, the one Shirley wears when a child comes in with mosquito bites scratched raw. *What have you done to yourself now?*

If only they'd just let her crawl back to her bed in the infirmary. She wants to bury herself again in the cool, clean, pressed linen.

"If Faye hadn't stopped you, you might have gone off in that canoe and drowned. Have you thought of that? Have you thought of how that would be for your parents?"

His tone is sharp now, has lost its chummy warmth. *But nothing happened*, she wants to say, though she almost wishes something had. Drowning seems preferable to twisting around on the hard metal chair waiting for the more awful questions that are sure to come: *What's this about being in love with Janet? What were you trying to do last night? Kiss her? That's what it looked like to everyone watching.*

"You were on the dock." Myron continues, relentless. "You were drunk as a skunk."

"I'm sorry," she wails, clutching her head. "It was stupid, stupid, stupid."

"Yes," he agrees and snorts. "I'm glad you realize that. We're getting somewhere if you do."

She stares at him again, at the nasty ironic smile on his lips, anger welling up. How could he not know how desperately idiotic and ashamed she feels?

"You say you were alone. You drank yourself into a stupor. Why?"

"Just for the hell of it."

"Well, well," Myron falls silent, fiddling with his moustache. "You are obviously a very troubled young person, Toni Goldblatt. Those first few weeks of camp you were having some difficulty adjusting, but that's not unusual, and then you seemed to settle in."

He flips open a file folder at the top of the stack in front of him, scans the page inside. "You got your Junior's swimming badge. You learned to paddle stern. You volunteered for the musical. You were liking camp better, weren't you?"

She nods.

"You developed a strong attachment to Janet Bloom. That's perfectly normal too. I believe she's been a good influence, all in all."

He says this with no particular emphasis. If he notices, he does not care to acknowledge the heat that flames Toni's face to the tips of her ears.

"I have to conclude these troubles of yours came with you to camp. There are some things we're not equipped to deal with at Camp Tikvah. Your parents will have to get to the bottom of ... the situation. I spoke to your mother this morning. She is coming to get you. Perhaps that's best. What do you think?"

Toni nods dully. Yes, it would be best. Facing her parents would not be half as bad as spending another minute at Camp Tikvah. Suddenly she longs for the sight of her father's car.

Myron leans his elbows on the desk, his cheek against his fist, and studies her with a strange expression as if unsure what to make of her. But the puzzled frown and the half-closed eyes also make him look sleepy, and she has the funny thought that he might nod off in this position. Then abruptly he jumps up and glides around to the front of the desk with surprising ease, considering he's so chubby and the space so narrow. She gets up too, less gracefully, rattling the metal chair. He puts his hand on her shoulder and pats it lightly.

"You're a decent girl, Toni, I'm sure of it. You need help, professional help, but you'll be fine." His voice swells with false heartiness. "Maybe one day you'll be back with us at Camp Tikvah. In the meantime I hope that all the good things you've learned and experienced here will serve you well."

The hand on her shoulder steers her toward the door. As she's about to exit, the hand grips and holds her back.

"I think I know where the booze came from. That guy in the kitchen. Alain Dubois. It's him, isn't it? Okay, you don't have to say a word. I can see it in your face. I never like when the kitchen staff fraternize with the campers."

One final squeeze to her shoulder and he pushes her out the door.

From beyond the screened windows of the Camp Tikvah office come the sounds of an ordinary day: yells from the baseball field, distant singing, an announcement on the P.A. about tonight's bonfire. Already none of this has anything to do with Toni. She slumps on the beaten-up vinyl couch and hopes her mother will arrive before any Tikvah-maniac can discover her here. *Hey, it's the sicko, the barfing drunkard, the …* No, she won't let herself think of the other names being whispered from ear to ear.

Farther inside the room, Bunny, Myron's niece, who is also camp secretary, pecks out a letter on a typewriter. Her ponytail quivers with the effort of concentration. Staccato bursts of tapping are interrupted by Bunny's curses as she stops to apply gobs of Wite-Out over her mistakes. She'd barely looked up when Toni entered the room with her duffel bag over her shoulder. Parked at the bottom of the steps outside is the suitcase into which Toni hurriedly stuffed all her belongings. What's taking her mother so long? Toni gets up to look out the window at the dirt road. She tries to will the family car, a black Ford Falcon, into view, but the dusty stretch of road remains empty. Then out of the corner of her eye she notices someone on the path. Her heart flips. It's Janet. Toni drops face-down on the couch, nose squashed against the vinyl, arms wrapped around her head like someone taking cover from an air raid. She knows it's an absurd position, but she remains so, barely breathing, as the door opens.

The typing stops. A long silence follows. Neither Janet nor Bunny says a word, but Toni imagines them exchanging looks and shrugs. Blood pounds in her ears as she waits and silently pleads—for Janet to leave, for Janet to stay. She feels the pressure of a thigh against her side as Janet lowers herself onto the couch. She hears the striking of a match, a long sighing exhalation. The smell of smoke in the room brings a wave of nausea to Toni's throat, but she wills it away. This small act of martyrdom pleases her.

"Hey, kiddo," Janet says softly. "Hear you're feeling pretty wrecked."

Toni doesn't answer. She presses her sweating forehead harder against the taut vinyl. The irregular tapping of the typewriter resumes.

"I know all about that. Been there." Janet chuckles. "Don't worry. It passes. You'll be yourself again soon. Drink lots of water and the crap will get out of your system." She sounds light-hearted and distant, like someone speaking to an invalid and obliged to be cheerful.

"No!" Toni hears herself groan into the cave between her elbows.

"No?"

"It won't pass."

"It won't?"

"I've got too much crap. I'm a stinking cesspool."

"You mean to tell me you'll have a hangover forever? After one little binge? Well, maybe not so little." Janet chuckles again. "But still ... "

"You know what I mean," Toni says fiercely as tears well up in her eyes.

Janet smokes in silence.

"You're not a ... a cesspool." Janet's laughter sounds awkward now. "You're just very young, you know. Sensitive and mixed up. Trust me. One day all this will be a funny story to tell your grandchildren."

A funny story. Does Janet really think so? Or is she just putting on the counsellor act? Toni longs to see Janet's face, but doesn't dare turn over. One look, one *wrong* look, out of those sea-green eyes would blast her to smithereens.

"Hey, come on now." Janet pats the top of Toni's head. A whimper escapes Toni's lips.

"Oh! Sorry. Tender, eh?" Janet pulls her hand away.

"You're not hurting me," Toni whispers, but Janet's hand does not return.

"I'd offer you the hair of the dog that bit you, but plain tap water is a better idea. Anyway," her voice sinks to a whisper, "I've got nothing left. You drank me dry."

"I'm sorry, so sorry," Toni wails, banging her forehead against the couch. "I'm sorry for everything. *Everything.*"

"Hey, don't put yourself down for showing some spirit. *Ruach! Ruach!*" Janet imitates a dining hall chant. A crazy hope catapults into Toni's thoughts. Perhaps Janet regards yesterday's scene as not so very horrible after all. Maybe they can still be friends. Toni rolls over to look up at Janet's droll grin. When her mouth relaxes, the cute chocolate freckle on her upper lip reappears, a tiny piece of Janet that Toni has come to regard as her own.

"I'm leaving today. Soon as my parents get here. I couldn't stay. Not after ... after all the things I said, in front of everyone."

"Oh, that." Janet waves her hand. "People babble all kinds of stuff when they're looped. Forget it. I have."

"Can we get together when you're back in the city? Could I come over to your place sometime?"

The smile fades from Janet's lips. She stares blankly at Toni for some moments and blinks.

"I'd hate not to see you ever again. Please."

"Hey! Of course you'll see me. I'll be playing concerts, you know. Might even come to your school some time."

"Could I help out with your concerts? Could I be a stage hand?"

Janet takes another drag and directs the smoke out of the corner her mouth in a long, nicely controlled stream. Her eyes fix upon the window above Toni's head.

"Concerts aren't like that. It's just me and a few friends with guitars. There's nothing to stage."

"I could carry your guitar. Or ... help with the lights?"

Toni can hear how desperate she sounds.

"Just come and listen. And bring your own friends."

Janet's tone is flat. What Toni fears most is happening right now. The gap between them has started to widen, and though Janet smiles her coaxing, joking smile, there's no connection. Instead, there's finality to the way she rises after a last friendly poke in Toni's ribs and says, "Be seeing you," and makes a point of singing out a hearty goodbye to Bunny too, as if the secretary is just as important to her as Toni. Then she's skipping down the outer stairs and all Toni can do is watch her go.

The bags loaded into the trunk of the car, Toni urges her mother to get going, but Lisa wants a private word with the director first. Lisa wears her shimmering green dress with the bolero jacket and a string of fake pearls that look real enough to fool Herr Rothschild himself. An outfit that means business. Toni slides down in the passenger side of the waiting car. Very soon the P.A. will announce the Tuck Shop is open and kids will appear—the twins even! *Hurry, hurry, hurry.* But Lisa takes her sweet time.

After an eternity, she finally stomps back down the stairs, plunks herself into the driver's seat, slams the car door, and starts the engine. They rattle along the pot-holed road, and Toni's temples throb with heat, misery, and the remnants of her hangover. She hopes her mother won't make good on the promise of a long talk during the drive home. She wants silence, oblivion, the landscape zipping by. Their progress down the dirt road is torturously slow.

"What a stupid little man," her mother says as she negotiates a turn too quickly and then steps on the brake, making Toni jerk forward. Everyone who annoys Lisa is "little."

"Covering up for his own incompetence. Puffing himself up like a toad. Immediately I saw through him. I looked straight into his eyes, and he could not look back at me."

Toni stares out the side window. The bushes along the road are coated with ash-grey powdery dust.

"I know his type. A petty official who tries to put the blame on others, but he could not fool me. I let him have it."

Now Toni can't help but relish the scene, as she imagines it: her mother's face growing darker and darker, her eyes filled with a terrible light, Myron realizing his mistake too late, cringing behind his desk, smiling stupidly with his peanut-goo teeth as a torrent of shrill, indignant words slaps down his feeble arguments, her mother like a magnificent tropical bird in her iridescent green suit, flashing pearls, and brilliant lipstick, showing up the mess in Myron's office. *You tell him, Mama!*

"Says we should send you to a psychiatrist. Never have I been so insulted."

What? Toni whips around, away from the imagined scene in the green blur beyond the window. She faces her mother, a sudden chill in her heart.

"Yes, a ... what do you call it? A head shrinker. For my daughter. Says you are troubled. My Toni! Does he think I don't know my own daughter? I thought this was a proper camp with proper management, I told him. Where was the supervision, I asked him. And where did that liquor come from? That he couldn't answer me. He's covering up for someone, himself for all I know. Maybe he keeps a bottle under his desk."

"No, he doesn't," Toni mumbles.

"No? So maybe one of his counsellors does. Maybe that Janet you so adore is the drunkard. Ha! I see I've hit on the truth. With one look, I see things. Not like that stupid director. A mother knows."

"Mama! Shut up, shut up!" Toni presses her hands over her ears.

"Okay, okay. Calm down, *Bubbele*. We'll talk properly later."

Toni slumps against the car door and closes her eyes tight. Lisa says nothing for a while. They pass a beaver swamp, a run-down cabin beside a small lake, a clearing with a weathered farm house, and some motionless cows.

"What an awful road," Lisa exclaims when a rock pops up against the undercarriage of the car.

"How long to the highway?" Toni asks.

"Soon, *Bubbele*, soon. I know you want to get home. I've made my yeast buns for you."

"I'm too hungover for yeast buns," Toni says.

"My poor chick. That girl was a bad influence. I could tell from your letters."

"You don't know anything!" Toni shrieks. She twists around, away from her mother, and leans as far as she can out the window.

"Get back in here," her mother says firmly. She rolls up the window part way when Toni slouches in her seat again. "Dirty air," she says, shaking her head over the clouds of dust they leave behind. Presently they come to a hardtop road between corn fields. The car glides along smoothly at last.

"I know one thing," Lisa says. "You think that girl is a goddess, and that's perfectly normal. Happens all the time with young persons your age. Nothing strange about it, no need to pay some head shrinker to tell us that. I just wish they'd supervised you better and didn't let you become so attached."

Rage surges in Toni's chest as she watches the rapid movement of her mother's lips, the indignant quivers of her head. Lisa finally pauses for breath, while coming to a halt at an intersection to the highway.

"I'm a lesbian, Mama."

Toni's sweaty fingers grip the under-side of the car seat. She holds on for dear life, like someone on a roller coaster about to take the downward plunge.

Her mother makes no move to turn onto the highway. For a few moments the car idles and there's nothing but the monotonous cheep of crickets in the fields and her mother staring at the windshield. Toni thinks she's going to be sick again. That wooziness in her stomach, and the air so still. If only the sullen sky would burst forth with thunder, lightning, rain. It just sits there, dark and bloated.

"Don't be crazy," Lisa finally says in a voice of quiet fury. "You are no such thing. Is that what he called you, that ugly little man?"

Lisa's foot presses on the accelerator so that the car jerks forward as she swings onto the highway.

"He didn't. But he knows. Everybody knows."

"Nobody knows you like your mama does. You came out of my body. You are a perfectly normal, good girl. Clean and decent, like you were raised. You don't even know what that word means, do you?" She glances sharply in Toni's direction.

Toni's face boils as she turns toward the window. They are moving swiftly now, bearing down on a lumbering half-ton truck.

"Of course I do."

Lisa utters a barking laugh. "*Mein Gott*, there are a million miles between admiring some older girl, as you did, and that other thing. You have not a cruel bone in your body. Such women are sadists. You understand? They are cruel, depraved. She-devils, not women." Lisa makes a spitting sound. "The Nazis selected them to be guards in the camps because they could be counted on to act like beasts. You have nothing whatever in common with those monsters. You will put such worries out of your head, do you hear?"

Her mother's eyes narrow, and she clutches the wheel fiercely, speeding up, then slowing down abruptly, as she changes her mind about overtaking the truck. She launches into another tirade about Camp Tikvah and Myron's chutzpah at refusing to give a refund for the two weeks Toni will miss. Then Lisa tells Toni about Julius's poor health, his ulcers, his lack of energy. They mustn't worry him with the details of this incident. He's been told that Toni has the flu.

Toni sits with downcast eyes, barely hearing a word. She envisions a flushed, hard-faced, leering woman in jackboots and a uniform, brandishing a whip over a row of naked prisoners. She-devil. A word she's never heard her mother use before. It is ugly, lurid, extreme, compelling in its accuracy, pointing to the depths of depravity and the vehemence of Lisa's feelings on the subject.

Toni's veins fill with ice.

chapter 11

All Toni wants is to drown in sleep, to fall into the depths of a black, suffocating void. Spread-eagled on her bed, she sinks into the torpor of a late-August heat wave. Across the city, lawns lie scorched, leaves droop, sparrows hide under hedges, their beaks open, gasping for air. Each day the radio announcer predicts a thunderstorm, but no rain comes. A faint smell of rot hangs everywhere. The whole world is dying. *Good.*

"Let's see a film," Lisa says. "The movie house will be air conditioned."

She fans herself with a folded section of newspaper as she stands in Toni's doorway.

"And then we could go to that new place downtown. The A&W. Hmm, *Bubbele*? What do you think? I heard it's very popular with the young people."

Toni hears the newspaper swish back and forth. She hears the coaxing in her mother's voice and something else not usually present, a hesitation, as if Lisa's unsure how to approach this deformed creature that used to be her daughter. The nausea, never far from Toni's throat these days, condenses. With her eyes shut tight, Toni shakes her head. Kids from school probably hang out at the new A&W. What can her mother be thinking?

"Well then, go to the Y. Go for a swim. You can't just lie there like an empty sack."

The newspaper slaps at the foot of the bed. A hand tugs Toni's arm.

After more exhortations, Lisa retreats, muttering curses against the foul, inhuman heat. She'll be back later. Not another word has been said about the topic that engaged them in the car on the drive home from Camp Tikvah. Not a word more will be said. A closed book. And did those things actually happen? Were they not like one of those lurid stories whispered from ear to ear in the bunk after lights out, growing wilder and more grotesque as each teller takes up the tale? Toni's fists, clenched during her mother's presence, relax, and she sinks back into lethargy. But her body just pretends. Even in slumber, a fluttering moth of anxiety knocks about inside her gut. When she wakes her jaw feels sore, as if she's had a rough session beneath a dentist's drill. She's been grinding her teeth.

After dark one evening, while her parents watch TV, Toni ventures out into the tepid air. Her feet take her to Decarie Boulevard, to the Snowdon branch of the Jewish Public Library, located in a commercial building upstairs from a deli. The library consists of a single, stuffy, book-crammed room and a wrinkled, doddering librarian, barely awake, her chin propped on the bridge of her folded hands. The librarian rouses herself at the arrival of this rare bird, a summer evening visitor and a young one at that, but Toni declines the offer of help. She slips away into a corner, carrying with her the most innocuous of books: the *Oxford English Dictionary*. She scans the entries and when she finds the one she's been searching for, huddles over the desk.

"Resident of the Isle of Lesbos … female homosexual … sexual attraction to a member of one's own sex … a perversion." And that's all. Nothing more beyond a few terse definitions. Still, she derives some satisfaction from seeing the word that has been rolling around in her mind for weeks—the word that sounds so much like a disease—in bold print. She stares until the letters stamp themselves on the backs of her eyelids.

Another day, while her parents are out, she rifles through her father's study and finds something useful at last: a thin volume of essays by Sigmund Freud. Her father has no particular interest in psychiatry, though, unlike Lisa, he regards it as a serious science. He's probably never read these essays. Freud was a Viennese Jew and a book hound; it was said the great man stopped to browse in the very shop where, decades later, Julius worked. This long-ago, fleeting, personal connection would be enough to make her father want some books of Freud on his shelves.

Seated cross-legged on the floor between the big oak desk and the filing cabinet, one ear cocked for her parents' returning footsteps, Toni skims the essays. The language is dense and convoluted, imposing and authoritative. Although she understands little, certain words jump out at her: *aberration, deviation, inversion, perversion, masochism, sadism, hermaphrodite.* There are terms that fascinate and repel. "Fetish," for example. What a deliciously hideous word, sounding like the German *fett*—fat, greasy. Freud rips away romance. He defines kissing as "contact with the mucous membranes of the mouth." With merciless precision, he details other contacts of organs and mucous membranes, grotesque combinations she could never have imagined. All humans are sick, it appears, but some are sicker than others. "I am an invert," she doodles on the pale skin of her thigh. She draws an upside-down stick figure with its head in a trash can. Then she furiously rubs at the marks with a spit-moistened hand.

There's one hopeful note in the sad litany. Freud says inversion can be cured by hypnosis.

On a listless afternoon, Toni sets out for the Jewish General Hospital on Côte-Sainte Catherine Road, about a mile from her house. Her mother thinks she's finally gone to the Y for a swim. She carries a plastic bag with her bathing suit, towel, hair brush, and a piece of her mother's strudel as she stands in the busy hospital lobby. A robotic voice calls for this or that doctor to come to this or that section of the hospital. Toni wanders down one hall after another. Finally, she finds the courage to tell a girl behind an information counter that she's mentally ill. Where is she supposed to go for that? The girl barely looks up from the form she's filling out to direct her to the emergency department. Toni's knees weaken. Emergency! She imagines men in white coats rushing at her to pin her arms in a strait-jacket and almost turns back. But she has come too far. Grimly, she trudges toward a set of double doors and ends up on a bench between a man with his arm in a sling and a weary mother with a feverish toddler.

She waits for two hours while almost everyone else in the crowded waiting room—those who were before her and those who came after—gets seen to first. At last a tousle-headed man carrying a cellophane-wrapped sandwich calls her name. She wonders if he's going to offer her the sandwich, but instead he ushers her into a little room and closes the door. The man carefully places his sandwich on the gurney and rests one of his haunches upon it, half sitting, half standing, quite close to Toni and looking down at her. He introduces himself as Dr Margoles and stretches out his hand. His handshake is damp. If it weren't for his unbuttoned white coat with the stethoscope in the pocket, she wouldn't have guessed he was a doctor.

"I'm an intern," he says softly, as if reading her thoughts. "Is that all right with you?" He's pasty-faced with watery, lashless eyes behind glasses, a hoarse voice, deeply sincere, striving to ooze reassurance.

She nods.

"Good." He draws out the word. He considers her for a long moment before adding: "What can I do for you?"

What indeed? The intensity of his stare, the soft unhurried manner of speaking, throws her off. One of his socks has rolled down, revealing a well-scratched mosquito bite on a bony ankle. She says nothing.

"You told the nurse you wanted to be cured of … of certain inclinations through hypnosis. Is that true?"

She can't bring herself to say a word. She wants to put her hands over her ears, shut her eyes, and crouch in a corner.

"Are you afraid of me?"

He leans forward. The watery blue eyes lock on hers. It occurs to her that he's starting the hypnosis treatment on the spot and that she ought to relax and let it work. She ought at least to try.

"No, I'm not," she answers.

"Are you afraid of men?"

The question is puzzling.

"No."

"Oh."

He seems a touch disappointed. Runs his hands through his straggly hair.

"Have you ever done anything with other girls? You know, experiments with touching, and so on?"

What can he be thinking? What does he take her for? "No!" she shouts, causing him to jerk backward and almost loose his balance as the gurney shifts. He re-crosses his legs and ponders her again with his spooky blue eyes.

"So it's just feelings you're worried about?"

Perplexed by the question, she remains silent. *Just* feelings?

"Do you notice boys at all? Do you notice them on the street, at school?"

She thinks of the guys in her class. How bunches of them burst into a room and start up a frenzy of drumming on the desks before the teacher arrives. They are certainly noticeable.

"Yes."

"You look at boys?"

"Sure."

"I see."

He clears his throat. Taps his chin.

"I think you should talk to your guidance counsellor when school starts. That's what he's there for. Kids your age have all kinds of feelings. Perfectly normal."

His tone has become crisp, matter-of-fact, the keen interest suddenly gone. She understands she is being dismissed.

"By the way, hypnosis is rarely used as a treatment anymore. Quite outdated," he asserts as he bends to scribble notes on a clipboard.

Toni slinks back through the emergency waiting room, past the rows of benches and the knots of people. All the jittery sense of daring that buoyed her up until this moment has left her. She feels stupid, like she's failed some kind of test, but also that she's been cheated out of a proper diagnosis. Perhaps she should have demanded to see a real psychiatrist. *Never deal with underlings,* her mother always says. But there's no way she could bring herself to ask for a second opinion.

A line from the Bible jumps into her mind—*Male and female He created them*—and she sees the perfectly formed, side-by-side couples of every species marching across a verdant new world. They march confidently through time, those proper beings, while the "it" she is watches frozen and alone from within the great void. The "it" belongs nowhere. Emptiness and chaos will follow it all the days of its life.

On the Labour Day Monday before school resumes, Toni hikes to Côte Saint-Luc Road. "Cote Saint-Puke" is what Janet used to call the suburb she grew up in. "Little boxes, little boxes, and they're all made out of ticky-tacky," she'd sing in a high, fast falsetto, cracking up the kids and counsellors gathered around her.

Toni loiters across the street from a classy, white-brick apartment building with an awning. Its name, "The Savoy," is written in gold on the heavy glass doors. She counts the storeys (fourteen) and the balconies (eighty-four) and keeps a hawk eye on who goes in and out. She's done this before, but always under cover of darkness, never in broad daylight. Doesn't matter any more. Doesn't matter if she's spotted during her crazy vigil. The game's up, or will be soon. For this very reason, Toni feels in her bones that this time, finally, she'll catch sight of Janet. All she wants is a glimpse of Janet's red hair disappearing through the glass doors and then to see blinds roll up in one of the windows. Oh, to be able to figure out which apartment is hers at last. But as with all the other times, the people who enter and exit the Savoy bear no resemblance to Janet. A light rain falls, steaming the streets, soaking through Toni's shirt. A few cars swish by. Hardly anyone's about. Perhaps everyone's still at their cottages in the Laurentians, drinking up the last drops of summer.

Tomorrow school starts again. Guys and girls in new fall jackets will throng the halls, eagerly sharing stories about their summer adventures. Whispers too. Whispers about something that happened at a camp. The story will have travelled from the A&W to the Orange Julep Drive-in to the halls of Northmount High School. Were Toni to pass by the huddled groups, a sudden silence would descend. Nothing said out loud, but everything known.

There's only one thing left to do. Death ends agony in one magnificent blast. Death cancels out sin, wipes the slate clean. In death you are pure. Powerful too, because death is mightier than the sum total of all your creepy thoughts and acts over a lifetime. Death takes everyone's breath away. Death says: *You see? She gave her all. Her suffering wasn't ordinary.* The dead are loved forever. They are the flame in the glass.

She trudges back to Snowdon, getting wetter and more bedraggled with every step. At Queen Mary Road and Westbury she pauses and casts her eyes uphill toward Saint Joseph's Oratory, the Shrine. As a kid, she used to love to sneak in with her buddies, to prowl around the vast, dimly lit chambers with their rows of flickering candles, the yellowing crutches of supplicants cured, and the urn in which Brother André's heart was preserved in formaldehyde. Her parents used to scoff at these attractions, calling them *goyische naches*, gentile diversions, but the mystery and the promise of miracles called to her. The black cross on top of the basilica seemed like a man with his arms outstretched in flight. She starts up the hill toward the Shrine and the veterans' hospital opposite, while the cars and rumbling buses hurtle by. She imagines ambulance sirens, priests, and nuns rushing forward, wounded soldiers watching the commotion below from their hospital windows. She imagines newspaper headlines. She smiles as she walks, calm and easy. Halfway up she teeters on the edge of the curb and waits with her eyes closed. Soon the Number 65 will come and, gathering momentum, will plunge down the long slope of Queen Mary Road. All she has to do is fall forward slightly, let go, let go. Beautiful oblivion at last. She sucks in her breath.

An engine roars, wind slaps her face, and thick exhaust enters her nostrils as she opens her eyes. The bus rolls down the hill and away. Her feet have remained plastered to the sidewalk. They are obstinate, these size-nine feet. They will not budge. They don't belong to her at all, none of her body does. She resents this rebellion of the flesh, yet can't help but feel amazed at the blind will that has revealed itself. At the pivotal moment, an overwhelming force shouted through every cell, drowning out the feeble instructions of her mind. So how do people kill themselves? How do they do it? She now sees that her own attempts will be hopeless. She is here, unremittingly here in this world. No point in waiting for another bus.

As she trudges toward home, she finds herself walking into Kalman's Five and Dime. The bell above the door announces her entry with a loud, jarring ring.

"Yes?" Kalman barks. He has dark bags under his eyes and nervous hands that unwrap a bundle of Yiddish newspapers on the cluttered counter. His mouth falls in sour lines as he sees her standing in a daze of indecision. Should she buy chocolate bars? Should she gorge herself? Her glance falls upon the display of school supplies on the shelves along the wall, and she wanders over. If she's got to show up at school tomorrow, she may as well have the gear. She spends every cent of two months' accumulated allowance on a set of Hilroy exercise books in five pastel colours, along with pencils, pens, erasers, and a geometry set. Kalman's voice purrs with new respect as he totals up these items and mentions each by name. Suddenly, his stubby, newsprint-grimed fingers bouncing over the cash register keys strike her as beautiful. A wave of gratitude washes over her and she wants to weep. She has a flash of insight. It occurs to her she could become a proper egghead. Not just ordinary, get-along-without-effort smart as she's been all along, but brilliant. So brilliant she becomes untouchable and is catapulted onto another plane.

chapter 12

Toni knows the paramecium. She has studied this charming pond creature inside out. There it lies before her in the grainy textbook photo: a single transparent cell, shaped like the sole of a shoe, marvellously intricate and ingenious. A universe unto itself. She covers the page with her hand and whispers the names of the paramecium's components; oral groove, cilia, food vacuoles, macronucleus, micronucleus. In the diagram beside the photo, the slipper-like body is outlined in bold purple, with paler shading for the internal parts, everything clearly labelled. In real life, the creature is minuscule and the colour of water. Even under the microscope, only its jerky, spinning movement gives it away. During biology class she took her turn peering down into the clever apparatus of revealing mirrors and saw slipping by, just beyond her magnified quivering lashes, the blobs of life held together by the thinnest skins imaginable, propelled by rafts of minute hairs.

"Ew. They're wiggling!" girlish voices squealed. "They're germs."

"No, sperm!" said one of the boys. "See the tails?"

"Chuck contaminated the slide. Stuck his hands in his pants, didn't you Chucky?"

"Eek! Disgusting!"

Toni Goldblatt, the Grade A student, the one who has re-made herself from the inside out, bent her face to the microscope's eyepiece and took notes. She allowed herself just the ghost of a smile at her classmates' shenanigans. There were no tails, of course, and the girls knew that, but pretended otherwise. To them the little organisms were just dots of nothing. They couldn't appreciate the wonder. Only someone like Mr Price could. Mr Price, the biology teacher, a fellow traveller in the realm of scientific pursuit.

Now, the evening before her mid-term, Toni reviews her biology text and lab notes, elbows on her desk in the bedroom that she has transformed as much as possible into a monk-like cell. Gone are the flouncy white bedspread of her mother's choosing and the matching curtains with all that superfluous trim. Instead, the naked pane of glass looks out at the March-bare tree in front of the house and hard-packed snow. Only the plain, white roller blind hangs at the top of the window, ready to be pulled down and blot out the world. A brown wool blanket stretches tightly over the bed, tucked neatly into hospital corners. Her books are arranged in alphabetical order. Pens, pencils, rulers stand erect in their black plastic holder, and stray papers are stowed in three-punch binders. Once upon a time, a few months ago, she was loose and lazy, her room cluttered, her mind a swamp. But the old Toni no longer exists. Peeled off like dead skin.

Sucking in a deep breath, Toni opens her loose-leaf binder to a blank page and quickly sketches the paramecium with its components and labels, exactly as in the diagram she's memorized. Mr Price would be pleased. His eyebrows would lift slightly, and his lips shape the words: "Clever girl."

Mr Price has a narrow, sharp, aristocratic face, wears horn-rimmed glasses, tweed jackets with leather patches at the elbows, and an expression of cool, scientific detachment. He can settle down the class with just one long, withering glance.

"The world doesn't care whether you pass or fail," he says, delivering his warnings in an almost cheerful tone. "No one gives a hoot. That's what you'll find out the day you leave school. Sink or swim, it's entirely up to you."

He perches on the end of the teacher's desk, lacing his long fingers around one knee, calm and aloof, yet Toni likes to think he gives a hoot about her. In the remote gaze behind his glasses she's glimpsed flashes of admiration for his star pupil. She's convinced they share an unspoken bond, a cool bright passion for knowledge. They are united in disdain for everything else—for the shallow, frenetic world of mini-skirts, electric guitars, the swinging British sound, Expo 67 fever, unisex hairstyles, the restless, unruly hordes at Northmount High. Others can get themselves into a lather about the latest Beatles album, *Revolver*. What has that to do with anything real, with study, facts, grades?

But Toni keeps such scorn to herself. To her classmates, she's quiet, studious, amiable Toni who doesn't mind if someone looks over her shoulder to copy a homework assignment. She used to get crushes on girls, but that was lifetimes ago. She's almost a member of a different species now. Almost like *My Favorite Martian,* the funny little guy from outer space in the TV series, who can do amazing tricks such as read a whole encyclopedia in seconds, but is baffled by the oddities of human emotion. Rude jokes, sexual innuendo, classroom flirtations flow right past her. Extraneous chatter. That's part of being clever.

Now, TV voices murmur through the wall. Her parents watch the late evening news in the living room. Earlier, her father stood in her doorway and asked if the volume was up too high. "Of course not," she told him, while rattling off definitions in her head. She saw him glance about her orderly room, reassured and pleased with her industry. Lately, a new understanding has grown between them, the understanding of two people who like to delve down into the quiet of their minds. They can sit together and read, producing no sound beyond the rustle of pages, the clink of a coffee cup. Occasionally, they still go for long Sunday walks while Lisa prepares dinner. He listens respectfully as she tells him about biological processes, osmosis, for example. He nods and rubs his goatee thoughtfully with a leather-gloved hand. He stoops a bit more than he used to, so that they are the same height as they walk along, shoulder to shoulder. Thrilled with her report cards, foreseeing scholarships, he doesn't probe or nag, as does her mother. He doesn't expect her to aim for more than a lifetime of honourable, dispassionate industry.

Fact by fact, she gathers up kernels of information like a harvest mouse building up a winter's storage. The paramecium has reproductive choices: divide itself in two or exchange nuclear material with one of its fellows. Very efficient. Very clever. There's nothing mysterious about becoming top of the class. It's called hard work. She plans to score a perfect 100 in mid-term biology, high nineties in everything else, and next year when the real test, matriculation exams, comes around, she'll be ready. By July next year, she'll have her photo published in the *Montreal Star* among the province's most outstanding students. There she'll be, one of the few females amid all those male faces, and printed beside her photo, a breathtaking grade-point average. Her parents will burst with pride. Everyone in the city will see the picture. Perhaps there'll be a phone call. *Hey, kiddo, remember me? I've never forgotten you. Wow, first in the province. Way to go.*

But she's been dreaming while precious study minutes have escaped. She compares her sketched diagram to the one in the text and finds she forgot to include the contractile vacuole, the sack-like pump that controls osmotic pressure. Without its little pump the paramecium would fill with water and explode like a balloon. Not good. She must redouble her efforts, review everything from beginning to end. In last month's test she made a stupid mistake that came from missing the obvious and robbed herself of a perfect score. Mustn't happen again. Focus, focus. In a recurring dream, she has seen herself with a blank exam booklet, her hand paralyzed, while her mind teems with memorized facts, tiny spinning organisms with lashing tails that jerk frantically and collide against the impermeable barrier of her skull. Meanwhile the wall clock booms out the seconds.

Focus, focus. The night has many more usable hours.

When her eyes grow bleary and words swim on the page, she resolves to refresh herself with the 5BX program. She found the Royal Canadian Air Force pamphlet at the bottom of a carton of books her father brought home from a thrift store. She was immediately drawn to the promise of fitness and discipline through five basic exercises to be done in the privacy of one's room, a mere eleven minutes a day. Toe touching, back swimming, sit-ups, push-ups, running, and jumping on the spot. There are charts and diagrams and tips. *Defeat the first desire to skip; then defeat all such desires as they occur.* A bull's eye adorns the top of each page. Toni intends to reach the lofty heights of Chart Six, when she'll be able to do a Russian-style kick squat and a flying push-up. The pamphlet suggests that after Chart Three, women should refer to the gentler XBX program, but Toni has no intention of doing so. The floor shakes as she crashes through her stride jumps. The door of her bedroom flies open.

"Are you crazy? It's almost midnight."

Her mother stands on the threshold and glares out of her mask of cleansing paste: two dark, piercing eyes surrounded by a meringue-like crust.

"I'm almost finished," Toni gasps as she flings her arms outwards.

"The Cheung family downstairs will call the police."

The Cheungs will do nothing of the sort. They are meek immigrants from Taiwan who never complain, but Toni tries to jump more quietly, nonetheless, on the tips of her toes, which will give her muscles more of a work-out anyway.

"*Mein Gott*, you go to extremes. It's not healthy."

Lisa's mouth stretches in a grimace. A flake of dried paste falls from the ghostly mask. Toni turns so she's facing the window, her back to her mother. Her feet thump down, her hands slap above her head, and she counts out the repetitions until she's done. Annoyed to find her mother still in the room, she falls to her knees to begin an extra round of push-ups.

"Do you want to look like an army sergeant?"

"It's my body."

"In my day, girls did gymnastics to become supple and graceful."

"Your day!" Toni snorts. Her biceps burn, her shoulders ache. *Don't force your body until it hurts,* the pamphlet warns on the very first page. But she wants it to hurt.

As she waits at the bus stop on Victoria Avenue, Toni goes over everything again in her head: the categories of protozoa, their methods of ingestion, excretion, movement, reproduction. She can visualize diagrams and text and even the exact page on which the text appears. She's almost like that Martian guy. Although she hardly slept, she's alert, mind buzzing, brain like a giant searchlight. As she mentally ticks off facts in her review lists, she observes the bedraggled line of passengers queued up along the soggy snow-banked street. They clutch their collars and hunch their shoulders against the wind. A man with hairy nostrils mutters that the bus is late. A big lady with patently false teeth hopes March will go out like a lamb. Three guys from her school try to shove one another into the soupy slush in the gutter.

When she turns away from this pathetic clutch of humanity to gaze across the street, a warm splash of colour catches her eye. Her body jolts awake. There! Over there, at the bus stop on the other side! A girl in a belted brown coat stands with windblown hair catching the sunlight. That flaming shade of auburn, that languid stance with hands in pockets and hip thrust out. It could be no other. After all this time!

Toni abandons her place at the front of the line and tears across the street, dodging a car that slides sideways as its driver slams on the brakes. The angry blast of a horn follows her as she sprints diagonally, uphill, bypassing the girl, her intent being not to approach head-on but to walk down past her, casually. She's not sure what she'll say when the girl turns her head. Perhaps nothing. She just wants to see, to be sure. With each step Toni's blood pounds harder.

Nyah, nyah! Not Janet Bloom. Not even close. The face that comes into view is broad and plain, with dull brown eyes instead of green ones. Toni's chest deflates, the disappointment is devastating, though it's been months since she chased such phantoms. She has not allowed herself to actively seek out Janet, but every so often she catches a fleeting glimpse, always illusory. The crazy thing is, months ago she could no longer clearly envision Janet's face. The image had gone blurry, which depressed her more than anything. The mad, weak, sicko part of herself longs to repossess the memory. Her drill-sergeant self does everything in its power to stamp that memory out.

When she gets to school, she finds an empty bathroom, slips into a stall, and retches as quietly as she can into the toilet. All that good food, her mother would lament. All that nourishing bread, cheese, cocoa, fruit, jam. But Toni is glad to see her breakfast go. It's been churning around in her fluttery stomach for the past half hour.

Although light-headed, sweaty-palmed, and bitter-mouthed, she breezes through the test. There's not a single surprise in the list of questions. The trick ones almost make her laugh, they're so obvious. She finishes early so has time to check and re-check her answers. Nevertheless, after handing in her paper, she walks away convinced there was one, small, slippery-tailed detail that eluded her. Maybe worth just a half a percentage point—but still!

chapter 13

Toni's father sits on the edge of his chair, angled away from the dinner table. He peers down at the evening *Star* clutched in his hands, his brow knit, his lips twitching as if the words he reads were live creatures jumping around in his mouth. Every so often one of them escapes.

"Nasser," he mutters. "Egypt ... Israel ... troops."

The potato soup at his elbow is growing cold.

"*Verdammt noch mal!*" Lisa fumes.

She doesn't approve of newspapers at dinner. At breakfast, in the kitchen, all right, she'll make concessions, but at dinner she likes a touch of civility, eating in the dining room, using a nice tablecloth and the shiny "good" cutlery. Tonight, too, in honour of spring, a centrepiece of red tulips adorns the table. They were wild ones that escaped the flower beds at Saint Joseph's and popped up in the strip of grass between the sidewalk and the wrought-iron fence. The drooping heads now hang over the lip of the vase, loose petals stirring in the breeze from the open window.

"If Papa's allowed to read at dinner, so am I," Toni declares. "My end-of-year exams are two weeks away. Two weeks!"

How could this have happened? She's been preparing for her grade ten finals for months.

"I forbid either of you to read at the table." Lisa points her spoon toward Julius's bowl. "I'm not reheating that."

Julius's eyes remain fixed on the paper. "'Nasser's forces gathered along Israel's border are combat ready,'" he reads aloud. "'The

Secretary General of the UN calls the situation potentially grave.' Potentially grave! Potentially! Hah!"

"What nonsense! Nasser's bluffing." Lisa raps her spoon against the table. "If you let every foul story in the newspaper spoil your appetite, you'll never eat. *Nu, schon!*"

Toni noisily scrapes back her chair and stomps to her room to retrieve her Latin text. Latin is her worst subject, the one that could pull down her grade-point average. Her only defence will be to memorize whole swaths of the material that could appear as a sight translation. Back at her place at the table, she whispers bits of the *Aeneid* while her parents continue to argue about the newspaper article.

"Nasser is a clown," Lisa declares. "The Israelis will give him a good *klatsch* like they did to the Syrians a few weeks ago, and he'll run away with his tail between his legs."

"Egypt isn't Syria. Egypt has a serious army. Heavy guns. And what about the Soviets? They'll mix in. They're stirring up the pot. No, no, no, you can't wish this away with one of your little *klatsches*."

Julius clutches his forehead and groans, as if Middle Eastern bullets have already begun to fly and his quivering nerves can feel the reverberations across the miles.

"You!" Lisa says, noticing Toni's open book on the table. "Put that away. For God's sake, you've become a fanatic. You can spend a few minutes eating dinner like a *mensch*."

"*Arma virumque cano*," Toni intones aloud, glaring back into her mother's eyes.

"Arms and the man, I sing, who, forc'd by fate / And haughty Juno's unrelenting hate ... "

The *Montreal Star* returns to the table at the next night's dinner, and the next, the headlines screaming louder every day. By the third week of May, the Middle East crisis has jumped from the bottom corner of the front page to top centre, pushing down other news, even the happy stories about the millions of visitors flocking to the newly opened Expo 67. Egyptian troops continue to mobilize. The UN has meekly withdrawn its peacekeeping forces at Nasser's bidding. Israel's Red Sea port is under blockade. War looms. There's no longer any semblance of normality in the Goldblatt family dining room. Editorials float over the bread basket and the scattered tulip petals. Newsprint mingles with chicken grease. Lisa and Julius bend their heads to study the dense columns of reportage and analysis while their hands mechanically raise and lower their forks. They both agree on the gravity of the situation. The debate now is over what must be done. Lisa is for action: swift, immediate, devastating. Pounce now while the Arabs are still spouting rhetoric and rattling their sabres, while there's a chance to catch them off guard. And if so much as one mortar shell falls on Tel Aviv, let the bombs rain on Cairo. Let the wrath of Israel's air force pour down on the mobs that boil through the streets and chant for the Jews to be thrown into the sea.

"Just what we need," Julius scoffs. "Some trigger-happy hothead like you to set the powder keg alight."

Toni tries to shut her parents out and sink into Virgil, but the edge in their voices slices through her concentration. She lifts her eyes from the march of Latin words in her textbook to their flushed faces. Her mother's head thrusts forward between hunched shoulders, her father's bald pate gleams with sweat. Something about their anxiety—more than run-of-the-mill worries—arrests her attention.

The problem with precipitous action, Julius explains with rising irritation, is the chain reaction sure to follow. If Israel attacks, the Arabs will close in on all sides. Nasser will shut down the Suez Canal and the Western powers will move to protect their oil supplies. The Soviets will jump in. World War III begins. Is that what she wants, Mrs Bomb-Them-to-Smithereens? Mrs Let's-Have-Another War? Does she want nuclear disaster and the Jews in the middle, again, and blamed?

"Who's the extremist?" Lisa shouts, jumping up from her chair. "*You* are. You, with your crazy, exaggerated scenarios. You're a defeatist." Her finger jabs. "World War III just because we defend ourselves!"

"Nasser has set a trap. Don't you see? He wants Israel to start a war."

"And you want to capitulate. Like Chamberlain did with Hitler."

"I didn't say do nothing. We must use brains instead of bullets. Find a diplomatic manoeuvre."

He taps the newspaper, open to the editorial page. The *Star* backs him up with its call for a cooling-off period.

"Diplomacy! Chamberlain was a diplomat. Was world war prevented? The gas chambers?"

Her parents continue to hammer away at each other as Toni slips off to do the dishes. War, she marvels. Real war. Not the history-book version where you know how things will turn out and the terrible events are over and done with. No, the coiled horror that has always lurked in the background of her life. And now Israel is in danger. The land of the Jews could be wiped out while the whole world watches on TV and reads the blow-by-blow in the *Star*. While she and her parents watch helplessly, pogroms of unprecedented fury could occur. Neither of her parents has said so, but she can feel what they fear in her bones. She stands with the dishrag in one hand, the soapy dinner plate in the other and wonders: Is it possible this ordinary moment of time is the ledge above the pit? *Can't be.* But why not? Blunt reality thunders down on you. The worst *can* happen. What else has she been hearing all her life? She shivers with a strange, cold excitement.

On Monday evening, Toni's parents prepare to depart for a giant rally on behalf of Israel at the Sheraton Mount-Royal downtown. She's surprised that her father has agreed to accompany Lisa. Normally, crowds appall him. Slogans and banner waving are not his style. But he grits his teeth and presses his fedora firmly onto his head. "It is necessary," he sighs grimly. "We must show solidarity."

Toni wasn't intending to go. She was looking forward to the precious silence that would envelope the empty apartment, peaceful hours of uninterrupted study. But at the last minute she jumped up from her desk, ran after her parents, pulled by an irresistible force. She has never been to a political rally. The Jewish community has never held one, as far as she knows. This is a once-in-a-lifetime opportunity.

As the buildings of downtown loom large, she becomes aware of hundreds of cars heading in the same direction. Soon she and her parents are hanging onto one another, following the streams of humanity that overflow the sidewalks of Peel Street and converge on the hotel. The lobby is packed, the elevators leading to the ninth-floor ballroom are mobbed. Julius starts to have misgivings, but Lisa leads the scramble up the stairs, and Toni pulls her father with her. No way she's going to miss out now. They manage to find a spot at the back of the ballroom, crammed full with people young and old, where, beyond the mass of heads and hats, a voice addresses them over a crackling sound system. The man speaks in impassioned, dire tones.

"Nasser is another Hitler. Jews everywhere must stand together. Israel must prevail or face extinction."

"What did I tell you? Didn't I say so? Didn't I?" Lisa, pressed against Toni's side, trembles while her hand clutches Toni's forearm, the nails digging in.

"It's roasting in here," Julius says, loosening his tie. "I hope there's a doctor or three in the house."

More speakers follow, representing this chapter and that committee of various Zionist organizations. One man wins Julius's nod of approval when he thanks Prime Minister Pearson for trying to bring about a session of the Security Council. Another man appeals for donations. Someone else calls upon youth to go to Israel in its hour of need. Unprecedented numbers have turned out for the rally, the crowd in the ballroom is told. There are thousands in the hotel, thousands more milling about in the street below. Toni turns her head this way and that, scanning faces in trepidation because, if the whole community has turned out, then *she* might be here too, somewhere in the crowd. And then, as if her two eyes were a fishing line, a hand waves. The hand belongs to a boy, shouldering his way toward her through the press of bodies. Before her stands Samuel from Camp Tikvah, the religious guy who used to join the select group in Janet's room and listen to folk music records. He still wears a black skullcap pinned to his lank hair, but his body has bulked up and his face has lengthened. Toni's instinct is to bolt. Besides Janet, there's no one from Camp Tikvah she ever wants to see again. And she's not even sure about Janet. But Samuel is upon her before she can move away.

"Hey, isn't this fantastic?" Samuel enthuses, as if they had just parted company a few moments ago. "Were you at the youth rally this morning at the Y? I saw tons of *hevre* from camp. We talked about getting a gang together to fly to Israel and help out on a kibbutz. If we can convince our parents, that is."

Samuel lowers his voice and winks in Toni's mother's direction and Toni sees Lisa is watching them with keen interest. At camp, Samuel was almost as awkward and shy as Toni was, but now, fired up, bouncing on the balls of his feet, his words tripping over themselves, he seems a different person. His eyes, after fixing on Toni's for a moment, dart back and forth over the crowd, searching out other familiar faces. She has the impression he remembers her only vaguely, as a fellow Tikvah-maniac, and that's good enough for him.

"Did you see Janet?" Toni brings herself to ask.

"I heard she's in Europe. Or somewhere." He shrugs. The news causes Toni's heart to plummet. *But why be so disappointed? Isn't it just as well?*

"Hank was at the rally this morning," Samuel adds. "Remember our waterfront director, Hank? I bet he's planning to go to Israel. Please God, I'll get there too."

An elbow digs into Toni's side.

"Aren't you going to introduce me?" Her mother wears a syrupy smile.

Reluctantly, Toni obliges. As if he can hear Toni's unspoken wish, Samuel says goodbye and pushes on.

"So who was that?" Lisa asks behind her hand.

"I just told you, Mama."

Don't get any dumb ideas.

After the speaker on the stage asks everyone to rise for *Hatikvah*, Toni hears the thunder of feet and scraping chairs and then the rumble of voices, faltering at first, gaining strength, swelling into a tide, brave and defiant. They all sing the Hebrew anthem about the hope of 2,000 years, and it seems to Toni the crystal chandelier above their heads shivers, sending rainbows of light across the ceiling. Or is it the effect of her tear-blurred eyes? The togetherness in the room is like the feeling on Friday evening in the dining hall at camp, but a hundred times bigger. One community. One people. Throw the Jews into the sea? Hah! They are themselves the sea. A force of nature. Unstoppable.

After the anthem comes the slow, suffocating shuffle of thousands out of the ballroom, through corridors, down the stairs. And though feet trip and elbows jab, there's barely any of the usual griping. Instead, they make a sober, dignified exit onto Peel Street, which is flooded with people. All move together up the hill toward Sherbrooke Street, banners and placards held aloft. "Israel, we are with you!" the signs say, "No to aggression" and "Free the Gulf."

And then, like a heap of ants scattering away from a nest, the crowd disperses, the great noise it has made swallowed up by the hum of traffic.

"Thank God that's behind us," Julius says, mopping his head with his handkerchief and resettling his hat. "One couldn't move. Not forward, not backward."

"The community showed its face. Finally!" Lisa exults.

Her father digs his fingers into the back of his head where the migraine has lodged. "It was necessary," he sighs.

For once, Toni feels more aligned with her mother. Community! The people! In that fine moment in the ballroom, she was transformed from a single-celled creature eking out its paltry life into part of a composite body, a multitude led by a pillar of fire.

"Will there really be a war?" Toni asks her father the next day. He's come late to the breakfast table, his face pale and clammy with migraine. His tie, loosely knotted around his Adam's apple, lurches up and down as he sips the chamomile tea.

"Very likely," he answers glumly. "Nasser won't back down. Israel can't accept a blockade."

The day's headlines read: "Soviet Naval Units Head for Mid East" and "Jordanian-Egyptian Defence Alliance Signed."

"Will Israel win?"

"Israel has no choice but to win."

But it is not exactly conviction she hears in his voice. More like grim resignation.

"Will the Americans help?"

He gazes back at her with infinite pity.

"The Americans don't have to help," Lisa says cheerfully over her shoulder as she butters toast at the kitchen counter. "Israel can beat the enemy all by itself."

Toni scours newspapers, both current and past issues that have piled up in the magazine rack. Some words are reassuring: Israel's steely resolve, the morale of its citizens, reservists hunkered down in sun-baked valleys, boy scouts delivering mail. Other passages sound less hopeful: Nasser promises a fight to the finish, the Palestinian Liberation Organization vows to leave few survivors, Iraqi and Kuwaiti troops are on the move, tourists and foreign embassy staff have fled, Israeli diplomats are floundering. What does it mean, what does it mean for us? That's the question she can't bring herself to ask her parents. At night, with her ear to the crack of her bedroom door, she catches snatches of their overseas phone calls to the relatives in Italy, to acquaintances in Haifa. Amid their shouts and arguments there have also been agitated whispers. She has the vague sense of preparations being made, contingency plans. What kind of preparations? She can't imagine. Her heart races painfully.

On June 1, 1967 the headline reads: "Arab Allies Mass as US Urges Talks."

All three of them pounce on the copy of the *Gazette* Julius bought at Kalman's corner store in the still of the morning, slipping out while Toni was still in bed. Her father looks drawn and hasn't slept. His hands shake as he flips pages. Toni leans over his shoulder to read. The UN creeps at its petty pace with a resolution introduced, a debate scheduled, a veto threatened, as tanks roll up to borders and guns take aim. Toni has to agree with her mother who splutters, "What a useless clutch of windbags," while her father bites his lips.

Lisa has ceased talking of a tactical first strike, since the moment for a surprise attack seems long past. But she still insists Israel will win.

"How can you be so sure?" Toni asks.

Her mother takes an unhurried sip of coffee before answering, her lips curled in a smug smile.

"I laid the cards."

Her father makes a sound as if a bone is caught in his throat. "The cards!"

Tomorrow is Toni's Latin exam. All her striving and sweating for a brilliant mark seem so childish now. War will come, the kind of war that shaped her parents' generation and perhaps will test hers, at least those of her generation brave enough to rise to the challenge.

"What's the point of exams when there's going to be a war?" she wonders aloud.

Her father's hand slaps down hard on the table.

"The point of exams! The point!"

His normally quiet eyes are wild. "You mean to tell me war should be an excuse to slack off? Precisely when war comes you must get your credentials. Precisely now—you mustn't waste an opportunity. What you hold in your head is all you can rely on in this world. Haven't I told you that often enough? *Nu?* Haven't I?"

Yes, he has, in jokes and maxims and words of praise for her diligence and occasional grumbled warnings. Never like this, with such desperate fury. Toni sits frozen, stunned.

"Let's all calm down," Lisa says as she rises and lays soothing hands on Julius's shoulders. "No need to get so excited. Of course Toni will do her exams."

Her mother shoots Toni a warning look that says, *Your father has come apart, we must put him back together.*

The next day Toni writes her Latin exam in a strange mood of detachment. When she closes her exam booklet, she has no idea whether she breezed through or mucked up and hardly cares. She rushes home for dinner and the evening *Star.* It is Friday night. Her mother has gone to some pains to create a festive atmosphere with candles, challah, the best dishes, as they used to do when Toni was a child and before their lives got so hectic with work and school. Nevertheless, after the meal, they all rush to watch the CBC news and sigh because so little is said about what's really going on. The coverage is mostly on the infernal, lumbering debate in the UN, which can't even bring itself to call for a cessation of hostilities.

On Saturday, they sift through every word of the weekend papers. On Sunday, there's neither a *Gazette* nor a *Star*, and they all prowl the apartment grouchily, on edge. On Monday, the war breaks out.

It's a strange relief to have war finally underway, though the early reports are far from reassuring. Fierce battles rage on three fronts. Each side claims victories. Air raid sirens sound in Cairo, Tel Aviv, Jerusalem, and other cities. Each side blames the other for starting the war. Israel says it's fighting for its survival. The US makes a surprise announcement of neutrality.

"The Americans won't help?" Toni asks, incredulous. "Even if Israel is really in trouble?"

Her father can only offer that look of infinite pity.

On day two of the war, Toni comes home from writing her biology exam to find everything has changed. Israel claims stunning early victories, the annihilation of Egypt's air force, a breakthrough in the Sinai. The claims seem backed up by the front-page photo of Egyptian prisoners under Israeli guard. But most telling is the Soviet Union's belated and urgent call for a cease-fire.

"Hah," cackles Lisa, eyes flashing gleefully. "Now you want a cease-fire! Now that we are winning."

She points her finger at the newspapers spread out on the couch as if the Soviet representative at the UN, the treacherous Fedorenko himself, were sitting there hanging his shameful head. Though Julius is not so certain that the tide has turned completely, he's visibly relieved. Toni performs 5BX jumping jacks up and down the hall.

No one sleeps that night. They drift about like restless ghosts, and every hour on the hour, they reconnoitre, bleary-eyed, in the kitchen for the radio news. Julius twiddles the dial in between announcements, now and then locating a station that broadcasts a bulletin. Each tidbit of information lifts them higher. Finally, even Julius can't deny that victory is at hand. Even he agrees the UN can go to hell. Let Israel smash its enemies. Once and for all.

Toward dawn, Lisa brings out crystal glasses and a bottle of Sabra orange liqueur that she bought in a burst of patriotism last week and has been hoarding for this occasion. They clink glasses, shout *l'chayim*, let the warm glow rise from their bellies to their heads. Humming *Hava Nagila*, Lisa pulls Julius and Toni to their feet and they link arms and stumble around the kitchen in their night clothes, slippers flapping against the floor. No one worries about the poor Cheung family down below who must be startled out of their sleep by the commotion above their heads. Despite his rumpled pyjamas and the unnatural flush of his cheeks, Toni finds that her father cuts a dignified figure. His noble bald head and greying goatee recall photos of the nineteenth-century European intellectuals who founded the Zionist movement. And her mother, how lovely and girlish she suddenly appears, her dark eyes laughing, her pink satin nightgown swishing around her hips. Toni collides happily against her parents, her father on her left, her mother on her right, swinging them this way and that in the drunken dance. What amazing times! She has entered history. She has fused with a huge and magnificent force. Nothing will ever be the same again.

Part III

Jerusalem

chapter 14

The bus bumps and lurches up the steep, twisty road through blasted rock, past rusted wrecks of armoured vehicles. Hairpin turns that make Toni's already queasy stomach flip. A stout hip presses into her side. The standing passengers stumble and grumble "Oy!" Just like Jews. Just like Jews anywhere. Unbelievable!

Still, who are these people? Soldiers loll over their kitbags. Matrons clutch squirmy toddlers and string nets of groceries. A black-hatted praying guy jerks in his seat. There are sweaty men with briefcases and newspapers held up to their noses. There are girls in flowered miniskirts that show off smooth, tanned legs. The driver wears shorts, sandals, a shirt open almost to his bellybutton. The faces are beautiful or ugly—spectacularly so, either way.

As Toni leans into the breeze from the open window, her hand slips into her pocket to feel for the postcard that has accompanied her everywhere for weeks. The dog-eared corners feel pleasantly furry. *This funny little country will blow you away.*

Hot, dry wind whips over her face. They are in hill country, far from the airport on the humid coastal plain. Graffiti splashed on the dynamited rock is written in the same ancient chicken-scrawl letters of the *Kaddish* prayer her mother keeps handy in the kitchen drawer back home. This too seems unbelievable.

"*Studenteet?*" a voice shrills into her ear.

Her seat-mate is an oily-skinned crone with sagging breasts and a tight yellow kerchief out of which have escaped bits of lank grey hair.

She jabbers, pitching her voice above the blare of peppy music from the radio, hung above the driver at the front of the bus. The old woman repeats "*studenteet*" more insistently this time. Toni nods and tells her where she's from.

"Ah! Ka-na-da!"

The woman pulls a sad face and makes her fingers walk through the air as if travelling a long distance.

"*Ima! Aba!*" she says tragically and slaps her hand to her cheek.

Toni stiffens in surprise. How would this woman know about Toni's fierce struggles to convince her parents to let her come to Israel for a year? It began last fall with some tentative musings at the dinner table about how some of her classmates were planning to take a year off before starting university to go to Israel to join a kibbutz. Julius had almost choked on a chicken bone at the idea Toni might do this. Lisa agreed, in principle, that Toni should visit Israel some day to round out her education, but certainly not any time soon. So Toni had dropped the subject. At that point she wasn't sure Israel would interest her anyway, despite the enticing posters from the Israeli embassy plastered around the neighbourhood. Then came the postcard from Jerusalem. It contained just a few brief offhand lines, but they acted as a summons, galvanizing her vague fantasies into iron determination.

Her acceptance by Hebrew University and the generous scholarship that came with it helped soften up her father. She disarmed her mother with a new-found Zionist fervour that so echoed Lisa's own. Still, both her parents grew frantic as the day of departure drew near, and Toni teetered between excruciating guilt and a desperate urge to get away. How good it felt, at last, to turn the corner of the corridor at the airport in Montreal. Away from her mother's scrutinizing gaze, from her father's foreboding eyes, she felt like a birthday balloon let loose. Now she shrugs and makes a hand-waving gesture at her seatmate on the bus.

"*Ima, Aba, shalom,*" she says. The final goodbye, the sobs and hugs and her own brief moment of panic, seem so long ago. At this moment her parents seem like outgrown articles of clothing on a closet floor.

The old woman returns Toni's smile with a sly one of her own, elbowing Toni in the ribs. She gestures to one of the young soldiers, twines two fingers together and babbles some Hebrew words. Toni catches the drift: romance, marriage. The woman assumes Toni will be on the lookout for a boyfriend. Her mother, too, dropped broad hints. *I wouldn't be surprised if my little girl catches a nice fish in the Israeli sea.*

Toni turns her head away from the woman to study the craggy peaks above the road, the forests of pines. She is saved from further conversation by the radio now cranked up to what must be the news, delivered by a sombre-voiced announcer. The bus goes still. Everyone listens intently, Toni's neighbour included. A few heads shake, mouths turn grim. Then static, a change of channel, more music. The old woman flicks the air with her hand as if to say, "Don't ask."

At last, the bus crests a final hill and squat buildings come into view along with TV antennas, carpets slung over balcony rails. Some girls at the front begin to clap and sing "Jerusalem of Gold," the song that has become like a second national anthem since the end of last year's war. At a dark narrow station with grubby kiosks and jostling crowds, the bus jerks to a halt. People scramble to their feet, grab for belongings. The air is suddenly thick with heat and exhaust. Toni's neighbour remains firmly planted in her seat, blocking Toni's way.

"*Yerushalayim!*" she exclaims, squeezing her eyes shut as she lovingly pronounces the city's name. Then she clutches Toni's arm and babbles urgently in Hebrew. A middle-aged man with a briefcase twists around and flaps his free hand at the woman to stop her stream of chatter. His deeply lined face and pouting mouth seem set in a perpetually sardonic expression, the look of someone utterly fed up with this world of disappointments. So his next words are a surprise.

"This is not Jerusalem, this station," he says in English. "You will see. Yes. Really."

He bows his head in thought. His forefinger shoots upward. "The ancient rabbis said 'Ten portions of beauty gave God to this world and nine of them fell upon Jerusalem.' You see those soldiers?"

He gestures toward a group on the platform greeting their comrades with hand slaps and shouts.

"They go through fire, these boys, without a murmur, but when they bring back to us the Old City and our Wailing Wall, they cry like babies. There is one Jerusalem now. One Jerusalem whole and complete."

His voice thickens, his eyes grow moist, his lower lip trembles as if he too would cry like a baby right there amid the press of passengers shoving forward to leave the bus.

Standing on the platform with her luggage amid the throng, Toni feels in her pocket yet again. The postcard, damp from the sweat of her thighs, touches back. The words lodged in her mind sing out: *This funny little country will blow you away. Ya gotta come.*

The man on the bus was right. She has seen towers, walls, gardens, stones like polished coins, light, and more light. Every day she roams the labyrinth of streets and gets lost anew. She drifts into a courtyard where geraniums blaze against shady walls and the sound of a flute spills from an open window. She turns a corner and stumbles into the downtown roar. She follows a stretch of new-laid asphalt to a field of thorns. She beholds a dazzling white building that has shouldered its way into vista of barren hills. And over there, tumbling down a sun-scorched terraced slope, a herd of goats, followed by a swarthy goatherd who looks as if he could have stepped out of the pages of the *Golden Treasury of Bible Stories.*

She roams like a smitten lover. She is one of thousands. From the four corners of the earth, young people, mostly Jews, have flocked to Jerusalem. They have come to be part of the miracle, the stunning victory of last year's war that has marked a new beginning for the homeland. The walls and fences that so lately divided the city have been torn down, forever, the people say. In vacant lots that were once no-man's-land, rolls of barbed wire wait to be collected, along with bullet-holed signs that read "Danger! Border!" The lots are criss-crossed by both Jews and Arabs seeking shortcuts into once-forbidden territory. New Jewish suburbs are shooting up, built by Arab labourers who carry baskets of dirt on their shoulders. Hammers ring out. Machines clatter.

At the *ulpan*, the intensive Hebrew course that will run through the summer, Toni learns about words within words: the Hebrew language is based on three-letter roots out of which blossom a profusion of nouns, verbs, and modifiers. Every name has a meaning. Jerusalem has many.

"What words do you find in *Yerushalayim*?" asks Michal, the *ulpan* teacher. "Yes, *shalom*. Exactly. And *shalem*. Very good. And notice the ending, *ayim*. This means two, a duality. Why? Ah, this is a question for rabbis and mystics. But you will see this ending in other words, and that is why I mention it."

Michal strides up and down, her gauzy skirt billowing, her long hands waving. Her skin, like that of most Israelis, bears the ravages of the sun—furrows, crow's feet—yet her eyes are bright, her gestures energetic, her voice vibrant enough to keep the doziest students awake through the long, hot morning hours. She teaches with a passion for every letter and phrase, the humblest parts of speech. Chalk sprays like sparks as she writes on the board.

Toni scribbles diligently in her notebook. *Shalom* = peace. *Shalem* = wholeness. The *ayim* ending means two. A suggestion of two cities in one, embedded in the ancient name. A case for the mystically minded, indeed. After just three weeks of Hebrew, she has two crammed-full notebooks to study, along with Michal's mimeographed handouts, newspaper clippings, and her well-thumbed dictionary.

In the evenings, in her dorm, Toni reviews and memorizes, trying to block out the chatter of girls in the corridors and that of Brenda, her bouncy, too-friendly roommate. Most of Brenda's companions are Americans like herself, who travel in packs to the Old City markets, to dances and suppers and Shabbat evenings with the guys at Hebrew Union College. They speak English amongst themselves, but also manage quite well in Hebrew because, unlike Toni, they learned the fundamentals at religious schools and youth groups. Toni lags behind. When university starts in two months, her lectures will be almost entirely in Hebrew. She's majoring in biology and will be competing for honours with native-born Israelis. There's not a second to lose.

Other than Brenda, Toni has only two possible contacts in the city, and she avoids them both, for different reasons. There's a Mrs Lieberman, related to Mrs Shmelzer, her mother's boss in Montreal. Mrs Lieberman lives in the well-heeled neighbourhood of Rehavia, and her husband is a doctor. Weeks before Toni's departure, Lisa began to talk about Mrs Lieberman: how to get in touch with her, when (*Not after lunch; Mrs Shmelzer says people sleep after lunch*), what to bring (*Flowers, one always brings flowers; very cheap in Israel*). Mrs Lieberman's address and phone number lie buried in Toni's empty suitcase. Toni has no intention of paying a visit. She can see herself being interrogated and fussed over. Detailed reports sent across the seas. Enough!

The other contact is an entirely different matter. Janet Bloom. She lives in Beit HaKerem, a neighbourhood between the university campus near the centre of town and the new complex of dorms on the western edge of the city. From the window of her *ulpan* class on campus, Toni can see beyond a sun-drenched wadi to Beit HaKarem's pines and red-tiled roofs. She resists the impulse that tugs her feet in that direction. Soon. But not yet. She wants more of a tan, more Hebrew under her belt, that tough, confident Israeli look, so that when she does finally knock on Janet's door, she'll hear, "My God! I never would have recognized you."

But Hebrew doesn't come easily. Toni slogs and strains, yet words refuse to march in orderly procession from her mouth, and she becomes tongue-tied at critical moments. Meanwhile, Brenda, her roommate, engages in easy conversation with Simha, the cleaning lady on their floor. Simha, a Sephardic Jew from Iraq, is short and squat, with swollen ankles and a rasping voice suited to her guttural Hebrew. Each morning Toni hears the slap-slap of Simha's rag on the terrazzo floors. Brenda asks after Simha's children. "Ai! Daughters!" Simha sighs. The oldest is twenty-seven and still no bridegroom. A tragedy! A scandal! Brenda argues the cause of the modern woman, while Simha counters with age-old wisdom.

"*Habibti*, listen. After twenty-four, a girl is overripe fruit."

Toni hears everything through the door that Brenda once again forgot to shut. Brenda's pronunciation is terrible—so Yankee, those broad vowels—but the words flow. To learn Hebrew, Michal says, you have to engage with the people: talk, ask directions, bargain, discuss, argue, don't be shy. Which is hard for someone who is.

And it's not just language that eludes her. There are mysteries in faces and gestures, encounters that make her feel out of her depth.

One day, waiting at a bus stop, Toni finds herself being scrutinized by three Arab workmen. They are dust-covered, leather-skinned, wear keffiyehs, baggy pants, torn shoes. There are men like these all over the city. According to Michal, they are grateful to have jobs and to be under Israeli rule, enjoying a much higher standard of living than their cousins in Jordan, never mind what their terrorist leaders say abroad. Squatting in the shade of a wall, they smoke and watch her out of eyes dark as new-laid tar. Are they angry, judgemental, leering? Toni becomes aware of her long bare legs sticking out of her shorts. A foreign girl's legs. Michal would say these people have to get used to modern ways. They can't live in the Middle Ages forever. The men make no gesture except to lift their cigarettes to their mouths and exhale the smoke. Yet their gazes drill into her. Toni wishes she could manage that quintessential Israeli gesture of disdain, a shrug and toss of the head accompanied by a sharp click of the tongue. *Tzuk!* But her mouth is too dry, her sense of rightness too uncertain.

Another day, Toni leans against a guard rail at a busy corner in downtown Jerusalem. She gobbles her falafel lunch while she watches the milling crowd. Most interesting to her is the group of girl soldiers clustered in front of the falafel kiosk. Stunning, every one of them, their gazelle-like loveliness not the least bit marred by the khaki pants and jackboots and the rifles slung over their shoulders. The girl soldiers lean into one another and laugh and rebuff the flirtations of passing boys. Their hands dance in the air as they shout over one another's voices. Their lips move incessantly. Wouldn't it be wonderful to march in a column with girls like these? To camp in the desert, become swarthy and muscled, and present herself at Janet's door one day: Captain Goldblatt in uniform.

"*Shalom, motek,*" says a voice near her ear.

Toni turns to see a ruddy, impudent face, laughing eyes. A boy is perched on the guard rail beside her, looking down. He's one of the *chakh-chakhim*, the greasers who gather on street corners and harass the passing girls. When did he show up? On his knee rests a paper bag of sunflower seeds. He spits out a shell, smiles, revealing strong, white teeth.

"Are you American?"

His voice is eager. His eyes gleam as he says "*Amerika-eet.*" She frowns as she considers how to answer. This dark-skinned boy is clearly a *Mizrahi*, a Middle-Eastern Jew. Michal told of how thousands of them came from Arab lands after '48, how the new State of Israel struggled to absorb them. For years they lived in tent camps and crowded housing projects. They are poorly educated and primitive compared to Europeans, Michal said, and there are "social problems," but, Michal insisted, the army is doing an excellent job of assimilating the second generation. Toni feels she should be kind to anyone who was raised in a tent camp. On the other hand, the *chakh-chakhim* are crazy for foreign girls, who are supposedly a softer touch than the hard-nosed Israelis. Better not to get involved. She shakes her head and looks away, hoping he'll get the message.

"Not American? Dutch? Swedish?"

He leans forward to catch her eye. She shakes her head again, more severely this time.

"So? Where are you from?"

He sounds miffed, as if Toni were the one being rude. At the same time, he inches closer along the rail.

"Nowhere!" she snarls, her patience gone.

"*Ooh wah!* That's exactly where I'm from. Nowhere. We must be neighbours. Huh? Maybe we grew up on the same street." He throws his head back to laugh. "You are so tall. Are all the girls of your country so tall?"

"*Chamor!* You are a donkey!" Toni spits. A feeble insult, childish, something out of the Hebrew language primer. She looks quickly toward the kiosk, but the girl soldiers have left. Perhaps she too should vanish into the noonday crowds. She strides up the long slope of Ben Yehuda Street, but she can feel him close behind. *He wants to follow? Fine!* She'll take him on a wild goose chase. Up and down the baking streets they go, around corners, and across intersections until her head rings, her throat aches, her eyeballs burn. The boy sticks like glue. He seems not the least bit out of breath.

"Hey, tall girl. What's the hurry?"

Having gone in a big circle and arrived back in the centre of town, at Independence Park Toni darts down a path between flower beds in search of a drinking fountain. As she bends over the fountain, the boy's face comes close, like he means to kiss her. Toni picks up a rock.

"Is it because you are a lesbian, you are so cold and heartless?" he says.

It takes several moments for the question to sink in. The Hebrew word is unmistakable—"*lesbeet*"—so, too, his ugly smile. As she stands dumbfounded with upraised arm, he jumps forward, rises on tiptoe, presses his mouth to hers, and shoves his tongue inside. He has a surprisingly large, fleshy tongue that licks in quick circular motions, seemingly not wanting to leave any surface untouched. His sly hand gives her right breast a squeeze. She jerks violently, but he has already sprung back on nimble feet and is dancing away.

"See, not so bad with a boy. Bye-bye, *lesbeet*," he calls over his shoulder.

"You have to go somewhere for *erev Shabbat*," Brenda wails. "You can't stay here all alone."

She's been trying to persuade Toni to come with her to a Hassidic-style happening with the Singing Rabbi from San Francisco. Brenda makes a tragic face at the thought of Toni staying behind in the abandoned dorm. On Friday evenings the building empties out as students join family or friends for a festive meal, and the halls become still as tombs.

Brenda has soft blue somewhat bulgy eyes and buck teeth over a wet lower lip. In honour of the Sabbath she's dressed in an embroidered Yemenite blouse, blue skirt, and dangly earrings, while her brown hair is done up in a loose French roll. She looks down upon Toni, stretched out on her narrow cot, with eager, good-hearted, gormless sympathy. Unbearable!

"I do have somewhere to go," Toni blurts out. "I'm visiting an old friend. Janet Bloom. She's a folk singer. She's on the radio sometimes."

"Wow! Neat!"

The words "folk singer" and "radio" have the desired effect. Brenda's jaw drops and her eyes fairly pop out of her head.

"Maybe you've heard of her?"

"No! I haven't. Sorry."

Brenda moans in apology as if it's a personal failing of hers not to have heard of Janet Bloom, but, in truth, there's no reason why she should. Though Toni pricks up her ears whenever she hears a female vocalist on the radio—in buses, cafés, the dorm—so far the performer announced at the end of the song has never been Janet.

"How do you know her?"

Toni hesitates, then tells her about Camp Tikvah (briefly) and of how last fall at a folk music concert at the Jewish Y she ran into someone who told her that Janet, of all people, had already made *Aliyah*. Toni ferreted out an address, wrote, and eventually Janet wrote back. Just the one postcard: "Hey there, Voice-From-the-Past. I've been performing around the country. Did a spot on the army radio show. Hoping for a record contract (keep your fingers crossed). This funny little country will blow you away. Ya gotta come."

Instead of signing her name, Janet drew a self-portrait in the form of a guitar with stick legs and arms (one waving) and above the fingerboard, a face framed by long, streaming hair.

After Brenda dashes from the room, Toni lies back on her bed and listens to doors slam, goodbyes called, the roar of departing buses, and the fading of footsteps on the street below. Shadows deepen. A stillness descends, broken now and then by a distant shout or blast of a horn. The encounter with the *chakh-chakh* replays in her head, thoughts of what she might have done differently, his parting shot: Bye-bye, *lesbeet*. The Hebrew word is almost identical to the English, but worse, overly familiar and indecent, like the boy's slimy tongue. She jumps up to pace the room, gaze out the window at the empty streets and the hills turning mauve in the failing light. The loneliness Brenda warned about sinks into her chest. She hadn't really planned to visit Janet just yet, but now the idea takes hold. Surely, after waiting so long and proving she's not too eager, and after such a miserable day, she has earned the reunion at last.

chapter 15

There are no buses after sundown on *erev Shabbat,* hardly any traffic on the eerily empty streets. Toni hikes the long winding road toward Beit HaKerem, and by the time she reaches the neighbourhood, black night has descended, snuffing out landmarks, blotting out street signs. She wishes now she could have phoned ahead, but who owns a luxury such as a telephone in Israel? Old-timers, not newcomers like Janet. After searching the well-treed but poorly illuminated streets, she finds the house at last, in a cul-de-sac on the edge of a wadi. No lights on the porch either. She has to feel with her fingers for a bell. She hears the slow shuffle of slippers, the creak as the door opens a crack, revealing a dim glow from the hall and an ancient face with a beaked nose and squinting eyes.

"Around the back," the voice croaks. "They have their own quarters. I don't interfere." Then, as Toni is about to retreat, the elderly figure leans forward to peer more closely.

"What are you? Boy or girl? *Ach,* never mind, as long as you are serious. We need serious young people in this country. We don't need freeloaders and lazybones, these, what do you call them, these hippies. In my day, we weren't afraid of work. Do you know what it means to work?"

The accent is familiar—German-Jewish—as is the tone, a cheerfully belligerent grumbling Toni has become accustomed to on street corners and bus line-ups. Everyone has to outdo the other in displays of fortitude and martyrdom. Before she can respond, the creaky voice mutters, "Go on! Around the back, I said," and the door is shut tight, leaving the porch in utter darkness again.

She gropes her way along a path at the side of the house to a walled garden at the back of which stands a low building, some kind of shed or garage, with double doors that stand slightly ajar. Candles flicker inside. *Flowers, one always brings flowers,* Toni suddenly remembers, and regrets she has nothing. She rubs sweaty hands against her shorts, steps forward, stumbles against a heavy object—a clay pot, perhaps— which clatters mightily upon the flagstone path and rolls back and forth with a slow, hollow sound. Somewhere a startled cat shrieks and the doors of the shed fly open and Janet stomps out, fists balled, shoulders hunched, a picture of fury, though the expression on her face is obscured by the gloom.

"You fucker," she howls. "You've got your bloody nerve."

Toni raises her hands defensively because those fists look like they're about to make contact with her head. But then Janet stops, freezes, peers intently.

"What the fu ...?"

"Janet, it's me. Toni. Toni Goldblatt."

Janet's hand covers her mouth in a gesture of wonder. Or is it dismay?

"Remember me? From Montreal. From ... Jewish camp."

"Right," Janet says finally, but without much conviction.

"You said I should visit. I'm so sorry. I meant to write, and then I meant to phone, but they said you wouldn't have one and that in Israel people just drop in, and I ... if this is a bad time ..."

"I thought you were David. You're his size," Janet says in a tone of accusation, as if, just by resembling this object of her wrath, Toni deserved a good dose of it herself. Then, turning on her heel, Janet makes a vague gesture over her shoulder which Toni interprets as an invitation to follow into the candlelit room. Janet flops onto a mattress laid directly on the bare tiled floor and heaped with rumpled bedding and cushions. She covers her eyes with her arm.

"Are you all right?" Toni asks.

"Yeah, yeah. Kind of bummed out at the moment. Make yourself at home."

Toni looks around for somewhere to sit. She finds herself in a low-ceilinged, spectacularly messy room, jam-packed with astonishing objects, none of which resemble anything so ordinary as a chair. There's a tall glass hookah, a clay drum, a pile of salt-encrusted driftwood, a spent mortar shell holding a bouquet of dried thistles, a fishing net draped across one wall and ornamented with broken seashells and coloured glass, a big round brass tray covered with dirty dishes, an empty tire lying on its side (the treads still gripping the dirt from its final encounter with a road), and a nose-less plaster bust of Elvis with a leather peace symbol covering one eye. There are empty cans and crumpled papers and books and butt-filled ashtrays and a bucket of soaking laundry and, in one corner, the ripped, foam-rubber-spewing back seat of a car. A mobile made of coat hangers dangles from the ceiling and gyrates slowly. And the whole crowd of objects—particularly the coat hanger mobile—casts crazy shadows in this flickering cave of a room.

Beside the wrecked car seat, Toni spies a passable leather hassock. Dragging it over near Janet, Toni lowers herself, sinks into the yielding material, almost topples backward but manages to hunch awkwardly with her long legs jack-knifed beneath her chin. She stares woefully at the dirty soles of Janet's feet, while Janet continues to lie on her back in bummed-out silence.

"I forgot how tall you were," Janet finally says from beneath her arm. "You really are as tall as David."

"Is he your boyfriend?"

Janet utters a strangled laugh.

"That sounds so high school prom and hearts and flowers. He's my man, I guess." Janet sighs.

Glancing around the room again, Toni now notices signs of this man. A leather cowboy hat hung over a lamp. Other masculine clothes. It had never occurred to her that Janet could be part of a couple. Awe, anxiety, and resentment chase one another around in her mind. Then something else in the room catches her eye: leaning against a wall, beneath a poster of three dancing Hassids, she recognizes Janet's old blond-wood, acoustic guitar. It's a comforting sight, like a long-lost friend, and she is almost inclined to give the Gibson a hug.

"What does David do?" she presently asks, not because she really wants to know, but for something to say.

Janet sits up abruptly, crosses her arms over her chest.

"He doesn't 'do'!" she says severely. "He just *is*. I mean, he does all kinds of stuff—gardening, religious studies, learning Arabic—but he's not into that achievement shit. He doesn't believe in identifying with a role."

Toni bows her head at this chastisement. When she's sure she's regained control of her voice she says, "Maybe I should go home."

"But you just got here!" Then in a gentler tone: "Don't go. Sorry. I'm not being the hostess with the mostess. My head's kind of elsewhere. Nice to see someone from back home. Really."

Janet rummages around in the bedding and locates a pack of cigarettes.

"Smoke?"

Toni lights up and tries to look like she does it all the time.

"Dubeks," Janet says apologetically. "Cheap Israeli brand. But better than nothing."

She takes a deep drag and contemplates Toni steadily out of her wide green eyes.

"Yeah, I remember you," she drawls, as if little bits of memory are clicking into place. "You haven't changed a bit."

The blithe assessment stings. Toni wants to launch into the tale of all the ways in which she has become a completely new person. Her eyes catch Janet's smoky green gaze and words fail her. Janet herself has certainly changed. Slimmer than she was at camp, her face still densely freckled but more finely sculpted, with sophisticated hollows and lines, and a grave, sad, distracted air. Her red hair is longer and less kinky than Toni remembers, cascading over her shoulders and down her back. She wears a loose cotton skirt and a gauzy blouse with a green and yellow pattern of swirling lines that seems jungle-like, bringing to mind some rare tropical salamander disappearing into the underbrush. There are beads and tiny mirrors sewn into the cloth. Janet's necklace of silvery coins winks in the candlelight.

"So what brought you here?" Janet asks after a fretful glance toward the rustling dark beyond the doors.

Has she forgotten the postcard? Her exhortations? *This funny little country ...Ya gotta come.* But perhaps she wants to know what motivated Toni to answer the call, why it touched a chord in Toni's heart. She rakes her fingers through her tousled hair. Where to begin? She needs to say everything, thoughts that have accumulated for months. She starts by describing her rambles in the city, jumps backward in time to the Six-Day War, the victory that suggested the hand of God—not literally of course, because she doesn't believe in that Old-Man-in-the-Sky stuff—nevertheless something big did happen. And Jerusalem! Four thousand years of history—battles, exiles, tragedies, dead-ends, the Jews kicked out, but never losing their ties to the land, and then she's back to the Six-Day War. She's no longer merely Toni Goldblatt, the kid from Snowdon, whose biggest accomplishment so far has been to graduate from high school with the fifty-dollar Steinberg's bursary. Standing on Jerusalem's sun-baked hills, she feels she's swallowed thousands of years, lived thousands of lives. All this she tries to express, waving her hands and leaning forward, the hassock half off the floor. She sees her listener's expression change from gentle indulgence to strain to a grimace of endurance. She is boring Janet to death.

"I'm so sorry. I talk too much."

She squeezes her hands together between her knees. Janet's face lights up in a genuine smile for the first time this evening.

"Same old Toni. It's okay. I understand where you're at." The smoke streams out of Janet's mouth in a sigh. "You're in the honeymoon stage. I felt a lot like you do when I came, which was just after the war. I didn't plan to come. Happened by accident. I was hitching around Europe, met up with this neat bunch of freaks and someone says, 'Let's take a boat from Athens.' Next thing I know, I'm on the beach in Acre. Far-out scene. People drunk with happiness because Israel didn't get wiped off the map. Strangers hugging one another. We had a *kumzits* that lasted weeks. But the euphoria wears off. The daily stuff catches up with you. You need elbows and a thick skin in this country."

"But you're a performer. You're doing so well!"

"Was doing well. Was starting to get somewhere." Janet frowns and bunches her necklace of coins in her fist. "Had this fight with my agent."

"You have an agent!" Toni marvels.

"Real asshole. David says the music biz is a rat race like any other. I dunno. Maybe he's right. I should do my own thing. Oh well, if my career was still on track you wouldn't have found me here. I'd be in Tel Aviv, where the action is."

After a forced smile, she sinks back into gloomy reverie. Toni is struck dumb by the glamour of Janet's troubles, this unfathomable otherworld of the music business. She imagines men with slicked-back hair and cigars, women in glittery gowns, fights in dressing rooms, mirrors smashed. A dozen questions dance on her lips, but all seem equally foolish. Finally, to break the silence, she asks, "Where's David now?"

"I don't fucking know."

Janet leaps up and paces back and forth in front of the doorway, head bowed, arms crossed over her chest. Her bare feet slap softly on the terrazzo floor. The movement of her billowing skirt makes the candle flames shiver. She stops abruptly, looks keenly at Toni as if noticing her properly at last.

"Hey, you must be starving. I am. I'll get some food. To hell with him."

Despite the long hike from the dorm and the lateness of the hour, Toni isn't the least bit hungry. Her throat feels closed to food, but she nods eagerly anyway and follows Janet across the patio and the garden to a galley kitchen in the main house. Janet loads a tray with salads, hummus, cheese, a loaf of rye bread.

"No booze," she apologizes. "That fucker was supposed to bring the booze."

They return to the patio where several wicker stools and a small wooden table wait under the gnarled branches of a tree. Janet lights lanterns and suddenly the garden is alive with dancing light and shadows.

"This is where we eat most of our meals. David does the garden. He rescued it from near death. We've got roses, cactus, bougainvillea, our own herbs. He pruned this fig tree. He's got the touch."

Toni makes out soft blooms against the foliage and breathes in sweet and spicy scents. The stone wall, about as high as her shoulders, surrounding the enclosure creates a cosy space, reminding her of bonfire nights at Camp Tikvah. Beyond the wall is the solid darkness of the wadi. How often Toni lay on her cot at the dorm or sat at Hebrew class at the university campus and tried to imagine this place, and now she is here, at last. Her jittery fingers pinch pieces of rye bread into a heap of pellets while Janet, leaning over the table, busily eats. It is a great piece of luck, Toni decides, that David has gone AWOL, allowing her this reunion with Janet on her own.

"I was saying that the euphoria about Israel wears away," Janet says, wiping her mouth with the back of her hand. "But not for everyone. David's still high on being in Jerusalem, the Holy City. Of course, he's just high, period. He lives in his own zone, a different level. Know what I mean?"

Toni isn't sure, but an uncomfortable truth strikes her. "You really like him."

She is appalled at how resentful her statement sounds, but Janet doesn't seem to notice.

"Huh!" is all that Janet offers as reply. A skeptical snort. Or a preoccupied grunt. Or perhaps a defensive "don't-remind-me-of-what-I-feel." But whatever the case, Toni's comment is a conversation stopper as Janet rummages for cigarettes, lights up, and drags deeply, eyes shut in concentration like a condemned man on a firing line trying to savour his last request. After a long pause, Janet's eyes blink open.

"So what is it you're doing here again?" she asks, her gaze drifting from Toni's face to the depths of the darkness beyond the garden wall, where trees rustle and a cool breeze wells up.

Happy to change the subject, delighted at another chance to present her new self—the grownup, scholarly, almost-Hebrew-speaking self—Toni tips forward on her three-legged stool. She babbles. She rearranges Janet's cutlery. She marches the army of bread pellets back and forth. A sudden stiffening of Janet's posture stops the army in its tracks. Janet's head shoots upward in a listening position, and now Toni hears it too, a faint whistling in the distance, which grows stronger as it approaches, resolving itself from a wispy sound into one of the Singing Rabbi's hypnotic melodies. The whistled tune is accompanied by the tinkle of glass.

"That's him!" Janet pronounces breathlessly. She stubs out her cigarette, smoothes her hair, straightens her shoulders and stares hard in the direction of the whistling. There's a scrambling by the wall, and then a tall, lean figure swings over and drops to the ground in a deft movement, noiseless, except for the clinking of bottles. "Hey, babe. How's it going? I see you got grub on the table. Sweet darling! I'm starved."

The voice is rich and deep. The words flow like melted chocolate poured from a vat.

"Where were you, you shithead?"

David grins, showing a flash of white teeth beneath a droopy black moustache. He removes a small embroidered cap, the kind worn by religious Jews in the Bukharian Quarter, and scratches the scalp beneath a shaggy mane of hair.

"Places, man. Places!" he says in a tone both emphatic and wondering, as if no other explanation were needed, but as if he is amazed at these vague, mysterious places he's been privileged to visit. With sinking heart, Toni notes he is undeniably handsome. Tall, but with a slight scholarly stoop, giving him a gentler air than the forceful Israeli masculinity common in the streets. He wears some kind of ethnic shirt of soft white cotton, a leather choker, patched jeans, and sandals. Big, gardener's hands. Arched, quizzical eyebrows. An impish cleft in his chin. Intense dark eyes.

"I could kill you. I could bloody well kill you."

Janet has reared off her stool and grabbed the butter knife and waves it menacingly toward his chest.

"Aw, don't be like that, babe."

He drops before Janet on one knee, opens his knapsack and pulls out several bottles of beer along with some kind of liquor, which he places at her feet. A pack of cigarettes follows. He adds a handful of change from his pocket to the offerings. Next, he starts to take off his shirt as if he means to give her that too.

"Oh quit it, you asshole."

But a grudging softness has come into her voice, and to Toni's astonishment she allows him to pull her down to the ground and envelope her in a hard embrace. His hair falls forward to cover both their faces.

"This is Toni," Janet says in a slightly breathless voice when they've staggered to their feet. David studies Toni with a frank, unsmiling curiosity that makes her blood rise. She's become accustomed to these cool, appraising looks—from young men in particular—who seem to want to figure out what's not quite right about her, what ingredient is missing. She stares back, jaws clamped tight, until his hand shoots out to enclose hers in a firm, manly grip, the kind of handshake one fellow might give to another. An unexpected spark of pleasure warms her chest. The keen look on his face is one of interest, not judgement, she realizes, and she can't help but be flattered. Introductions over, David opens the beer he brought, squats down on a stool, and helps himself to supper, including the leftovers on Janet's plate—the crusts and smeared hummus. He stuffs food into his mouth with his fingers, eating heartily, smacking his lips, and wiping his hands on the legs of his patched jeans.

"You're famished," Janet says, surprised. "I thought you'd have eaten by now."

"Went to the *Kotel*, lost track of time. What a trip. People dancing, singing, high on Shabbas. Aw, man, you should have come."

Janet considers him for a long a moment.

"You said you were going to synagogue." She pauses. "Meet anyone?" Her voice is guarded.

"Yeah." He chews thoughtfully and swallows. "Elijah the Prophet. After the *Kotel*, I went up the Mount of Olives. Sat on a wall above the cemetery. Black as tombs all around me, and across the valley the lit-up city floated in mid-air. Elijah said to me: 'Far fucking out!' Those were his very words."

All this is said deadpan. Janet makes a face and finally smiles. She pushes a teasing finger into the cleft of his chin.

"Aren't you a scream."

"Anything else to eat?"

Wordlessly, Janet slips off her stool and pads across the flagstone patio. She returns with another plate of tidbits from the fridge. While David eats, she sits close beside him, touching his arm and shoulder and watching the food disappear with obvious pleasure. At the end of the meal, David picks his front teeth with the edge of the long fingernail at the end of his pinkie finger. Toni stares in fascination. It's a custom for Middle Eastern men—both Jewish and Arab—to grow that one long nail, so uncouth to European eyes, Toni knows. She has not seen a single Western Jew thus equipped. David smiles and belches loudly.

"The Bedouins consider burping a compliment to the host. Opposite of Western culture where bodily functions are dirty. I consider the human body holy, don't you?"

Toni detects a glint of merriment in those studying eyes.

"Sure. Every hole is holy," she banters back at David.

David guffaws and nudges her hard, so that she nearly falls off her wicker stool.

"Toni really is spiritually minded," Janet says, smiling at them both, pleased to see them getting along. "She's nuts about Jerusalem."

David beams. "Thought you might be. Could see that you've got depth. I can read a face pretty well."

"This town is too serious and uptight for me," Janet says peevishly. "I prefer gritty old Tel Aviv."

"Jerusalem will grow on you, babe. Give it a chance."

David takes one of her hands in his own big paws and traces the lines with his thumb.

"These lines don't lie. I see you discovering your deep-down soul. I see an amazing spiritual journey on the way."

He presses Janet's palm to his lips. Janet sucks in her breath and her body seems to melt toward him. Jerking her head away, Toni studies the ghostly white roses by the garden wall.

"It's late," she says. "I should go."

"Should or want to?" David drawls. "'Should' is the most evil word in our vocabulary. William Blake said, 'Better to strangle an infant in its grave than to listen to the dictates of should.' He said something like that, anyway. Are you telling me you *want* to leave?"

"Three's a crowd."

At this, David and Janet both burst into laughter. Janet reaches across the table and pats Toni's hand.

"You're a sweet kid. Have some more beer."

The three of them clink bottles together.

"So, what's your trip, Toni?" David asks, folding his hands behind his head and stretching his long legs out in front of him. "Whatcha seeking?"

Not wanting to repeat the tale Janet found so tedious (Six-Day War, being part of history, blah, blah), Toni focuses on her university plans, her excitement about being accepted into a science program. David utters an unimpressed "humph" that seems to say you'll soon be rid of those illusions. An awkward silence ensues.

"David's got a degree in philosophy. He's been to graduate school too," Janet says.

"Dropped out of graduate school," he corrects her. "Flew the coop. Whoosh." His hand arrows through the air to suggest a plane taking off. "Couldn't stand the bullshit. Univer-shitty. That's where they try to stifle independent minds."

Toni tries to take this in. Dropping out seems almost criminal, an act of breath-taking recklessness. Yet David clearly has no regrets. He relates some of the adventures he's had since chucking his exam booklet into the garbage and sticking out his thumb on the open road. He camped with the Navaho in the desert and on a houseboat with a fisherman who could have been Hemingway's twin. He did an ashram. Got busted in Paris. Wooed a girl in Rome. As he talks, David rocks his body and his hands tell the stories along with his voice. In a country where everyone talks with their hands, his fluid gestures still seem unusually expressive.

By and by, he pulls a silver-foil packet the size of a sugar cube from the lining of his embroidered cap. From his pocket he produces a penknife and a metal pipe.

"Ah," Janet murmurs happily. "I've been dying for some shit."

"Moroccan gold." David chuckles. "The best."

He shaves the lump with his penknife, fills the pipe, and lights up, filling the air with a burnt hay aroma. The pipe passes from hand to hand. Toni hesitates for just a heartbeat. The intimate glow of the lanterns, Janet's dreamy smile, and David's nodding head snuff out silly admonitions from another lifetime about frying one's brains and landing in jail. She clutches the pipe, sucks hard, and explodes in a coughing fit as the hot smoke sears her lungs.

"What a waste," Janet says with a shake of her head, but David instructs Toni in the art of taking small, manageable puffs and holding them down as long as she can. She waits eagerly for something to happen, and presently—is it her imagination or is it real?—she feels light as thistledown, heavy as clay, aware of the bigness of her body but not unpleasantly so. After what seems a long time, Janet rises and drifts toward the path by the side of the house, her palms uplifted as if feeling for rain from the cloudless sky. David gets up too, encircles an arm around Janet's waist and beckons Toni to follow.

They walk out the front gate, across the road, to a border of wild cactus bushes along the lip of the wadi. David leads the way through a gap in the bushes, down a narrow sloping path into black nothingness. Clusters of lights glitter here and there on the hills in the distance, but immediately around them solid gloom presses in. Janet takes Toni's hand as they stumble along, single file, over stones and between thorny plants that scratch their bare ankles. They reach level ground and stop. Then Toni is on her backside in soft cool dust. She smells the remnants of a campfire, hears the silky rustle of nearby olive trees. The vast dome of the sky blossoms with stars.

"Where are we?"

"Our favourite spot," Janet's voice says through the thick dark.

"The centre of the universe," David chortles.

A match flares to reveal David's pursed lips sucking on the pipe, his eyes crinkled against the smoke. Janet snuggles up against his shoulder. A few moments later—or has an hour gone by?—the three of them lie flat on their backs, their bodies radiating outwards like spokes in a wheel, heads touching. Toni breathes in a cloud of heavenly scents— hash, smoke, dust, the dry grasses and thistles of the field, the lemony fragrance of Janet's hair—each smell perfectly distinguishable and also beautifully blended. Laughter rolls around beneath her ribs.

"Good vibes, eh?" David's elbow nudges her side. "How d'you like my city so far?"

"Your city? How come it's your city?"

David mimics her tone of indignation. "How come it's *your* city?"

Again he and Janet burst into giggles.

"It's the City of David. Okay?"

"Okay," Toni agrees. She's feeling most agreeable.

"And my name is David Konig. King David. Get it?"

He tells them a story. In ancient days, Jerusalem belonged to a Canaanite folk called the Jebusites. King David conquered them but did not drive them out, marrying one of their princesses—Bathsheba—and absorbing them into his people instead. Jerusalem, a central point in the lands of the Israelite tribes, became his capital to which, with much fanfare, he brought the Ark of the Covenant. The King himself led the procession, dancing out in front to the tambourines and drums.

"Guy was a fucking genius," David says, exhaling smoke with a whistling breath. "He had vision. He got down with the people."

Janet's sweet voice pierces the night. She sings an old Hebrew folk song Toni remembers from camp about David, King of Israel. In Janet's mouth, the childlike ditty becomes a wistful ballad, exquisitely tender.

How very odd, Toni thinks, to be here, enveloped by the magical darkness, stoned out of her mind and talking with Janet and David, as if the three of them have been pals forever. Earlier today she was grasping for connection, and now—is this really now? Or are they back at a campfire under the stars? Or is it another time altogether, 200 generations ago, when King David wooed the lovely Bathsheba? Where have they landed, the three of them? At the bottom of a crater in their own dusty, sweet-smelling planet, while her room at the dorm is as distant as the moon.

Later, as they clamber giddily up the steep path toward the winking lights of houses above, Toni stops abruptly to announce to Janet, "I'm not the same, you know. Not like I was back then. I want you to understand."

Her voice swells with earnest avowals. Janet squeezes her hand.

"It's okay, it's okay. I know."

chapter 16

Rush out of Hebrew class. Slap along the flagstone walk in sandalled feet. Hurry, hurry, hurry, across the lush campus lawns, past splashing fountains, rose gardens, white marble buildings, down dusty shortcuts and into the sun-parched wadi. Scramble along the rocky, dusty path, up the thorny slope, through the gap in the tangle of prickly pears, to the little house in the cul-de-sac. Heart thumping, throat parched, head a-throb with the heat.

"You again," Mrs Katz, the landlady, croaks. She keeps watch in the shade of her porch during the day, dozing in her chair. Still as a gecko until she hears the sound of shoe leather on pavement, then she twitches awake.

"Very good. Give that other one something to worry about. She's too snooty."

The old lady cackles. Off her rocker, Toni thinks, not for the first time, as she hurries down the garden path to the whitewashed cinder-block hideaway with the green metal doors.

"Knock, knock," Toni calls breathlessly, though the doors stand wide open.

"What's this knocking shit?" David roars.

She helps herself to water from an earthenware pitcher on the floor, drinking straight from the jug in big gulps, the cool liquid spilling onto her shirtfront. No formalities required. In this room, formalities are forbidden. In the daylight, the room's colours come to life—the reds, purples, greens of the fabrics from the Arab market, the deep rust of Janet's hair, the cool turquoise of the walls. David chose to paint the room this particular shade of blue-green, soothing as the sea and popular throughout the Middle East, except in the homes of European Jews, where all plaster is treated with mildew-fighting whitewash.

Seated cross-legged on the mattress while strumming her nylon-stringed guitar, Janet looks up and smiles vaguely. David, beside her, bends back to his books. He seems to be reading several at once. There's a volume open in his lap, others scattered about, bristling with notes. Toni thinks of her father in his cherished library, how he would approve of David's voracious reading appetite, though perhaps not of books left open, face down on the floor in spine-cracking positions, or the choice of titles. There are texts on the Kabbalah, Hassidism, Sufism. There's Buber, Heschel, Hesse. *Siddhartha* and *I and Thou* and *The Prophet* by Khalil Gibran. There's also a tattered paperback—Leonard Cohen's *Beautiful Losers*—which David found when it dropped out of some hippie's knapsack at the central bus station. An excited smile plays across David's lips as he reads, rocking back and forth, yeshiva-style, and humming a Sabbath hymn in soft falsetto beneath his breath. The white Bukharian cap embroidered with doves and vines in gold and silver threads—so much groovier than a plain old yarmulka—adorns his head.

Toni plops down on some cushions and pretends to be engrossed in her Hebrew homework, but she's too distracted to study. She steals glances at her friends instead, at Janet, who often turns toward David as her fingers strum gentle chords that take up the theme of his hymn. Janet seems fascinated by David's keen concentration. Her eyes are puzzled, envious, resentful, and tender, by turns. And he appears as unaware of her gaze as she of Toni's. The moment stretches out, strangely sweet and melancholy, reminding Toni of a scene painted on a vase that arrested her attention at the Israel Museum. Three damsels chased a hunter who chased a lion who chased the damsels, round and round, all of them with limbs extended, frozen in motion.

They lie on their backs on the mattress in the afternoon heat. The oscillating electric fan sends intermittent puffs of soupy breeze across their flushed faces. David, in the middle, passes the joint to Janet on his right and Toni on his left. The butt end is flattened and soggy from three pairs of lips. The fan hums. The coat-hanger mobile jangles. A jingle-jangle afternoon. Hey, Mr Sandman.

"Eilat," David murmurs as if answering a question that's been brewing in his mind. "Let's go to Eilat."

He talks about the freaks camped out year-round on the beach, about the wind-carved copper-coloured mountains and how everyone shares food and dope while the sun fires their brains into incandescent wires and visions shimmer upon the horizon of the Red Sea.

"Better than acid, man. That's how the prophets … that's how Jesus …" He hoists himself up into a half-sitting position, his eyes aglow. "Or, hey, we could do Sinai, climb the mountain where Moses saw the burning bush, saw God face-to-face in the thundercloud. And there's Nuweiba, an oasis where the Bedouins hang out."

"But I want to go to Tel Aviv," Janet groans.

"If you want a city, we'll go to Haifa and see the Bahai Temple. You've never been to the Bahai Temple? Shit, man. Shit!" He thumps the mattress with an enthusiastic fist while his lips stretch in a white-toothed grin.

"Listen here, David Konig. I want the AdomDom Club and Dizengoff Square." Janet props herself up on one elbow, her brow puckered, her voice grown petulant. "I like the crowds at midnight, and there's always a party at someone's apartment, and then after the party, there's the beach."

"Fuck Tel Aviv," David says as he plucks the roach from between

Janet's knuckles and grunts with disapproval that's it's gone out. "Tel Aviv's all tar from the tankers, diesel smoke, tired, jaded, soulless rot under a manic mask, built on the dunes fifty years ago and an old whore already. Safed, man! Okay? Dig Safed! Layers of history, yet glows like a young bride. Twisty streets, mountain views, Galilee air, mystic caves, Kabbalists. Then just down the road, there's Tiberias, Lake Kinneret, palm trees, fishing boats, Byzantine churches, groovy kibbutzim."

"But I can't go anywhere," Toni wails. "I have to go to *ulpan*."

There is a long, speechless, fan-buzzing moment as her companions take this in, followed by laughter, bone-shaking, knee-slapping, teary-eyed laughter. But they're not being mean, their merriment embraces their little-big friend, so that now she too starts to giggle, starts to howl. The spark for the mirth no longer matters; it's the contagion, the fire. Laughter is like energy that excites molecules, causing them to collide and form new bonds.

Arm in arm, bumping hips, they saunter down Jaffa Road. David holds them close—Janet on his right side, Toni on his left—to form a solid unit, commandeering the sidewalk. How good to belong to a tribe of three. They hoot at the offended looks of passersby. Their feet follow the steady stream of shoppers, worshippers, soldiers, tour groups, schoolchildren, families on outings, all in a holiday mood and heading for the same destination, the heart of Jerusalem, the ancient city that lives within the massive stone walls. At the arched portal of Jaffa Gate, the crowd bunches together as it presses through to the bustling flag-stoned plaza.

Saturday morning. In the Jewish part of town, metal shutters cover shop fronts and Sabbath stillness reigns, but here in the Arab city the markets boom. Delivery men trundle hand carts, vendors shout, barefoot boys balance trays of pita on their heads. Amid the swarm of tourists, black-hatted Hassidim rush toward the Wailing Wall and a group of pilgrims troops after a brown-robed monk.

"Dig this!" David shouts over the general commotion. "If I never see L.A. again, I'll die a happy man."

He pulls them into the stream of humanity squeezing itself through the narrow main street of the bazaar. "*Keef halak,*" he roars to the shopkeepers, pronouncing the Arab words of greeting deep in his throat with authentic flare. Dark-skinned faces break out in smiles.

There were times when Toni wondered about her welcome in the Old City. There were subtle, troubling signs—an aggressive tug at her sleeve, an old man's deliberately aimed gob of spit, a veiled woman's hard-eyed stare—but now she sees only the cheerful atmosphere of brisk commerce. Wearing a wide-brimmed straw hat, granny sunglasses, and a dreamy smile, Janet trails her fingers over the profusion of goods that spills out of stores: baskets, blouses, rugs, trinkets, sheepskin jackets still smelling of sheep. Vendors erupt with eager offers, "Please, lady. Come in. Take a look. Twenty lira, but for you, lady, fifteen."

As if called forth to demonstrate that all is peace and love in the Old City, a youth steps out of a doorway and throws himself at David with cries of joy. There are shouts and hand slaps. David presents Samir, the boy who has been giving him Arabic lessons. Samir has narrow hips and clear skin, with a ghost of a moustache on his adolescent upper lip and a smile like a neon sign. He wears a patterned short-sleeved shirt tucked neatly into tight black pants and battered plastic sandals, and he's good looking in his way, though he reminds Toni of the *chakh-chakh* in Zion Square. She imagines neither youth would be pleased with the comparison.

"You are most welcome here," Samir says, touching his forehead and his heart and nodding politely at Toni, then turning to Janet with a warm, worshipful gaze. His eyes linger on the red hair that billows from under Janet's hat. Toni is suddenly aware of how Janet's hair stands out in this world of covered-up women.

"*Walla!* You are a lucky man," Samir says to David. "You have two beautiful women and I have none."

He beats his chest with his fist. David laughs and Janet flashes a lovely, unself-conscious smile that makes Toni uneasy though she couldn't say why.

"Come with me," Samir urges. "I have something for you."

He takes them downhill to the part of the market covered by vaulted roofs where the air is dark and cool, penetrated only by narrow slits of sunlight. At last they stop at a tiny record shop with Arabic music albums displayed in crates and racks in the store's entrance. The album covers show musicians dressed in formal suits playing ouds, violins, flutes, accordions, and some instruments Toni has never seen before. Samir chooses a record with a photo of a matronly woman in a glittering gown. At his bidding, they sit on low stools in front of the shop, sipping cardamom-scented coffee in miniature cups while a throaty, passionate female voice wails from the shopkeeper's record player. David listens intently, swaying in his seat. Samir sings along while gazing at Janet and holding the side of his head in an attitude of ecstasy. To Toni, the music sounds as if it's on the wrong speed. Notes rise and dip and wobble. The strained look on Janet's face shows she's no fan either.

"You like?" Samir asks, when the song comes to an end.

"Not much," Janet admits.

"But that's Umm Kulthum!"

"The greatest female vocalist in the Arab world," David says.

"The greatest in the whole world," Samir corrects him. "You want to be a famous singer, Miss Janet, so you should learn from Umm Kulthum."

Janet rolls her eyes and David winks, as if begging for her indulgence.

When they are ready to leave the café, David proposes a walk along the ramparts at the top of the Old City walls. He and Samir lead the way, their heads leaning toward each other as they engage in conversation. Janet and Toni follow several paces behind, making their way over cobblestones worn slippery by multitudes of feet.

"Is he going to be with us the rest of the day?" Toni asks irritably. The blissful symmetry of the three of them together has been broken.

"Oh, he's not so bad," Janet laughs. "Samir's in love with the West, you know, even though he makes a big deal about his own culture. He's torn this way and that. Envies our freedom and prosperity, then overcompensates by lecturing me about Arabic music."

"I don't like the way he looks at you."

"He means no harm. Looks are free. I wouldn't let him ball me, though. I don't like him enough for that."

There is something in the matter-of-fact way Janet says these last words that shocks Toni into silence. As if a proposition has been made and rejected, but not, perhaps, with the finality one would hope for. And that harsh, crude phrase, *ball me*. She's relieved when they arrive at the foot of a thick tower in the crenelated walls, and she can focus her attention on the flight of steep, narrow stairs that twist up the tower.

The views from the top are magnificent. A landscape of fawn-coloured terraced hills dotted with olive groves rolls out to the south and east. A fainter line of hills marking the Judean desert shimmers in the distance. Within the walls lies a jumble of rooftops, TV antennas, graceful domes and minarets. David tells them how Jerusalem's walls had been breached many times until finally Suleiman the Magnificent built solidly enough to keep Christian invaders out. The defence held until the arrival of the British during the First World War.

"General Allenby got off easy. He never had to fight his way into the city, not like the Israelis did last year. By the time Allenby's army got here, the Turks had high-tailed it."

"The Jordanians, they abandoned us too," Samir says. Everyone turns to him in surprise. "Yes, they fought, but they began too late. And then they left us to be conquered." His tone is bitter, his eyes clouded.

"I thought you didn't like Jordanian rule," Janet says.

"The Jordanians, they neglect us, yes. But now is worse. Now we are under the rule of dogs."

Silence falls over the group. He notices their shocked faces and lifts his hands in supplication. "I don't mean you, of course. I mean the soldiers."

"Israel is full of soldiers," Janet says coldly. "It has to be."

"Yes," Toni spits. "Exactly."

"Hey man, you've got to see the big picture." David claps Samir on the back. "The Jews were meant to come back into their city. It's part of the Big Guy's plan." He points heavenward. "Anyway, the soldiers won't be around forever."

He adds some words in Arabic, but Samir smiles ruefully.

"Your Arabic is not so good, my friend. Even not in my language and not in yours, are you making sense."

Though he continues with them on the walk along the ramparts toward Dung Gate and the plaza in front of the Wailing Wall, he has become a brooding presence. When they reach the steps to the road filled with throngs heading for the plaza, Samir takes his leave and Toni isn't sorry to see him go.

The Wall, the *Kotel,* rises high and wide, ancient and everlasting. Crowds dance, sing, bob in prayer before this last remnant of the ruined Temple, destroyed 2,000 years ago, but never abandoned or forgotten. The Wall is a mirror of the Jewish people itself, Toni can't help thinking, a testimony to their endurance. Once, worshippers stood before the holy site in a garbage-strewn alley while shitting donkeys ambled past. Under Jordan's rule, Jews were banned altogether. But a year ago, the victorious Israelis bulldozed all the houses that crowded up against the Wall and built a plaza. Now there is space for celebrations, for busloads of tourists. A space illuminated by spotlights and guarded by discretely placed soldiers on rooftops.

"Far out," David yells, eyes shining, fist punching the air. His demeanour is unremarkable amid the general exaltation. A conga line of yeshiva boys dances by, earlocks flying. When they've passed, David pushes his way through the crowd to the section in front of the Wall, demarked by metal barriers, where the men pray. Toni and Janet see him greeted by a white-bearded fellow who hands him a prayer book and skull cap. Then he becomes one with the mass of bodies, jerking, swaying in prayer.

"Did you want to go up?" Janet asks.

"I'm not really religious."

"Me neither. But it's kind of cool to be there. Come with me?"

Janet, suddenly shy, glances up at Toni. It is a plea. *Oh*, a voice answers deep in Toni's heart.

Together they enter the smaller area sectioned off for women worshippers and find themselves up against the massive limestone blocks, smoothed to a golden sheen by countless hands through the ages. Above them, grasses and shrubs sprout from crevices, doves coo, swallows swoop. The entire lower reaches of the Wall bristle with little bits of paper on which supplicants have written prayers and wishes and stuck them into the gaps between the stones. Every so often one of these notes flutters to the ground like a fat snowflake to join the litter at their feet. It is said that the *Shekhinah*, the feminine emanation of God, hovers eternally by the Wall. *What nonsense*, Toni can hear her father say. *God reads notes?* And yet something is happening here, a thrum of energy. There is something so sweet and touching in the way

Janet places her palm against the block in front of them and bends her head in silent concentration, as do the dozens of women all around.

Out of the general hubbub, a divine voice emerges, high and fluid, a voice to melt stone. Janet's eyes remain closed as she sways and sings softly to herself and the bit of Wall in front of her face. Toni inches closer until her arm almost touches Janet's and then she recognizes the song—a big hit on Israeli radio, Biblical verses set to a peppy contemporary melody. Janet's voice gathers strength. She starts to snap her fingers. Women around them begin to murmur in consternation. "Quiet! Unseemly!" A woman must not distract the men on the other side of the metal barrier. The hissed chastisements egg Janet on. She sings louder. The men's section starts to rumble. David, who has edged closer to their side of the barrier, grins and gives a thumbs up. "Atta girl," his lips say. Janet tilts her head upward and lets her voice soar.

"Shame! Shame! Get away, you whore. This is a place of worship, not a concert hall."

Black-hatted men cover their ears. Others, with shaking fists, press against the barrier. Women swarm around Janet, who continues to sing, oblivious, it seems, while Toni pushes back with both hands at the crowd that would threaten Janet. Toni shoves and jabs and yells, enraged, trembling, and exalted because she's protecting Janet: Captain Goldblatt at the ready. Over her shoulder she catches sight of David, holding his laughter-filled belly.

Afterward, they celebrate with glasses of arak and dishes of pistachio nuts in a quiet courtyard of the Armenian quarter. "But maybe we shouldn't have, maybe one should…" Toni tries to collect her thoughts as her companions hoot and cackle while a sombre-faced waiter looks on.

"That moronic word again," David sneers. "*Should!*"

chapter 17

Toni's pocket holds the letter that came with her monthly allowance cheque. The page, filled with pointed questions in her mother's steeply slanted hand, brings to mind Lisa's manner of leaning forward with arms planted on the breakfast table, her strident voice. *Who are these new friends you spend so much time with? Why haven't you contacted Mrs Lieberman? Why don't you write more? Or call? Surely you can get hold of a phone at the dormitory.* Of late, Toni's letters home have indeed been sparse. Her mother has a knack for jumping to the wrong conclusions. At the bottom of the page, in the narrow space Lisa had left him, is the usual brief, courteous greeting from Toni's father. *Work hard. Watch out for the sun.* Etc. Toni skimmed the letter and cashed the cheque.

"She's such a snoop," Toni declares to her friends as they sit beneath the fig tree. "She's not even embarrassed about being a snoop. She says, 'A mother needs to know.'"

Late afternoon sunlight slants into the garden. Deep shadows pool. One of David's creations—a tin can head with glass bead eyes and a ragged smile—peers out of thick foliage.

"Can't let go of her baby," David says.

The table is covered with his cigarette-rolling apparatus: tobacco tin, grass pouch, papers. He deftly strews, rolls, licks, seals, makes a supply of tobacco-laced-with-pot joints for the three of them. He raises a knowing eyebrow. "She needs to live out her life through you. Needs to suck your blood." He makes a slurping, vampirish sound.

Toni is struck dumb by the ghoulish image, a harsher assessment of her mother than she actually meant. But maybe he's right. Lisa's expectations have been driven by reaction to old wounds and losses, deprivations and failures. And she's not unique. That whole generation tries to hitch a ride on its children's wings, and must be shaken off or no one will fly.

"My mother couldn't wait to get rid of me," Janet says. She flicks ash toward her plate and misses, and it scatters onto the table instead. "I'm the black sheep because I don't make nice. She told me to shape up or ship out. The cold bitch."

Toni stares, amazed. Her own mother could never be called cold. She remembers being clutched and sobbed over at the airport before leaving for Israel—embarrassing at the time, but not without its comfort. Poor Janet. And broke too. The lovers live on what? Some meagre savings. David's occasional sales of hash. Life is cheap in Israel, but still. An expansive wave of tenderness washes over Toni's heart. She reaches into her pocket, pulls out a wad of Israeli lira notes, and places it in a crumpled wad on the wicker table between Janet's and David's plates.

"For the food," she says. "I've been eating here every day."

The lovers exchange glances. The lavish pile of money far exceeds the value of the simple fare Toni has consumed with her pals.

"For the dope too," Toni adds, lest her offer be rejected. "Don't forget the dope."

She's ready to get down on her knees and beg them to accept. David tips back his stool, folds his hands behind his head, and closes his eyes in contemplation. His black hair, bound in a pony tail, gives him a sleek, canny look, like a wolf. Janet studies the purple bougainvillea that cascades over the back wall. At last David speaks.

"It's the nuclear family that screws people up. And the western obsession with individuality. Communes are the way to go. Everyone equal."

His big paw reaches out and pockets the money. Janet remains in her faraway trance, as if this transaction has nothing to do with her.

"So move in with us already," David says. "There's plenty of space."

For a moment, Toni thinks he wants her to move with them into the shed. She sees herself curled up at the foot of their mattress bed like a pet, like another piece of flotsam and jetsam in their room. But no, he means for her to rent a nook in the main house where Mrs Katz, a widow, lives alone. If she agrees, as David is sure she will, Toni would no longer have to schlep back home in the evenings to the dorms in Kiryat Hayovel on the western edge of town. After all, they have become a kind of family. An alternative family. The more David talks, the more inspired he appears, eyes burning, hands chopping the air. Janet's eyes are downcast. She lifts her head to peer at David, and a funny laugh falls from her lips, expressing something between incredulity and affection.

"You beautiful lunatic," she says.

Although she would have preferred a stronger endorsement, Toni allows herself a whoop of joy.

I'll make her see it was a good idea. I'll make her see.

At first, Mrs Katz drives an impossibly hard bargain for allowing Toni the privilege of sleeping on her living room couch and the use of a couple of shelves of a linen closet. But when David lets drop that Toni's parents are from cultivated German-speaking Europe, the old woman's bushy eyebrows shoot up in appreciation and her price drops. She herself hails from Frankfurt. She approves of Toni's short, sensible haircut, easily maintained through a cold-water wash over the bathroom sink. A well-bred, serious-minded person, Mrs Katz decides.

Not the type to squander hot water with absurdly long showers. Not like a certain someone. The wizened face scowls at the curtains of hair that tumble down Janet's shoulders. Janet rolls her eyes toward the ceiling. A deal is struck. Toni's signature joins the others on the rental agreement.

The first night in her new abode, Toni lies stiffly on the narrow couch, acutely aware of strangeness—the heavy, dark-wood furniture looming around her, its dull gleams, the snore of her landlady in the adjoining room, the erratic tick of a dying clock. A portrait of one of Mrs Katz's relatives reminds Toni of Grandma Antonia. Toni vividly envisions the stern face, though it has been years since Grandma's picture was anything more to her than a brown shape on her parents' bedroom dresser. Now, once again, Grandma stares through the darkness, tight-lipped and inscrutable. Now she glides out of the picture frame and down the hall. She flies across the garden, cackling as she goes, to stand before the shed where the lovers lie enfolded together. Her claw-like hands grasp the handles of the metal doors. She rattles and rattles until Toni's eyes fly open to behold a shaft of dawn light penetrating the shutters of the living room window above her couch. An early bird peeps plaintively as if it wants to come in.

Pulling on a sweatshirt, Toni creeps into the garden, which is misty and grey, cool and slightly damp with dew. She lowers herself onto a wicker stool and watches as shapes gradually reveal themselves: the long spiny spears of an agave plant, the lobed leaves of the fig tree, the gentle outline of the garden wall, the latched metal doors of the shed. She sits and waits and sometimes she paces. At last the doors of the shed scrape open. Janet staggers out, pale and squinty-eyed, holding her hands up against the blinding light of day. "Gotta pee," she growls as she lurches past Toni across the yard. Janet is not a morning person. David emerges soon afterwards, bare-chested, flinging back his arms in a luxurious stretch, and then cocks his head quizzically at Toni, at the flush creeping up her cheeks.

"I wanted to see the sunrise," Toni says.

"Hm," David muses, rubbing his thumb up and down in the cleft of his chin, while in his eyes there's an intelligent gleam.

chapter 18

Kotz, Michal scrawls on the blackboard and stabs her finger against her palm to indicate a thorn. "*Ketz,*" she says with hand-wiping gestures that cause Toni's classmates to murmur knowingly: "the end." "*Kayitz,*" the teacher declares as she points through the window at the white-hot sky of summer. Toni listlessly copies the three words that share a common root and are bound in a web of connotations. Summer means the end of the growing season in the arid Middle East, the time of scorched earth and the rule of thorns. Her classmates call out other words related to the root letters that Michal has underlined, but Toni's gaze drifts to the window that looks toward the wadi and the beckoning treetops of Beit HaKerem in the distance. Yes, thorns pierce the flesh like summer's heat pierces the body as the end of love would pierce the heart, she muses. When her attention returns to the moment, she finds the class has gone on to discuss other subjects. She's behind in all the lessons but can't make herself care. Time creeps so slowly in *ulpan.* At last she is free to dash out the door.

Janet barely looks up when Toni arrives. She's seated on the mattress amid a chaos of bedding and sheet music, coaxing notes from her guitar.

"Shit, shit, shit," she moans when her fingers slip and a bass string squawks. She's trying something difficult, a Spanish-sounding melody with complicated rhythms and arpeggios. Her left hand splays awkwardly over the frets. As quietly as she can, Toni lowers herself onto the battered leather hassock to listen. David's off somewhere in the hills on his own, so she and Janet are alone. *Sing,* Toni wants to say, but restrains herself. It's been a while since Janet made any effort with her music. Of late, she's been sleeping away half the day and spending the other in a trance of dope. "I'm so lazy," she said one evening when David proposed a hike into town. She leaned way back on his arm so he had to hold her up or she would have fallen over. She was like a rag doll, with her head upside down, her hair dangling.

Now, Toni hunches forward to lose herself in the lovely ripple of guitar notes, in the warm tones of Janet's hair, the dance of freckles on her face. Six on Janet's forehead, three on her chin, that one in the bow of her lip, dozens on her cheeks. Counting seems almost like touching.

A squeak. A buzz. The music stops.

"Why can't I play? Why can't I play?"

Janet rubs her sweaty hands against her shorts. She thunks her head backward against the wall, causing Toni to feel the "ow" in her own skull.

"You need a break," Toni urges.

Janet flings the guitar away from herself onto the bed, where it falls with a groaning hum. She stomps over to the record player in the corner, clicks it on, drops the needle onto the groove of a spinning LP. Judy Collins' pure soprano singing "Both Sides Now" pours into the room.

"Listen to that," Janet says miserably. "She's so good, she's not even human."

"But you're just as good. Better!" Toni cries out, though Janet frowns, as if the overblown compliment distresses her. How could Janet, golden-throated Janet, doubt herself? "I love your voice."

Janet picks up a hand mirror from the clutter on the bed and studies her own face.

"Maybe I should get that chemical peel my mother always wanted me to have."

"What!"

"I look like a bowl of cornflakes. Especially in this climate."

"I love your freckles."

Janet barks out a laugh. Her knuckle grazes the spot on her lip in an unconscious erasing gesture.

"I'm glad someone does. Ah, shit." The mirror skids across the floor. Janet's shoulders slump. "I don't know what's wrong with me. I just wish I could … I just wish …"

"What do you wish? Tell me. Tell me."

Janet seems on the verge of pained revelations. Toni moves to the edge of the bed, trembling with eagerness to hear, to know, to console. She reaches out her hand despite the acid voice inside that tells her to stop. Too late. When Janet raises her head, a guarded look has come into her eyes, a wariness that chills.

"Let's go find David," Janet says crisply and jumps to her feet.

He is not hard to find. He's seated upon the low wall of a lookout in the nearby Jerusalem forest, engrossed in a book. The lookout is on a summit, affording splendid views of tree-covered slopes, the soldiers' cemetery below, and brown, uncultivated hills in the distance. Every tree around them was planted in recent decades by the young state of Israel—part of the pioneering effort to transform barren lands into a sea of green. It is a beautiful, if unnatural-looking, forest of wind-sculpted pines and pointy cedars, all much the same size. The trails are dotted with plaques to Zionist notables and donors. David has mocked the bloated dedications: "The Leonard and Mintzy Sugerman Grove. In appreciation of their generosity, blah, blah." Yet it is here, at this popular lookout, he often positions himself. A shaft of late-afternoon sunlight penetrates the branches above to gild his bowed head. You'd think he'd planned for them to find him thus.

When he looks up, his glittering eyes still hold that other world of the spirit he's been immersed in: Hasidic tales, mystical teachings.

"These guys blow my mind."

David waves his book aloft and giggles with nervous energy. "Their stories shake you, wake you. I might join a Hasidic sect. I could get into that. The Conservative Judaism I grew up with is pablum. But this stuff is *real*."

"David," Janet says, looking him straight in the eye, "I'm going back to Tel Aviv."

She's breathless from her quick tramp uphill, and the words have tumbled out, more abruptly than she meant them to, perhaps. Now she stands, feet apart, arms across her chest, and waits. Toni stands stricken. Janet's news is a blow to the gut. But after lowering the book to his lap, David just cocks his head and gazes back evenly. The excitement has vanished from his eyes, replaced by something dull and hard.

"Okay," he says.

"Okay?"

"If that's what you want."

His mouth smiles.

"Will you come too?"

"No," he answers. He draws the word out, the tone reproving, like a parent telling a child it can't have that toy and ought to know better. His face continues to smile in that bland, distancing way. When Janet remains silent he adds: "This is where I've got to be." He inhales deeply, as if to indicate the nourishing, soul-expanding quality of the air of Jerusalem. "This is where I can breathe."

"Well, I can't. I'm suffocating. I'm stagnating."

"If that's how you see it." He shrugs.

Janet's stance wilts. Gazing bleakly at the hills, she looks like someone who has painted herself into a corner. Neither of them pays any attention to Toni, whose nails dig deeply into her agitated palms. They don't consult Toni because, after all, this doesn't concern her. It's between the two of them. None of her business.

And just like that—through a word, a look—their tribe of three is blown apart, all these weeks of togetherness, chaff in the wind.

She attempts to give them space, so they can spend their last days together, so they can't blame her for interfering. She hears urgent murmurings, long silences. She knows it makes no sense, but at some level she blames herself for driving Janet away. Was it not that moment when her craving for closeness came to the surface—*What do you wish? Tell me*—that tipped Janet over the edge? Despair whispers that this is so, every waking moment. Now, she slips away early to *ulpan* and returns late. She passes like a ghost through the kitchen and avoids their communal place beneath the fig tree. She hopes that Janet is just a little bit aware of her sacrifices.

One evening, David shouts into the house, "Goldblatt, get your ass out here."

A bottle of arak, glass tumblers, and dishes of snacks cover the wicker table in the centre of the garden. The candles flicker in the clay lanterns that hang from the tree. It's party time, a final blow-out to bid goodbye to Janet and wish her well in her new life in the gritty, party town of Tel Aviv. David raises his glass in a toast: to Janet, to freedom, to life. Janet, wearing a dazed smile, chugs back her drink.

"We'll miss her, won't we?" says David, shooting Toni a look of keen insight. "But when you love someone, you've got to let her go."

Toni gulps from her glass. Arak and water, a milky mixture, deceptively smooth. It numbs sadness as it fires the belly.

Although the fierce heat of an August day has abated, the air still feels clotted and nothing stirs—not a leaf, not a withered blade of grass. It is one of those nights when people drag mattresses onto their roofs, complaining they can't draw a proper breath indoors. From the top of the garden wall a feral cat yowls, and the sound is like a distillation of all the longing in the world. David throws his head back to produce a startlingly realistic imitation. Janet offers her own rendition, her lips puckered into a tremulous "O." Toni falls off her stool to collapse in hysterics at Janet's feet. Just like old times. Tomorrow is a mirage. Only now exists.

They drink and eat and smoke and *kibbitz*. Then Janet jumps up, teeters a moment, and executes a shuffling dance-step toward the shed whose doors stand open, revealing the deeper darkness inside.

"I wanna listen to some music, you guys. Something groooovy."

"I've got just the ticket," David says, flashing his teeth in a swash-buckler's smile. "Guy I met the other day gave me an album of a California band. Far out stuff. Where d'you think you're going, Goldblatt? Party's not over yet."

Gathering Janet and Toni in a wide embrace, he ushers them both over the threshold of the room. He switches on a small lamp whose shade is draped with a crimson shawl so that the light cast is a soft, lurid glow. He squats and rummages through the records spilled around their portable record player, there's a crackle of static as he drops the needle into place, and then the room fills with the most outlandish sound. Electric guitars squeal and groan, drums crash, the tempo is erratic, fast to slow to one high-pitched note pulled out like a scream. David stands in the middle of the room and starts to sway.

"Acid rock. The real trip."

He punches a fist in the air as he dances, his black hair swishing back and forth over his face. Janet watches a moment, then steps forward with a defiant grunt. Her limbs hang loose, she shakes, shimmies, flings herself about, competing with David in the game of wild abandon.

"Come on, girl. Get in the groove."

David pulls Toni into the circle. After a few faltering steps she becomes accustomed to the screeching, discordant music. It has penetrated her entire body. She becomes the yowl, the shriek, the shudder of the instruments, though she's nowhere near as loose as the other two. Still, they're all connected, energized by one another and the unearthly electronic sounds. Drops of sweat fly from David's forehead. He strips off his shirt and clasps his hands behind his head, displaying his lean, tanned chest. Janet meets his eye and pulls off her own top, then her bra, tossing the garments behind her into a corner. All she wears now are her shorts and a string of glass beads that swings one way as her bare breasts, startling white against a ruddy tan, swing the other. The beads clack together like snapping teeth.

Toni drops her eyes, lifts them again, unable to stop staring at the wild, passionate, essential Janet. She takes a panicked step toward the open door. Suddenly there's not enough air in the room. Her heart pounds like a crazed animal. A stifled shriek escapes from behind her clenched teeth.

"She's freaking out," David says in the steady voice of a doctor delivering a diagnosis. Janet stares blankly while David grasps Toni's arms, gently pushing her toward the mattress on the floor. This takes an eternity, the long journey backward, step by step, until the edge of the mattress bumps against her ankles and she collapses under David's weight. His strong hands grip her shoulders, forcing her to lie still. The ceiling spins, the walls squeeze inward, sweat trickles down her sides. She's crying now, with hard, dry sobs that wrack her breast.

"Easy, easy," David purrs, then to Janet, "Get over here. Hold her hand. She's really freaking out."

Obediently, the half-naked Janet comes to sit on the other side of the mattress, leaning over Toni and crooning "Easy, easy," adopting David's tone while she limply holds Toni's hand in her own. Through her tears Toni sees Janet's bewildered face framed by a mass of frizzled hair. Two blobs of mascara run from the corners of Janet's eyes. The San Francisco band still screams from the record player.

"What is it, girl? What's bugging you? Let it out." David coaxes, his

American-accented "out" sounding like a sympathetic "ow."

"I want … I want … " Toni moans, surprised to hear herself, because it's not her, it's some trapped creature calling from the depths.

"Go ahead. Say it," David urges. He massages her right palm with his strong thumb while his glowing eyes fix on hers. "You've been bottling up your feelings for so long, haven't you, little girl? I know. We know, don't we, Janet? It's okay. Let it flow."

Abruptly Toni's tears stop. The feeling of being seized by the throat is back. David turns to Janet.

"Kiss her."

Janet regards him open-mouthed. She's drunker than Toni realized. Her face wears a bleary, unfocussed expression. But to Toni's surprise, Janet leans forward and kisses her, a quick, light brushing of the lips. The cool glass beads tickle Toni's neck. She's too astonished to say a word.

"You call that a kiss? That prissy little thing? Come on, Janet, do it right," David sneers. "Don't be such a prude."

"What's going on, David?" Janet asks slowly, a suspicious look dawning on her face. She sits up, arms crossed over her naked chest. "What are you doing?"

"I'm trying to help our little friend here. Have a heart. She's a virgin, for Chrissake." He says this as if virginity were an affliction. Toni tries to struggle off the bed, but David wraps his arms around her from behind, as if she were a mental patient to be subdued.

"Easy, easy, girl. Trust me."

Janet looks past Toni, fixing David with a hurt and hostile look.

"Leave her alone. This isn't funny."

"That's right. It isn't. There's a tortured soul here. All closed up like a fist. She needs you, Janet. Loosen up." David sounds genuinely mournful, as if he himself were the lovelorn supplicant. Toni stops struggling and looks for Janet's answer, wondering despite herself, what if? What if Janet could be persuaded to kiss her properly?

"Come on," he urges.

Janet chews her lips, and her eyes dart from Toni to David. Then her face hardens and her fist swings wildly. She misses him and clips Toni smartly on the ear.

"You pig."

"That's not very nice, Janet," David, says releasing Toni. "You hurt our little friend."

"And suppose we get off on each other, eh?" Janet shouts. "What if we decide to leave you out? Zee two vimmen, zey are so beautiful together! Ooh-la-la!" she says. "So what do we need you for?"

And before he can respond, she rises up on her knees and kisses Toni again, harder, more deliberate this time, trembling with anger, her chin colliding with Toni's. Yet her lips are soft as rose petals, as Toni always imagined they would be. When the kiss is over, Toni falls backward. From the far corner of the room comes the shrill wail of an electric guitar being fingered on the high notes.

"Cool. You chicks go for it. I'm already gone."

David rolls off the bed to rummage on the floor for his shirt. "I wasn't angling for anything," he adds in an aggrieved tone. "You've got a petty streak in you, Janet. I just want us all to be happy. Free of hang-ups."

Standing above them now, his shirt hooked on his forefinger and hanging over his shoulder, he addresses himself to Toni.

"You're not going to chicken out, now, are you? You've got to act. You can't just dream."

Looking from him to Janet, seeing Janet stiffen, Toni lunges forward like someone trying to grab a prize at the same time she realizes it's all wrong, insane. But her body is already in motion. Before she can stop herself, she plants a sloppy kiss on Janet's lips. No, not her lips. The side of her mouth. Janet wipes her face with the back of her hand and regards Toni in frosty silence. Suddenly they are back at camp, in that other crazy moment of drunken collision. Leaping to her feet, Janet snatches the scarlet shawl draped over the lampshade, wraps it around her bare shoulders, and stomps from the room. Her back retreats across the garden. She yanks open the back door to the main house and shuts it firmly behind her. David shrugs, a gesture that says, *Hey, I tried, didn't I, didn't I try my best?* The lamp, robbed of its fine, red-cloth covering, reveals a plain, parchment-coloured shade, scorched on one side. The light cast is harsh and cold, exposing the ugliness of the topsy-turvy room. The San Francisco band continues to grind out another variation of its plaintive, cacophonous howl.

Janet has slept on Toni's couch in the living room. David has withdrawn to the garden with a blanket and pillow (but not before he first cocked his head to Toni in invitation and grinned at her appalled rebuff). Toni has the turquoise room to herself. Mercifully, much of the night is gone. For a while she sinks into stunned sleep, wakes to a raging thirst and needlepoints of sunlight poking through the slits of the metal doors. She's trapped in a dream. *How did I get here, how do I get out?* The turquoise-painted walls have turned a sickly colour, like the powdery bloom of bread mould. Despite her pounding head, she hurries into the house to kneel beside Janet's blanket-wrapped figure on the couch. The eyelids flutter open, revealing red and teary eyes. They shut again quickly.

"Janet, I'm sorry."

Empty, used-up words.

Janet's hair is a bird's nest tangle. Smudges of makeup linger on her pale cheek. Yet she appears particularly beautiful now, concentrating with all her might on some private place inside herself, her fine bones showing beneath her skin. And merely witnessing this seems another transgression.

"Goodbye," Toni says, stepping backward.

Janet remains tense beneath her sheet with her eyes squeezed shut. It's clear she has no intention of opening them again until Toni has taken her sorry, unwanted self away.

chapter 19

She has to laugh at the name: Hotel Vienna. There's nothing remotely Viennese about this dingy room with the cracked, smoke-grimed ceiling, the tattered bedspread complete with cigarette burn-holes she can put her thumb through, the drunkenly tilted wardrobe, the naked walls, and dusty floor. A faded sign above the hotel entrance, tucked away on a side-street off Jaffa Road, beckons to transients and lowlifes with little money and fewer expectations. Down the hall is a shared bathroom that reeks of urine and Flit bug spray. In the alley below, cats hiss and fight over scraps of garbage. But all this ugliness soothes in a way. Like a "fuck you" scrawled on a wall.

Lying atop the bedspread in the stillness of the morning, Toni takes perverse satisfaction in her surroundings. *Look at you, insect! You got what you deserve.*

The hotel room's squalor is partly her own. She has contributed scattered unwashed clothes and remnants of take-out meals. Her stale smells mingle with those of her predecessors. The one bright spot is the forty-ounce bottle of Stock brandy on the windowsill. She's saving that for tomorrow when downtown becomes deserted for the Sabbath and there's nothing else to do.

Gradually the city awakens. Traffic rumbles, feet hurry across the pavement, metal shutters over shops rattle open, newsboys call out the name of a local paper: *Ha'aretz! Ha'aretz!* She pulls on some clothes and slips downstairs into the lobby, trying not to draw the attention of the desk clerk, a young woman with heavy makeup, blood-red nails, and a suspicious pouting mouth, who always wants to know how long Toni plans to stay. Fortunately, her attention is elsewhere. "What's your problem?" the clerk barks into the phone. She doesn't notice when Toni steps past and out the front door.

She meanders this way, that way, while all about her people full of energy and purpose hurry to their daily tasks. She wishes she could do a better job of pretending to have somewhere to go. What if she's recognized? What if someone from the *ulpan*, or worse, David Konig, calls out from the throng? She imagines him tracking her. "Why are you avoiding me?" he would say, all innocent and hurt. "What's the big deal?" Her reedy figure would be easy to spot. More than ever she feels conspicuously tall—an anomaly in a land of short, compact people.

She veers off the main road and drifts toward the district of the ultra-orthodox. Jews dressed as they did in the nineteenth-century ghettos of eastern Europe spill through the streets, wearing black frock coats, black hats, flowing beards, and earlocks, *payot*, spiralling down the sides of their preoccupied, stern-looking faces. The men rush past her averting their eyes, as required by their strict code of conduct. Women in sack-like dresses and tight kerchiefs herd flocks of young children. Weeks ago—it seems like months—Toni came here with David and Janet on a Friday evening. They stood together on a street corner while the sky turned a luminous royal blue and the joyful clamour of prayer issued from a dozen synagogues. Now she passes the same little courtyard where they had stopped to peek into windows and spy on housewives fussing over the Sabbath meal preparations.

"*Golem!*" a shrill voice calls.

She turns, startled. There's no one in the courtyard but a very small boy seated on a doorstep. He has silky white-blond earlocks and a skullcap that covers his head like a black bowl. He sucks his fingers and stares at her with wide impudent eyes.

"What did you call me?" she asks the boy.

"*Golem*," he says again, unfazed.

Freak, monster, Toni silently translates to herself. A lava of words bubbles up in her brain. *You little shit, you pompous little asshole with your inherited pretensions to superior morality. I'll give you the evil eye like you've never seen before.* She gnashes her teeth, takes a step forward. The boy's face crumples. He runs across the courtyard blubbering, "Ima, Ima, Ima." The moment, for the short time it lasts, is ridiculously satisfying.

"I want to join the army," Toni declares.

Behind the desk in a big noisy room at the Ministry of Defence sits a girl soldier with officer's stripes on her shoulders. At other desks, girls in khaki uniforms type letters and answer phones.

"Why?"

The question erupts, brusque, incredulous, from the officer's mouth. A question Toni hadn't anticipated.

"Because, I … I love this country. This is my country."

The officer waits for further explanation. She has short, dark curls, cherub cheeks, a cupid mouth, and shrewd Slavic eyes. Her small, competent-looking hands are folded over the passport and other papers Toni has given her.

Taking a deep breath, Toni launches into a monologue in both Hebrew and English about her desire to become a real Israeli, to integrate totally, and about her admiration for the military, her patriotism. As she rattles on, her face prickles with heat despite the big ceiling fan that whirls above. The officer eyes her with intent curiosity.

"But you are enrolled at the university," she says. "You have the stipend for foreign students."

Toni stammers that she is willing to pay it back, that it doesn't seem fair that foreigners get a head start at the university while Israelis have to go to the army first. The officer's brow furrows.

"Fair? You have funny ideas. If you are entitled to something, why not take it?"

She leans forward confidingly, eyes brightening, and says she herself intends to study abroad one day. Paris. London. Has Toni ever been? She smiles for the first time in their conversation. The digression strikes Toni as some kind of test. She swallows hard and tells the officer her goal is not merely the standard two years in the army but an additional year with the pioneering brigade that sets up border settlements. She's willing to go wherever posted. She's not afraid of death. Her interlocutor draws back with a frown at the word "death."

"You must take a psychological test to join the army," she says sharply. "Did you know that?"

"Yes," Toni lies. "I know." She hopes the officer doesn't notice the blood draining from her face.

"Let me ask you a frank question." The officer leans forward again. Her eyes narrow. "Have you been drinking?"

Toni jerks up in her seat. "No!"

Well, maybe a bit, she has to admit. Hours ago. But she's not drunk. She'll take any test to prove it. Sweat from her armpits trickles down her sides.

"I suggest you think this over a little longer," the officer says. "Talk about it with your parents." She pushes Toni's papers forward, wrapping up the interview.

"I'm rejected for the army?" Toni tries to keep her voice steady.

The officer makes that "*tzuk*" sound, that disdainful click of the tongue. "It's not for me to reject or accept," she says with a shrug. "We have nothing to do with recruitment here. You wandered into the wrong department. I'll give you the address. But I suggest you not make a hasty decision. The army is not as romantic as you think. Look!" She motions to the typing clerks behind her. "Does this look romantic?"

The officer rises and calls for one of the typists to accompany Toni back outside. "Good luck," she says.

The flash of pity in her eyes hurts more than if she'd uttered words of contempt.

The Arab boy, Samir, is here, in her room. He found her stumbling around the warren of alleys in the Old City at dusk. He could see she was sad. And lost perhaps? He offered to help. He said it was not good for a girl to walk the dark streets alone. She let him lead her up from the belly of the market to Jaffa Gate and then she let him follow her all the way to Hotel Vienna, up the dim stairway, into her room. She didn't care.

Now Samir does a little wiggling barefoot dance around the room, one hand on his stomach, the other waving above his head, and Toni can't help but laugh. Her first real laugh shared with another human being in what seems an eternity. They collide together in hilarity.

"You are a fine girl, Miss Toni, very fine and beautiful too. Perhaps no one has ever told you about your special beauty? You must not be sad."

His eyes glow with the ardour he once bestowed on Janet, a look hungry and pleading, but also a bit ruthless, inflamed by a need not easily thwarted. She couldn't care less about this either. Tipping her head back, she guzzles the last of her brandy from the bottle and wipes her numb mouth with her numb hand. As soon as she puts down the empty bottle, he's on top of her, squirming, tugging, panting, struggling with buttons. His eyes express urgency, and also the astonishment of someone who cannot believe his luck. He murmurs words in Arabic that sound like endearments. To her surprise, he says her name. *Toni.* It strikes her as odd that he should remember her name.

His fumbling fingers tell him she is a virgin, which he acknowledges with happy cries. A Jewish virgin, a Western girl, offering him the gift of paradise. But he must not reveal his inexperience. He must pleasure her too. She senses this thought dawn on him as he attempts to kiss her. A mouth like warm glue.

"Hurry up before I change my mind," she growls.

She hasn't a smidgeon of doubt that she could roll him off the narrow bed and fling him onto the hard-tiled floor if she wanted. But she chooses to remain passively spread-eagled instead. She wants free of her virginity. Away with it, away with fairy tales of virginal innocence and Prince Charmings. Be gone, too, the myth of wedding-night tenderness. Such tales have nothing to do with her, never did. But this hard, sordid pain she's invited into herself, courtesy of Samir, is truly her own experience. This is something she can fully possess.

And now she floats away to another place, another time, a damp forest floor with Arnold straddled on top of her, trying to break her will with his punishing thumbnail. *I win*, says her unfeeling flesh.

A few wild thrusts and Samir is done. The dead weight of his spent body sinks heavily onto her own. She pushes him off roughly, lets him know it's time to leave. The molten bliss in his eyes hardens into a look of displeasure. She is telling *him* to leave? Yes, he'd better go before the hotel manager comes to kick him out. She's not supposed to have guests, certainly not male ones. Samir scoffs at the warning, as well he might, since Hotel Vienna is clearly the kind of place where all manner of trysts occur. The mist of romance in his face has totally vanished.

"You are hairy," he sneers, with a contemptuous glance between her legs. "Like a monkey. Arab girls remove all that hair before they give themselves to a man. I have drunk from a dirty cup."

"Get out," Toni roars. "I'll call the police."

She's on her feet, the whole stark-naked length of her towering above the bed, brandishing the bottle she so recently drained.

He wastes little time in pulling on his pants, nervously opening the door a crack, and peeking into the corridor. He casts a stern look in her direction as if to say, *I'm not running away, see, and I'm certainly not letting you boot me out, because I'm the one in charge here.* Then he scampers down the stairs.

She is alone with the thick smells, the lingering ache in her groin, the dingy smoke-grimed room. On the ceiling above her head, a riot of insects executes an endless dance of repetitive loops.

Hours later, she wakes to the noise of pounding on the door, a coarse female voice shouting, "Open up. Open up."

Toni's head feels like a well-kicked soccer ball, her tongue like burnt toast. The woman refuses to identify herself and keeps pounding until Toni opens the door a crack. The clerk from downstairs stands upon the threshold, arms crossed over her chest.

"I need the room," she says curtly. Her eyes roam up and down Toni's scantily clad body and scrutinize the havoc beyond. Her mouth wears a nasty little smile. "You have to leave."

"What? Now? Why? I paid you. I paid you yesterday for the whole week."

"I don't want you here anymore."

Her sandaled foot taps the floor. She scowls with sour self-importance.

"But why?"

The clerk bares her teeth, the same grimace she uses when she aims her spray of Flit at a scuttling cockroach.

"Don't pretend innocence with me, *habibti.* That boy last night. I know where he's from. You sleep with Arabs. You can do whatever you want, but not in my hotel."

Your hotel? The question floats into Toni's mind, but she's too stunned to say a word.

To telephone overseas is no simple matter. She has to go to the Central Post Office, wait in a long queue to book her call. The huge, vaulted hall, built in the British mandate days, booms with echoing voices, a mirror of the chaos in her head. When her turn comes at last, the man behind the window tells her she's in luck. Usually, one has to wait hours, even days, but a phone line has become available. She can go directly into the booth. "Well, do you want it or not?" he snaps, seeing her hesitation. She enters the cubicle.

Fear grips her heart as she waits for the connection to go through. Not that she doesn't want to talk to her parents. She does, she's been longing to hear them again—her mother's passionate exclamations, her father's dry cough and reserved questions about her health. She aches for the reassuring familiarity. But what to tell them? She hasn't been able to string a story together.

I want to go home.

But why? What happened?

I have no money, nowhere to live.

But how can that be?

No matter what explanation she concocts, she suspects the hurricane blast of parental concern will be more than she can bear. She hopes that somehow, through the course of the conversation, the right words will come.

The phone's metallic cry, reverberating through the cubicle, runs through her like a jolt of electricity. She picks up the receiver. Through the hiss and crackle, she hears her mother.

"Toni? Is that you? *Gott sei dank!* Thank God, thank God, you called at last. I've been trying to reach you for days, but no one could tell me where you were. You disappeared off the face of the earth. I've been going crazy."

"Mama, it's okay," Toni says, her voice shaking. "I'm all right, everything's all right."

"Oh, my poor child, my poor child."

"Don't worry, Mama. Calm down."

An agonized sob vibrates in Toni's ear. Toni's neck prickles at an uncanny thought. Her mother's sixth sense! Does she know? Has she had visions of her daughter at Hotel Vienna? Impossible! Yet a sick foreboding invades Toni's gut. Something's going on.

"Mama?"

"Oh, Toni, Toni."

The voice fades.

"What is it, Mama?"

Dead air. Toni wonders if the connection has been suddenly interrupted. Then her mother again, loud and clear, though trembling.

"Your father, Toni. Something terrible has happened."

Who is this hysterical, blubbering creature at the other end of the line? She's not the mother Toni has known all her life. Why doesn't her father take the receiver out of her hand? Why doesn't he do something to bring her back to normal?

Part IV

Loulou's

chapter 20

Two strange figures await her amid the throng on the other side of the glass partition in the arrivals hall of Dorval Airport. A man's hand shoots up in a wave. Toni pushes forward through the automatic doors, through the gauntlet of greeters.

"*Mein kind!*"

A small, frail body collapses against her, arms cling, a head of permed hair shakes beneath Toni's chin, tears soak through her shirt. Toni awkwardly pats the heaving shoulders. The noisy crying seems to last forever. People are forced to step around the bottleneck created by the long, gangly girl and the little bawling woman. To Toni's relief, this woman, this mother transformed into a sobbing alien, finally lets go to fish for a Kleenex in her purse. She seems small and crumpled. The man who stands beside her, a burly, sweaty-faced fellow in a dark suit, steps forward, half smiling, half grimacing. His moist brown eyes shine with sympathy.

"I am your Uncle Franz, Francesco they call me in Italy. I wish I could have met my dear niece in better circumstances." He speaks a carefully enunciated English. The accent is similar to that of her parents. He encloses Toni's hand in his two big paws and squeezes so hard it almost hurts. "Be strong," he says hoarsely. "Your mother needs you now."

Her mother has covered her wet eyes with a pair of white-rimmed sunglasses too big for her face and a bad match for her smart black dress. The choice of accessory is so unlike what she would naturally wear that Toni wonders if she picked up someone else's sunglasses by mistake. Now the drawn face with the large dark shades tilts up at her, looking almost comical, like something out of *Mad Magazine.*

"I'm afraid we have to rush, dear. Franz will take your suitcase and get the car. I brought you some clothes. From Mrs Shmelzer. She picked out what she thought suitable from her racks. Very kind. Hopefully they will fit. You're thinner than I remember, but the tan is nice. We'll both go together to the ladies room. Come!"

With each sentence Lisa seems to recover her composure a bit more so that the last word, though a croak, sounds almost like her old self. She hooks her arm in Toni's and, half-leaning on her daughter, half pulling, leads her down the hall toward the washroom. Behind the locked door of the cubicle Toni unpacks a large paper bag with tissue-wrapped parcels: a black wool jacket and skirt, a satiny gold blouse, pantyhose. The shoes are in a separate plastic bag. Dress flats with a satin bow. Vaguely she remembers them and the last time she wore them, at her high-school graduation. Her mother must have dug the shoes out from the back of Toni's closet.

"How am I supposed to wear this outfit?" she complains. "It's gotta be ninety degrees outside."

Lisa is silent on the other side of the partition.

"Mama, are you still here?"

A loud snuffle.

"It's the best we could do," her mother says shakily. "The fall fashions are in. No summer things left. You don't have to wear them for long. But hurry, please. *Ach, Ach!* We're late."

Standing barefoot on the cool bathroom tiles, Toni wrestles with the pantyhose, tight as tourniquets, while the crotch hangs down to mid-thigh. Nothing else fits well either, the skirt too loose, the jacket too short. The floor heaves up and down with the motion of the plane still lodged in her body. Her mother paces outside the cubicle. Click,

click, click, go her high-heeled shoes. Toni remembers being a child in a department store dressing room, forced to try on some hateful new outfit, and not wanting to show herself, as she doesn't want to now. She just longs to slump down onto the toilet seat, give in to the wave of fatigue. But she can't, of course. The funeral has been delayed as long as possible. When she does emerge, her mother gives her only one swift distracted glance and Toni is relieved that, for once, her awkward appearance is beside the point. Together they rush to the waiting car.

"I told them you would come," Lisa says over and over as they drive down Decarie Boulevard to Paperman's Funeral Chapel. "They made noises that the burial should go ahead without you. I absolutely refused. What is the difference, a day this way or that?"

By "they" she means the rabbi, the Jewish burial society, the synagogue president.

"It is the Jewish law," Uncle Franz sighs as he steers with one limp hand guiding the wheel. His eyes gaze wearily at the busy road in front of them. He drives the Goldblatt family car much faster than Toni's father ever did, with a casual nonchalance, leaping from lane to lane. It occurs to Toni they might end up an interesting headline for tomorrow's newspaper: *Fatal Crash on Way to Funeral*. Lisa echoes her thoughts.

"This isn't Rome, Franzel. Slow down before you kill us."

He smiles sheepishly and eases up on the gas pedal after passing a large, rattling truck.

"Burial must, if possible, occur within seventy-two hours," Franz continues. "Something to do with release of the soul."

"His soul will be happy to see Toni."

Her mother chokes on a sob and can't continue. She turns around in the front passenger seat and her gaze glues itself onto Toni's in a relentless, pleading way. Toni coughs hard into her fist so she doesn't have to keep looking into her mother's red-rimmed eyes. Just before they arrive at Paperman's, her mother dons a small black hat with a half veil. Toni is glad because the bottom part of her mother's face doesn't look as bad as the top part. The bottom half, with the freshly lipsticked mouth, almost seems normal.

She is amazed at the crowd in the funeral chapel, turns cautiously around in her front row seat. A full house. Who are all these men in suits and skullcaps, women in sober, elegant dresses with matching accessories? Faces she doesn't recognize. What do any of them have to do with her father? He never had friends. He was an intensely private man. He dealt with clients, exchanged pleasantries with neighbours, patted children and dogs, but that was it. Never did he go to anyone else's funeral. Yet here are all these proper-looking people, speaking in hushed tones, looking as if they know what to do and how to rise to this grand occasion: death.

The rabbi and the cantor arrive at the podium. The coffin is rolled in and the entire assembly stands in one great rustling motion. When everyone sits down again, the cantor begins to sing. He's a slight, pasty-faced young man with a trim black beard, a black hat, and a surprisingly powerful set of lungs. He pours out a mournful lament, the high tenor dripping emotion, burlesque in its grief. She wishes he would stop. Her father, were he here, would cringe too. "Weeping and wailing and gnashing of teeth," he would mutter. Beside her, Lisa quietly sniffles with her fist pressed against her mouth. Toni searches for some echo of feeling inside herself. Nothing. Silence.

The rabbi speaks of a good man, a family man, hard-working and successful, though he came to this country without a penny. A man who witnessed the disaster that befell our people in Europe, the greatest iniquity of modern times. And yet this man remained steadfast in his commitment to life and Jewish values. He was devoted to learning and books, amassed a large library. The rabbi fails to mention that not a single religious text graces her father's shelves. Gazing dramatically left and right, the rabbi continues in this vein, as if he wants to convince everyone, or perhaps just himself, of the logic of his statements.

After the service, Toni, her mother, and Uncle Franz climb into the back seat of the limousine that follows the hearse. There's just the three of them and the driver and all that empty space in between. They sit in silence, her mother pressed close. Toni wonders that her mother could find comfort in this robot of a daughter sitting rigid beside her. Raindrops zigzag across the limo's smoked glass windows. The rain seems to pull the heat up from the ground and the oxygen out of the air. A smell of steamy asphalt filters into the vehicle as they inch along. A funereal pace. For the first time, Toni understands what that means.

And now they stand in front of a neat, rectangular hole in the ground with a mound of sodden earth beside it and the coffin suspended on straps above. Black umbrellas have mushroomed all around. The rabbi chants a few more prayers. A worm wriggles near Toni's foot. The coffin is lowered by two workmen cranking a pulley. The rabbi throws in a shovelful of earth that hits the wood with a dark thud. He passes the shovel to Franz who sweats and grunts as he labours. Lisa totters forward, hoists the shovel with effort and manages to tip a bit of earth into the hole. Her mother's difficulty with the shovel strikes Toni as almost shameful. When her turn comes, she works with a fury, flinging earth into the grave, and doesn't stop until Franz gently takes her arm.

Back at the apartment for the *shiva*, Toni is once again astounded. Her home has been transformed. The living room has been rearranged so that the furniture circles like prowling wolves around two low chairs positioned against the faux fireplace. Platters of food cover the dining room table: bagels, lox, cheeses, pastries, fruit. There are people everywhere. She recognizes a few: Hadassah ladies, a woman from the Y, Mr and Mrs Jacoby who used to come for Passover. Mrs Shmelzer, hands clad in yellow rubber gloves, stands at the kitchen sink, ready to attack a stack of dishes. Mr and Mrs Cheung have wandered up from the duplex below. Their two young boys stare wide-eyed while sticking tightly to their parents' sides. Uncle Franz booms over the din, "... for a week, yes, only a week. Back to the business in Merano ... there are two of us, two brothers, but Wilhelm is not entirely healthy himself." Strangers jostle in the hall, line up for the bathroom. There are greetings and laughter and a party atmosphere. Her so-very-private father would be appalled. "*Ohne mich*," he would say, "without me," and would sneak off down the stairs. And she wants to follow, to find him, wherever he's gone. But other than his home and his office, where could he be? He had no other refuge.

Someone guides her to one of the low chairs, the seats of mourners, beside her mother. A plate of finger sandwiches is placed on her lap. "Eat!" someone commands. "You need your strength."

"Here is Elsa Eisemann." Her mother croaks like an old lady. "You remember Elsa, dear? She gave you a ride last year during the blizzard. Oh, Elsa, thank you. I know. There are no words. No, I don't believe the doctors did all they could. I will demand an inquiry ... when I'm a little more myself. Quick? Yes, it was quick. Merciful for him. For me, not so. Yes, thank God she's here. I thought I'd go mad."

Lisa grabs Toni's hand and a damp wad of Kleenex presses between their two palms. Mrs Eisemann's eyes brim with good will.

"If you need anything, dear, you know where I live."

Toni has no recollection of her whatsoever.

One by one, people come forward to lean over them, to nod or shake their heads or pull some kind of sad expression. Some, the men especially, look like they're at the dentist. Lisa makes it easier for them. She talks and talks, filling up uncomfortable silences. Although her voice is barely audible and she has to pause for deep breaths, she doesn't stop talking.

"His heart. Why his heart? He never had troubles with his heart. I found him pacing like a restless tiger, pale as porridge. He thought the burning pain was his ulcer. It would pass, he said. He didn't want to go to hospital. But when we arrived at the Jewish General, they made him comfortable and were going to do tests. And then, a young doctor comes over, and tells me he's gone. Just like that. I wanted to speak to the chief physician. That young doctor didn't look old enough to shave. But they told me it would do no good."

Over and over, Lisa relates disjointed details. To some of the women she relates how diminished her husband looked afterward when they allowed her to see the body, how shrunken, how shortened. "What did they do to him?" she wails and sinks onto the bosom of one of her friends.

Ladies kiss Toni's cheeks. Men pat her on the shoulder. People tell her she must be strong for her mother's sake. Toni tries to look strong. She squares her shoulders, clenches her jaw, ignores the cramps in her legs and the wooziness in her head. When she feels the urge to pee, she resists because, for some absurd reason, she's afraid to leave this spot beside her mother.

An odd-looking little man approaches them. He has soft, pink cheeks, silky grey hair to the nape of his neck, and bangs, like a minstrel from merry old England. A black beatnik beret adorns his head. He introduces himself as Richard Abbott, owner of Browsers' Paradise, a recently opened antiquarian bookstore on Park Avenue that Toni's father apparently visited several times in the past month.

"Such a fine man, he was," Mr Abbott says, clasping his hands together. Heavy rings gleam on the fingers of both hands. A paisley ascot billows from the collar of his pearl-grey shirt. He seems out of place amid all the soberly attired solid citizens in the room.

"I'm new to the business of antiquarian books," Mr Abbott says breathlessly. "Mr Goldblatt set up my accounts. He told me about the

shop he owned long ago in Vienna. I told him we should become partners. He thought I was joking, but I wasn't. Oh, I would have liked him
for a partner. A practical man. But he had his sentimental side too, as
all collectors do."

Mr Abbott hesitates and appears wistful. He waves his ringed hand
at Toni. "Do come down to the store sometime, my dear."

Then he slips away into the crowd. Lisa gazes after him scornfully.

"Your father would have never taken any kind of partner, let alone
an odd duck like that."

Mr Cheung and his tiny wife approach. His English is better than
hers and she appears very shy, so he does the talking while she simply
nods again and again, a frozen smile on her anxious-to-please face.

"We brought some chow mein. I put in the fridge."

His round face gleams with perspiration as if speaking these words
has cost him great effort.

Lisa thanks him profusely, putting her hands out to both of them.
When they have turned their backs, she wrinkles her nose at Toni. Lisa
hates Chinese food. She used to complain to Julius about the foreign
smells seeping up through the front hall.

A sampling of desserts is placed on Toni's lap. Suddenly weak
with hunger for sugary things, she begins to stuff herself. She can't
get enough. Cherry Danish, fudge brownie, pecan tart. Her mouth is
full of caramel cream when she sees a familiar duo emerge from the
press of bodies in the room. A jolt of recognition shoots down her
spine—the Nutkevitch twins, Angela and Sharon. The sweetness on
Toni's tongue turns to mud. She is trapped with her back to the wall.
The twins glide inexorably toward her and then, since all chairs are
occupied, they sink to their knees on either side of her like supplicants
before a throne. Toni hastily swallows and rubs her sticky fingers together.

"Hi, Toni. Remember us?" one of them murmurs softly.

They are chic and magazine-cover gorgeous as always, in dark, well-cut (but not identical) silk suits, their lovely faces framed by glossy brown shoulder-length hair. Their brows knit with concern. If their purpose is to mock her, they are doing a good job, because the sympathy act appears sincere.

"So sorry about your father."

"I can't imagine what you're going through."

"Mum reads all the obits. She told us. We couldn't believe it."

"No one in our family has died yet. Both our *bubbehs* and *zaydehs* are still alive."

There is a pause as they wait for Toni to respond.

"Yeah, well, almost no one in my family is," Toni says. "Alive, I mean. Just about everyone is dead."

She breaks into a chuckle, as if this were a very good joke. The girls' mouths drop open. They look shocked, but awed and humbled too, as if confronted with a stupendous mystery, a horror they can't possibly grasp, and are aware of their own inadequacy.

"I'm so sorry," one of the twins whispers in a hushed voice. "I wish … I don't know what to say."

Toni bites her lips over her own idiocy. The twins aren't here to mock. How could she think such a thing?

"That was stupid of me. I'm sorry. It's not so bad," she finishes lamely. A twitch awakens in her cheek. They are still gazing up at her in reverence.

"Don't sit on the floor, for Godsakes. There must a chair somewhere." Toni glances around wildly, but all the seats are taken by older people who surround her mother.

"It's okay." A hand lightly touches hers. "We don't mind. I'm Sharon, by the way. It's still hard to tell us apart, I know." She smiles and waggles her fingers in greeting and Toni notices a glittery flash—a diamond ring. Is it possible she's married?

"We heard you went to live in Israel and had to rush back because of your dad. How awful." Real tears shimmer in Angela's eyes.

"It's nice of you to have come," Toni says after another awkward silence.

"Of course we came," Sharon says, with genuine warmth. "We've known you and your parents since, since forever, even though it was just for little bits at a time. I remember your dad from when we lived on Maplewood. That nice hat with the little feather he used to wear. Remember that, Angie?"

Which hat are they talking about? The grey fedora with the blue and black feather, or the straw boater with the tiny tan-coloured plume? Or some other hat that long ago bit the dust? It seems important to know, but she can't bring herself to ask.

"It seems like ages ago we were all in camp together," Angela suddenly says. "You never went back to Tikvah, did you?"

Toni searches Angela's face and finds no apparent memory of their old animosity and the disgrace that exiled Toni from camp. Have they truly forgotten? Did those incidents loom much larger in her mind than in theirs? Or have those ugly events simply become irrelevant, a time of childish things they can all put behind them because they are grown up and different people now?

"We skipped one summer of camp," Angela continues in a chatty tone. "Then we went as junior counsellors. I wish we'd gone to Israel instead, like you did. That sounds so exciting. Was it fantastic?"

"You could go to Israel next summer," Toni suggests, avoiding the question.

The twins look at one another. Sharon giggles, while Angela rolls her eyes.

"Shari's got herself engaged. Can you believe? She's way too young. She's my baby sister, you know. Came out of mummy's tummy after me. The wedding's supposed to be next June. But I might go to Israel on my own afterward. I'd like to try a kibbutz. Hey, don't look so surprised. We can live separate lives. We're not the Bobbsey Twins, no matter how it looks."

The twins chatter about Sharon's fiancé and about how they'll both be starting at McGill in a few weeks and how Angela wants to get into drama. Last year, she played Abigail in their high school's production of *The Crucible* and became hooked. They are the same animated, confident, gorgeous twins as ever, yet different. Harmless, and kind of sweet. They ask questions about Toni's life in Jerusalem, seem genuinely impressed that she learned enough Hebrew to get by on the streets within a couple of months.

Their admiration makes Toni all the more aware of how utterly she failed in Israel. She so wanted to fit in. She'd been drawn to the solidity of the place and the straightforward message of the Jewish homeland. But there were layers and layers of complexity beneath the simplicity, she realizes now. She was undone by subtleties she could barely fathom.

"Hey, did you ever run into Janet Bloom when you were in Israel?" Angela asks. The question seems to have been asked in all innocence.

"No," Toni says quickly, her face burning.

"Too bad. But you must have heard of her while you were there. She's a star, or almost a star, anyway. Our cousin who's at the Technion in Haifa told us about hearing her on the radio. I always knew she'd make it big. She really has talent."

Angela sounds just a bit wistful, as if Janet's talents cast doubt on her own and as if there's only so much stardom to go around.

"Will you go back to Israel once your life gets back to normal? Oh, God, how can I say something so stupid? Life back to normal! It's not so simple, is it? I'm an idiot."

Angela touches Toni's hand again tentatively. The twins look at one another. There's a brief moment of hesitation, during which the old telegraph system between them seems at work. They come to a decision of some sort and Sharon speaks.

"Listen, call us anytime. We can go out for burgers. Or a movie. You've got to meet Joe."

Angela writes down their phone number for Toni on a paper napkin. Toni thanks them again for coming and mumbles something about getting in touch. When they take their leave after paying respects to Lisa, Toni crumples the napkin in her fist and leans back on the chair. She's bathed in sweat, exhausted by the encounter. Her mother leans over.

"Wasn't it nice of them to come? I always liked the Nutkevitch girls. You should stay in touch."

"They are nice," Toni agrees, while knowing she'll never call. They're still of a different world than her own, though what her own world is she couldn't possibly say.

And now, filled with a strange agitation, overwhelmed by the heat and closeness of the room, she has to escape. She bolts from the apartment into the gravel driveway behind the building. Mr Cheung and his boys are there. They've changed into shorts, T-shirts, and running shoes, and are washing the Cheung's white Pontiac. The boys seem to have had a soap fight because bits of foam cling to their clothes and shoes. Mr Cheung holds a spurting hose. As soon as he sees Toni hesitating in the doorway, he fires some command to his sons in rapid Chinese, rushes to turn off the outdoor tap and hops over to her.

"How are you, Miss Goldblatt?" he says, as if they haven't seen each other for days.

"I'm okay, I guess."

She sucks in a gulp of sticky air. Although the showers of the morning have come and gone, the day remains hot, humid and still, with a dense bank of clouds overhead. She'd forgotten a summer sky could be anything but fiery blue. Was it really only twenty-four hours ago that she stood on the tarmac at Lod Airport saying goodbye to the fluttering Israeli flags? The air was hot and humid there too, yet entirely different, shot through with the wetness of the sea and a hundred indecipherable Israeli smells. Now this place called home is the one that seems foreign.

"Say, do you have a cigarette?" she asks Mr Cheung.

"I don't smoke, Miss Goldblatt. I am so very sorry."

His almost hairless eyebrows bunch up in concern. Something about the earnestness of his apology and the funniness of his round, kind, very Chinese face beneath his fresh-from-the-barbershop crewcut catches her off guard. The weeping comes in painful snorts and gasps. He puts an arm around her. The top of his head barely reaches above her shoulder, yet she collapses against him, allowing him to support her weight as the crying spell engulfs her. Through her tears she becomes aware of the two young sons watching from behind the hood of the dripping car, their staring eyes filled with a deep, dark wonder.

chapter 21

Her father is alive. The whole story of his death was a big mistake, a tragic mix-up caused by broken words received through a faulty telephone line. Nevertheless, all is not well. He's been cut in half. The top part of him, his torso, balances on the edge of a white-sheeted gurney, while he stares down to where his legs should be. He mumbles, "I'm sorry, I'm sorry," as if apologizing to his missing legs. Toni wants to rush over and say, "It's my fault, Papa. All mine!" But she can't move or speak and he refuses to lift his eyes. Which is just as well because she's leaking blood. A dark stream oozes from her bellybutton, down her limbs and out from under the cuffs of her pants to form a viscous pool on the floor. Her childhood buddy, Arnold, arrives to play bellybutton games. He's up to his old tricks, fumbles under her shirt, wants to press his thumb into the tender cavity. He'll make the leak worse. *Get off! Go away! Papa will see.*

She wakes and remembers everything: her father's death, the new fear ballooning inside her. Fear is a growth in her belly, a dark lump that expands relentlessly. It is real. It cannot be wished away. The last day of the *shiva*, awareness struck that her period might be late and she thought of what was planted that strange, drunken night at Hotel Vienna. The boy from the Old City sneers from afar. She barely remembers his face, yet his presence engulfs her. The encounter she perceived through brandy-befuddled senses takes its revenge. *You thought you could pick me up and then throw me away like a market-stall trinket, well that's not how it works,* habibti. *I'm in charge, see? The boy's in charge. I had fun, but that's not good enough. I had to leave my mark.*

Every day she has checked between her legs and been overwhelmed by the sordid implications of a clean wad of toilet paper. The pink, damp folds of her private parts seem deceptively normal, unsullied. But clean on the outside means trouble within.

What will she do? She can't think. Panic grips her gut as she huddles beneath the blankets in her still darkened room. Panic hurts. It is a crescendo of pain beneath her navel, a wave of nausea in her throat. She groans aloud and opens her eyes, this time for real. She has cramps. She has soiled her pyjamas and sheets. A familiar sharp, gory smell assaults her nostrils. Despite the impulse to retch, she swoons in relief. Ordinary discomfort and mundane mess—this she can deal with. Later, as she lies abed with Midol and a hot water bottle, a nugget from the *The Facts of Life and Love for Teen-agers* floats up from the depths of memory. *Don't start feeling sorry for yourself. You'd be a lot sorrier if you never did menstruate …*

She is grateful for "the curse" this time, all right. She lolls in gratitude while reviling the boy who caused her so much anxiety just when Papa, only Papa, should have been on her mind. The little creep. His filthy lust interfered with her life. It's his fault she hasn't been able to mourn. He stole tears that belonged to Papa. She stews in her loathing. But after a while her rush of anger exhausts itself, and then Samir's words come back to her: *My friend, even not in your language or in mine are you making any sense.*

A memory from her last day in Israel floats into her mind. During the bumpy bus journey from Jerusalem to Tel Aviv, some Arab villagers came on board, including a very pregnant young woman dressed in the traditional head-to-toe garb. Since all the seats were taken, the villagers—mostly men—crowded the aisles, and a few of them squatted down onto their bundles and suitcases, but the young woman remained on her feet. As the bus lurched forward again, she clung with one hand to the support rail and held her swollen belly with the other. Toni began to rise to offer her seat, but an Israeli man pulled a reproving face.

"What are you doing?" he said. "She is used to standing. You will only embarrass them."

He wore a satisfied, disdainful smile, as if to say, "What can you expect of Arabs?" Toni struggled for a moment with doubt, but all that had recently happened threw her into confusion and so, not wanting to create a spectacle, she kept her seat. And yet, during the whole rest of the trip she was uncomfortably aware of the large-bellied, precariously balanced woman behind her in the aisle. Now she wishes she hadn't listened to that man, but what did she know? And what does she know still of fairness and rightness and wrongness in that crazy little country?

The start of autumn is etched into the yellowed, spotted leaves of the maple outside. The street below is still. Kids are in school, mothers shopping, dads at work. Toni wanders into the living room, which is neat and spotless, thanks to her burst of zeal yesterday when she flew about with dust cloths while her mother, still in her housecoat, sat blank-faced in the breakfast nook. Now, from the kitchen, comes her mother's voice speaking sternly into the phone.

"I have the letter from the doctor, Mr Epstein. It was not a pre-existing condition. Nothing that was diagnosed. When will you send the insurance cheque?"

Her mother appears in good form this morning, busy with the business of death that continues well after the funeral. They spell each other off, it seems. One day Lisa copes, another day Toni does, though at times they both walk around like zombies. Why the cleaning fit yesterday? Lint bothered Toni. Shrivelled leaves on the carpet were an outrage, as were the messy piles of unread copies of the *Montreal Star*.

Her mother said to throw them out, but Toni couldn't. Someone would want to read them. *Someone.* The living room smells of furniture polish, Windex, emptiness. She wouldn't have thought absence could be such a presence, a silent, invisible intruder, creeping up behind you to say "boo."

Before returning to Italy, Uncle Franz said to Toni, "You must come to visit us. Merano is a jewel in the autumn. I will take you to the Dolomites. You must bring your mama. Why do we live so far apart? A shame!"

He shook his large head and smiled with his mild, sweet eyes. Toni was struck anew by the difference between him—big, gentle, easy-going—and her petite, firecracker mother. Over the years her father had suggested that Franz was something of a dimwit, but Toni now thinks otherwise. When it was time to say goodbye, Uncle Franz embraced Toni in a bear hug, the kind of hug that made her feel instantly bereft when he let go. In the past, she had never questioned why her mother took trips to Italy on her own, why they'd never gone as a family. When Toni asked, Lisa stiffened and her mouth turned down.

"He put it off," she said, her voice bitter. "Too busy, too expensive, he wanted to save for your education. Always something. But finally, finally, we were going, all of us. Next summer. We planned for you to fly from Israel and meet us in Rome. He promised."

She wailed these last words and anger rose in her eyes.

"The problem wasn't the money, of course. It was going back. He never wanted to set foot in Europe again. Yet he bought books from Nazis. I'm sure some of them were Nazis, though he laughed at me when I said so. He paid German agents to buy him books. He spent a fortune on long-distance calls. *Ach!*"

She shook her head and waved away these thoughts with three swift motions of her hands.

But Toni has no interest in a trip to Italy. She hasn't the energy.

The memory of Uncle Franz has faded. She slumps onto the couch, flinging aside the cushions she so carefully arranged yesterday, lights a cigarette, and flicks ashes into a pot of African violets on the coffee table. Her mother, dressed in a good blue suit with a coral necklace at her throat, marches in.

"Why must you smoke?"

"Why not?"

"It's an ugly habit. Unhealthy. Makes a woman look coarse. Your father wouldn't like it."

Toni glowers at her mother. The new weapon: the wishes her father can no longer express.

"I'll go out then," Toni shrugs, "if it bothers you so much. I don't have to smoke in the house."

"Oh no, *liebling*. Don't go."

Her mother's face, taut and determined a moment ago, comes apart. Her cheeks sag, and dark circles show through the makeup under her eyes. Worse is their naked desolation. Lisa wraps her arms around her daughter in a hard, desperate grip. Toni has heard her mother say on the phone to a friend, "I have no future. I live for my daughter now." Those words lie in Toni's soul like cement. Her father would never have said such a thing. *It would have been easier if she'd been the one to die first.* A sickening thought, but there it is. Like a bad smell from something rotten behind a wall.

An apparition approaches in the hallway, a white-robed figure with arms outstretched, walking slowly through the murky corridor. The figure stops, lifts its hands and utters a wail like a soul descending into hell. Toni freezes. A cold fist grips her heart. Her reason has been shattered. The two of them—Toni and the apparition—confront each other in silence for an endless moment.

"Mama?" Toni finally says when her jaws work loose.

"Oh, Toni, it's you."

The apparition remains rooted to the spot, but transforms itself into her mother in her cream-coloured, brushed-nylon housecoat.

"Oh, my dear. I thought ... For a moment you looked so like your father. Those pyjamas ... like his."

"I thought *you* were the ghost."

They clutch each other and laugh. Their laughter is a series of shuddering gasps.

"So who gets the bathroom first?"

"Age before beauty."

Toni dips her head in a bow. Her mother tweaks her ear as she staggers past.

Afterward, they sit across from one another in the breakfast nook, the single bulb above the stove casting its muted glow. Neither can sleep. One of those nights. Lisa thinks she might have become distracted and forgotten to take her tranquilizers. ("Because, without them, it's no use.") She reaches over to touch Toni's cheek.

"You're too thin, *Mausie*," she says. They both fall silent. *Mausie* was *his* term of endearment. Her mother jumps up to make the tea, a blend of chamomile and verbena from Europack Deli. When she sits again, she begins to talk, her eyes wide and dark and fixed on some spot on the wall beyond Toni's head.

"Our early years together come back to me, as if it were right now. As if all these intervening years were a dream, and I have just awoken. I smell the blossoms along the Tappeiner Weg, the lovely landscaped path above the river in Merano. I hear the rush of the water, feel the mist on my cheeks. I see Julius pluck a red hibiscus, big as a teacup, to present to me. I scold him, because, of course, you're not supposed to pick the flowers. We continue, up, up, the steep path, breathless, as he pulls me to the top. From up here, you see everything—the ring of snow-capped mountains, the town in the valley, the red-roofed houses, the vineyards, the orchards. Roosters crow. Church bells ring. And the sun pours down. And the blue, blue sky. Oh, you can't imagine how beautiful. A garden of Eden. As if the war never was, nothing bad ever was."

Her mother's fist presses against her chest like she is trying to contain her beating heart. She tears her eyes away from the spot on the wall to look at Toni.

"Merano is in the north of Italy, you know, in Tirol; once it was part of Austria. There were plenty of Nazi sympathizers among the Tirolers, who longed for reunification. When Franco was courting Hitler, Merano was the first Italian town to expel its Jews. So it had its poisoned past, this Eden. But with defeat, the rats had to crawl back into their rat holes. I saw the town with fresh eyes and so did your father. All was washed clean by the sun, the mountain air, the new era. We walked freely through villages where before we would have been terrified of betrayal. We dined in open-air *tavernas*, beneath arbours. Julius would spend his last lira on a meal of pasta and wine. He had recovered from an illness and was like a man born anew. He was witty, gallant, charming, passionate. Yes, passionate. The war was over. We were alive. For me, those years were the best. I would have found a way to make a new home for us in Italy, as my brothers did, but Julius wanted to leave Europe. And he had a falling out with my brothers—it's not important what about. A man's pride is so delicate. He wasn't quick to anger, but he could hold a grudge forever. We came here. The beginning was hard. We struggled, but we succeeded. It seems to me now the better our success, the more he became cautious, closed within himself. All his *meshugas* developed in this country where he believed we could have a fresh start. As if he was afraid to lose everything again."

Lisa sucks in a deep breath. Toni fiddles with the salt cellar, twisting and untwisting the cap, scattering the white grains, as she absorbs

her mother's words with growing unease. Her mother's disappointments were always apparent, but never so clearly spelled out. She had
had something grand once and lost it. He was witty, gallant, charming,
and passionate, the man who took himself away. The man Toni never
knew. *This isn't fair. You henpecked him, you pushed him into his shell.*

"He wasn't always gloomy," she says instead.

"Ach, ya. We had our moments," her mother sighs. "Funny thing is,
he didn't mind reminiscing about our nice times in Italy with me. As
long as it remained there." Her mother stretches her arm, palm outwards, to indicate a distance.

"As long we did not discuss a real trip to the real place. The same
with Vienna. But he could talk about places and people we once had
known. He remembered my home town of Karlsbad very well. Now I
don't even have that, someone with whom to share those memories.
Ach, never mind. One has to look forward. Forward."

She fixes Toni with a piercing gaze. Her clenched fist raps the table,
making the teacups rattle.

Her mother is thankful to hear that Toni doesn't want to go back
to Israel, that she doesn't care about missing a year of university. A
flurry of emotions passes over Lisa's face: guilt and worry, along with
relief, and then a dull, unfocused bewilderment. Toni vows she'll get
a job and apply to McGill next year. Avoiding specifics, she lets it be
understood she has her own reasons for staying put. She expects the
questions: *Where were you those two weeks in August? The landlady
on Bialik Street had no idea. What was going on?* Before the questions
can be asked, she volunteers a vague story about a camping trip in the
Sinai. Her mother swallows it, too convulsed with grief to probe. Getting away with her sins is a relief, but awful, too. A poisonous snake
of a story has gnawed at her mind since the day she heard the news in
Jerusalem. *Papa was sick with worry about his daughter gone missing,*

and that is why his heart failed. The fact that her mother's frantic calls to Mrs Katz on Bialik Street came after his heart attack doesn't still the accusations within. He must have known, or suspected, or feared. He never wanted her to go to Israel in the first place.

"Mama," she blurts out in her anguish. "It's my fault."

She begins a confession—or at least tries to—about the truth of her disappearance, how bad she was, how terrible she feels, and how she wishes she could apologize to him, but her mother cuts her off.

"You are not to blame. Nonsense. Put that out of your mind at once. Of course he worried with you so far away. So did I. When did we not worry? That has nothing to do with what happened. He had a … what did you call it? A cardiac infraction."

"A myocardial infarction."

"That's it! You see?"

Lisa pounces on the scientific name as if it were some kind of answer and absolution.

"He had a bad heart, and we didn't know it. The doctor should have known, but then your father was not so good about going to the doctor. Regrets do no good. One has to look forward."

Then her mother's flare of spirit fades and she slumps back on the bench, staring at her cup of tea, confounded by the sight of the whitish brew. In her distress, she added milk. She never takes milk in her tea.

The door to her father's study stays shut. Her mother has taken out the papers she needs and works at the kitchen table on the bits and pieces of wrapping up a life. Forms. Bills. Phone calls. In a furious swoop, she had ransacked drawers and closets, packed up his clothes for the Hadassah bazaar and left the bags in a row by the wall on his side of the bed. And there they remain. As if she's forgotten the next step. She sleeps on the living room couch (when she sleeps). The bedroom has become dangerous, a minefield of memory. The study is worse. She can't face the room that contained so much of him. Then, one morning she tells Toni in a tone of flat finality, "Take a look through your father's books and keep whatever you like. I'm selling the rest. I'll get a dealer in for an evaluation."

Toni is shocked. It seems a sacrilege to even contemplate dislodging the books he so painstakingly collected over the years. Every few weeks, a package would arrive from far away. He would carry the parcel to his study, a slight bounce in his otherwise solid step and open it carefully. He would lift the book to the light, examine its pages, and record something on an index card. Then came the ritual of placing the volume on the shelf according to some system of his own. The rows of books always stood silently at attention. They were his children and his sanctuary. And now, her mother wants to just tear that all apart?

As if reading Toni's thoughts Lisa says, "He put nothing in his will about the books. I was surprised. He made every other kind of provision. I don't want them, and I don't want to keep them as a museum."

Bitterness, long-harboured resentment, sours her voice.

When Toni enters the study, she's greeted by the room as her father left it, ordered and ordinary. The big oak desk, scratched and dented and familiar as her father himself, stands by the window. On it are objects that speak of a lifetime of methodical work: the big ink-stained blotter that covers most of the desk's surface, the goose-neck lamp, pens and sharpened pencils in the pencil tray, his glasses case, his watch. The cushion on the swivel chair bears the imprint of its years of service. The workspace is embraced on two sides by floor-to-ceiling shelves of books. Nothing creates such an effective sound barrier as books, her father used to say.

Where to start? She feels like a marauder come to pillage. As she leafs through antique books by some of his favourite German authors, she finds notes on which her father jotted down where he found the volume, when, how much he paid. The sight of his handwriting—the small, neat, closely spaced letters—arouses a sudden craving.

She rummages through his desk drawers, through the stationery, ledgers, files, index cards of addresses, boxes of cheque stubs, to-do lists. She's not sure what she's looking for exactly. Something personal, something beyond the dry, factual notes.

Interspersed among his businesslike items she finds strange hoardings: cellophane wrapped crackers, Melba Toast and cookies, packets of sugar, salt, ketchup, vinegar, coffee whitener. The kinds of things provided free of charge at lunch counters. In a bottom drawer she finds an unopened carton of Camel cigarettes. But her father never smoked, at least not that she knew. She opens a pack. They are stale. She lights up and nearly faints—she hadn't realized how stale. The cigarettes must have lain in the drawer for years. What sort of catastrophe did he think to fend off with this odd assortment of provisions?

A discovery in another drawer—letters she sent from Israel—sears her with guilt. Such a small bundle, and filled with such chatty nothings. On the top is the postcard of the Dead Sea Scrolls with belated greetings for his sixty-first birthday. She continues to poke around, but finds nothing more of interest. What she wants, she realizes at last, is something addressed to *her*. A letter in which he explains himself. She recalls something the funny man—Mr Abbott, the bookseller—at the *shiva* said about her father: "He had his sensitivities." A complete stranger seems to know her father better than she does. A fury surges inside. Her mother is right. Sell the books, truck everything out, erase all traces of the father who wasn't really here anyway. She slams the drawers shut.

She is about to storm from the room when she notices something tucked into the corner pocket of the large blotter. She snatches it up, then almost wishes she hadn't. It's an old snapshot, cracked and faded and vaguely familiar. The photo shows a young girl of about eight in a lacy white dress and white stockings. Her hands are clutched in front of her stomach, as if she's just been told to stop fidgeting and is doing her best, but the results aren't entirely successful. Her hair is parted to the side, creating a severe, boxy look, the fashion of the time, and topped with a floppy white bow. On the girl's face is a guarded, brooding expression. Toni recognizes Papa's younger sister, Ida, the one who, along with her parents, was among the first to be taken away when deportations from Vienna began.

Something was terribly wrong with Ida, Toni remembers. Her mother once said that her father grieved for his little sister more than for anyone else. He grieved for the sufferings he witnessed throughout her brief life and for the agonies of her end. These are the facts Toni grew up with and that always seemed both unremarkable and filled with a deep, mysterious horror. Toni's childish questions drew reproachful adult silence, and eventually her curiosity about Ida became dulled. She accepted that here was a riddle, one of many, without an answer. Looking now at the photograph, her heart sinks because she realizes that this brooding Ida holds a family secret. *Something wrong with her. Something shameful. An inherited defect of some kind.* Was this the reason her father would sometimes look at Toni with despairing concern, then avert his eyes? Some days later, she brings the photo to her mother.

"What was the big deal about Ida?" Toni asks, affecting a casual air. "She wasn't normal, right?"

Lisa looks up from a legal document, startled. She peers at Toni over the tops of her glasses.

"Why was Papa ashamed of her? Don't pretend he wasn't. I know he was."

Lisa says nothing. She purses her lips, thinking. Then her shoulders twitch in a little shrug as if she's come to a decision.

"He was not ashamed. Ashamed is not the right word. He was careful. This wasn't something to talk about. He didn't know if the condition would come up again in another generation, or whether the information could be used against us."

"What are you talking about?"

"Whether there might be consequences for you, when you wanted to marry. He lied, you see, on the immigration application, the part that asked for a medical history."

"Papa lied? About what? Tell me." Toni leans forward on the built-in table of the breakfast nook, bracing herself.

"All right. All right. I'll tell you, but you must keep this to yourself. Ida was epileptic."

Toni stares at her mother, not comprehending.

"The poor child had fits," her mother explains.

"Is that all?"

"That is enough. Perhaps nowadays there's better treatment, but in our day such a child couldn't go to a regular school and had to be watched every moment. It was considered a terrible defect. In the Nazi time, anyone—even pure Aryans—suspected of carrying this condition was sterilized. The procedure was called the *Hitlerschnitt*. The Hitler cut."

"The Nazis were crazy. Everybody knows that. But why the hush-hush afterwards?"

"Always they ask on forms if there is this or that in your family history. We agreed it was better not to say, just in case they would refuse to let us into Canada. And God forbid someone should find out now and take the citizenship away."

"Mama! That's so medieval. Epilepsy is just a common illness. You make it sound like possession by the devil."

"Of course, an illness, an inherited illness," her mother sniffs. "It was hard enough to get into this country. You have no understanding."

"But no one could take our citizenship away because of something like that. This is Canada, 1968. We're not in Nazi Germany."

"Maybe not," her mother concedes. "But prejudices still exist. It is better to be on the safe side and—"

"And keep deep, dark secrets?"

"No. We don't make a secret. We simply don't need to tell this story. One day you will meet a man you want to marry, and if you tell him this, he might change his mind. Don't give me such a look. Of course it could happen."

"But you married Papa! You're not being rational!"

"My instincts told me it would be all right to marry your father. Not everyone has such strong instincts. I knew any baby of mine would be normal in every way."

Toni sits down on the bench across from her mother, stunned. Ida merely had a condition that today would be controlled with medication. What would her mother think if she could see into the state of her daughter's heart? Toni pushes the question away. Back into the dungeon of banished thoughts it goes.

chapter 22

Only the front end of Browsers' Paradise is all set up. Displays of art books catch the eye on bright, white shelves at the front of a long, narrow room. A rocking chair invites the customer to bide a while. The cash register sits on a desk by the door, unattended, save for a fat grey cat with a baleful gaze. Its yellow-eyed stare seems to say, "Come in for Pete's sake, if you're coming, but close the door. There's a draft." The cat appears to be the sole proprietor until Toni spies Mr Abbott at the back of the room stooped over heaps of books. Stacks of precariously balanced, unopened cartons cover the floor. Teetering piles clog the aisles between shelves. Toni breathes in the smell of dust and fresh paint as she stands in the doorway holding a heavily laden shopping bag.

"Miss Goldblatt, what a lovely surprise," he warbles. Today he sports a red beret, worn at a rakish angle, and a loosely knotted ascot in a red-and-cream paisley print. Silky grey hair lifts like wings as he rushes forward to greet her. His several rings glitter.

"Still a bit of organizing to do." He waves toward the disordered piles and boxes. "And I've got a basement full, too. I go to an estate sale and can't resist. Whole libraries sold in lots. Much of it dross, but some pearls too. I suppose you wonder where I'll find room." He waves again toward the towers of books. "Turnover, my dear, turnover. Once people start to buy, there'll be space for these orphans."

"I don't suppose you want any more," Toni says, raising her shopping bags for him to see. Inside she's stuffed Langenscheidts' German-

English dictionaries, Churchill's six-volume series, *The Second World War*, and *The Decline and Fall of the Roman Empire*. The books are in fine condition and the series complete.

"Very nice," Mr Abbott murmurs as he examines her offerings on the desk with the cash register. The grey cat decamps with offended flicks of its tail. "They were your father's, weren't they?" And when she nods, he lifts his hands in protest. "But you should keep them. You might find them handy. You're a student, aren't you?"

"Not right now. I'm looking for a job."

"Money worries?" His mild blue eyes seem genuinely concerned.

"Nah. Just the way it worked out." She shifts from foot to foot. "We're selling all his books," she blurts out.

"All?" Abbott's eyelashes flutter. "You don't mean that, surely?"

"I do," she says gruffly. "I don't read German. My mum doesn't care for his books. She's negotiating with Mr Heinemann on a price."

"His Wassermanns? His Georg Hermanns too? Oh dear, that is sad."

Abbott puts his hand on the side of his head as if the news has disturbed the delicate workings inside. "I suppose you know the type of authors your father liked to collect?"

"Not really."

"Your father had a soft spot for Jewish German-language authors of a certain vintage who'd lost their audience because of the war or whose careers were nipped in the bud or who'd fallen out of fashion. Authors who no longer fit with the time. Wassermann was one such. He was a giant in his day, according to your father. And now, who reads him, who's heard of him? Georg Hermann, who died in Auschwitz, is a similar case. Another of your father's favourites, Hermann Ungar, was a rising light in Czechoslovakia during the brief democratic era. His works are shunned there now. The communists, you see? They don't care for Jews. Oh, there are many others."

Abbott makes an expansive gesture to conjure up the multitude of books by persecuted, obscure, and has-been authors in her father's library.

"He collected a few pure nobodies too. Writers who weren't particularly good—he told me this quite frankly—because he felt sorry for them. Isn't that sweet?"

Abbott flashes a smile. Toni experiences a prickle of irritation. Her father loved those who in some way failed. She doesn't see the glory of this at all.

"Thing is, it doesn't matter anymore," she says harshly. "Doesn't matter who he liked and why. He's gone."

"Well!" the bookseller says, taken aback. "Well." He gives his head a small shake as if trying to dispel her cold pronouncement. "The monetary value was never the main point, you see? To your father a book was a soul and each had intrinsic value. He was on a rescue mission of sorts. To rescue those crushed by fate, destined to oblivion, by at least giving them a place in his library. Quite a quixotic fellow, your papa. I must admit I rather fell in love with him."

Toni is surprised to see a fat tear slip over the rim of Abbott's left eye and roll down his soft cheek. Her father would be mortified by such a display.

"How well did you know my dad?"

"Not well enough," the bookseller answers with a tragic air. "But I understood. The collector's soul, I understood. Oh, my dear." Mr Abbott honks into his handkerchief. "Young people can be hard. Do keep a few of his books for yourself. You'll be glad you did when you are older."

Abbott squeezes his hands together in appeal. Toni laughs. She can imagine her father commenting dryly. *A comical bird, that one, but harmless. I give him a year before he's bankrupt. You realize not a soul has entered the store since you did.*

"You say you need a job," the bookseller says, throwing his hands high as if struck by an inspiration. "How strong is your back?"

"I'm very strong," Toni answers, squaring her shoulders. "I do the 5BX program, the one used by the RCAF."

"Well, then. I could use a helper. You're just the one."

"Really?"

"So many boxes to bring up from the basement. I'm a walking ad for Ben-Gay ointment, my dear. And I'm sure you could handle the cash better than Mr Pickwick." He gestures toward the grey cat, who has resettled in his spot. "And I have no doubt books are in your blood. Just a matter of bringing out the latent potential."

Abbott dances about, gesturing with excitement.

Six months. That's how long he'll last, she hears her father saying. But Mr Abbott's elation is contagious, and a job's a job. Her very first. That's something at least.

chapter 23

Sunday morning in the deep-freeze of winter—it's the worst day of the week, worst time of the year. Toni surveys stark trees, sidewalks of hard-packed snow, cars with black slush frozen into the wheel wells. All this beneath an iron sky. She leans her forehead against the frosty windowpane until her whole face aches. On weekdays and Saturdays, she can busy herself with her bookstore job. On Sundays, there's nothing but long bleak hours of empty freedom. "Get together with some other young people," her mother urges. "Join a club. Why don't you call the Nutkevitch girls?"

Nothing changes.

Her mother has gone to the Shape-up class at the Y—Toni can see them, a roomful of middle-aged, leotard-clad women, upside down, doing the "bicycle" to a tinny recording of the Beatles' "Lady Madonna." Hips propped on hands, legs churning the air with desperate determination. Pedalling to melt away fat, to banish sorrow. But fat clings and sorrow sticks. A woman of a certain age without a man is pathetic. No one says so, but everyone knows.

Toni prowls about the house. Picks up yesterday's paper—"Students Riot at Sir George Williams University"—throws it down again, then flips on the TV for ten seconds of *The Galloping Gourmet*. She drifts into her mother's room. The closet door stands open. Her mother's clothes have strayed across the rod. Months ago, bags stuffed with her father's suits, coats, sweaters, and shoes were finally sent off to the Hadassah bazaar. Toni has his watch, which she asked for as a memento.

The twenty-year-old Swiss Omega was his first big splurge in Canada, part self-indulgence, part prudence. It has seventeen jewels, a stainless steel casing, a black leather strap, and the last letter of the Greek alphabet stamped in gold beneath the number twelve on the watch face. A watch like that would help him look like a solid citizen, inspire the trust of clients, he must have thought. Toni punched an extra hole in the strap to make it fit her own wrist.

On what was once her father's side of the closet a single suit remains, along with one white dress shirt, a tie on the otherwise empty tie rack, his felt fedora on the shelf above, and a pair of black shoes on the floor. A complete outfit. Do the dresser drawers also hold one of everything? Socks, underwear, pyjamas? So that were he to suddenly materialize, he'd be perfectly equipped to walk out into the world? She can't bring herself to look.

The suit her mother has saved is of good grey wool, shot through with blue and silver threads, and without a speck of lint. When did he last wear it? Toni can't remember. She's never paid much attention to male attire before, but now she admires the subtle pattern of the pinstripes and the fine cut of the cloth while her heart aches. This mere thing has outlasted its owner. Oh, the mute, useless endurance of inanimate objects! The cruel emptiness of sleeves! She has a sudden craving to see the suit filled by a living body.

Lifting the jacket from the hanger, she slips it on. Not a bad fit. A bit roomy across the shoulders and around the middle, perhaps, but the sleeves are about right, reaching to the midpoints of her hands. What's not right is her faded orange T-shirt beneath the beautiful jacket. She tries on the dress shirt, buttoning it right up to her chin. The pants now. She must have the pants. A thrill of the forbidden flutters beneath her ribs. She steps into the trouser legs, zips up the fly, pulls tight the belt, though it's too long for her slim waist. The pant cuffs flop on the floor. She wriggles her bare feet into the black shoes. Better. The tie next, a lovely silk one with blue, white, and wine-coloured stripes. Her nervous fingers improvise a knot. She completes the picture with his grey felt fedora.

Hands in trouser pockets, legs astride, Toni surveys herself in the mirror behind the closet door. The sight is both eerie and exhilarating. She looks downright handsome. Were her mother to walk in the room right now, her screams would shatter glass. Toni feels she has overstepped some limit, regressed into a childish game of dress-up, but one that perverts the very idea of childhood and human dignity. *What a naughty devil!* She winks at herself, a wink that thrills as it appalls. How would her father feel to see her thus? Does he look down reproachfully from some heavenly realm? *But he's not here. He's gone.*

An old, familiar sadness washes over her. She remembers this from long ago, the terrible anguish that would engulf her in the presence of her father, leaping from his skin into hers. They would be happily walking hand-in-hand on a blustery April day to the Belgian pastry shop on Côte des Neiges Road, perhaps rhyming off some comical verse from a German storybook. Suddenly, she would sense a difference, perhaps a release in the pressure in his hand, an uneasy shifting of his head. That was all it took for the atmosphere to change, and they would carry on in strained silence. She could sense the pain of loss in his bloodstream, a dripping away that whispered: *You are alone, no happiness lasts, happiness is merely an illusion causing you to drop your guard, so that when the blow comes—as it must—it will fall harder than you can bear.* And now that old gloom lives on. A dead brown smell, detached from its source, concentrated in the fabric of his suit, seeps into her body once more. Hastily she removes the outfit, puts everything back exactly as it was before, after a thorough going over with the lint brush.

Several days later, she sits behind the cash register at Browsers' Paradise observing "the boys." That's how Mr Abbott refers to a group of odd young fellows who frequent his store, often just before closing time on Saturday afternoons. They have narrow waists, sensitive features, giddy manners. They eye one another hungrily while leafing through slim volumes of avant-garde poetry or glossy photos of God and Adam sparking one another on the ceiling of the Sistine Chapel. Mr Abbott doesn't seem to mind their presence, though they rarely buy the expensive books they like to finger. He smiles indulgently and pats their cheeks. Some time ago, Toni realized these young men were homos. She was disgusted, of course. She was disgusted because anybody would be—it was a natural reaction—but also because this lot was so bloody blatant. They carried on right under Mr Abbott's nose. Once, down in the basement, she heard a strange, unwholesome ruckus from behind the bathroom door. Bristling with indignation, she warned Mr Abbott that a certain type of clientele might scare off other customers. He put his hand to his chin and contemplated her with gentle blue-eyed consternation.

"They do no harm," he murmured vaguely.

Did he know, or didn't he? She couldn't be sure. It seemed quite within his character, that of a kind little elf, to look beyond the depravity to the human being underneath. She decided to tolerate the boys for his sake.

She's become used to them now. She even enjoys the excitement they bring into the shop, the innuendo that goes over her head but that charges the air with a sense of daring and fun. Lately too she has become intensely curious about their secret lives.

This evening, two of the regulars—Brian and Winston—are in the shop. Brian sits in the rocker with Mr Pickwick sprawled on his lap in a posture of ecstatic abandonment. Winston bends over them. The two boys stroke the cat, their fingers ploughing through the long grey fur, and giggle while Mr Pickwick purrs at full throttle.

"You going to the Blue tonight?"

Winston straightens and smoothes back the long blond hair that has tumbled forward into his flushed face.

"Where else?" Brian shrugs. "Hope springs eternal."

He lowers his voice and whispers something Toni can't hear. The "Blue" they're talking about is the Blue Nile, a nightclub in the seedy section of Sainte Catherine Street East that features bars and strip-tease joints. From afar Toni has glimpsed neon signs that depict nude, female dancing legs kicking up and down. She leaves her spot by the cash register and approaches the rocker and gives Pickwick a flick under the chin.

"Hey, fellas," she says as casually as she can. "How'd you like some company at the Blue tonight? I've got this old suit of my dad's I tried on the other day. I'd blend in—look just like one of the guys. Wouldn't it be a gas?"

She kneads the cat's ears the whole time she speaks. When she's done her little speech, she dares to look at Winston. His arms fold over his chest and his mouth twists into an expression of amused surprise. He and Brian exchange glances.

"Well!" Winston says dramatically. "Well! I never thought I'd live to see the day. I could see her blending in. Eh, Brian? Don't you think?" He gives a mighty wink. "But believe me, darling, you'd really be much better off at Loulou's."

From this casual remark, Toni learns about a world beyond anything she had ever imagined.

chapter 24

Loulou's is on a marginal strip of Dorchester Avenue, an area in transition: part commercial, part residential, with ma-and-pa grocery stores and shabby rooming houses that have seen better days. A few blocks away, Sainte Catherine Street hums and glitters, but in this pocket of the city the traffic is sparse. Only now and then a shadowy figure rushes by with collar pulled up against the ear-chewing wind. Toni stands on the corner behind a telephone pole, scanning a row of modest buildings that are neither one thing nor the other: neither swanky downtown, nor racy east end, neither English nor French, but something in between. The linguistic dividing line used to be Saint Laurent Boulevard—the Main—but lately the French have come west. A new sense of pride and entitlement has awakened among the masses, bringing their fast, loose-vowelled lingo into territory that was once almost exclusively English. Among the thoughts that tumble through Toni's brain as she lingers in the shadows is the question of what language they speak at Loulou's. If French, she's not sure how she'll manage because, though she did well enough in the subject at school, there's a world of difference between passing an exam and understanding the argot of the street.

Toni trots back and forth, casting quick glances at the door that will lead her to happiness or perdition. It's on the ground floor, half hidden by a long flight of outdoor stairs. The sign above is so discreet it's easy to miss, spelling out Loulou's Lounge in faint, flickering blue neon, a colour like the last light of an evening sky. If you weren't looking for that sign, you'd be sure to miss it, and even now it seems like a mirage. She has lingered on the corner and wandered around the neighbourhood and frozen her butt for over half an hour. The evening is slipping by, and still she can't make her move. She watches as several couples arrive, knock, and are admitted, while a brief gust of chatter and music blows into the street. Then silence once more. Blank walls and a dark closed door.

Finally, numb of toe, trembling of limb, Toni scoots across the road and into the gloom beneath the outdoor staircase. Shortly afterward, she hears footsteps, someone striding down the street, who stops just inches away from Toni's hiding place and stands in the ghostly pool of light cast by the neon sign. It's a woman with dark, handsome features—long, strong face, hawk's-beak nose, conquistador's mouth, thick eyebrows. Her hair is cut in a short masculine bob, and she wears a black leather jacket that gives extra heft to her square shoulders. If she's noticed Toni, she pays no attention, but instead whisks out a comb from her back pocket and rakes it along the sides of her head. One hand combs, the other smoothes in quick, self-assured movements. On the pinkie finger of one of those powerful hands a gold ring flashes. Toni holds her breath, weak with excitement. She's aware that had she seen this manly woman on Saint Catherine's an hour ago she might have thought her freakish and averted her eyes. But now, suddenly, perhaps because of the place and time and the gesture with the comb, Toni sees something new, the compelling appeal of ambiguity. It is a face that breaks the rules.

The woman draws herself up, trots down the steps, and raps a smart tattoo on the door.

"*Ben,* Juanita! *C'est toé!*" a deep, heavily accented voice booms out. "About time. Get your ass in here. Your gang's waiting."

They speak English at least.

Again, from inside, banners of carefree noise issue forth—clinking glasses, laughter and dance music—and are abruptly cut off when the door slams shut. Toni's heart thunders against her ribcage. Perhaps, beyond this threshold, an underground of toughs, gangsters, and freaks awaits. Army boots and switch blades and bearded ladies. Perhaps she's arrived at the gates of hell, but she must go forward. She hurls herself at the door, pounds with her fist.

The door opens a crack and a pair of eyes sweeps up and down her like a policeman's flashlight, taking Toni's measure.

"*Ouai?*" says the same husky voice that greeted Juanita. And when Toni just stares, "You look for someone?"

"Can I come in?" Toni breathes.

The door opens a touch wider. The person behind the voice leans forward into the gap. In the dim glow of the entranceway, Toni makes out a tall, hefty build, a broad face, a squashed-in nose, and a thatch of straw-coloured hair tumbled over the brow. Shrewd lines crinkle the corners of the eyes.

"How old are you, kid?"

"Eighteen," Toni answers, without thinking to lie.

"Tell me another! Anyway, even if you are eighteen, you're under-age for this *établissement*. And you're wearing jeans. I have a dress code. No jeans."

"I didn't know."

Toni swallows down the sob rising in her throat. She notices now that her interrogator wears wine-red slacks, white loafers, and a gaily patterned shirt with the sleeves rolled up. There's a heavy gold chain around her neck and another on her wrist, but these ornaments look more like weapons than jewellery.

"Tough luck," the woman snorts as the door begins to close, but Toni's foot juts forward of its own accord, wedging itself against the jamb.

"But I'm a friend of Juanita's."

The words have come out of nowhere.

"Heh? That so?"

The woman sounds doubtful, nevertheless she turns and shouts, "Hey Juanita! *Viens icitte.* Someone here says she knows you. Ever lay eyes on this kid before?"

The Spanish-featured woman appears in the doorway. She has shed her leather jacket and now stands before Toni in a man's suit—solid black, the pant legs pressed into razor-edge creases—and a white, open-necked shirt. She regards Toni blank-eyed, stone-faced, and Toni can only look back at her in trembling silence.

"Sure, I know her. This one's trouble," Juanita finally declares in a slow, firm voice.

"Thought so," says the doorkeeper, crossing her arms over her chest. She has biceps as big as Toni's knees.

"But I'll keep her in line. She'll answer to me. Give her a break, Rick."

Juanita still doesn't crack a smile, though a twinkle has come into those obsidian eyes.

"*Eh, ben,* it's cold standing here. Come in if you're coming."

The door swings open.

Toni's in.

Hand clamped on her shoulder, Juanita steers Toni through a long, narrow, crowded room with dark-painted walls and wreathes of smoke snaking up toward the ceiling. There's a bar on one side, a small scuffed-up dance floor beside a juke box, and a few tables at the back where Juanita's friends sit waiting.

"Hey gals, look what the cat delivered. Fresh meat. Okay, this here's Maggie. That's Rhonda and Renée. Me, you already know, right? So what's your name?"

Toni tells them.

"A first-timer, gals, fresh from her mommy's tits. 'Course I know.

Saw you shivering under the stairs with your eyes big as hubcaps. Welcome to our den of iniquity."

Juanita bends in a mocking bow.

"Come sit on my lap, honey," Maggie says, winking and patting her knees. She's a chunky older woman—forty at least—with short, curly, muddy-brown hair. She's wearing a tartan blazer with brass buttons and a lapel pin that's halfway between a cross and a dagger.

"Don't trust Juanita, she's an animal, but I don't bite. Not unless you ask nicely. Har, har. Poor kid, doesn't know what to make of us. She's going to faint or run screaming out the door."

"No I won't," Toni mutters, but sidles away from Maggie to an empty chair near the other two—Rhonda and Renée—who sit pressed close together like lovebirds on a wire. Rhonda, who's clearly the "guy" of the couple, though she's pink-cheeked, baby-faced, and skinny, extends her hand for Toni to shake. The grip is surprisingly firm. Her sweetheart ignores Toni. In her own way she is as arresting as Juanita. Renée is tiny and ultra-feminine, wearing a low-cut cocktail dress that shows off the tops of voluptuous breasts but also a knobby hump at the summit of her spine. She hunches at the table, a cigarette balanced between white fingers that end in scarlet nails so long they curve inward. Heavy makeup, swirls of stiff black hair, a pouting mouth, and a seemingly permanent morose expression complete the vampish picture. Rhonda's arm rests protectively on the back of Renée's chair. They seem an unlikely couple, the one an exotic bird, the other like a little boy dressed up for a birthday party in a blue suit and red bowtie. Toni can imagine her mother's hissed verdict: *Grotesque.*

"So am I right?" Juanita says. "Scared shitless?"

"If I was, I wouldn't tell you," Toni answers, trying to keep the quaver from her voice.

This earns her a burst of friendly guffaws. Soon she's clutching a beer, puffing a fag, soaking up the repartee and gazing eagerly around the room. A truth slams down upon her mind like a pot lid finding its pot. She swoons with the euphoria of a Newtonian discovery. Every last soul here is female. The fact is no less remarkable for being obvious.

The chatter in the room is both in English and French. She sees a great variety of girls and women. Almost no one's wearing jeans; Rick wasn't lying about her dress code, but otherwise everything goes—casual pants, dark turtlenecks, mannish suits, mini-skirts, slinky gowns, sturdy winter boots, elegant pumps. Some patrons seem indistinguishable from the chic set that parades down Sainte Catherine Street on a Saturday afternoon. Some wear the wool ponchos, black berets, and owlish glasses of college intellectuals. A few are similar to the gang she's with now—carefully turned out and differentiated to resemble the male or female of the species. Some faces are plain, some attractive, and a few are heart-stoppingly beautiful. Toni finds herself seeking out those special faces. Their loveliness strikes her as especially poignant here in this warm, smoky room, sealed off from the outside world. Her senses keenly alive, she thinks she might be turning into the kind of animal Maggie alluded to, but she has no regrets. And this transformation has happened almost instantly, as if the air at Loulou's were a secret, powerful potion that made you anew.

"Look at the eyes on this puppy. It's rude to stare." Maggie cuffs her gently on the side of the head. "Are we boring you, miss? At least you don't claim to be doing a project. You can't imagine how many of these college kids come in here claiming it's just for medical research. They want to study us and find a cure. You look like you caught the disease. She's cute like this, ain't she?"

"Not your type," Juanita chuckles as Maggie leans across to Toni and Toni pulls away.

"But, *dites moi*, what type is she?" Renée inquires disdainfully, emerging from a tête-à-tête with Rhonda. The two had withdrawn into a private world of whispers and teasing smiles. "She's got no style." Renée waggles a finger to indicate Toni's outfit of jeans and baggy sweater, ornamented with a flower-patterned silk scarf she'd slipped from her mother's drawer and awkwardly tied around her neck before leaving the house. She'd been trying for the ascot effect—it always looked so stylish on Mr Abbott—but her knot was all wrong. She'd had no idea what to wear.

"This new breed of girls that comes around, they're so vague." Renée waves her hand dismissively. "Not one thing or another, neither ladies nor gentlemen, something in-between. A bunch of 'its.' What are they here for? Are they for real or just tourists? I like to know who I'm dealing with when I come to the club." She regards Toni with disapproval from beneath long black lashes and purple-powdered lids.

Stung, Toni is about to retort in anger, but a warning gleam in Juanita's eyes keeps her quiet.

"Don't take what my better half here says too personally," Rhonda pipes up. "The little lady gets upset, and I don't blame her. We're sick of those women's libbers. They want everyone to look the same. They don't talk to us, you know." She indicates an earnest circle of women near the bar. "We've all been living the life for years. That crowd more or less just got here, like you, but they act like they own the place. They go to the university, so they must know it all. But hey, maybe you'd rather be with them. Go where you please. Don't feel obliged."

Toni has no desire to join the college girls, whose backs seem pointedly turned against Juanita's corner and who seem as snooty as Rhonda suggests. A beer is coursing pleasantly through her veins. Her table mates are unlike any people she has ever met: exotic and strange and thus thrillingly beyond the bounds of ordinary judgement.

"I've never been here before," Toni says, sliding carefully past Rhonda's last comment. "So I didn't know what to wear. If I had a suit like Juanita's, I'd wear that."

A cheer goes up at her table. Juanita slaps her on the back. When they ask whether she has a job, she says she's a store clerk, doesn't mention it's a bookstore or that she's been accepted for the fall term at McGill. A fresh round of beers and a cocktail for Renée appears on the table, ordered by Juanita. Toni tries to whip out her wallet to pay, but Maggie pushes her hand down.

"Watch yourself, kiddo. Don't insult Juanita. You've been lucky so far."

Toni buys the next round. The night wears on, heats up, as girls take to the dance floor. Arms entwine, foreheads touch, lovers gaze deep into one another's eyes. Toni focuses on the beer bottle in her hand to keep from staring too obviously through the smoke haze at the sensuous scene. Juanita winks and leans toward Toni in a brotherly fashion to point out characters and explain the ropes, her voice low and confiding.

"Rick there, she grew up in the bars, was a bodybuilder once, tough as nails. She knows her business, how to keep out the creeps, how to make the crime bosses happy, how to handle the cops. They don't raid like they used to, but still, Rick wasn't shitting you, you're underage, and so are half of the ladies in this establishment. Anyway, them cops don't need no excuses. They can walk in here anytime, wham, lights go on, everybody who doesn't skip out the back door gets hauled off in the paddy wagon. Nine times out of ten, no charges, but you've spent the night in the slammer anyway with those pigs jeering and feeling you up. But, like I said, Rick takes care of us. She can sniff out a spook a mile away. If the lights flicker on and off, that's the signal. You dive for the back door, or if you can't, at least make sure to let go of the girl you're dancing with. Now, about the no-jeans rule, that's to keep the place classy. Some of our kind can be tough customers and Rick, she likes a nice clean club. No fights, no drugs. You want to do hippie drugs, you go out into the alley. Act in a way Rick doesn't like and, believe me, she'll take you by the scruff of your neck and fire you out on your ass.

"Renée doesn't know what you are, but I spotted you right off for butch. You'll be fine. Have yourself a girl in no time. See that knock-out blonde in the silver dress? She's a stripper at Babylon's and a little more besides. We were an item once, but I stay away from rough trade now. Not worth the hassles. Every woman's beautiful when you get her clothes off. Women are easy. Want to know a secret? Straight women are easier. I've had dozens—factory girls, secretaries, horny house-wives."

"Don't believe a word she's telling you. She's a fucking liar," Maggie slurs, having returned from a trip to the toilet and a fruitless cruise around the room. Her face is flushed and sweat gleams along the edges of her close-cropped mop of curls.

But Toni does believe—because of Juanita's suave ducktail, her hawk's-beak nose, her smooth, easy manner, and her hands, most of all her hands, which are strong, well-manicured, a subtle blend of male and female, and full of knowledge. These are hands that have held a dozen manual jobs, brushed sweat off the flanks of racehorses, wielded brooms and rakes, guided taxis through snowstorms, and, with the same light, sure touch, unzipped the backs of numberless gowns. Toni would give her life-blood to possess such hands.

When a waltz plays on the juke box, Rhonda and Renée get up to take a turn. Renée, whose natural stance is to be thrust forward be-cause of her hump, rests her chin on Rhonda's shoulder and presses her ample bosom up against her partner's flat chest. Looked at from a certain perspective, they could appear as caricatures, but Toni feels the heat between them, sees the bold tenderness with which Rhonda caresses her lover's deformity, how they exchange sly smiles and nestle closer together, as if the bony protrusion at the top of Renée's spine were a secret erogenous zone. Embracing couples float through clouds of blue smoke. Elvis croons from the juke box. Normally, his saccharine voice would give Toni the creeps, but now it's part of the charming scene, of the melancholy and longing that flows through her.

In the ladies room, she encounters a drunk Maggie, who manages to reach up and plant a beery kiss on Toni's mouth before Toni can push her away.

"Aw, sorry, honey, sorry. I'm terrible, I know. Bet you wish you never came through that door."

In mid-apology, Maggie again gropes for Toni's waist and is again rebuffed, more roughly this time.

"Lay off," Toni mutters, but adds, "I'm glad I came."

She is less offended by the kiss than she would have thought. Maggie's lips were surprisingly gentle. And despite the older woman's lumbering drunkenness, there's dignity along with the mischief in her eyes. Toni decides she would happily endure a hundred such clumsy come-ons for another night of magic at Loulou's.

chapter 25

The club has become her beacon through the long, grey week. During the hours in which she dusts shelves, sorts books, writes out receipts, Toni dreams of women brushing hips in a smoky room. On Saturday nights, she drives down to the dimly lit area around Loulou's and finds a dark side street on which to park. Crouching low, she changes into the button-down shirt and herringbone blazer she bought at the men's wear department at Ogilvie's. Around her neck she knots a wine-coloured tie. A peaked black leather cap completes the outfit. Then she dashes through the frigid air to the door beneath the stairs. A quick tap-tap and she's welcomed into the warmth and laughter, the embrace of that throbbing, hidden world. As she leans against a pillar by the bar and scans the scene for faces new and familiar, she feels her shoulders broaden, her body stretch to its full imposing height. All week long she's been a muted, grubbing Cinderella. Here, at last, she can be a prince.

Juanita's gang hails her and she strides forward, proud to be loyal to the old guard at the club and to be considered under Juanita's tutelage.

"When you're interested in a lady," Juanita says "you have a drink delivered to her table and then, when she turns to see who it is, you nod. Don't grin like an idiot. Give her a look, like James Dean, steamy and cool at the same time. When you dance, you lead, right? You're the gent. Don't forget that for a second or it breaks the spell. Once you get her home, you'll be fine, little brother. Had my first when I was fifteen.

She was an older woman, married. We fucked all night while her husband lay drunk on the floor."

Just the word "woman" coming from Juanita's mouth, flavoured with her Spanish accent (*woo-mun*), conjures up delectable visions; Marilyn Monroe blowing kisses or Sophia Loren, hot-eyed, full-lipped, from the film *Marriage Italian Style*. Juanita's ease in tough streets, the hint of hard knocks in her past fills Toni with envy. How perfect to live for the moment, nothing but the moment, with that earthy, essential élan of the prol.

A few weeks after her first appearance at Loulou's, the story comes out that Toni's Jewish. A chill falls over the table.

"Little rich kid, eh? Shoulda known," Maggie says, narrowing her eyes. "She's come down our way to slum."

"I'm not rich," Toni says fiercely, while realizing a truth she's known · all along—she's of a different class. They would regard her home in Snowdon, her university savings fund in the bank, even her job in a Park Avenue bookstore with suspicion. Maggie and Rhonda are factory workers, Renée waits on tables in a diner, Juanita is on the dole. Her last job was in the stables at Blue Bonnet's race track. Until now, no one has asked Toni about her background. It's understood Loulou's is where you leave the outside world behind. And so it would have remained if she hadn't opened her big mouth to boast about the beautiful girls of Jerusalem.

"Goldblatt, hmm," Renée muses. "Jews always have names with gold and silver in them." The big boss at the shirt factory Rhonda works in happens to be a Mr Silverstone. There's no malice in Renée's voice. She's quite unaware of the nonsense she's spouting, and so Toni sits flummoxed. Juanita rubs her chin thoughtfully and says nothing.

"I have to work. My mother has to work," Toni says doggedly, then adds, "We don't go to synagogue or anything like that."

Instantly her face flames as if her blood is in revolt against her words.

The last time she tried to make her Jewishness less offensive to others was when she was a kid playing with her gang. In those days too, "Jewish" was an accusation, though of nothing specific. Toni would use the line about not being religious to prove she wasn't like those Nutkevitch girls. They were the real Jews. A sick feeling rises in her throat.

"I was born Jewish, and I ain't ashamed of how I was born," she says, with a defiant thump of her fist on the table, while a nervous inner voice sneers, *Oh yeah? Since when do you use words like 'ain't'?*

But Juanita breaks out in a husky "bravo!" She claps her hands slowly. "We're none of us ashamed of how we're born, eh, ladies?"

Everyone nods and the subject is changed, though the tightness in Toni's throat remains. Her new companions are at ease with bald, ignorant assertions. A term her mother would use springs to Toni's mind. They are *primitive.* Gaily, innocently so. Sooner or later the masks must fall. She pushes these thoughts away, grateful when Juanita leans over and points out a pretty, long-legged woman in a short skirt, seated alone at the bar.

"That's Marie. She's on the loose. Broke up with her lover. Go for her before someone else does."

"Don't you want her yourself?"

"Ha! Don't worry about me. I got other fish to fry."

So Toni leaps from her seat before she can lose her nerve, and swaggers off to the bar, conscious of all the spectators appraising her performance.

"Manhattan for the lady, please," Toni tells the bartender. She straightens her tie and makes her approach.

"Hi, doll. Don't think I've ever seen you here before," Toni says in her deepest, most suave voice. There's an empty chair beside Marie, but Toni doesn't sit. Instead she leans forward, as she's been coached, elbow on the bar, biceps flexed. Cool and steamy. She whips out a pack of cigarettes from her pocket and taps the pack so that one fag is thrust forward like a finger extended: *take me*. Marie helps herself, her lips curling slowly upward. She's an older woman, thirty at least, with sad eyes, a smirking mouth shiny with lipstick, and a long, willowy body. Amazingly, she seems happy to see Toni turn up. Soon they're on the dance floor, swaying to a hot new number by the Supremes. When a slow song starts, Marie tugs on Toni's tie to pull her close. Applause and wolf whistles erupt from the table in the back.

"I like my partners tall," Marie sighs in Toni's ear.

She smells of patchouli and vermouth. When her bosom meets Toni's dead on, a wave of heat floods Toni's groin. Her head swims, her knees are mush, but she tries not to give anything away. After a few more dances, she drives Marie home to an apartment building just east of downtown. In the flickering light of the elevator, Marie's lips are the luscious colour of plums. The polished steel wall behind them mirrors two romantic figures, one in a close-fitting feminine coat, the other in a jacket and rakish cap. Marie's nyloned knees brush against Toni's legs just as the elevator door purrs open on a long, dimly lit corridor. Toni staggers out, follows Marie down the hall. Marie smirks and fishes in her purse for her key. And then the air grows thick. The knot of Toni's tie presses against her throat. She feels a rush of absurdity and sordidness. Instead of Marie's eyes, she sees Janet's—haunted, miserable, shocked, accusing—the way they looked out at Toni that morning after the night of disastrous gropings. It's one thing to play the game at Loulou's, to wear the uniform, perform the moves, evoke cheers from her buddies, another thing to contemplate being naked with a stranger. Two strangers actually: the one she's taken home, the other within her own skin.

Who am I? Neither male nor female, neither fish nor fowl. Outside God's creation. Not even the tiniest twig on the evolutionary tree. An unclean spirit. An It.

"I gotta go. It's not you, you're beautiful but ... I ... " Toni searches for an excuse. "There's someone waiting," she mumbles lamely.

She bolts for the emergency stairs.

"You two-timing fucker!" she hears Marie shout at her retreating back.

Tiptoeing in sock feet into the house, Toni encounters her mother in the corridor. Dark circles like bruises lie beneath Lisa's eyes. She clutches her housecoat to her throat and shivers with the March cold that Toni's brought in through the door. Or perhaps what makes her tremble are the forebodings and haunted dreams that assailed her during the long hours in the empty apartment.

"It's late. Where were you, for God's sake? Couldn't you have phoned? I was asleep, of course I was, but a mother sleeps with one eye open. You stink of smoke. And what is that? Perfume? Feh! A vile one. Like that stuff they burn in churches. Why didn't you ask for my nice cologne?"

Before Toni can reply, Lisa continues: "But really, where were you? You can tell your old mother. I'm happy you're going out more, meeting people finally. It's good one of us finds a little joy. For me it will be when I dance at your wedding. Who were you with? Someone special? Don't give me that look. A mother knows. You were in a club of some kind. You think I never did such things when I was young? I tangoed the night away at Café Max in Prague, a downstairs bar with a live jazz band. I broke a few hearts ... so long ago. But tell me, do you have to wear such mannish clothes?"

She reaches out to grasp the collar of Toni's pinstriped shirt. The blazer, tie, and cap came off in the car and are hidden in Toni's rolled-up winter jacket. Nevertheless, her mother looks Toni up and down and for a moment anxiety clouds her eyes, a terrible doubt seems to break in, then is pushed away again.

"I know, everything's topsy-turvy now. Boys have long hair, girls wear overalls, young people on the street look like they're going to a masquerade ball. Never mind. Come have a cup of tea with your old mother. And then you must sleep."

Lisa puts the kettle on and continues to babble, filling up the silence while Toni suppresses yawns. Bone tired, she wants to fall into bed, but she can see her mother is like a wound-up top, desperate for contact. And despite her weariness, Toni relishes the comfort of tea in the kitchen, her chattering mother in her housecoat across the table. A dignified grief is etched on her mother's face, an Old World beauty filled with grand tragedy and resolve.

When at last Toni stumbles to her feet, her mother reaches up to hold her face between her hands.

"Sleep well, *Bubbele*."

Her mother can have no inkling about Loulou's. It's beyond her horizons. But had things gone further with Marie, would Lisa not have sensed something? *A mother can tell.* Toni cringes at the thought. Her body aches with thwarted desires. She doesn't know how she'll face the gang at Loulou's next week after tonight's humiliating performance. She tosses on the searing embers of anxieties before tumbling at last into merciful sleep.

Part V

The Ghetto and Beyond

chapter 26

A poster on a bulletin board stops Toni in her tracks, arresting her brisk journey across the university campus. Normally, she doesn't bother with the announcements that compete for student attention like waving hands. There is always so much going on: hootenannies, protest marches, poetry readings, football games, frat parties, film nights, talks on everything from Mao to meditation. When do these people have time to study?

During orientation week the entire freshman class assembled in the gymnasium for a pep talk by the rector. He stood at a podium, a remote stick figure in a grey suit, but with a voice that boomed over the sound system.

"Look to your left, look to your right," the voice thundered. "Imagine those people gone. Only a third of you will graduate. The rest will fall by the wayside."

Skeptical titters ran through the crowd, but Toni believed him. The rector's gloomy warning confirmed what she already knew, how much easier it was to go under than to stay afloat. She'd missed a year, was no longer in the groove of disciplined study. Only iron will could save her. She bought thick notebooks for each of her courses: Introduction to Biology, Bio Lab, Organic Chemistry, Plant Morphology, Psych 101. Inside the front covers she stapled schedules and campus maps and reading lists. She shunned the carnival-like distractions.

This day in mid-October, she's in a rush to get to Psych 101, a popular course held in an auditorium that fills up quickly. If she's late, she'll have to stand in the lobby and watch the professor on closed-circuit TV. Yet something about the poster has caught her eye.

"Sisters Unite!" shout the big red letters. "Rise up against patriarchy! A talk by Marsha Dvorak from the Women's Liberation Collective of Columbia University. Basement of the Unicentre. Thursday, Oct. 19, noon. THIS IS A WOMEN-ONLY EVENT!!!"

The poster includes a black-and-white photo of the speaker defaced with a moustache, a forked beard, horns, cartoon boobs. After "Sisters Unite," some wag has penned "and get up-tight." Other graffiti include: "cunts *über alles*," "butch bitches," "cocks unite to cure feminine frustration movement!" and most ominously, "We're coming to get you!" In a different tone, someone has neatly printed a question beside the "women only" restriction: "Isn't this discrimination too?"

Beneath this poster on the bulletin board, scotch-taped to the wall and lacking the administration's stamp of approval, hangs a densely typed mimeographed sheet proclaiming a manifesto by S.L.A.P. (Sisters Linked Against Patriarchy).

"Man, the oppressor, is responsible for war, violence, domination, capitalism, conformity, privilege, supremacist ideology. Womyn, the nurturer and original force of civilization, has been raped, abused, exploited, silenced, imprisoned in suburbia and the family. We are non-hierarchical, non-exploitive, anti-bourgeois, anti-doctrinaire, freedom-loving, joy-affirming."

At the end of the thirteen-point manifesto comes an invitation to another event: "Hex-in against the Annual Engineering Students' Miss Sensation contest. Disrupt this pageant of degradation. All wimmin welcome."

Surprisingly, this manifesto has not been defaced, perhaps because all those words leave little room in the margins for commentary and because the mimeographed sheet is hard to read. One has to stand close, bend down, pore over the blurry blue lines. A strange fascination roots Toni to the spot. She's heard mutterings about Miss Sensation in campus corridors and even at Loulou's, which she still frequents—her one indulgence—on Saturday nights. The manifesto's call to arms and the nasty comments on the Marsha Dvorak poster set off a storm in Toni's head. She imagines brandishing a baseball bat at thick-necked engineering types who threaten the women's lib meeting. The fantasy gathers force and she quivers with righteous anger. Then checks her watch. Damn! Better hurry.

As she cuts across campus, feet swishing through crisp autumn leaves, she notices a cluster of women by a fountain. She recognizes the impassioned, gesticulating figure of Francine, ringleader of the radical feminists at McGill, and a regular at Loulou's. Before she can swing away, they notice her too. Francine stops in mid-sentence to call out her name. Reluctantly, Toni approaches.

"You're coming to our protest action, right?"

More than Francine's words, it's the tone that rankles. The smug assumption, the veiled threat. The radicals claim Toni as their own because they've seen her at Loulou's. Supposedly, she has no choice but to fall into line.

"I have a lecture," Toni says, balling her fists in her jacket pockets.

"The action is on a Friday night," Francine says reasonably.

"I'll be preparing for my lab."

"A lab is more important than women's liberation?"

Francine's eyebrows arch upward above her granny glasses.

"I didn't come to college to fool around. I came for an education. Anyway, I'm not a witch."

Francine ignores this last comment. "Our event is very education-al," she says. "Whereas what you get in the lecture halls is a bourgeois, conformist message to uphold the patriarchy." The other women nod. Francine's bright, intelligent eyes fire out challenges. "Don't tell me you get the respect you deserve as one of the few women among all those male chauvinists in the science faculty."

Toni sees herself in the lecture hall with the rows of conservatively dressed, studious young men who generally ignore her because she's neither one of the guys nor dating material. Which is just fine, thank you. She doesn't want their attention.

"I'm not oppressed. If I do my work, I'm treated as an equal."

"But you're so hooked into the system, you don't see what it does to you."

Francine's tone drips with pity now. She bares her teeth in an ingratiating smile while scanning Toni's attire, taking obvious note of each concession made to traditional femininity: a purse, a bead choker, a satin blouse whose shiny cuffs peek out of the sleeves of Toni's wool pea jacket. The outfit is designed to conform to campus trends and contrasts markedly with the clothes Toni wears to Loulou's. A "gotcha" look gleams in Francine's eyes.

Toni glares back. "Can't chitchat any longer. I'm in a hurry."

"Maybe you're afraid to be seen with us? Afraid of what the straights might think?"

"You're right. I don't want to be seen with a bunch of commies."

Toni stalks off. There's a lot more she could add. For example, that she's heard the same rant against bourgeois education from one of the biggest male chauvinists in the hemisphere, a guy called David Konig, who uses hippie rhetoric to manipulate people, women especially, into abandoning their wills. And what's so bad about getting a degree, having a profession, instead of ending up a lowly paid stenographer in an office or a freeloading drop-out? She fumes to herself throughout the psych lecture while she leans against a wall in the lobby and frantically, awkwardly, scribbles notes about Pavlov's dog.

At Loulou's, she's become a lone wolf. Though she still clinks bottles with Juanita occasionally, Toni's not with that gang anymore. She got bored with the repetitive conversation, the hollow jokes, and they with her lengthening silences. Now she keeps her own company, nursing an air of mystery, her nose in a beer, one of a row of quiet, steady drinkers at the bar. She's got no time for entanglements anyway. She escapes to the club just to refresh and recommit herself to her serious long-term affair with her texts. Juanita comes by sometimes for a chat. She and Toni have maintained cordial relations, bound by some instinctive code of honour. The loyalty persists, though Toni's a college girl and could be viewed as one of "them," the new guard crowding out the old-timers. Loulou's has been changing, and fast. Every Saturday brings a fresh wave of kids from the suburbs and campuses. They are cute, though stridently unisex or studiously weird, and Rick has relaxed her standards to accommodate the new crowd. Anything goes—jeans, overalls, plaid shirts, beads and hippie tresses, Mao jackets, Che Guevara berets, army surplus togs. Rick shrugs as if to say, "*Ben*. What can you do?" She's got too much business sense to resist a rising tide.

The Saturday night after the Marsha Dvorak talk and the Miss Sensation pageant, Francine and her pals breeze in, lively and energized by the week's events. (A photo of them chanting, fists raised, upstaging the beauty queens at the pageant made the front page of the *McGill Daily*.) They wear austere outfits in keeping with their revolutionary zeal and butch haircuts, but woe to anyone who calls them butch. The buttons on their berets say, "Stop sleeping with the enemy" and "Sappho was a right-on woman." These gals buy drinks, though. They make Rick's cash register sing as they chatter and laugh and have a grand old time with their revolution. A couple of the militants begin distributing a flyer; it's the S.L.A.P. manifesto. Toni pushes it away.

"No thanks."

She sees Rick accept the flyer with a good-natured smile.

"*Ouai*. Don't need to tell me men are pigs. That's why I make this bar for girls only. What's that? Girls are women? Got it, *ma petite. Ex-actement!*"

Toni watches Rick slip the manifesto behind the counter—straight into the garbage no doubt—and smiles to herself while chugging back her beer. She's in that nice, numb state of inebriation when everything strikes her as delightfully absurd. Raised voices nearby wake her from her daze. An argument has broken out at a table by the back. Toni stands up to look over the heads of gathering spectators.

"Those shoes aren't made for walking, sister. High heels are a trap of the patriarchy. Liberate yourself."

Francine is haranguing Renée.

"Show some respect for the lady," Rhonda bellows. She's risen from her seat, drawn herself up to her full height—which doesn't amount to much—and jabs her finger upward into Francine's face. Renée has remained seated, her mouth turned down in an expression of disdain while her fingers pluck at Rhonda's sleeve as if to say: "It's not worth the trouble."

"Lady!"

Francine shakes her head and sighs as one would with a child painfully unaware of its foolishness.

"That's right, she's a lady. Better watch your tongue," Toni growls, pushing her way through the circle. Numbness has given way to righteous anger. Francine turns to face her.

"You think that's a term of respect? *Ladies* are patronized. *Ladies* are put on pedestals and turned into objects. And to think women are doing that to their sisters. It's pathetic. These women here have been brainwashed by double oppression, sexism and classism. But you! You should know better."

"I do. I know disrespect when I see it. I know commie talk when I hear it. If you were a real butch, I'd belt you."

A mighty wind fills Toni's chest. The joy of the fighting cock.

"Trouble with you is you're male-identified," Francine says with quiet scorn. "A repressed, fucked-up, bourgeois, imitation man who feels threatened by the revolution because it'll strip you of your privileges."

"See this?" Toni yells, raising her fist. "This ain't no imitation."

A hush falls over the group, a look of thrilled expectation illuminates the faces, even those of Francine's friends. The promise of drama grips them all.

But then a powerful force grabs Toni from behind, pinioning her arms, practically lifting her off the floor, and, in front of the startled onlookers, she's frog-marched to the rear door. A firm, adroitly planted foot on her backside thrusts her over the stoop and into a cluster of aluminum trash cans below. Lids scatter and clatter. The heavy door slams. She finds herself on the ground, holding her gravel-grazed hands to her chest, blinking her beer-dazed eyes in the dark. Flung like a rat into the alley. She immediately starts to shiver. The air is damp, unusually cold, with a whiff of approaching snow, and she's in her shirtsleeves.

"Shit!" she says aloud.

"Got some if you want," says a voice close by.

Toni starts and rattles the trash cans again. A squatting figure leans against the alley wall. Toni sees a coat with floppy sleeves, a peaked cap like the kind she herself sometimes wears, pulled low over a forehead, a glowing ember at the end of a hand. A familiar aroma reaches her nostrils. The ember rises toward her.

"Good weed. It'll take the edge off," the squatting girl says.

Toni ignores the offer and flings herself at the steel-clad door, grabbing the handle. Locked. She pounds with her fists and kicks with her feet. The thick metal barely reverberates.

"Rick, let me in! I need my jacket."

"Save your strength. Godzilla never lets anyone back in same night she's tossed her out."

"But I need my jacket."

Toni hammers some more at the door. She hears muffled music and chatter inside.

"I wouldn't do that or she'll blackball you."

"Yeah?" Toni wheels around. "That what happened to you?"

"Hell, no. I'm just having a date with Mary Jane. Couple of tokes left if you want."

Again the hand reaches up. The girl's small face wears the irrepressible, gleeful grin of the pothead.

"I don't touch that crap anymore. With booze you know what to expect."

"Damn right. Booze is reliable. The ten-minute glow, the two-hour daze, the rage, the blues, the black-out, the hangover. That was quite a crash landing by the way. Like in a Road Runner cartoon."

"Very funny."

"Hey, was I laughing? Did you see me laugh?"

The girl addresses these questions to her left hand which she's curled into a fist and holds up in front of her face. Out of the corner of her mouth, she mutters the answer in a high, nasal voice, ventriloquist style, "No way, José."

"Right. Thought so," the girl says in her normal voice, still addressing her fist.

"You wouldna laugh, Seenyor, to see someone so abused and tormented," the fist says in a Mexican accent. The curled fingers and thumb wiggle to imitate a speaking mouth, like Shari Lewis doing her Lamb Chop puppet.

"No, I wouldn't. I really wouldn't," the girl solemnly nods, but then her fist uncurls, her hand flies to her mouth, and she bursts into snorts and snickers.

"Fuck you," Toni says.

"Nice to meet you too. Name's Robin."

The oversized coat and the boyish cap, along with the seedy

atmosphere of the alley, make the girl look like a street urchin in a Dickens novel. Her merry eyes observe Toni.

"You part of Francine's crowd?"

"Francine's crowd! They wouldn't like to hear that. They don't believe in leaders. They're against hierarchy. Let's see, where do I fit in? Am I politico, hippie, artsy-fartsy, or just a garden-variety pervert? Whadja think?" Robin addresses her fist again.

"Leedle bit of everytheeng, Seenyor," the fist says. "You are schizoid, no?"

"If I'm schizoid, what are you?" Robin asks the fist.

"My name ees José Jeminez," the fist bleats, like the sad-faced, stand-up comic from *The Ed Sullivan Show.*

Robin looks up to see if Toni's laughing yet and, finding she's not, grins and shrugs. "Don't worry. I'm not certifiable."

A violent bout of the shivers seizes Toni again. She stamps her feet, hugs herself, and rubs her jacketless arms, muttering, "Shit, shit" between chattering teeth.

"Poor baby! Take this."

Robin has risen and peeled off her coat, which she drapes over Toni's hunched shoulders. "Come, put it on," she coaxes, as she stands before Toni in her open-necked flannel shirt. "I'll go around through the front and get your jacket. Rick will give it to me. Meet me by the stairs. We can go for a burger if you want. Nothing like food to warm you up. Anyway, I've got the munchies real bad."

Though tight across Toni's shoulders, the dark wool coat, still warm from the girl's body, cuts the damp wind and brings comfort. Toni trots up the alley behind Robin's retreating figure. Her beer glow has dissipated, replaced by wobbly knees and a dull sense of gloom.

A short while afterward, Toni and Robin sit facing one another in a booth at the A&W on Sainte Catherine Street, demolishing the midnight special: cheeseburgers, fries, large mugs of root beer. Each savoury bite revives Toni's spirits. Robin too eats with gusto, her cheeks rosy, her lips shiny with grease. She's not exactly knock-you-down gorgeous, Toni decides, but captivating in her own way. Dark, intelligent eyes, funny upturned nose, good skin, long black hair fastened in a loose ponytail, bold, unplucked eyebrows. Her manner of talking is quick and bright with a teasing cock of her head now and then. The name suits. There's something of the plucky bird about her.

Between mouthfuls, Robin tells Toni who among the women's libbers and Marxist-Leninists that frequent Loulou's are living together or have slept with one another and so weaves a tangled web of relationships in which she too has been involved. If Toni thinks those women are sexless missionaries, she's sorely mistaken. The love juices flow as freely as the rhetoric. They are an incestuous bunch of sisters, which can make for tortured sessions at consciousness raising groups. Still, they're more loving than hurtful of one another, Robin insists, and the urgency to fix a broken world keeps the bonds strong. Robin is in full sympathy with the revolution—who wouldn't be, she asks—but without waiting for an answer sighs and admits that lately the intensity feels stifling. The imperative to make all personal acts political takes up so much energy. She wouldn't mind an uncomplicated roll in the hay that doesn't have to go through the feminist-analysis shredder in the morning. As Robin says this, she licks her thumb, and something about her direct look into Toni's eyes hits like a hammer on a gong. Toni feels her face heat up.

"Me, I only date femmes," she says gruffly and takes a huge gulp from her mug. The fizzy drink explodes into prickles at the back of her head. She has to close her mouth quickly to swallow a cough. When she glances Robin's way again she can see she's being observed with amused interest.

"How do you define 'femme'?"

Robin strikes a pose, chin on fingertips, eyelashes fluttering. Then another: eyes wide, mouth in an "O," hand on heart like a damsel in distress. Another still: face sideways, smile vampish, the tip of her pink tongue peeking from the corner of her mouth. The mimicry is perfect, the contrast with the boyish flannel shirt, absurd. Toni guffaws, but the tightness in her chest intensifies.

"Seriously, I'm curious. I've never actually talked to someone who's into the butch-femme thing. It's kinda out of style these days. What about it turns you on?"

"Oh, well, you know. The ultra-feminine look. Dresses, makeup, glamour. I couldn't date a girl who looks too much like I do. Opposites attract."

Blood rushes up Toni's neck, into her cheeks, her eartips, in an inferno of embarrassment. She's suddenly aware of how tall, rangy, and big-boned she is, compared to Robin's delicate features and petite form. How stupid to have brought up the subject of dates.

"Opposites attract? Only opposites? Really?" Robin grins. "Is that what they teach you in biology? So how come mice don't mate with elephants? Or ballerinas with road workers?" She shrugs. "I think everyone's potentially androgynous. Straights go out of their way to accentuate differences to shore up heterosexuality. But to each her own. Personally, I like the surprise package effect."

"What's that?"

"Well, when a woman's got plain clothes on, she's like a mystery present in a brown paper wrapping. You get her home, undo the wrapping and, wow! You discover the lovely, soft body underneath. More seductive than satin and lace. At least to me."

Suddenly, with great clarity, Toni imagines Robin lying back on a bed, her black hair loose, her plaid shirt unbuttoned. The faded green-and-brown flannel contrasts with the freshness of her skin. At the base of her throat is a delicate hollow into which the tip of a tongue would so nicely fit. Then Toni realizes she's staring at that very spot and her heart begins to pound without mercy.

"I guess the libbers have brainwashed me," Robin is saying. "I like a sense of equality. Oh well. It's late." She yawns without covering her mouth and the scrunching up and subsequent relaxation of her face are enchanting. Like a magic trick. "Time to get a move on, I guess."

When the waiter comes with the bills, Toni tries to pay both.

"But why?" Robin asks, eyes wide. "This isn't a date, is it?"

Toni bites her lip and agrees to go Dutch. While they're getting up from the table, Robin asks where Toni lives.

"In Snowdon. With my mother."

"Oh my God, that's so butch!" Robin's hand flies dramatically to her heart. "Do you have a curfew? Don't look so mortified. Just kidding. Can't help myself. You're so kiddable."

Snow flutters down from the heavens when they emerge onto Sainte Catherine Street. Like a zillion white moths, fat flakes fill the air, pull the city into the premature embrace of winter. There's no wind, just this steady, dreamy rain of white. Feathery snow blankets roads, sidewalks, tops of cars, windowsills, mailboxes, fallen leaves. The traffic has thinned. A few cars sail by with a hiss of tires on roadside slush. The sky between the drifting flakes is pearly grey and luminous.

"Oh," Robin cries. She flings her arms wide and tips her face heavenward. "Wow."

Her long black coat flaps as she gambols about. She grabs Toni's arm.

"Let's walk! Let's walk!"

Down Sainte Catherine Street they scamper, past darkened shops, lampposts haloed with glitter, Saturday night stragglers rushing home. They slip and slide on their smooth-soled shoes. Snow settles on Toni's hatless head, creeps down the back of her neck, and she shivers, but she isn't cold. At Eaton's department store, whose displays are well-lit despite the hour, Robin stops to mock the mannequins in fur coats. She contorts her limbs into ridiculous poses, hip thrust this way, elbows that, fingers splayed. She pirouettes, toppling backward against the window glass, and Toni doubles up with laughter. In that moment Toni sees how appreciative laughter energizes Robin's antics, how Robin's spirit blossoms like a plant in the sun, and Toni feels the delicious power of being sun-like in her attentions.

They meander down side streets. Where are they heading? Nowhere, it seems. Wherever their feet will take them, for as long as this mood of abandonment lasts. Nothing matters to Toni but this white magic all around and this bold frolicking imp at her side. They walk through alleys where snow transforms garbage into cuddly creatures, down the middle of streets following tire tracks of packed-down slush. Robin's unabashed chatter—now pure clownery, now interesting revelations—is a key that turns locks. Toni finds herself talking too, about adolescent longing and high school misery. Stories of pain and loneliness that shared become badges of honour.

"Yeah, that was me, all right. It was hell ... "

How wonderful to have a hell to describe to another who understands and nods and grins. And interrupts so charmingly.

"Jewish camp, no kidding? You're Jewish? So where are your horns? Don't tell me you don't have horns, I'll be very disappointed. According to the nuns, I've been hankering for the devil all my life. I'm a failed Catholic, thanks be to Christ. Came out at boarding school. The Sacred Heart convent on Côte des Neiges. Yes, the building on the hill that looks like Dracula's castle. I was sixteen. Me and my roommate Mona cuddled under the covers at night, dying with lust and fear because Sister Agatha patrolled the halls in running shoes and held onto her rosary beads so you couldn't hear her coming. Mona finally cracked. Guilt ate her up. Made me join her in self-imposed penance. Cold showers, kneeling on bare floors, fasts. We'd make love, then she'd wake me in the night for Hail-Mary marathons. Looney-tunes. But I couldn't let her go. Thought I'd have to throw myself out the fourth-storey window. Finally, Mother Superior realized something was up and sent Mona home. Exhaustion, they said. Maybe she had the saint's calling, but in the meantime she was suffering from nervous strain. We were to pray for her *mens sana in corpere sano*. I begged my parents to take me out too, which they did, thank the Goddess. Best thing for me, going back to a normal school with normal delinquents. What about you? Did you see that counsellor again? Did you and her finally get it on?"

"Well, sort of. It was, it was in Israel," Toni falters.

"Outta sight! And?"

"A long story. I'll tell you another time."

"Ah, the pain of first loves," Robin says gently.

On and on they drift, through a night as dazzling as the Milky Way. Presently, they're on Sherbrooke Street, heading for the massive stone gates of the university. Robin falls silent, lost in thought, though she walks with purpose. Toni doesn't ask where they're going, but a hunch grows and her heart beats fast. Beyond the snowbound campus they arrive at a neighbourhood called "the Ghetto," a moniker that always struck Toni as odd. Nothing here calls to mind the seething ghettoes of medieval Europe. Elegant rowhouses of grey stone line the quiet residential streets. Some buildings were once manors but have since been subdivided and served as digs for generations of students. Long outdoor staircases with graceful wrought-iron banisters stretch from the street to upper floors. At the bottom of one of these Robin stops.

"Here's where I live."

Toni can't speak. All through their long walk, she's been chanting an inner prayer: *Take me home with you. Take me home.* Now, as they stand at the foot of the snowy stairs that lead to Robin's door, Toni grasps the icy banister to keep from sinking to her knees.

"Your feet must be freezing." Robin smiles and begins to climb the stairs. "Mine are. Coming up?" Toni clings to the banister.

"But you're shaking like a leaf. What's the matter? Why don't you come?" Robin descends a few steps and peers at Toni's face. "You look like you've seen a ghost. Say something. Oh no! Now I've got it." Robin strikes her forehead. "You're a virgin. 'Course you are. Why didn't I realize? All that butch-femme bravado and the way you were blushing at the restaurant. I thought it was shyness, but shit, you're not even out."

"I'd like to come up," Toni manages to mumble.

"Uh-uh. Not a good idea. I'm not feeling motherly right now. Virgins are famous for falling in love with whoever brings them out. Instant enchantment, like in *Midsummer Night's Dream*. Snap, and you're in love with whoever flicked your switch. It gets too personal and complicated, see? All I want is a fling, an easy fuck, not to have to feel responsible. Oh shit, don't look at me like that. Why weren't you upfront?"

"I'm not a virgin."

Toni feels herself blush to the roots of her hair.

"Your nose is growing. Men don't count. If you've been fucked by a man, it doesn't count."

"I won't fall in love. I promise."

Toni grabs Robin's sleeve.

"You must think I'm full of myself," Robin says, gently pulling herself free and taking a step backward. "I've just seen a lot of intensity lately. And I don't believe in love anymore. It's a trap, makes people possessive. Slaves."

"Just this once. I'll go home right after … "

She tries to think of a promise to convince Robin that the need ripping through her body isn't dangerous. Other nights, when she stood on the doorstep of someone willing, she was the one to turn away, overwhelmed by her desires. Yet it was nothing to what she feels now. Terrified. Incandescent. Filled with a hot white light. Sure in her bones that only good can come of this. Unable to say it out loud.

"Aw, look at you. You make me feel like a bitch. All right then, Goofy, come on up."

Does she just feel obliged, Toni wonders, as one would feel obliged to take in a stray cat? But the hand that reaches out and grasps Toni's is sure and firm and transmits a more heated invitation than words alone could do. Toni's heart hammers harder. Robin in the lead, they ascend the long, snowy staircase toward a red wooden door at the top. Inside, they creep down the hall so as not to wake Robin's roommates, and arrive at a tiny bedroom whose narrow space is almost entirely filled with a wide, low bed. Robin lights candles, one after another until the room is ablaze, then pulls Toni down. They swim into the deep warm sea of a kiss.

"What do you like?" Robin whispers when they are naked. "Tell me."

"I don't know," Toni confesses, amazed to hear herself tell the truth. "It's my first time ... like this."

She shuts her eyes and waits for Robin's reaction, the I-knew-it accusations about Toni's virginity. Everything could be over before it has begun.

"Right, your first time."

Robin sighs, producing a long, warm, tickling breeze that sets everything inside Toni a-quiver.

"Well then, we better go slow. The first time is really important."

She has left the known world. She is waving goodbye, this time for real. Behind her, the certainty of pyramids. Before her, the wilderness, the dry, brown earth, crags and thorns. No shelter here. No history to hang onto. Only space and silence and the freedom to be naked. She is no longer the chosen. She chooses. The flood of heat. The thunder of her heart. She is home.

chapter 27

They never use the "L" word. Banished is the sentiment that creates mountains of expectations and sinkholes of grief: Love. Ooey-gooey love. Beware the romance industry, Hallmarks, Harlequins, the patriarchal capitalist plot, the cleaving that turns women into docile imbeciles, emotional weaklings, slavish consumers of everything from overpriced lingerie to washing machines. Love equals monogamy equals aping the straight world's idea of marriage (egotism à deux, imprisoning domesticity).

Though they have excised the word "love" from their vocabulary, "lover" is okay. Lovers can be bold, sexy, sophisticated, spontaneous, non-exclusive, free. Lovers don't wallow or cling. Lovers aren't "in" anything. They are just themselves.

Toni, the lover, strides across campus toward the Ghetto. Walking tall. She *is* tall. She is stretched out to her full glorious height, never again to shrink into herself like a faint-hearted turtle. She wants a gift to bring her honey. But what? Flowers? *Verboten.* Flowers to Robin would be like bacon to a rabbi. Chocolates? Another romantic cliché. She follows the trail of dirty slush into a grocery store and cruises the aisles. Beans, par-boiled rice, instant mashed potatoes—the staples of student diets. There must be something. Finally, she settles on a Sara Lee banana cake from the frozen foods cooler. It has a thick, golden layer of frosting. Sweet and sensuous, yet neutral. But will Robin be pleased? Toni hurries from the store plagued by doubts over the hard, icy package tucked under her arm.

At the bottom of the long outdoor staircase leading to the magical red door of Robin's apartment, Toni pauses to catch her breath, compose her face, think of casual opening lines. *Hi, doll. How's it going? Brought a little something for dessert.* At last she can wait no longer. The staircase shakes beneath her bounding feet.

"Oh!" Robin says. "It's you." Her brown eyes register the guarded surprise of someone who finds an uninvited guest on her doorstep. Panic stabs Toni beneath the breastbone. Did Robin forget their date? But the impish face breaks into a grin. "Kidding. Just kidding. Jeez, you're so easy!"

How lovely Robin appears, a woodland sprite in a plaid flannel shirt and men's work socks, her glossy, unpinned hair spilling over her shoulders. They sit on the edge of Robin's bed in the small, overheated room, and all Toni's efforts to calm herself come undone. They've been going out (if that's what it's called) for more than a month and still Toni trembles as she did the first time. She swabs her sweaty brow with the back of her hand. Robin apologizes for the overheated room, says the window is stuck. Toni leaps up, glad to have a chore to perform for her sweetheart. She yanks and pummels the stubborn sash until a cool hand touches her arm.

"Hey, Goofy. Save your energy for something better."

Robin's eyes are wide and dark. And tender. So amazingly tender. They tumble upon the bed.

How is it possible, Toni wonders anew, to penetrate that soft vulnerable place in Robin and deliver not pain but pleasure? A miracle. Her lover's body arches, the navel smiles, a deep-throated groan echoes through the room. They take turns taking all they need from one another, then they fall into velvet sleep.

Later, howling with laughter, their naked, unequally sized bodies wrapped together in a bed sheet, they lurch across the hall to the bathroom. The walls are painted metallic red—the red of accidents, of lipsticked temptresses—and there are candles, incense holders, and ashtrays. There's a poster of John Lennon in wire-rimmed glasses, another of Janis Joplin in feathers and beads. Robin squeezes gobs of raspberry bubble bath into the gush from the faucet of the big clawfoot tub. Mounds of foam swell as the water pounds. Clouds of steam fog the window, shutting out the winter night. Robin has bath sports to teach, games with washcloths, soap, toes. Where did she learn to play so deliciously? With other girls? Jealousy! *Verboten.*

They soak until their fingers pickle, passing a soggy joint from hand to hand.

"I think I'm starting to corrupt you a little," Robin says.

Later still they attack the Sara Lee cake. They eat straight from the aluminium container, clashing forks, letting the flavours explode on their tongues and in their marijuana-soaked brains. Mesmerized, Toni watches Robin's buttercream-shiny lips move in rhythmic chewing. Her own mouth moves in exactly the same way, the same pace, as if drawn into a dance. How wonderful. One mind in two bodies. The union of souls. *Union? As in marriage? Hush. Shush. Don't spoil the moment.*

Toni explains the magic of photosynthesis as exemplified by chains of formulas and diagrams of cells packed with chloroplasts. She rhymes off the multi-syllabic molecules proudly, as if she had discovered them herself. Though she can see Robin's face has gone stiff with boredom, Toni talks faster and faster. Her lover yawns mightily. She hops up from the bed, away from Toni and the fat, densely printed textbook between them.

Robin is into arts, drama in particular. She has no head for facts and formulas, and like much of the ill-informed world, finds science a bit sinister despite its usefulness. Science run amok leads to nuclear bombs and lobotomies, she argues. Look at her dad, a doctor, and a prime example of cold, patronizing hubris. Plus, she feels sorry for the rat in the maze, the dog in the cage, the chimp attached to wires. She almost wept over the experiment on the nurturing-deprived rhesus monkeys. The photo in Toni's psychology text showed a deranged baby monkey cowering in a corner and rocking on its haunches. Toni had to admit she too was disturbed by the forlorn expression on the animal's face, but how else is science to advance?

Now, with a flick of her toe, Robin flips open the lab notebook Toni left on the floor and grimaces. The page shows diagrams of dissections including one of the urogenital system, with vaginal flaps pinned back to expose the cervix.

"Poor kitty!" Robin's voice throbs with tragedy.

"It was a mouse, not a cat. Anyway, it was long dead. We didn't hurt it."

Robin doesn't look convinced.

"One day I might discover the gene for gayness," Toni jokes.

She's thinking about the astounding breakthroughs of recent years, electron microscopes, the structure of the DNA molecule. Because of such leaps in technology and knowledge, Toni Goldblatt, a mere first-year biology student, might be better equipped to someday unravel the mysteries of the organic world than Einstein could in his era.

"Then what? Aborted fetuses? Exterminations of defective carriers?" Robin's tone is combative. She pulls a sweater over her head in frowning silence. With a stab of panic, Toni realizes that Robin is about to depart.

"Can I come watch your rehearsal?" Toni pleads. She ought to study, but she's not ready to let Robin out of her sight just yet. And she knows Robin always likes an audience.

"Sure." Robin offers a faint but forgiving smile.

Toni wishes she had words to convey her love of biology. The bigness of the field drives her, the depths, and the mysterious intimacy too. She once read a heart surgeon's memoir. The surgeon described an outdated technique for saving patients in cardiac arrest by cutting open the patient's chest cavity and manually massaging the failing organ to restore its rhythm. An incredible sensation, the memoirist wrote, to hold a quivering heart in one's bare hands. Yet all of biology is like that, Toni thinks; it's a breathtaking closeness to the essence of life. True, most of her course work is drudgery. The number of interlocking mechanisms in a single cell alone staggers the mind. She reviews and memorizes and digests, but every so often is struck by pure astonishment. You go down, down, down to the basics—atoms jostle against each other, electrons skip out of their orbits, new bonds are formed, complexity grows. Out of unfathomably tiny bits of matter and energy comes a whole universe. And life? Surely it's more than the sum of inanimate parts. Will that mystery someday be unravelled? The quivering truth within?

Although enrolled in English literature at McGill, Robin's real passion is an experimental troupe called the Oh Theatre. Several evenings a week, the eleven members of the troupe meet in an empty loft near the harbour in Old Montreal. They rehearse a piece, written by the director, about a family hiding out in a bomb shelter in the aftermath of a nuclear holocaust. Robin plays an angry daughter who argues for going up to check on what's left of the outside world. Her lines are impassioned pleas for freedom. A theme song plays between acts: Dylan's "Let Me Die in My Footsteps."

The lone spectator, Toni sits in the shadows on a heap of old rolled-up carpets as she watches, entranced. How can Robin give so much of herself in public? How can she make herself transparent to people she hardly knows and eventually to an audience of strangers? Robin rages, falls on her knees, digs her nails into her scalp, and sobs in a heart-wrenching manner. Toni wants to leap up and put her arms around her darling. Before she can do so, Robin lifts her head and she asks in a weary voice, "Overdone?" Toni is indignant when the director nods in the affirmative.

After rehearsal, she and Robin stroll through the narrow streets of Old Montreal, past all-night jazz joints, head shops, art galleries, basement cafés. Robin has introduced Toni to this chic part of town that not so long ago was just a drab business area by day and a den of crime by night. The district, with its old stone buildings, has a European feel. Toni confesses her dream of taking Robin to Vienna someday. She can speak some German, and remembers her father's stories; she could act as a guide, showing her sweetheart the Imperial Palace, the boulevards, parks, the street where the Jews had to scrub the sidewalks, the bookshop where her father once worked. She imagines how Robin would ache with sympathy.

"Let's go next summer," Toni enthuses. She takes Robin's hand and slips it into her jacket pocket so that their two hands can nestle together.

Robin laughs lightly and pulls away.

"Next summer is a long way off."

"So tell me about him," her mother says casually.

The command fails to register at first. The words are as meaningless as the dripping of the tap at the kitchen sink, the muttering of the 7 a.m. news. In a fog of weariness, Toni nurses her second cup of coffee. Her mother sits opposite in the breakfast nook, dressed for work in a smart wool dress adorned with a bright silk scarf. Lisa more or less manages Shmelzer's Ladies' Fashions these days. She supervises the sales staff and the seamstress, handles transactions with suppliers. Months ago, she changed her hairstyle yet again, dying it black with one dramatic wave of white in the front to remind the world of her losses, yet still appearing chic. The elegant hairdo frames a face with eager eyes and a bright, coaxing smile.

"*Nu?*"

Him? Uh-oh.

"What are you talking about?"

"You think I'm blind? You think I don't see what's obvious, not just to me who reads you like a book, but to the whole world? My little girl is in love."

For a second, Toni swells with the pleasure of her joy acknowledged. Then she remembers what's at stake. Cruelly awake now, palms sweating, she whisks the hands that had caressed Robin's body mere hours ago under the table. As if her mother might guess what those hands have been up to.

"You have blossomed like a rose. You smell of love. See? I say the word and you blush."

"Bullshit. I'm not blushing," Toni counters. Her cheeks are on fire.

Her mother barely raises an eyebrow at the strong language. Her face maintains an expression of pleasurable expectation.

"I'm not in love. I don't believe in love. It's romantic garbage that turns women into slaves."

"Oh dear." Her mother shakes her head knowingly. "All right, not love. But you like someone. And you're spending a lot of time with him. And he makes you happy. That's no crime, my darling. You mustn't be so afraid of your heart."

"I go out with a bunch of friends, that's all. Just friends. I wish you wouldn't try to poke into my head."

"Finish your breakfast. Don't run away. I'll leave you alone if you don't want to talk. I only wanted you to know I am happy to see you happy."

She gives Toni a two-eyed wink, squeezing both eyes shut and opening them rapidly again, a special signal of approval and delight dating back to Toni's childhood. Then, seeing her daughter has clammed up but good, Lisa makes a great show of burying herself in the newspaper.

She turns pages, scans articles, hums along with the Mozart concerto on the radio. She smiles as if she were the one glowing with the deep-down beautiful secret. They sink back into companionable silence, but presently a voice across the table asks Toni, "What's his name? Surely you can tell me that."

For some reason—perhaps because she's still addled from last night's pleasures—Toni drops her guard.

"Robin."

There. It's out. The name she chants to herself day and night. Two syllables that can demolish her mother, wreck their home. Toni's tripping tongue has gone heavy and dry, and her heart hammers without mercy as she waits for the explosion.

"Robin," her mother muses, still smiling. "That sounds British. Is he British?"

"No," Toni mumbles. "Not exactly."

Lightning bolt averted. Of course. Robin Hood, Christopher Robin. It doesn't occur to Toni's mother that Robin could be a girl.

"Robin," Lisa repeats with a nod of approval. "Very sweet."

Toni grins despite herself. She could hug her mother for saying Robin's name is sweet. Immediately afterward she frowns and jumps up from the table. Behind her mother's falsely casual air, she can see all the other questions lined up and jostling forward: *Where does he live? What does he do? What does he look like? Who's the family? Is he Jewish? When's the wedding?*

"I'm late," Toni blurts. "I've got to get to class. I've got a mid-term. Where's my book bag? I can't find my book bag."

Just as Toni's hurrying out the door, her mother warbles in her most engaging manner, "Bring him home for Shabbas dinner sometime."

Later that day, at Robin's place, Toni admits her regrets. She'll have to pay dearly for that liberating moment of truthfulness. Her mother will be like a bloodhound on the scent. She'll lay traps and ambushes, won't be put off. Not without a mighty effort, anyway.

"But I wouldn't mind coming to dinner," Robin teases. "I like Jewish food. And I bet I'd like your mum too."

"Yeah, I bet you would," Toni says mournfully. "She might have liked you too."

Toni hunches on Robin's bed with her chin in her hands thinking of all that's been lost. It would indeed have been nice to bring home her "best friend" from McGill for a Friday night meal, for candle-lighting and blessings over wine and bread, her mother whispering the prayers, then rushing out to the kitchen to fetch a feast of savoury dishes. It would have been delightful to see her mother and Robin on their best behaviour, charming one another, to bask in the glow of a budding relationship between the two people she cares about most. She can imagine her mother telling stories of her past, her escapes and survival and Robin's wide-eyed interest and respectful murmurs. Robin would recite Shakespeare while playing footsies with Toni under the table. Alas, now none of this can come to pass.

"Why not?" Robin asks, without cracking a smile. "She's invited me. Remember?"

"The Robin she invited is a boy. Remember?"

"So tell her the truth. You have to sometime. Get it over with. I did."

Robin shrugs, as if nothing could be simpler. Tell the truth. Face the consequences. No big deal. Toni stares at her beloved in dismay.

"But you and your family are estranged."

"That was their choice, not mine. A major shitload, but I got over it. At least I'm free to be myself. Don't have to pretend to be something I'm not."

Toni knows the story of how Robin came out a year ago at Christmas dinner. Her father had just finished sharpening the carving knife and was ready to slice into the golden-brown bird. After Robin's pronouncement, the knife remained raised in the air. A horrified silence fell upon the room. Her mother folded her napkin and in a quavering voice announced she would just check on the mincemeat tarts in the oven. When the kitchen door closed, Robin's three brothers and two sisters erupted in jeers. Their father thundered for quiet. He didn't want to hear another word and insisted they have a normal, proper, family Christmas dinner. The subject was soundly dropped as they passed dishes, piled their plates. During the flaming of the Christmas pudding, one of the brothers made a reference to fruitcakes and her mother had to take a pill and one of the sisters burst into tears. On Boxing Day, after the last visits of the relatives and exchanges of gifts, Robin's father offered her a deal. She could discreetly seek psychiatric help for her "identity crisis" at the Allen Memorial Hospital, but, if she refused treatment, she would no longer be welcome under his roof. He would set her up in an apartment and pay for her college tuition—provided, of course, she didn't disgrace the family with a public scandal. In other words, he offered her hush money. She accepted the offer and never looked back. "They can all go to hell," Robin says.

Toni admires Robin's courage, her kiss-my-ass attitude. Amazing, to walk away not just from parents, but from a pack of siblings and relatives too. Robin implies that Toni should be able to act with similar boldness. But their situations are so different. *Different how?* Toni can't explain. So now she just lets her chest fill with misery and apology as she says to Robin, "I don't want to come out to my mother. Not yet."

"Suit yourself."

Robin puts on her Janis Joplin record, cranks up the volume so that the bass guitar buzzes the window pane. She rocks her shoulders and smiles to herself as Janis howls out a number about a ball and chain.

chapter 28

Lisa plays solitaire at the dining room table while Toni studies for a mid-term exam. Slap, slap go the cards, a soothing sound along with the creak of wood as their bodies shift on the old pine chairs. Her parents bought the dining set at Morgan's department store bargain basement soon after they came to Canada; it has been part of Toni's home for as long as she can remember. The room smells of freshly brewed mocha, of strudel, and the last of the Sabbath candles that just burnt themselves out. Her mother remains pleasantly in the background until she declares, "I have discovered why you won't tell me about your boyfriend."

A snort of hot coffee flies up Toni's nose. She coughs and sputters. *What now?*

Her mother doesn't look up, continues to arrange cards, though she's no longer engaged in the game of solitaire. Face-down rows of three lie before her—the old fortune-telling pattern—and as she turns them over one by one, she focuses intently on each revelation, her lips moving as if in silent conversation with herself.

"He isn't Jewish," her mother says, while she taps a jack of spades with her forefinger and nods her head. "I was starting to worry he's a criminal, a hoodlum. Or he's deformed with one eye that stares and another that wanders. But my daughter wouldn't fall in love with a thug or a freak. I realize now it's much simpler."

"Mama, lay off. You begged me to stay home more, so I'm home. I have an exam. I have to study. I told you I broke up with him. It's finished. Okay? I don't have a boyfriend."

"No, it is not finished."

Her mother shakes and shakes her head with small emphatic movements so that for a moment Toni thinks she's developed a tremor. "You are so infatuated, yet full of secrets. You make up stories, hide, try to distract me, look as if you'll faint when the phone rings." Her mother sighs and lifts her head. She looks at Toni with deeply wounded eyes. "Don't tell me I'm wrong. There should be no lies between us. You are my daughter. All I have left in the world."

Her mother's chin quivers. Toni sits speechless.

"You think I won't understand, but I do. Love makes people foolish. It's natural and beautiful, all the same. I am not prejudiced, but naturally, I want you to marry a Jew. For one thing, it would make your life easier. When two people share the same culture, when both face the same challenges from the outside world, when they can take certain points of view for granted in the other, there is a basis for trust. It's not the same between people of a different background. One day out of nowhere can come an ugly surprise, an innocent-sounding question— 'Why do you Jews do this or that?' A casual remark, but it cuts to the bone. The *chazer-fus*, the little pig's foot pokes out, we used to say. The worst is when the children are born. It becomes so complicated."

"Mama, stop!"

Her mother closes her eyes and takes a deep breath.

"A mother can only wish for the best and advise, but not force her will. Since I'm on the topic of advice, let me say one other thing. Nowadays, girls do everything with boys. Free love. The Age of Aquarius. Ha! You think I don't have eyes and ears? Young people think they have changed the world. Every generation thinks so. Believe me, believe your old mother. A girl needs to hold back to maintain the boy's respect. All right now. Don't look so offended. I've said my piece. Follow your heart. But stop this skulking around in the shadows."

Toni stares down miserably into her lap. She hears the soft slap of cards against the table.

"I see something else," her mother says after a long silence. "He is shorter than you. Well, that's not so terrible either."

A strangled laugh bursts from Toni's lips. The room seems wobbly and her head feels as if the coffee she's drunk has gathered at the back of her skull, defying the laws of physics and digestion, and is about to explode. *Tell the truth.* Easy for Robin to say. Robin's parents have a slew of other children. They can afford to let one go. And Robin can afford to let *them* go because someone's sure to break rank and take her side. Already this has started to happen. A brother called to invite her to a pub crawl. An aunt hinted she's trying to get the father to relent. For all their uptightness, Robin's folks lead normal lives. When they see smoke rise from a chimney, they don't think, *Hitler's ovens, lost relations.* Robin doesn't have to answer to slaughtered millions. Or to a mother who reminds her several times a day, "You are all I have left."

Now Toni's mother sweeps up the cards and places them back in their lacquered wooden box. After another long look into Toni's face, she sighs.

"Just remember I can't help but see what I see. Even though this fellow isn't what I had in mind, I'm aware of your happiness, and my heart is glad. Bring him home for dinner. I don't care if he's a Mongolian pygmy, I'd like to meet him."

Toni bends her head to her notes. Her hand moves across the pages to highlight key words and phrases with a yellow felt-tip pen. Her lips recite, "Mitosis: the process by which a cell duplicates its genetic information ..." *You would wish for a Mongolian pygmy, if you knew. You would hold out your wrists and say, "Slash them, go ahead."*

"... pairs of chromosomes condense and attach to fibres that ..." *No, worse. You'd stand there with a face of devastation.* "... pull the sister chromatids to the opposite sides of the cell." *And you, Mama, are all I have left.*

What? What was that?

Toni's hand with the felt-tip pen freezes in mid-air as this last startling thought drifts through her mind.

But that's not true. I have Robin.

Sunday morning. Late. Toni can tell by the stale taste of the air in the room and the throbbing redness beyond her closed lids. Reluctantly, she opens her eyes onto a sun-drenched room. Light glints off the ice-glazed roofs and snow-heaped balconies of the Ghetto. Although it's March, the city still lies in the grip of winter. Within a few hours, perhaps even before she's managed to pour enough coffee into her gut to become fully conscious, the sun will have sunk again toward a blood-red horizon. Spring break is over. Final exams approach. She should rise. She should force herself to creep away from Robin's sleeping body and get over to the library. When she tries to move, a stab of pain travels down her occipital nerve. She imagines this nerve as a tightly wound vibrating guitar string. She imagines all the cones and rods of her retina clacking together like castanets and the vitreous jelly quivering.

Last night was a mistake in a long series of mistakes. Earlier in the day, the Oh Theatre set up an ambush in a busy shopping centre. The troupe gathered in Place Ville Marie in the midst of the Saturday rush and, without sets, props, or warning, launched into their play. It was the scene in which the family gazes up at the ceiling of the bomb shelter and wonders what's going on outside. The idea was to shake people up, break down the barriers between audience and actors, between the stage and the everyday world. Some shoppers stopped to stare and to glance uneasily at the cement above their own heads. Other people just elbowed past. It was the troupe's third such venture into guerrilla theatre. Toni watched the whole production, half irritated, half bored since, by the third time around, the caper had become stale, at least for her. For the troupe, it was still an incredible high to jolt passers-by out of their self-absorbed trajectories. Afterward, all the theatre people went to someone's house to toke up and then to a blues bar in Old Montreal. After that, back to the loft for more partying. Toni tagged along to the bitter end because Robin expected her to. Or was it because Robin didn't?

Scenes float up through the fog of memory: Robin dancing erotically with one of her acting buddies—a girl with long blonde hair, high cheekbones, violet eyes. Supposedly straight. The two pressed up against each other making kissy faces. Was it merely another performance, or did a current of real desire run beneath the show? Couldn't have been too serious, though, could it, because Little Miss Glamourpuss is not the one who spent the night in Robin's bed. Toni remembers draining the last drops from a bottle of Johnny Walker. She remembers a taxi, the long difficult ascent up the slippery outdoor stairs to Robin's apartment, leaning on Robin's shoulder. Just Robin, or was there someone else? Several people? Did the party continue in the kitchen or was that merely a dream? She slides her hand sideways, reaching for Robin, and finds instead a cool expanse of taut bedsheet where her girlfriend should be. She opens her eyes again. The room is empty.

"Robin!" she croaks. "Hey, Robin."

Peals of laughter from the kitchen. Creak of the floorboards in the hall. Slam of the front door.

"Robin! Where the fuck are you?"

She'd go see for herself, but her head feels like a bag of mud.

The door of the bedroom swings open and Robin waltzes in, bright-eyed, rosy-cheeked, perky, smiling. And stark naked. Toni heaves herself into a sitting position.

"What are you doing?"

"I was about to take a bath. Wanna join me?"

"Who were you just with? I heard someone."

"Oh. That was Monica. We were saying goodbye."

"Like that? You said goodbye like that?"

Robin's breasts have never seemed so bouncy and impudent. The nipples stick out, to the left and to the right, like signs pointing in opposite directions: *They went that-a-way.*

"No, silly. I was wearing a towel."

Robin rubs her hand hard over Toni's head.

"Ow. That hurts."

"Poor baby. You look like shit. Come, a bath will do you good."

"Monica spent the night here? She slept here?"

"Not exactly, no. She didn't sleep and neither did I. We were up all night. Talking."

Robin's eyes appear calm, untroubled, unwavering. A wall of glass.

Talking? What kind of talking? What kind of churning of jaws and flapping of tongues went on from three in the morning—or whenever this started—all the way to now? Robin's gaze remains steady and impenetrable and Toni recognizes the look, the hard glaze of false innocence. She has worn that mask herself a thousand times in her mother's presence. But now is not the moment for confrontation. Her head is too sore, her stomach too wobbly, her nerves too frayed. Later, when she's got her strength back. Then she'll get to the bottom of this business with Monica. She lies back on the bed and groans. It is a groan that gives voice to her excruciating pain, a groan that she hopes will pierce Robin's heart with pity and make her fall on her knees with guilt. Instead, Robin leaps onto the bed and springs up and down on the tips of her toes like an acrobat on a trampoline.

"Let's take a bath. Let's take a bath."

Toni's aching head flops like a rag doll's against the pillow.

"Ow, ow. Goddamn it. You're killing me."

Toni grabs one of the jumping ankles and Robin stops bouncing, though she doesn't sit down. Toni can't bear to look up at that animated face, so out of sync with her own. That's the problem, isn't it? They are out of sync these days. Whatever Toni's mood happens to be, Robin's is sure to be the exact opposite. Rolling over on her side, Toni fumbles around on the bedside table for her watch. Where is it? A flutter of panic. Then relief, when the trusty Omega tumbles out of the hip pocket of her jeans, which lie in a heap on the floor. Her fingers close around the cool metal. She holds the watch to her face—12:35 p.m. Not so bad. The day isn't shot. There's time for aspirins, coffee, a heart-to-heart with Robin, a kiss-and-make-up session, and a long, hard slog at the library afterward. Perhaps this Monica is just a trifling interest that can be nipped in the bud, and Robin hasn't so much to atone for after all. Hangovers make one paranoid. As Toni starts to strap the watch to her wrist, Robin jumps up and down again. A prancing foot kicks the watch right across the room.

"You bitch," Toni screeches. "That's my father's watch."

She rolls out of bed, crawls on hands and knees to grope amid the dustballs beneath the desk.

"Did it break?" Robin asks. She doesn't sound nearly as contrite as she should.

"I don't know," Toni says. Holding the watch to her ear, she can hear the quiet tick, tick, tick, intimate and reassuring as a heartbeat. "It's okay, I guess. But you *might* have broken it. You might have *broken* the most important thing I own."

She glares through the tears that have welled up in her eyes. Robin still looks quite chirpy and unaware of any transgression.

"Come on, sourpussy. I'll give you a massage. I'll wash all your grouches away."

Toni teeters on the edge of full-blown anger, then takes the hand

Robin reaches out to her. She loves Robin's hands, so small but strong and clever. A massage would be just the ticket. And, yes, a bubble bath and Alka Selzer and a big, steaming mug of coffee brought to the edge of the tub. Plus a clear, unequivocal explanation of what happened last night. Wrapping herself in a sheet, she follows the naked, prancing Robin out the door.

They lean back against the porcelain on their respective sides of the tub, limbs touching, but no warmth coursing from one body to another. The bubbles have hissed and popped into nothingness. What's left is thin scum on tepid water. Robin places her wet feet on either side of Toni's face, squeezing Toni's cheeks so that her lips lift up from her teeth.

"Come on. Let's have a smile."

Toni pushes the playful feet away.

"I hate you."

"You have no reason to hate me. You've chosen to see things a certain way."

Robin rests her head against the edge of the tub and gazes up at the ceiling. Toni wonders what other interpretation there could possibly be.

"We didn't sleep together," Robin had said. "But there's an energy between us. I think it's something we'd like to explore."

Explore! Yeah, right! Such a benign clinical expression like a couple of Girl Scouts on a trail-blazing expedition.

"You've got the hots for Monica. You're sick of me. Why don't you just come clean?"

"I'm not sick of you." Robin sighs. "I told you a long time ago I don't believe in exclusivity."

"You can't be involved with two people at the same time. That's bullshit."

"Okay. If that's how you feel."

Robin's tone sounds flat and final, as if something's been decided. A wave of panic surges in Toni's chest.

"She's straight, you know. Anyone can see that. She's just playing games."

"Then you have nothing to worry about."

Robin's lips twist in a thin smile. The tap drips. John Lennon peers smugly through his wire-rimmed glasses, while Janis Joplin offers her stoned grin. Lazy drops of water trickle down the steamed-up window beyond which the sky blazes an annoyingly cheerful shade of blue. Toni hurls a sponge toward the Lennon poster. It hits the wall with a wet plop.

"You want to try your chances with her, but keep me in your back pocket in case things don't work out."

"Don't make me out to be the bad guy. You're the one always making excuses. You've got to study. You've got to run to your classes, run to your mother. But you want me here waiting like a good little wife."

Robin steps out of the bath and into a towel, rubbing herself thoroughly, paying special attention to the bottoms of her feet, before marching away. Toni pulls out the plug and hugs her knees while the scummy water inches down her body, leaving her feeling heavier and heavier, colder and colder. She remains in the tub until the last trickles gurgle down the drain.

"You never complained before," she whimpers to the empty room.

chapter 29

The coffee tastes like ashes, like the black wet muck left after a camp-fire has been doused. The toast is bad too, brittle, dry, foreign matter in her throat. Toni can't fault her mother. She got up early and made her own breakfast, but the meal went stale before it reached her lips. Her mother sits on the opposite bench in the breakfast nook, sip-ping from her favourite miniature gold-rimmed cup and munching and skimming the paper as if everything were normal. And so it is. The same Europack Deli-brand mocha they've been drinking all their lives, made in the same stove-top percolator. The same bread as always, a sturdy German-style farmer's rye, toasted and thickly buttered. It's Toni's tastebuds that have changed. Gone flat.

Head propped on her hands, Toni gazes down at her open text-book, which shows an electron-microscope photograph of something that looks like blood-red spaghetti: cilia on the nasal epithelium. The text blurs. The photo pulses. Her own nose hairs prickle as the tears rise. Who cares about any of this? She's tired of science. The only rea-son the book is here is so she can avoid her mother's well-meaning questions and prying eyes.

Across the table, the coffee cup clinks in the saucer. Her mother clears her throat.

"It's all over," she pronounces. "I know. You don't have to say. Your heart is broken, and you think you never will be happy again. But you will be, I promise. Listen to your old mother."

Toni steals a peek through the veil of her fingers and sees her mother nodding, sees the pressed-together lips, the sad, knowing gaze. She ducks her head again and draws in her breath carefully. Before she came into the kitchen, she'd managed to clean up her face and swallow her sobs, but now they threaten to engulf her once more.

"Believe me, this is just a passing storm. He has given you a taste for love, which is a valuable thing. So he has served a purpose. For the rest, goodbye, good riddance."

Toni's throat constricts.

"You'll find another. You have no idea how young you are, my darling. And he doesn't deserve you. I knew that all along. I never did care for him."

Toni gasps in astonishment. "What are you talking about, Mama?" She balls her fists in sudden fury. "What do you know?"

"I know that a man who refuses to meet his girlfriend's mother is worthless. *Nu?* Don't you agree?"

Lisa arches her pencilled brows and lifts her chin, exposing the creases on her aging neck. Her gold earrings glint in the morning light. She is a well-dressed lady prepared for her predictable, manageable milieu, where spring fashions follow upon fall, customers are malleable, wholesalers can be harangued, and staff can be cowed. A world of Hadassah meetings, gym classes, shopping sprees, ladies' lunches, good deeds, and smart deals. A world in which sons and daughters come around by and by, and despite detours to ashrams or road trips or hippie happenings, eventually find their way to the wedding canopy—the only possible happy ending.

"There is no *him*," Toni spits. "There was never any *him*. Can't you get it, Mama? Do you have to be so stupid?"

There. Said. Done. An unnatural stillness fills the room like the terrible moment after the bomb has dropped and before the bloodied survivors start to scream. Toni clutches her head, heels of her hands pressed into her eyeballs, and waits for what comes next. But she doesn't care, she really doesn't care anymore. Bring on the wailing and railing, the scolding, the threats, the pleas. *Have you no shame? Your poor father must be twisting in his grave. Promise me you'll never do such filthy things again. Promise me you'll get treatment. It must be hormones. It must be bad influences. All you need is the right boy. We'll find you a boy.* Pointless. Specks of dust in the wind, such rebukes and lamentations. They cannot change the immutable fact of the hand she has been dealt. *I am what I am, and I'm not sorry. I can't be.* This is the bedrock of her existence now. It is good to feel its hard-edged presence.

The bench on the other side of the nook creaks as her mother shifts her weight. Silence, awful silence, like a dangling sword. Toni is afraid to look up, but she must, though her heart hammers violently now. Her mother's eyes are wide open and strange, revealing the bewildered pain of a wounded animal. No fight there, or flight, just a sinking resignation instead. It is the look her mother wore during frozen moments in the first few months after Toni's father died. Toni came upon her once, standing stock-still in the living room, the watering can in her hand angled tipsily above the African violets. She gazed down at the plants as if she had never seen such things before and couldn't understand how this leafy profusion came into existence on the coffee table. The hand holding the can trembled, and water dribbled from the spout onto the polished wood surface, but she neither poured properly nor put the can down. She just stared. At that moment, Toni rescued the watering can, put her arm around her mother, and broke the spell. Her mother sank against her in relief. No such rescue is possible now. She is no longer a daughter.

"I'm sorry, Mama," she says in her anguish. "That was mean, how I said it. I didn't intend to be mean."

"But you were."

The tone is flat. Not a reproach exactly. More a statement of fact.

"It's not how I meant to tell you. And I *have* wanted to tell you. I wish I could make you understand it's not so bad, my life."

Toni stops. It occurs to her that perhaps she's assumed too much and there's still a need to spell things out.

"You do understand what I'm talking about, don't you?"

A noise comes from her mother's throat. A sour laugh.

"I'm not quite as stupid as you think."

It is then Toni realizes her mother always knew. Or knew for a long time, in any case. In some deep-down place she knew, as one knows about death and disaster, that one can fend them off for only so long. Now the thin veil has been ripped away, the fiction that fed hope is gone. This is how things end. A single pronoun spoken out loud becomes a breath that extinguishes a flame. Something vital and precarious is snuffed out forever. *She always knew.* All those assertions about the wedding-to-be were just empty bravado. But this does not make the situation any easier. On the contrary, the unspoken words stand between them: *I always knew you would disappoint me.*

"Do you want me to go away, live somewhere else?"

What other act of contrition can she offer? But her mother seems genuinely puzzled by the question.

"What good would that do?"

Toni has no answer. They both lapse into silence again. Lisa rubs her left hand over the knuckles of the right, back and forth, rhythmically. Toni stares down at the stale slice of rye. It has stiffened into a curve like a palsied hand. It is the colour of dead skin. At last her mother speaks.

"So there's no boy. So that's not who you've been mooning after all these months."

"No. But she did make me happy for a while. I got a taste of love. You were right about that."

Again the bitter laugh.

"Is that so?"

Toni twists a paper napkin into a corkscrew.

"This isn't something I can change." Then, more firmly, "Even if I wanted to."

Toni searches her brain for more to say, words of explanation, reassurance, and sees that none are wanted at the moment and perhaps none are possible. The hollowed-out look in her mother's eyes warn that she has taken in all she can and must digest her disappointment and that she wants to do so in private. Her slumped shoulders bear the signs of a sorrow settling in.

"Aren't you late for class?" she says heavily. And then the odd afterthought, "Don't forget your lunch. It's the brown bag in the fridge."

Everything between them is finished.

And yet, that very night her mother confronts Toni in the hall during their mutual sleepless prowlings.

"Is she worth a sliver of your fingernail? Is she worth a single hair of your head, this person who makes you soak your pillow with tears at night? I could have told you right away she is not."

"You can't tell me who's good for me, Mama. That's not how it works."

Toni speaks gently, as if to a child. In the dark it is better. The gloom that blurs edges, veils faces, makes them more familiar to one another.

"You bow down to this goddess. For what? For heartache."

"I didn't choose heartache."

"You choose to throw away your life."

"It's not a choice ... it's ..."

"It's unnatural!"

"Natural to me. I can't pretend anymore, Mama."

"I can't pretend, either. I can't pretend I don't want something better for my only child."

Stalemate.

Nevertheless, it is an opening, this outburst. Familiar territory, the resentment and anger and the fierce, unwavering maternal claim. Their old lives are shattered, yet something endures.

Neither of them talk about *it*. The subject, quietly acknowledged but avoided, becomes like an awkward piece of furniture they negotiate during their daily rounds. A bleak Passover comes and goes without even a toast drunk to Elijah the prophet. By silent mutual agreement, Toni and her mother shun the holiday that more than any other links Jews to their past. As a child, Toni loved the festive meal and ceremonies. Her father would read from the *Haggadah*. They ate matzah and bitter herbs to remember the afflictions of their ancestors under Pharaoh and grew merry on the four cups of wine. During the song that enumerates the blessings of the Exodus, Toni would yell out the chorus—*Dai-daiyenu*, it is enough; each blessing on its own suffices. Now, Lisa's grim face seems to say, there are only curses to which to apply the phrase, *daiyenu*.

They nurse their separate griefs in their bedrooms at either end of the apartment. When they speak at all, it is of neutral subjects, Toni's classes, Lisa's day at work. Toni spends long hours at the library. Where else is there to go without a lover? As far as Lisa knows, her daughter could be anywhere. Toni makes no announcements. Her mother asks no questions. But the first Saturday night that Toni feels ready to go back to the club, she becomes aware of her mother's hovering presence. Lisa stands in the doorway as Toni irons a pale blue cotton shirt to military crispness. She watches with folded arms as Toni fluffs up her bangs and smoothes the sides of her dark, pixy-cut hair. Out of habit, Toni had almost locked the bathroom door for privacy, but then deliberately left it open. All those years of sneaking around. *I can't pretend any longer.* Lisa makes no comment as Toni pulls straight the kiss-curls that the girl at the beauty parlour took it upon herself to shape. She can feel her mother appraising her outfit with new eyes.

"I'm going to the club," Toni declares gruffly. She waits for the question: *What kind of club?* She has not decided how to answer.

"I just ask for one thing. That you be discreet." Her mother pulls her arms tighter across her chest. "You don't have to advertise. Understand? It is no one's business."

"You want me going out with a bag over my head?"

"I don't want you to draw unwelcome attention. I don't want you to go anywhere police could be watching. You may think this country is so free and just, but there are limits to what people will tolerate, and you will give them excuses to make you a victim. I won't have it. It's not fair to me either."

Toni regards her mother with surprise.

"It's 1970, Mama. We're not in the thirties or in redneck country. People live and let live in this city. Okay, okay, don't get excited. Of course I'm careful. The place I go is perfectly safe. Don't worry."

She looks back into the mirror unable to bear her mother's stony expression, which masks a rising hysteria.

"I've been doing this for quite a while, you know. No big deal."

She laughs awkwardly, leans forward, as if she's found something on her face that needs closer inspection. "There have never been police at the club," she lies.

She remembers Juanita's stories about raids and, while she's witnessed none herself, she has not forgotten the instructions. *Drop your partner. Head for the back door.* The possibility of a police invasion at any moment adds to the excitement of a night out at Loulou's. She remembers other battle tales she's heard over beers and cigarettes and the bravado of loud laughter, tales of betrayal at workplaces, jobs lost, homes wrecked, assaults by thugs. Still, what her mother envisions is a distortion. Her mother sees spies in every corner, entrapment agents, morality squads, witch-hunts, jackbooted thugs. The cruel knock on the door in the middle of the night, the round-up, the cattle car. These are the visions permanently stamped on her mother's mind. Nothing can erase them, not even Trudeau's grand statement a few years ago about the state having no business in the bedrooms of the nation. Toni promises to be discreet because it never occurred to her to act otherwise. But she knows the promise will do little to allay her mother's fears. Suddenly she pities her parents because of all the things they felt obliged to hide, their primitive suspicions and knee-jerk paranoia. They truly come from another world, a starker one, the shadows of which no amount of modern light could ever dispel. But it is their world, not hers. Between then and now lie not merely more than twenty-some years, but a whole new universe of hope, promise, brilliance: Martin Luther King's "I have a dream" and Trudeau's "Just Society" and "Ban the Bomb" demonstrations and draft dodgers and psychedelic art on the sidewalks of Montreal. She looks at her mother. For a moment, she has again that strangely fearful but exhilarating sensation she felt at the airport almost two years ago when she was on her way to Israel and waving goodbye.

chapter 30

Her favourite spot in the library is the row of desks by the fifth-floor windows overlooking the main campus grounds. From here she can look down at students criss-crossing the soggy grass on their way to classes, heads ducked against a slanting April rain. Through the smoked glass that gives everything a grey, other-worldly appearance, she can watch the budding branches toss, the flag atop the arts building flap and clouds scud across the sky. And see none of this, really, because her mind is busy sucking up information from the pages spread out on the desk. Today she has a 751-page book to review. She's allotted half-an-hour per chapter, with ten-minute breaks, and has devised a method of self-quizzing that includes closing her eyes and recreating diagrams from memory.

She reads the heading called "Mistakes in Meiosis," turns to the window, and tells herself about the errors that can occur during the formation of reproductive cells. In the separation of minute chromosome strands, the wrong number—too many or too few—can result. Or the structure can be wrong—an inversion, a translocation—leading to defects, diseases, seeds that cannot grow, but also, every so often, a brilliant new form of adaptation. Millennia of incremental steps created biologic diversity. Mistakes are part of the scheme. A defect in pigmentation, for example, led to the camouflaging white fur of Arctic animals. A flush of euphoria warms her cheeks as she not only finishes her chapter five minutes early but envisions the universe as a single, pulsing, unfathomably complex organism. Ah, that's science fiction. But it's fun.

She puts aside the plastic ruler which she uses to guide her eyes down the columns of text, laces her fingers together, and has a good stretch. The desks in front and behind her are occupied by the bowed figures of other plodders. Papers rustle, pens scritch. The pretty girl in the black beret two desks over won't look up; she'll never give Toni a smile. All strangers. All the lonely people, the song goes. The library is a heap of self-focused ants who wrestle with their personal grains of sand. She hardly knows anyone in her classes. Her fellow science students are a conservative, unengaged, buttoned-down lot, mostly male, with a sprinkling of straight-arrow girls. They have their house parties, beer nights, and football games.

She desperately misses Robin. She misses the heady moment of entering Robin's apartment, the lavender-painted bedroom, the scent of pot, perfumed candles, Robin's skin, and Robin's loopy grin. And the excruciating thrill of never knowing whether Robin was completely hers. She misses that too. Oh, and the chaos of tangled bed sheets, the gurgles of the radiator, the wail of Joplin through the walls, the fall-down-on-the-floor giggle fits, the sexy dancing together at Loulou's, and the acknowledgement in the faces of the women who greeted them there, the eyes that said, "They're a couple." (Even though Robin had decreed they weren't.)

She has the impulse to run down to the lobby of the library, find a pay phone, make a call.

Oh, Goofy. Is it really you? Imagine, I was just thinking of you too. Guess I can't get you out of my mind.

Yeah, sure. Dream on, idiot.

The Omega, which she has unstrapped and laid flat on the table, reads 5:45 p.m. Fifteen minutes, not the allotted five, flew away. She let herself sink into the quicksand of fantasy, that swamp that lurks beneath the surface of her will. She sees herself flubbing the exam, blowing the scholarship. Then what? No love, no degree, no career, her whole life a total flop before it started. Her eyes fix on the second hand, its steady, heartless march in a circle that repeats and repeats itself. *Oh, Papa.*

Yearning stabs suddenly as she envisions him hunched over his ledgers. She sees his long bent back, one side of his bald head shiny from the light of the goose-necked lamp, the other side in shadow. He would have loved the fine, modern library she's sitting in now, the bland white fluorescent light, the sound-absorbing beige carpets, the long orderly rows of book-filled shelves, the soft rustle of pages being turned, the silent music of a million books and hundreds of busy brains. She sees him writing his numbers into ledger columns, subjecting himself without question to the steady grind of work. There is submission in the stooped shoulders, but dignity too. He looks up and offers her one of his pale, sweet smiles, a touch of irony in the corner of his mouth as if to say, "Well, I wasn't a rocket scientist, but I endured as best I could, and you have to admit, you're glad I did."

She remembers how, when she was a child, he showed her a newspaper clipping about scientific research in Antarctica, the most inhospitable place on earth and yet a kind of paradise, he tried to explain, because the only human presence was an international brotherhood of scientists working together for the common goal of knowledge. He told her that if a person were able to live more than one life, his second existence would be as a researcher alone in his hut on the ice with his measuring devices and the great, grand sweep of a frozen continent before his eyes.

"Take me with you, Papa," she'd said, and he'd replied, quite gravely, "All right then, we will both go together in our second lives."

How many thousands of times must he have glanced at the face of his Swiss watch, anxiously, perhaps, because the hour was late and there was so much work to be done? But he would have been soothed, too, by his ingenious little device of interlocking wheels that converted the vast, chaotic stretch of time into an orderly series of moments. She looks again at her textbook and is ready to study. Soon she is deep into the chapter on viruses and bacteria.

By next stretch break, daylight has faded. The smoked glass gives back her faint reflection. A revelation dawns, a decision. There is something she must do, something she wants keenly. The conviction has been growing for weeks in the deep earth of her subconscious, but only now, because of some inner readiness, has it burst into the light. Her mother may not entirely approve, but it can't be helped. She'll get over it. She's shown herself to be far more accommodating than Toni ever thought possible.

"I need to move out, Mama. I need a place of my own."

The statement comes out in a tone of cold finality. Her mother draws back as if slapped in the face. They both stare at each other, stunned.

"Do I interfere with your life?"

Her mother bangs her cup down into its saucer. Her eyes are dark pools of hurt.

"You come and go as you please, all night long sometimes, and do I say a word? You have the use of the car. You talk to me when you want, ignore me when you want. I ask no questions. I don't pry."

"Mama, it's got nothing to do with you. I just need to be on my own. To be independent. Because … I can't explain. I need—"

"You need to run away from your mother."

"Not run away. Just be in a different place. I'll visit. Every Friday night if you want."

Toni squeezes bits of rye bread into pellets between nervous fingers, but her voice is even. She's surprised at how certain she feels, and justified in her certainty, though lacking clear words of explanation.

She now feels self-conscious in her mother's presence, aware of all that her mother thinks and feels and keeps to herself. They were closer when they were lying to one another. The truth has made them strangers.

"I know you'll never understand," she says miserably.

Her mother gives her a sharp look.

"You don't want to go back with that, that person, do you?"

"No, no. It's got nothing to do with her either. Believe me, that's completely over."

Toni sighs. Everything's over but the heartache.

"Because you'll regret it if you do. You'll be going backward, not forward. Always in life you must go forward."

"But that's it, you see? I left home once when I went to Israel and now I'm back here. I've gone backward."

"Don't twist my words."

Her mother jumps up and starts scrubbing the counter top beside the stove. She shakes clouds of Dutch cleanser out of the can and attacks the surface with frenzied zeal. The sponge in her fist hisses and spots of white powder land on her good wool dress. Toni stands up too, wondering whether she should try to say more or let her be.

"Mama, look ... "

"How are you going to pay for this whim, Miss Independent? *Nu?* Are you going to use up your college fund so you can live on your own? The money your father worked for so hard? What about your ambitions? Everything you throw away. My dreams you destroy. Your father's dreams too."

Lisa rips the burners out of the stove. The burner guards clatter into the sink. She up-ends the toaster, yanks open the crumb tray, and crumbs scatter over the just-wiped-clean counter and linoleum floor. It is refreshing to see such energy. Toni chuckles at the sight of her mother's head lowered and her shoulders hunched up. The maddened-hen look, her father used to say.

"Mama, calm down. I won't use up my college money, okay? I've still got savings from my job last year, and I'll work this summer. I'm sure I've done well in my exams, so I might get a scholarship. There are lots of cheap apartments in the student ghetto. I'll share a place. All I want is a room, see?"

"You have rooms here. Rooms and rooms and more empty rooms."

The burner guards rattle as her mother scours them with steel wool, the abrasive grey paste covering her fingers, doing God-knows-what damage to her carefully manicured nails. She grits her teeth and screws up her face in a fury of concentration. Water spurts from the faucet. Toni approaches, lays a tentative hand on her mother's shoulder. The hand is shaken off. Lisa leans into the sink and away from her daughter. The stiffness of her body and the contortions of her face say there's no point in pursuing the discussion any further.

All right. Be like that. You prove my point.

Toni hardens her heart and gathers her resolve.

The cold war continues when Toni returns from classes that evening. Her mother moves about the house as if Toni weren't there, as if she'd already departed. Sloughing her off. She has prepared supper for herself, a meal for one: leftover chicken drumstick, tiny portions of rice and peas, eaten without sauce or butter. A prisoner's rations according to the standards of the Goldblatt household, a meal of affliction. She eats in stony silence while Toni cooks herself an omelette and toast and then, just to underline her own position, pulls out everything of interest from the fridge: pickles, salad, cold cuts, apple strudel.

Her mother, who has finished eating before Toni gets to the table, retreats into the living room to work on a piece of embroidery. Passing by on the way to her room, Toni sees the frown of concentration as Lisa threads her needle. The white piece of linen in her hands is a runner. Over the years she has made several of these with themes of flower baskets and birds to match the Sabbath tablecloth that still gets hauled out for the occasional festive meal. She works in utter silence, but Toni can hear her thoughts: *Here is the trousseau that is not to be. My life's labour wasted.*

The next day is the same. And the next. Toni could stay out late to avoid the chill at home, but she decides that to do so would be to capitulate. She decides instead to stay home and ignore the psychological warfare. She plunks herself on the couch to watch an episode of *Ironside* with Raymond Burr playing the role of the wheelchair-bound detective with the steely resolve. It's her mother's favourite show, but Lisa doesn't join her daughter in front of the TV. She storms in with the vacuum cleaner, pushing the sucking mouth around chair legs and corners, filling the room with the machine's clatter and whine. The message is clear: *You want to leave? Get out then. Go. I don't need you. I don't want you, ungrateful child. Why are you still occupying my furniture?*

Toni presses her hands over her ears to block out the noise and fixes her eyes on the screen. She will not be cowed. She will leave in her own sweet time when she's ready. It is her right. Deep down, though, she wonders how long she can swallow the poison. Her mother is the stronger one, armed with the conviction of the insane.

Toward the end of the week, Toni comes home to find her mother engaged in some kind of project on the kitchen table. The newspaper lies open to the classified section. She wears her reading glasses and holds a yellow marker. Beside Lisa's elbow is a notepad with a list of phone numbers.

"I won't have you living in a hovel," she coolly announces before Toni can ask any questions. "You must get yourself a decent place. I can see a few possibilities."

Tap, tap goes her pink lacquered nail over the page of the newspaper, pointing to various ads she has circled. Apartments for rent. Her voice sounds firm and rational, free of hurt and accusation, as if the cold war had never happened and she's just picking up where they'd left off when Toni first declared her intention to move. *What is she up to? What now?* Toni feels herself once more out-manoeuvred, the ground shifting around her. She distrusts the nonchalance in her mother's face. Too many times it has masked depths of bitterness that reveal themselves a moment later in an annihilating barb.

"You don't have to do this, Mama. I'll look for my own place."

"There is not much time. You'll want to get settled before summer begins. Here's what I suggest."

Toni is about to give her an argument, but sinks onto the breakfast nook bench instead.

"Find something for the first of June, after your exams. Start looking right away. There will be lots of vacancies, especially where students live."

The voice that delivers this advice is calm, practical, resigned.

"Rent an apartment, and if you need to share, you be the one to choose the roommate. Advertise for the kind of person you want—someone quiet and clean and so on. Well, I leave that up to you. That's your job. Just don't take in any louts or freeloaders or drug addicts or pushy types. And you must have a written agreement. I'll speak to my lawyer about that. What I want to emphasize is that you should select, not be selected. This gives you better choices."

The strategy makes sense. Toni remains quiet, still not sure whether to believe in the forgiveness implicit in her mother's words.

"Heaven forbid I should chase you out. But if your mind is made up to go, then you must start your search immediately. You have no time to waste."

"Will you be all right on your own, Mama?"

"Me? All right? Why should I not be all right?"

The motherly head rises, the jaw stiffens, the eyes blaze.

"*I* am not some delicate egg that needs to be coddled. *I* have taken care of myself all my life. *I* have survived Hitler. Have I not? Have I not?"

Lisa's fist crashes down on the table. Toni ducks her head and stifles the wild laugh that such tirades inspire.

"But you! You have a lot to learn, Miss Know-It-All, Miss-Let-Other-People-Walk-All-Over-You. Yes, that's you. Don't give me an argument. In one way or another, that's what happened with that girl. I could smell it. Well, you better learn to stand up for yourself. You better learn right now. My daughter must not be a dish rag."

"Yes, Mama."

"Why do you smile? There is nothing funny."

"Yes, Mama."

When they have finished their discussion on apartment hunting and rise to leave the table, Toni bends low to envelop her quivering, indignant, five-foot-two, stand-up-for-herself mother in a hug. The first proper one in ages.

chapter 31

In the end, she settles on a bachelor apartment in a modest, low-rise building on Hutchison Avenue, a little east of the Ghetto. The bachelor is slightly more expensive than shared accommodation would be, but there are fewer hassles. She really doesn't want to deal with roommates. After she and her mother scrub the place from top to bottom and apply a fresh coat of paint, it looks cheery enough. The amenities include a galley kitchen and a balcony of sorts in the form of a fire-escape landing on which she places a potted geranium, the biggest and most thickly blossomed plant from her mother's collection. The pink blooms shake in the early June breeze, soaking up the warm sunshine, and look plucky and bright against the austere black of the metal rails.

Her furniture consists of the desk from her room at home, the fold-out couch her father used to nap on in his study, some bookshelves Mr Abbott gave her, and a small table-and-chair set her mother found at the scratch-and-dent sale at Eaton's. Toni tried to argue she could eat perched on a stool in front of the counter between the kitchen and main room, but her mother insisted a home was not a home without a proper table. Robin has given her scented candles, a couple of plush, tasselled cushions, and a poster of Virginia Woolf.

"I'm not supposed to let in any louts or freeloaders or drug addicts or pushy types," Toni had said when Robin came by.

She'd been rehearsing the line all morning and thought she did manage to say the words with a reasonable lightness of tone. Robin smiled, ignored Toni's attempts at stoic reserve, and reached up to plant a kiss on her mouth. Toni knew Robin too well by then to read a great deal into the kiss. All it meant was: *Now that the messy stuff is over, I officially grant you permission to join my tribe of ex-lovers so we can simply be friends.* After Robin left, Toni thought her heart would break all over again, that the emptiness of the apartment would crush her to bits. She took a long walk through the downtown streets, bought herself a jumbo steamed hotdog on Saint Laurent Boulevard, and felt a little better. She went to a poster store and, after searching through the Picassos and Mirós, the James Deans and Marilyn Monroes, she bought herself a map of the night sky. She liked the foreign-sounding names of the stars and the idea of learning patterns that had guided explorers through the centuries.

The star map looks down from the wall beside her bed, giving her something to contemplate when she's tired of reading but not ready to turn off the light. Opposite is a photo from her Jerusalem days of a cat on a garbage bin. She has contact sheets full of famous Israeli landmarks, but the cat has always been her favourite. For some reason the scrawny figure with the shoulder blades sticking up through loose skin, the lowered head, the tense stance, the wide, watchful eyes encapsulates Jerusalem for her. Everything is distilled in that defiant, unblinking stare: mazes of lanes and walls, vistas of dry hills, the searing sun, the thorny cactus, the choking dust, the cries of vendors, the pungent smells of sage, Turkish coffee, and dung. Curses and arguments, life on the boil. "You can never forget me," the photo says. "May your tongue cleave to the roof of your mouth if you try."

Toni has never read a word of Virginia Woolf. According to Robin, the British author was a lesbian at heart, if not fully in the flesh, and a brilliant, stunningly beautiful almost-lesbian at that. Toni was instantly captivated. The black-and-white portrait shows a young woman in profile, pale, delicate featured, sad-eyed. Her hair is done up in a loose, old-fashioned bun behind her head, exposing an elegant neck and a pretty ear. Virginia graces the wall above the dining table. Toni considers the poster a kind of tribute to what she had with Robin, but it is nice for its own sake too. Something lovely and female to look at while breakfasting alone.

When her mother saw the Virginia Woolf portrait in pride of place above Toni's table, she screwed up her lips and seemed unimpressed even after Toni explained who the great lady was. Her mother said nothing, only glanced up at the portrait with a certain resentment Toni only understood on Lisa's next visit. Her mother arrived with bagsful of additional house-warming gifts; cutlery and pots and pans, but also a collection of family photographs in five-by-seven stand-alone frames. There was a copy of the photo of Grandma Antonia that had dominated the bureau in her parents' bedroom. There was a snapshot of Toni's father, younger than she'd ever remembered him, looking handsome and energetic in an open-necked short-sleeved shirt, his suit jacket flung over his shoulder. He stood on a path against a background of lush woods—a pause during a ramble on the Mountain, no doubt. Another photo showed Toni's parents standing close together at some fancy dance party, both dressed to the nines. A fourth was of Lisa holding Toni as a toddler on her lap.

"Why must you have pictures of strangers in your apartment?" her mother asked, placing the photos around the room. "Isn't your family good enough?"

Toni accepted the offering, while making it clear Virginia would remain where she was. When her mother left, Toni repositioned the family photos all together in a line on the ledge of the window overlooking the fire escape and the back lane.

Toni has come to agree with her mother that it's good to have these familiar faces in the room. They provide a kind of company and reassurance. In certain moods, Toni sticks out her tongue at her stern-faced grandmother whose disapproval she always took for granted, though they never met. But she also rather admires the strong features, the set jaw, the unflinching eyes. Sometimes, when she glowers defiantly into the mirror, she finds a certain, pleasing resemblance.

The photos of her mother inspire arguments.

"Look here, I know what you're thinking," Toni says to the doting, young-mother face, half submerged in a pale mop of toddler curls. "You wish I could have been normal. You're resigned but not happy. Too bad. I like girls. Okay? That's how I am. Can't be changed, and I wouldn't want to change anyway because then I wouldn't be me. See? I'd be some other person. It would be like I'd never been born. And I can't wish that on myself, not anymore. You think my feelings are unnatural. Well, guess what? Nature is a lot weirder and more complicated than you think. There's homosexual activity among monkeys and dolphins. The female spotted hyena has a fake penis. There are birds that kill their young. Nature isn't good or bad, it just is. You can't use biology to make moral arguments. And anyway, plenty of people do things that are a lot stranger than what I'm doing. Just look at the classified ads for orgies and wife swapping and swingers' clubs, if you don't believe me. As for grandchildren, they're just not in the cards."

By this point in the lecture, Toni is jabbing her finger and shouting. The photo mother continues to look back with the same benign, unruffled, slightly besotted expression as before, and Toni slowly simmers down. This framed mother is manageable, after all. But so is the real-life parent back in Snowdon, comfortably removed, yet just a phone call or bus ride away.

Strangely, she cannot bring herself to talk out loud to the picture of her father. Often she catches his eyes looking through his glasses across the room at her, eloquently tender, yet veiled in his impenetrable mist of reserve. It still enrages her that he could take himself away without a word. He will forever remain unreachable. Although her reasonable brain tells her otherwise, his elusiveness seems a retribution for—what sin exactly? The sin of her own vulnerability. He would have been far less judgemental than her mother, and yet, and yet. If only she could assure him she will be okay.

Among the books that line her bookshelves are several of the novels by out-of-fashion German-Jewish authors her father liked to collect and that Mr Abbott persuaded her to save. "You might develop an interest some day," Abbott had said. She doubts it. She is sure the dense German prose of a bygone era will always be a colossal bore. But these books seem as good a memento of her father as his Omega watch. Seeing the grey spines with the German titles makes her see her father as he caresses the cover of a cherished volume, cradles it in his hands. The smell of the aged pages, in particular, brings him back. An odour of mustiness, sorrow, regret, and yearning. Now and then she sticks her nose into one of those tomes and sniffs. She feels sweetly close to him then.

Along with the photos her mother gave her, Toni has put out a few of her own. On her cork bulletin board above her desk, she's tacked the row of four playful mug shots that she and Robin and Monica recently took together for a lark in the photo booth at Woolworth's. There's also a colour shot of the girls' softball team Toni recently joined and one she rather likes of herself alone. It shows her in her gear, baseball cap pulled low over her eyes, fielder's mitt held up, ready for action. She's grinning boldly and, she has to admit, she doesn't look half bad.

Now, on this sunny Sunday morning in June, seized by a fit of perfectionism, she attacks her apartment with an arsenal of cleansers until every speck of dirt has been pounced upon and every surface gleams. Despite this frenzy of work, excess energy still hops beneath her skin, so she dashes into the streets. There is solace in the hum of traffic, the variety of people strolling by, the smell of cars, dust, French fries, lilac blossoms, and new-mown grass. She loves this neighbourhood—a mix of residential buildings and shops, old and new—in the heart of the city. The campus is close by, her summer job at Browser's Paradise within walking distance, the wooded paths of Mount Royal a short hike uphill. Just minutes away there's Loulou's—newly named Loulou's Disco and bursting at the seams on Saturday nights with enticing women from every part of the city. She loves the bustle of the main streets and the seedy look of some side streets, where down-and-outers smoke butt-ends on rickety staircases and hippies jam with bongos and guitars. Each time she goes exploring, she discovers some new delight: a nifty tobacco store, a café that features live music, an all-night pool hall, a delicatessen with the best smoked meat in town.

Her growling belly leads her to Schwartz's, into the steam and clatter, the mess of jostling bodies and boisterous voices that shout out their orders and argue in Yiddish. Elbows on the counter, she sinks her teeth into a sandwich piled high with thinly sliced, juicy smoked meat slathered in mustard and topped with a fat dill pickle.

"Nice and tasty, eh?" says an old codger by her side. He lifts his rat's nest eyebrows and winks to his friend. "Vot en eppetite."

"See how the *schmaltz* runs down her chin? You want for me to lick it off, *Maedele*?"

The two men chuckle as if they've reached the pinnacle of wit. They know she's Jewish—knew the moment she walked in the door, could read the shared ancestry in her face—and they treat her accordingly, with the friendly-rude-lewd manner reserved for one of their own. They are part of the décor, these wheezing letches. Toni shrugs and continues to chew. *One of these days I'll walk in here with a sweetie on my arm, and won't your ogle-eyes pop?* She savours the thought along with the taste of smoked meat on her tongue.

After Schwartz's, Toni wanders over to Sainte Catherine Street to join the parade of Sunday strollers, young folk in beads and feathers and leather fringes who crowd the sidewalks to see and be seen. What a city! Montreal in the summer of 1970. There are hookahs and puzzle rings in window displays. There are saffron-robed Hare Krishna guys in Phillips Square. There are jugglers and drummers and psychedelic murals. Music is everywhere, in jazz clubs, Latin clubs, blues joints, *boites à chansons*. "*Mon pays*," cries Gilles Vigneault from a car radio. "Let it be," croon the Beatles. "I'll be there," chant the Jackson 5. Everyone, but *everyone* is included in those songs.

She finds herself searching for members of that other tribe she belongs to. *You perhaps? Are you?* A game of fantasy and hope. The passing faces give back nothing. Never mind. Already, after a short month in her new digs, she has become one of the downtown people, hip and cool and ready for adventure. She continues to saunter and to scan faces, in tune with the mood of the throng. The air pulses with messages, the exchange of countless secret and not-so-secret glances, the hunger in every heart for connection.

And then, incredibly, it happens to her too. A head turns, recognition flashes, a pair of eyes lock onto her own. The girl in the crowd slows down. A moment ago she wore a dull, closed, almost surly expression, but suddenly she blazes with interest and a delicious smile lifts the corners of her mouth. Is this someone Toni knows from the club? Or just a stranger whose soul reaches out across the void? *You. Yes, you. I know.* Spinning around on her heels, Toni tries to give chase, but the current of bodies moves too swiftly, the girl has vanished. It doesn't matter; the animated look on the girl's face was real and staked a claim, if only for an instant. For blocks and blocks, Toni carries the energy of the fleeting encounter in her squared shoulders and striding feet, and she knows the unknown girl must do the same.

For the moment, *daiyenu*, it is enough.

GABRIELLA GOLIGER's first book, *Song of Ascent*, won the 2001 Upper Canada Writer's Craft Award. She was co-winner of the 1997 Journey Prize for short fiction, a finalist for this prize in 1995, and won the *PRISM international* Award in 1993. Her work has been published in a number of journals and anthologies, including *Best New American Voices 2000* and *Contemporary Jewish Writing in Canada*. Born in Italy, Goliger grew up in Montreal. She has also lived in Israel and the Eastern Arctic, and currently divides her time between Ottawa and Victoria, along with her long-time partner, Barbara Freeman.